ALSO EDITED BY JOHN JOSEPH ADAMS

THE MAD SCIENTIST'S
GUIDE TO WORLD DOMINATION

THE MAD SCIENTIST'S
GUIDE
TO
WORLD
DOMINATION

Original Short Fiction
for the Modern Evil Genius

EDITED BY **JOHN JOSEPH ADAMS**

TOR®

A TOM DOHERTY ASSOCIATES BOOK · NEW YORK

THE MAD SCIENTIST'S GUIDE TO WORLD DOMINATION

Copyright © 2013 by John Joseph Adams

Tor Editor: James Frenkel

Design by Heather Saunders

A Tor Book
Published by Tom Doherty Associates, LLC
175 Fifth Avenue
New York, NY 10010

www.tor-forge.com

Tor® is a registered trademark of Tom Doherty Associates, LLC.

ISBN 978-0-7653-2644-7 (hardcover)
ISBN 978-0-7653-2645-4 (trade paperback)
ISBN 978-1-4299-8845-2 (e-book)

First Edition: February 2013

Printed in the United States of America

0 9 8 7 6 5 4 3 2 1

COPYRIGHT ACKNOWLEDGMENTS

CONTENTS

FOREWORD

CHRIS CLAREMONT

As far back as the *Iliad* and the *Odyssey,* as far back as Shakespeare and Marlowe, right on up through the present day, the best heroes are defined by their villainous adversaries. The admiration we feel for them is more often than not defined by the quality of the threats they confront and ultimately overcome.

Think of the stories we tell, in our imaginations, on the playground—who's more cool: Ming the Merciless or Flash Gordon? Darth Vader or the whole of the Rebel Alliance? Khan or Kirk? Magneto or Professor Xavier? Who among these characters do we remember most when the story's told? Who's made the strongest impact? Whom do we secretly admire, even as he (or she) terrifies us? Who seems to have the most *fun?*

In most adventure fiction, be it drama or melodrama, the hero is defined very much by his (or her) adversary. The hero, sadly, is the more passive figure, forever waiting for the villain to set the plot in motion, to then take whatever actions are necessary to forestall it. The better the villain, the more impressive their assets—whether personal, being mentally and physically superior to the hero, or collective, in that he commands an impressive force of underlings—the more heroic his adversary becomes in taking a stand against what appear to be overwhelming odds. And, of course, in emerging triumphant.

Things get even better in stories like those in this anthology, where the villain strides masterfully into the category of Mad Scientist. You can find yourself confronting Dr. Moreau on his island where he's busy reducing living people to the size of children's toys. Or twisting the concept of villainy against itself, as was done in *X²: X-Men United,* wherein the mutant heroes allied themselves with Magneto against an even greater threat, that of William Stryker. At story's end, one adversary is slain by the other, who then betrays his allies, leaving them all to die. Two mad scientists, two heinous villains, one richly dramatic climax. What more could audiences ask for?

For the creator—the writer—the wonderful thing about such characters is that they offer the opportunity to dance across both sides of society's line between "good" and "evil." We craft the world as we want it to be, invariably a nice place full of nice people, and then introduce a tangible threat. The beauty of the mix, of course, is that we have the opportunity to play with these tropes—for example, the villain might seriously tempt the hero to switch sides, or to use a more classic description, seduce him to the dark side of the Force. There's a seminal power in that temptation—the hero might fall and the villain triumph. By the same token, the hero can reach out and tempt the villain to renounce his evil ways and thereby redeem himself, perhaps by taking a stand against a greater evil. Or simply walking away from the life he'd lived until now, so as to start anew. That aspect of this primal conflict became the linchpin of the character of Magneto in the *X-Men,* giving him a power and depth rarely seen in comics and film as he was brought to tangible life by Ian McKellen.

Either way presents the audience a story rich with dramatic tension, in that you don't know until it actually happens how the tale's going to end. It keeps us reading (or watching) and leaves us eagerly awaiting the opportunity to come back for more.

But of course, the conflict—between good and evil, if you will—is just the tip of the proverbial iceberg. Right beneath it is the equally primal question: *Why?* What takes a soul and casts him, or her, one way and not the other? Why is one person compelled to be a villain and another the hero? We see Macbeth as a noble man in the opening scenes of Shakespeare's play, an admirable warrior, yet by Act Five he has become a veritable monster. True, he's won a kingdom as the three witches foretold but in the process he's betrayed king and colleagues, slaughtered friends, betrayed all he believed in, and cast his soul to ruin. And throughout, we can't take our eyes off him. Not only that, he gets the best lines.

So here we have a clutch of stories presenting a view of life from the perspective of the mad scientist or evil genius. Some are conquerors, others criminals; some look like normal folks, others wear costumes. All are delightfully fascinating. They're the dark side of our soul brought to life and cast into a realm where the inevitability of their defeat is *not* a given. As the saying goes, it's fun to admire forbidden fruit but you should never forget that there's a reason it's forbidden in the first place. And it's not because someone's being selfish.

We let ourselves admire these mad scientists because we know that in the end they'll lose. Trouble is, what we think we know isn't always the case. They're scientists, which means they're always looking for answers. They're proud, resourceful characters, determined to brave new pathways and even more dangerously to try the wholly unexpected. Does that make them evil? Or just one step ahead of the rest of us?

So enjoy these stories, your brief wander through worlds where the rules may not be as predictable and dependable as you might prefer. Just be careful. The tiger is a lovely animal but shrouded in that physical beauty are the muscles and fangs of a predator. To its eyes, you may well be prey.

Admire all you wish—but take care not to become the next main course for dinner.

THE MAD SCIENTIST'S
GUIDE TO WORLD DOMINATION

CATEGORY: Secret Identity Management
Variables

RULE 967.2b: Managing Your Love Life Is No Easier for
Geniuses

SOURCE: Professor Incognito, Instigator of Martian
Rule

VIA: Austin Grossman

*Our first journey into the realms of madness looks reasonable
enough. How crazy can an itemized list really be? Well, in this
story, a simple list of Professor Incognito's apologies reads like the
confession of a remarkably evil genius.*

*Professor Incognito likes to live the lifestyle of any classic su-
pervillain. He's got secret rooms and hologram projectors, midnight costume changes, and plans for sentient tigers.*

*There's just one barrier lying between him and perfect happi-
ness: his fiancée. Is there any way to explain to her that beneath
his mild-mannered façade as a physics professor, he's got the skills
to take over the galaxy? Is there any way to reconcile a relationship built on lies? And should he wear his costume to their next
couple's counseling appointment?*

*Beneath the humor, this tale asks a more chilling question:
What role do secrets play in our relationships—and do we really
want to know everything about our partners? It doesn't take a
genius—evil or otherwise—to fear the consequences of a love built on
lies.*

PROFESSOR INCOGNITO APOLOGIZES:
AN ITEMIZED LIST

AUSTIN GROSSMAN

If you're receiving this message then you have probably made a startling and disturbing discovery regarding the nature of my scientific work.

Please forgive the unsettling nature of my appearance—the holographic projector is my own invention and probably very lifelike apart from the change in scale, which I believe lends a dramatic effect. I understand if it initially gave rise to confusion, panic, or small-arms fire. Needless to say—I have to add this—your puny human weapons are powerless against me.

I am recording this because I just gave you the key to my place, and although we've had the "boundaries talk" several times these things still happen and I wanted to have a chance to explain.

To get this far, you must have found the false wall I put in at the back of the bedroom closet. You must have pushed aside the coats and things, found the catch and pulled it aside to see the access shaft and the rungs leading downward to an unknown space deep beneath this apartment complex.

Did you hesitate before descending? Perhaps you still supposed this might be a city maintenance tunnel—strange, but surely more plausible than what followed. You must have started the elevator manually. (I've always admired your resourcefulness at moments like this.) And then you would have had to guess the combination to the vault door; tricky, but then of course you would know your own birthday. So maybe then you realized where you were, as the vault door opened and the rush of escaping air ruffled your black hair, and you crept inside, lips parted, flashlight at the ready. And you heard the electrical arcs sizzle and smelt ozone, and the glow of strange inventions cast a purple light onto your face, and you found yourself standing inside my secret laboratory.

Maybe this is for the best, you know? I think you should sit down—not on the glowing crystal!—and we can talk. This may take a while but fortunately the silent countdown you've triggered is quite lengthy.

I completely agree that this is very legitimate breakup material. I know that's what Kris would say—will say—she's said it about a lot less. Plenty of people—say, InterPol or the federal government, or the Crystal Six—would take matters much, much further. They've certainly tried.

This isn't the first time I've faced discovery. Secret identities are fragile things; you set up a dividing line in your life that can collapse in an instant, that can never be reestablished. You yourself have already come close to the secret so many times, come so close to stumbling into the clandestine global conflict that is my nightly pursuit.

(The hero Nebula came close to unmasking me in Utah, before I lost her in the depths of the Great Salt Lake. In Gdansk I matched wits with Detective Erasmus Kropotkin. But always I knew you, Suzanne, were the greatest threat to my domination of the world.)

In any case, I'm afraid this knowledge will do you no good. As I am constantly having to inform people.

I said "explain" but I think I really mean "apologize." And, truthfully, most of my apologies aren't very sincere. Typically I make them just before or after an unspeakably evil act. Before hurling a helpless superhero off a tall building, I say things like, "Please forgive my rudeness," as a kind of facetious witticism, a quip to break the inevitable tension.

I'm going to try and be more sincere this time, partly on the advice of our Doctor Kagan but also out of a sense that if I owe anyone on this terrestrial globe, which I will shortly crush with the burning talons of pure science, an apology, it is you.

So I'd like to issue this apology regarding my rudeness, a boilerplate phrase but maybe on this occasion it can stand in for all the small inevitable, innumerable items that must go unsaid in this list: toilet seats left up, dinners missed, gestures of tenderness that went unmade when they were needed most. And, yes, for the mighty and terrible engines that must, even now, be warping through the ether toward your pitiful planet.

In the interest of precision and sincerity I'd like to itemize this list as far as possible, which I know is a little too much like one of our counseling sessions. I know you're probably going to break up with me again. But please, bear with me.

• • • •

I, Professor Incognito, hereby issue apologies regarding the following:

RE: ANY CONFUSION YOU MAY BE EXPERIENCING AT THIS MOMENT
It must be a shock to learn that the person you think of as your hardworking, decent (perhaps a bit dull) fiancé is in reality the terrifying, fascinating, inexplicably attractive figure of Professor Incognito. You've heard of me, I suppose? A name synonymous with evil and brilliance the world over? I hope so. I made a point of mentioning it enough times.

I think—and I think Doctor Kagan would agree—that this might be really, really good for our relationship. You often spoke of a remoteness about me, a part you simply couldn't reach. Maybe that was the reason you were attracted to me in the first place, that you sensed on some level a mysterious unknowable chamber you couldn't find a way into. On some level you guessed what it might be, that I had hidden away my glittering machines, seething chemical vats, the mutation ray in a place you'd never reach.

Of course you did. People have levels, you would say. Engineering levels, generator levels. Hydroponics.

RE: WHAT HAPPENED AT DINNER WITH YOUR PARENTS THE OTHER NIGHT

Your father's remarks about Martians were both irresponsible and uninformed, but that's no excuse for how I reacted. But, and at the risk of repeating myself: the Martians are an ancient and noble culture who built golden pyramids long before human life appeared in North America.

RE: ANY SLIGHT UNAVOIDABLE DECEPTION

It didn't start out this way. In the beginning everything was much as it appeared to be. I was a young physics researcher with a hopeless crush on a brilliant colleague. It would have been ridiculous, even if I weren't five foot four, even if I weren't maybe the most awkward individual on the planet. I would never have dared speak to you. That first kiss outside the student center is still as miraculous to me as the sunrise might have been to our primitive ancestors, long before science simultaneously cleared everything up and made it all more confusing.

And it's strange because it was on the very day of that kiss that I had the first whisper of the insight that would make my career, crack open reality, and ultimately lead us to this conversation.

I knew, before anything else, two things: one, that it was the greatest scientific discovery in a hundred years, and two, that you could never, ever be told of it.

RE: OUR DATE ON THE EVENING OF JANUARY 25 2007

Yes, I was irritable and distracted at dinner, and I didn't listen properly to your story about Eileen and the paper's managing editor, whatever his name was, which I think, in retrospect, was more entertaining than I gave it credit for. It's not an excuse, but that was the day of my first experimental proof of concept. I had discovered there is—layman's terms: a gap in the world—a space between the atoms . . . if you knew where to look for it. A scientific principle with endless applications for the manipulation of matter and energy.

I could have told you about it, and I didn't. I still don't entirely know why. There were legal reasons, of course; you would have been an accessory under the law. And my secrets were dangerous. I'd be protecting you as much as myself. But I'll be honest: as my career progressed those reasons came to matter less and less. I know now that I can protect you in other ways, that the law can be bought, my enemies crushed or intimidated.

You were the most important person in my life, the one who knew me most intimately. Why couldn't I tell you? Maybe I was afraid you would contact the authorities. Or steal my ideas. Or call me insane.

Maybe I knew you wouldn't choose me if you knew everything about me. And maybe being in love means you never get to be a whole person again. The moment we met I became two people: the one I decided could be with you, and the one left over, the person I am by myself. A person who I could never, ever let you meet, and who became the greatest criminal genius the world has ever seen. I used to marvel at that fact that you *didn't* have a hidden side, that you're the same all the way through. How can a person not have a secret and glorious part of themselves that the world absolutely must not see?

In three more weeks I had a working blaster, and we met to see *Hannah and Her Sisters* at the Regent. I fell asleep on your shoulder, dreaming the genetic code for a race of sentient tigers.

RE: RUDDIGORE

I don't know how we each ended up thinking the other was a light opera fan. And in my defense, the reviews were very positive—I think the word "rollicking" appeared more than once. Believe me, I died a trillion deaths as we sat there together and watched undergraduate theater majors milk a comic Gothic pastiche for cheap laughs.

It was late fall, and when we met outside the theater your cheeks stood out pink against your dark green overcoat. We left our coats on inside, and all I remember of the play was feeling the cheap stiff wool of mine brushing up against your shoulder. Afterward, I walked you back to your dorm and we lamely joked about how bad it had been, and you couldn't see how flushed my face was.

That was the day my prototype force field stuttered into life, and I'd laughed and fired a dozen test bullets, then had to blame the gunpowder smell on my roommate's cigarettes. You sent me home.

Pausing on your doorstep, I looked up at the stars, clear and bright in the Midwestern sky, and began to formulate the glittering digital architecture that would become Craniac XII. But I foresaw neither its first words, nor its tragic final act.

RE: THE FATE OF YOUR MUCH-VAUNTED CAPTAIN ATOM.

Ah ha ha ha ha ha ha. Well, maybe I won't apologize for that.

(There are frequencies of sound inaudible to the unaugmented senses of homo sapiens. But you knew that, didn't you?)

RE: MY METHODS

Crude, perhaps? Not so wholesome as you would prefer? You don't even know the history of the world I live in and the conflict that formed it. The moment you commit a crime in a costume you see new truths about the world. You probably think Mage-President Nixon never reached the moon.

Consider: Do you remember that weekend, we drove for four hours in a snowstorm to visit your brother and his wife. We went the last two hours without talking, not angry—just in a shared reverie as the world darkened and we felt like the one warm dry place in an infinite plane of blue-white snow and black trees and wet, gritty highway.

You didn't know it, but Iluvatar was following us—one of the Mystic Seven—but she knew I wasn't going to try anything. She lagged behind, further and further back into the dusk and the storm.

We drove on. I thought about how much power an Unspace generator could make; I thought about what kind of treads a cybertank should have to cross this terrain, and if your brother was going to be a jerk to me the entire time, and how many human skulls would go into making a really nice throne, and whether there was enough power in all Unspace to get me through this weekend, and if Craniac XIV could untangle all the messed-up stuff in your family.

RE: ANY INCONVENIENCE I MAYBE CAUSING YOU

Yes, well, you see, I haven't mentioned it but you may be staying here quite a while. Don't try to run. Do feel free to explore, though. Given what you've said about my housekeeping in the past, I think you'll be pleasantly surprised.

You know I don't like to boast, but I'm really pretty proud of this place. I broke ground on the first chamber and a simple ventilation system while you were at your mother's in Baltimore, but since then it's actually gotten quite extensive. When the construction robots really got going, it all just spiraled—a generator room, shock chambers, plasma containment, the xenoapiary, the panopticon, the emergency launch tubes. The catacombs below the lower level seem to be naturally occurring, but I never quite got to the bottom of some funny seismic readings. Best not be too curious.

What you're seeing is the real thing I built during the better part of our life together. We'd see a movie or have our study night and around 2 a.m. I'd come back here, get into costume, and duck into the secret passageway.

Sometimes I'd still be spacey and distracted for a while but I eventually I'd shake it off and spend three or four hours adjusting the nutrient fluid for a dinosaur embryo, or trying to tune in to the exact broadcast frequency of a dying star, or laying the plans for another sub-basement. I'd get the robots going on the next phase then emerge through one of the four exits on Linden Street to see the sun coming up. I'd get a coffee then hurry through the quad to introduce freshmen to the basic equations of sound propagation. Then home to sleep, to wake up in the afternoon to see you again.

It was perfect in a lot of ways; I'm sad it's over.

It wasn't easy. There were more last-minute costume changes than I can tell you. We'd have coffee and I'd be shaking off the effect of a stun-ray, or waiting for news of my unmasking. The heroes knew for a fact I lived in this area. Captain Atom even snooped around our department at school, asking after anyone who kept strange hours, had strange ideas and perhaps a lack of interest in social activities. It would have been obvious if only they had been looking for a real person—they were looking for a stereotype. My precautions were effective but I think you were the real reason they never picked up on who I was.

I liked being your boyfriend. There were the times when it was absolutely the most blissful moment a person could have to leave the lab and know I'd be having a dinner with you. When we walked in the street holding hands, I'd want to check to see if people were watching just so they'd know how lucky I was.

And then, of course, there were the times when I felt like I was trapped inside a collapsing star which is in my own brain and threatened my ability to even think original thoughts, when it felt like I'd made the most awful mistake in the world.

I know there must be a way to have a relationship that truly works, and I have faith that, with your understanding—and the aid of my Martian allies—we can find it. (More on that presently.)

RE: WHAT OUR COUPLES THERAPIST CONSIDERS AN INADEQUATE EFFORT AT COMMUNICATION

I understand why you left, that first time. You knew there was something missing, and I knew it too. I just couldn't tell you.

There have been a hundred moments when I was on the brink of telling you. I tried to say the words out loud. I knew you were a physics major and all, but I didn't think you'd be into it—power and wrongdoing—it was too strange. And I admit, a part of me worries that if I told you about it, the secret part of me would disappear.

And it's too complicated now. If I'd just told you at the very start, maybe you could have understood, but now? After the diggings and archenemies and sea planes . . . If I started now I'd have to explain how I came to speak Mandarin and what happened to my original eyes. It's gone a little far.

I have my problems with Doctor Kagan, as I know you do too, but we agreed to keep seeing him and we will, although that may prove more awkward in the days to come.

RE: THE BREAKUP, MY REACTION TO SAME, AND THE ENSUING STATEWIDE "CARNIVAL OF CRIME" (SO-CALLED)

I think it was harder on me than it was on you. I tried to channel the feeling into my work. I went out and met new people and tried new things. I no longer had to sleep or take breaks except on missions and to make my teaching schedule, which I'm proud of having kept up. It's harder than you think for a being of pure scientific evil to hold regular office hours. You remember the day I asked you to take me back? You can thank Detective Kropotkin for that humbling moment. The night before, I had snapped the lock of his office door and was busy dusting his things with my nanotech powder. It happened that Kropotkin was waiting for me. He'd come in to work late, unable to sleep. He stood in the doorway looking especially seedy, a checked wool coat pulled on over his pajamas, but the revolver steady in his grip. It's so obvious Kropotkin is an asshole, even his allies feel sorry for him. He honestly thinks living alone and playing drunk chess on the Internet makes him a tragic hero.

Seeing him there, with his sad little grin, I realized something worse: He thinks he understands me. He actually thinks we're melancholy companions and rivals in a long dance of good and evil, law and chaos. And seeing him, I felt that I was, indeed, looking into a kind of mirror, but only in that I was turning into a pathetic cliché. I realized that the person I am with you, is also part of the person I am.

The next day I showed up at your work and told you I'd changed, and for once I was telling the truth. I know you don't want to be serious again too soon, but there are a few things I think you should know.

RE: THE KRIS THING

Do you remember the time when we were forty minutes late to dinner with Kris and—who was it? Bryan?—and you didn't speak to me the whole ride over except to remind me that the 3A is a toll road and you didn't have any change? God, did I hate you then, and I'm sure you hated me, although I bet not as creatively.

And of course we got to the restaurant and the moment we got there, you were all smiles and I joined in as much as I could, thinking, *god, relationships are a grotesque charade.* No one had a bad time even though the conversation was warped by Bryan's inability to leave even marginally ambiguous statements unclarified, and we were there maybe three hours. By the time we left we weren't fighting any more; not for any reason, we just weren't.

I was hoping it would work the same way once I subjugate your planet's military.

RE: THE SUBTLE, NEFARIOUS MEANS BY WHICH I LURED YOU HERE

You didn't really think I gave myself away by accident, did you? Am I that sloppy? You saw the laser burn on my jacket lapel a few days ago. You caught a millimeter of costume poking out from beneath a shirt-cuff at the fund-raiser. (I know you did.) All carefully calculated to pique your interest, I assure you. And then I left the secret door open just a tiny crack, just enough for light to leak out.

I knew you'd find me eventually, darling.

Titanium steel bolts are sliding into place to secure the vault door behind you. Don't be alarmed, and please don't break anything. I've been decent so far, and I've taken your abilities into account.

I suppose now it's time to talk about what happened three weeks ago.

You were away at one of your conferences, and I took the occasion to do a little more digging. Plunderbot and I were making a tertiary excavation on the south side, nothing serious, just laying in more server space and another heat sink, you know? Then we uncovered a power line that isn't found on the city maps. We dug around it, followed it a few hundred feet until we struck a wall of reinforced concrete. We looked at each other, wordlessly, then I cut into it, making a cylindrical opening, and stepped through into a cool, air-conditioned, well-lit corridor.

It was an underground complex.

I explored further, ready for anything except what I found. That's right, Suzanne, or should I say . . . *Nebula*? I should have known it was you under that cheap disguise. The way you smell when I lean close to you, like no un-enhanced human could.

RE: ANY MOMENTARY DISCOMFORT YOU MAY HAVE SUFFERED

The rearrangement of molecules is never a pleasant experience. The disorientation will fade presently. Please be patient until your powers return, at which point if you choose, you can totally start smashing things. But I just needed to feel that I was heard (as Doctor Kagan would have it) on a few final points.

RE: THE FIGHT WE HAD THE OTHER DAY

I'm sorry we both got angry. I shouldn't even have been robbing that stupid museum. It was a bad day. I'm glad we got to talk, even if it was just a "curse you" and "you'll never get away with this" thing.

RE: THE MARTIANS

Okay, elephant-in-the-room time. I, for one, choose to welcome our new Martian friends and overlords, and this is a personal choice I hope you'll be able to respect. Believe me, I know how unpopular this particular stance is going to make me, but I don't think it's right to bring politics into our life together. "Overlords" is a loaded word these days, and I know that's hard to get past. But you know what else is hard to get past? A glowing, golden, invulnerable Martian force field. Political views are, in my view, of secondary importance, once you see an ant grown to a hundred times its normal size.

I know you've noticed a change in me since the breakup. I've been trying new foods, learning a new language, working out. I've got a tracker in the muscle of one arm, and some really cool glowing rocks at home that you won't like at all. Surprising how things can change, just all of a sudden.

I have new friends now, you'll be happy to know. Lots of them. They're an old civilization; they watched us evolve from domed palaces on their homeworld while writing sonnets and sitting under musical crystalline trees. We have long conversations about real stuff: love, philosophy, lasers. I might have let you in on it before but I've been a little busy. They can look just like us, you know. They can look like anything they want to.

Maybe this isn't working for you right now, and I can deal with that. I'm not sure I have room in my life for another friend at the moment. In time, yes, I think you will regret your insolence. Possibly on the asteroid I have picked out, where you'll be mining sodium. No rush, we'll clear this up under the benevolent world government we're planning. That is, once we're done ending world hunger and, oh, I don't know, curing cancer? You'll be in the minority soon enough.

I worked hard on making this Martian thing happen, way before it was considered cool, and now that I've gone on record I know what the question is: Do I expect special treatment? I think it would be natural for them to call upon people who understood them from the first, for positions like, I don't know, administrative director of planet Earth. Honestly, it's not for me to say. But if you think they're not listening right now, you're kidding yourself.

Here's what I'm saying: Maybe this movie isn't about me at all. But it should be. The brave one who knew it was all a lie about the Martians, who was the first to stand up and say, hey, call me crazy but I think we can make this work. And maybe this is a lost cause, but right now it doesn't look like it to me, so we'll just see who wins this one, fair fight and no regrets. Don't judge; you don't know what's going on in those saucers. It could be pretty great.

RE: WHAT IS ABOUT TO HAPPEN

Well, I suppose this part is the most predictable, isn't it? It's a political transition; I think that's the most sensible term. And there's a place for you. I got specific with them on this. Their ideas on gender roles aren't what you call progressive, but that's exactly what a policy of engagement drives. A two-way street, right? Cultural exchange.

Oh, and the uniform. I've laid out some stuff for you to wear, and probably you'll think it's going too far, but, you know, if you're into it, it's traditional where they come from. I know it's a little skimpy, but we'll be altering the weather on this planet soon. I do have two-sided tape someplace. And the headpiece is adjustable. Totally one hundred percent optional.

RE: EVERYTHING, THE FATE OF THE ENTIRE WORLD, AND WHATEVER

I won't feel bad about the conquest of the Earth; not the destruction of the Capitol Building, or the White House; not tripods stalking the wheat fields; not the sodium mines or the humiliation of your primitive military forces, nor riding in triumph in my robot steed along lower Broadway to Times Square where I will personally accept the surrender of all seven leaders of the UN Security Council. I'm just sorry we wasted so much time that could have been ours, together.

I know we don't talk much about the future but I have some proposals to make. We've talked to Doctor Kagan about models for an adult relationship but it seems to me we've been a little unimaginative.

Here's what I'm saying: It would be terrible if someone were to find any of the equipment in my laboratory. Maybe they could comprehend what it was in time to stop me. It would be perfectly understandable if that person were to appropriate my inventions to use against me. Such a person would earn my undying enmity! In fact, I would be forced to consider that person my nemesis. We'd still fight on a regular basis. (I have a working mirror maze, if that makes a difference to you.)

The choice, Nebula—Suzanne—is entirely yours: everlasting enemies on a post-Barsoomian Earth, or co-regents of the North American province of the Greater Martian Solar Empire? I don't want you to feel obligated, but yeah, I'm putting myself out there.

I could really commit to this, you know? Long-term. It's not what you pictured, but be honest: Wouldn't you have been disappointed with anything else? Shouldn't there to be something more to a person than what you see walking around every day—an alternate self, a secret identity or two, or twenty. We've all had the dream where you find another room in your house you never knew about—if you found it, what would be in there? I thought hard about what that might be, and I've done my best to give it to you—something really cool, something scary and brilliant and mysterious all at the same time. Every single day.

Austin Grossman's first novel, Soon I Will Be Invincible, *was nominated for the John Sargent Sr. First Novel Prize, and his writing has appeared in* Granta, The Wall Street Journal, *and* The New York Times. *He is a video game design consultant and a doctoral candidate in English Literature at the University of California at Berkeley, and he has written and designed for a number of critically acclaimed video games, including* Ultima Underworld II, System Shock, Trespasser, *and* Deus Ex. *His second novel,* You, *came out from Mulholland Books in 2012, and his short fiction has also appeared in the anthology* Under the Moons of Mars: New Adventures on Barsoom.

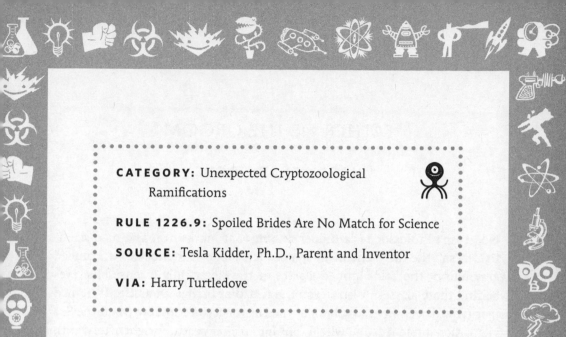

CATEGORY: Unexpected Cryptozoological Ramifications

RULE 1226.9: Spoiled Brides Are No Match for Science

SOURCE: Tesla Kidder, Ph.D., Parent and Inventor

VIA: Harry Turtledove

No matter who you are, planning a wedding is hard work. After all, it's not easy bringing together two people with different lifestyles, grooming habits, and hobbies. But at least the bride and groom are in love. The truly difficult process is the unification of their families. With all the tension between the parents and siblings, it's amazing more weddings don't end in funerals.

Our next piece is all about how hard it is to adjust to new in-laws. It's expected for the bride's and groom's parents to struggle getting used to their new roles in their children's lives. But for Professor Tesla Kidder, it's not so much a challenge as an . . . experiment. And for a man who has devoted his life to the creation of bizarre inventions, experiments can be very dangerous things.

Here is a cautionary tale about pre-wedding jitters gone horribly awry. It might even be enough to make you appreciate your own father-in-law.

FATHER OF THE GROOM

HARRY TURTLEDOVE

No, it isn't Professor Tesla Kidder's name that marks him as a mad scientist. It isn't the ratty, chemical-spotted lab coat or the shock of uncombed gray hair or the gold-rimmed glasses or the electrically intense blue eyes behind those glasses. It isn't even the fact that he has an assistant named Igor (who'd been in grad school at the University of Moscow when the Soviet Union imploded, and who'd split for greener pastures right afterward).

No, indeed. It's none of that. By his works shall you know him.

Consider, if you will, the stop light. Perhaps I should say, consider if you can. The stop light plunged an area with a radius of 1.378 miles around his Tarzana laboratory into darkness illimitable, absolute, and—it rapidly transpired—unrelieveable. That circle might be a black hole yet if the cheap AAA battery with which he powered his gadget hadn't run out of juice after a couple of hours.

Or consider his room-temperature superconductor. Professor Kidder was convinced the world would beat a path to his door (now that it could see the way again). Better he should have stuck to mousetraps. No matter how super his conductor was, who needed the poor android in an age of automated trains?

Then again, you might—or, if horror disturbs you, you might not—want to contemplate his motion censor. It did just what it was designed to do, and froze the Ventura Freeway into utter immobility at morning rush hour. Once people noticed (which, given the usual state of the Ventura Freeway at morning rush hour, took some little while), an irate CHP officer pounded on his door and demanded that he turn the goddamn thing off. Traffic eventually resumed the uneven baritone of its ways.

I'm not even going to talk about his microcosmic green goddess. That's a whole 'nother kettle of sturgeon. And some things are better left to the imagination.

I will tell you that lately Professor Kidder has got more and more interested in DNA and genetic engineering. This worries you? Let me tell you something—it even worries Igor.

You might imagine that, with such splendors on his *curriculum vitae,* Tesla Kidder lives alone, cooking in Erlenmeyer flasks over a Bunsen burner. You might, but you would be mistaken. He is happily married to Kathy, a smashing blonde, and has been for lo these many years.

How? you ask. How? you, in fact, cry. Well, to put it as simply as possible, Kathy is a bit mad, too, or more than a bit. Proof? You want proof? She breeds Weimaraners for a living. What more proof do I need?

They have a son. He looks like Tesla Kidder, except his shock of uncombed hair is brown and he wears contact lenses instead of mad-scientist specs. His name is Archimedes. Some people would get a complex about that. Young Kidder just goes by Archie. He smiles a lot, too. He's the most normal one in the whole family—not *normal,* mind you, but the *most* normal.

He majored in physics and minored in chemistry at UCLA. Maybe they'll issue him those gold-rimmed glasses when he starts going gray. Or maybe not. He's head over heels in love these days, not trying to cypher out the best way to turn the moon into a giant economy-sized bowl of guacamole for God's next Super Bowl party.

His beloved is a smashing blonde named Kate. Like father, like son? Well, yes and no. For one thing, Kate is allergic to Weimaraners—and other dogs, and anything else with four legs and fur. For another, she's about as far from mad as you can get. While Archie's doing the research for his doctorate, she's finishing her MBA.

But she sure said yes when he popped the question. The two-carat rock in the engagement ring he gave her didn't hurt, no doubt. And if Archie didn't explain that his father had synthesized it from two carrots, well, can you blame him? When the wind is southerly, he knows which side his bread is buttered on.

Kate and her folks (he does real estate; she's an investment banker) immediately started planning the wedding. The German General Staff may have worked harder planning Hitler's invasion of the Low Countries and France. Then again, they may not have. This was going to be The Way Kate Wanted It To Be.

Or else.

You might think such elaborate—even anal—preparations would put Professor Tesla Kidder's wind up. Mad scientist, after all, is traditionally a (small-*l*, please) libertarian kind of job description. For the longest time, he just smiled and nodded and went along.

And why the hell not? All he was was the father of the groom.

At a wedding, the father of the groom is as vestigial as your coccyx (unless you happen to be the nonbaboon sort of monkey, anyhow). All he has to do is show up at the rehearsal and the ceremony and drink. That's it. He's not even drinking booze he's bought, because the bride's family foots the bill.

Oh, he has to get a tux, too, in case he doesn't have one or eleven hanging in a closet. But that's okay. Mad scientists tend to look dashing and distinguished in formalwear. Here, for once, Professor Kidder conforms to a rule. He'll try not to let it happen again.

Sadly, Kate also conforms to a rule. The daughter of a real-estate whiz and an investment banker is much too likely to think she has the world wrapped around her finger. Sure as the devil, dear Kate owns a whim of iron.

Archie Kidder has noticed this, proving he isn't quite blind with love or some other related four-letter word. He labors, however, under the delusion that getting away from her folks and alone with him will cure her of this, proving he is as near blind with love or some other related four-letter word as makes little difference.

His cousin Stacey has also noticed this, since she is going to be one of the bridesmaids. She is not blind with love or some other related four-letter word for Kate, even though she introduced her to Archie (which is why she is a bridesmaid). In fact, now she is rather regretting that. The more Kate issues *diktats* about bridesmaids' dresses and such-like wedding arcana, the less in love (or some other related—oh, hell, you know) with Kate she becomes. She's starting to get pissed off instead.

Now, bridesmaids' dresses could piss off a saint. And if you are currently visualizing a pissed-off saint in a bridesmaid's dress, you are indeed the kind of person for whom this tale is intended, you poor sorry sod, you. But I digress. Bridesmaids' dresses have the twin virtues of being expensive and, more often than not, wearable only once, because bridesmaids' dresses look exactly like, well, bridesmaids' dresses, and like nothing else under the Andromeda Galaxy. Most bridesmaids' dresses come in one of two categories: the Bad and the Worse.

In Stacey's opinion, Kate was innately oriented toward the Worse. What's more, since it was her wedding, she was damn well going to ram the Worse down everybody else's throat come hell or high taxes. Attempts to reason with the daughter of a real-estate hotshot and an investment banker went the way you would imagine: into a stone wall at high velocity.

Stacey was not pleased. Which is putting it mildly. "She's going Bridezilla on us, is what she's doing," she said at a family gathering.

Now, Stacey is, all things considered, a sweet kid. She made a point of not saying this where Archie could hear it. But she didn't make a point of not saying it where *Professor Tesla Kidder* could hear it.

Oops. Major oops, as a fatter of mact.

Up till then, Prof. Kidder had been occupying himself the way he usually did at family gatherings: comparing and contrasting the flavors of various single-malt scotches. After comparing and contrasting enough of them, he could forget he was at a family gathering. And Kathy could pour him into her van and drive him home. He'd get hair from Weimaraners' coats on his own coat, but there are worse things. A few, anyhow.

If he'd done a little more comparing and contrasting, he wouldn't have noticed Stacey's snarking. If he had noticed, he wouldn't have cared. But he did, and he did, respectively.

You could see his ears quiver and come to attention. (No, he hasn't genetically engineered himself. Mad scientists *like* being mad scientists, except when they turn themselves into giant tarantulas or something. This is a mad writer's trick called hyperbole—I think.)

"Bridezilla?" he murmured in tones that spread nervous indigestion from Woodland Hills all the way to North Hollywood and beyond. "A metaphor perhaps worthy of reification. Yes, indeed." He's not the kind of mad scientist who goes in for *mwahaha,* but if he were he would have thrown one in there.

At most family gatherings, he would have been the only one there who had any idea what the hell *reification* meant. And the terror that, uh, terrorized the Northridge Mall might have been averted. But Igor, who was along because the story kind of needs him to be there (and also because he kind of has the hots for Stacey), hadn't learned English halfway. Armed with his rich vocabulary, he proceeded to ask precisely the wrong question: "Are you sure that's a good idea, boss?"

It was precisely the wrong question because mad scientists are always sure their ideas are good ones. It's part of what makes them mad scientists. "Of course I'm sure that's a good idea, dammit," Professor Tesla Kidder declared, at something over twice his usual volume.

"Well, I think we'd better be going," Kathy said brightly. She could tell when the comparing and contrasting might be getting a touch out of hand.

But all the way home Prof. Kidder kept muttering "Reification" under his single-malt breath. Since his smashing blond wife didn't know what the hell it meant (she rather thought it had something to do with East and West Germany getting together not long before Igor escaped the XSSR), she didn't worry her pretty head about it. She didn't worry about Weimaraner hair, either. She *likes* Weimaraners, remember. Nope, Tesla isn't the only mad Kidder running around loose.

. . . .

A bride and a bunch of bridesmaids constitute a giggle, which is something like a gaggle but shriller and squeakier. You can recognize giggles because they descend on bridal shops and malls with open credit cards. They are going to have fun, and somebody else is going to pay for it. But, to quote from the Gospel according to Theodore, don't worry; I'm not going political on you.

Instead, I'm going to the Northridge Mall with Kate and Stacey and the rest of the girls. And at the same time, thanks to the miracle of narrative, I'll also go to Professor Tesla Kidder's laboratory.

Kate is saying, in a voice that puts some of the bridesmaids in mind of a slightly off-center grinding wheel working its slow way through a fat nail, "No, you're not going to use those handbags. You're going to use these over here." *These over here* are larger and homelier and cost more. One of the bridesmaids has the gumption to point this out.

Kate's face curdles into an expression that would make even love-addled Archie think twice if he were there to see it. She wheels out the heavy artillery: "It's my wedding, and we're going to do it the way I want to."

Stacey's mouth forms the word "Bridezilla" once more, silently this time. Two other bridesmaids read her lips and . . . giggle. What else?

Professor Kidder reads her lips, too. Hooking his laboratory up to all the surveillance cameras in the mall is child's play for a mad scientist. Hell, Igor handled half the design work on the device that lets him do it, and Igor isn't even a mad scientist. He's just an Igor. (And of course Professor Kidder reads lips. Read lips? Professor Kidder practically *writes* lips. He's a mad scientist's mad scientist, Tesla Kidder is.)

He frowns. "Someone should do something abut this personage," he says. No, he's not talking about Stacey. "Something . . . instructive." He nods to himself, liking the word. "Yes. Instructive." And he remembers another word he likes: "Reification."

"You shouldn't take too much on yourself, boss," Igor says quickly. "Once the strain of the wedding is over, she'll be fine."

But Tesla Kidder isn't listening anymore. Not listening is another hallmark of mad scientists. Professor Kidder thinks. Then he explodes into experimentation. No, no, not literally. It has happened to a mad scientist or three, sure. Not to Prof. Kidder. He's a *carefully* mad scientist.

He pulls a mouse out of his lab-coat pocket to test the genetic recodifier he's cooked up. You don't keep mice in your pocket? Too bad. I already told you the lab coat was ratty.

Everything works at least as well as he hoped it would. Igor has the privilege of hunting down the recodified mouse. A fire extinguisher keeps him from suffering anything worse than second-degree burns.

He passes on to Professor Kidder a piece of advice from his student days in the vanished Soviet Union: "Make sure they can't trace it back to you."

"Interesting," Tesla Kidder replies. "I don't believe they know I'm working on a long-range genetic recodifier."

"Urk," says Igor. He hadn't known that himself. He hadn't imagined such a thing was possible. He is, after all, only an Igor.

"I didn't plan to field-test it so soon. Still and all, under the circumstances, no doubt it's justified. No doubt at all." As I've mentioned before, Prof. Kidder doesn't come equipped with doubts. It's . . . a lodge pin, like.

Being only an Igor, Igor does have them. "What about Stacey?" he asks. He also comes equipped with the usual male ductless glands. Anything happening to Archie Kidder's cousin would be a great waste of natural resources, as far as he's concerned.

"Tcha!" Tesla Kidder says, which may mean anything or nothing—he's a master of mad-scientistspeak. He pulls from a shelf not anything or nothing, but something, definitely something. To Igor, it doesn't especially look like a long-range genetic recodifier, but who the devil knows what a long-range genetic recodifier is supposed to look like?

Prof. Kidder flicks a switch on the something. He adjusts a dial, then another one—fussily, till they're both just right. Then he punches a button. The something makes a noise. It isn't a great big noise. Then again, it isn't a great big something. A beam of light shoots out. Professor Kidder scowls. That isn't supposed to happen. He pushes another button. The light vanishes. He checks the rest of the instrumentation. By his satisfied grunt, the something still works.

Which means we return to the mall. Kate and the giggle of bridesmaids are in Bed, Bath and Beyond, discussing scented soap. (Testing the recodifier on the mouse and calibrating the long-range version do take a little while, you know.) To be precise—which we'd better be, in a story involving a mad scientist—Kate is discoursing about scented soap. A bad habit, discoursing. Kate is firmly convinced of the superiority of lime to frangipani, sandalwood, or any other scent in the explored universe. Very firmly convinced.

One of the other bridesmaids whispers to Stacey, "She's even starting to look like a lime."

"It's just the fluorescent lighting." Stacey, after all, has spent time around a mad scientist. She's tried to explain impossible things before.

But it's not just the fluorescent lighting, and things keep right on getting impossibler. Kate's complexion goes from lime to Hass avocado: dark green and bumpylumpy. More and more bumpylumpy. Scaly, even. Where has that muzzle come from, with all those sharp teeth? To say nothing of the tail? No, we have to tell some kind of tale of the telltale tail, but not much.

Kate starts to say something else, presumably more about the magnificent wonderfulness of lime. What comes out, however, isn't exactly English. It isn't even approximately English. It's a bubbling shriek of about the volume you would use if you wanted to set Mount Everest running for an air-raid shelter.

What else comes out is a blast of fire. It's Kate's very first one, so it's not a *huge* blast of fire. But it's plenty to set several cardboard boxes burning, and it's plenty to make the giggle of bridesmaids stop giggling and start running. Running like hell, if, once more, you want to be precise.

The Bed, Bath and Beyond sales staff also opt for Beyond, and at top speed, too. Their customer-service training does not involve dealing with dinosaurian monsters, even ones that just stop in for soap.

Kate follows them out of the store. She hasn't fully figured out what's happened to her. Well, neither has anyone else but Professor Tesla Kidder, and he's off in another part of the narrative somewhere. She tries to complain. More bubbling shrieks come forth. So does more flame. Lots more flame. She's getting the hang of it.

When you are on fire, a man once said from agonizing personal experience, people get out of your way. And they get out of your way even faster when you breathe fire. Panic roars through the clothed mall-rats of Northridge.

"Run for your life!" a woman screams. "It really is Bridezilla!"

How can she tell? Simple. On the second digit of Kate's left forepaw (not the fourth, because the forepaw has only two digits once the genetic recodifying gets done) still sparkles Archie Kidder's two-carat rock.

And when people aren't running, they're aiming cell-phone cameras at Kate and zapping the stills and videos to every TV station and newspaper in town (lots of the former; not much left of the latter). Some of them even think to call the police, the fire department, and the SPCA.

Media frenzies have been built from less. From much less, to tell you the truth. Cars, vans, and all the helicopters not covering the latest freeway chase—say, about as many as the Brazilian Air Force owns—converge on the Northridge Mall. "Dinosaur runs amok!" a blow-dried airhead shouts breathlessly into his mike. "Details after this message!"

Before the impotence-drug commercial can even finish, Professor Tesla Kidder's cell phone blorps. Yes, *blorps*. Mm, how would *you* describe the noise a theremin makes? And what else would a mad scientist use for a ring tone?

"Yes?" he says.

"No," his wife tells him firmly. "I don't know what you've done, but stop doing it. Undo it, if you can—and you'd better be able to." She hangs up before he can get out even one more word.

And, before he can put the phone back in his pocket (no, not the pocket the mouse came from—mice gnaw on phones), it blorps again. Once more, he raises it to the side of his head. "Yes?"

"Dad!" Archie sounds reproachful, not firm. That may be even worse. "Fix it, will you please? Kate'll be fine as soon as the ceremony's over and the pressure's off. C'mon!"

So much for *Make sure they can't trace it back to you.* His family sure doesn't have any trouble. The police and fire department don't know him as well. Even so . . . How much damage can a real Bridezilla do in a mall? How expensive will that damage be? Tesla Kidder is a mad scientist, but he isn't a stupid scientist. No way, José.

His calculations take but a moment. "Oh, all right," he says, and, if he sounds a trifle sulky, it's only because he is. Back into the pocket goes the phone.

He recalibrates the long-range genetic recodifier. The police don't call. The fire department doesn't, either. No one pounds on the laboratory door. (Remembering Moscow nights, even Moscow nights under *perestroika* and *glasnost,* Igor is relieved.) No reporters show up asking for comments. They're all too busy trying to sound blasé about this Mesozoic irruption into the bastion of modern American capitalism.

Prof. Kidder pushes the button on his device again. No annoying extraneous beam of light this time. Tesla Kidder beams himself. He's fixed that, anyhow.

We return, then, to the mall to await developments. The Kateosaurus with the flashy engagement ring has just flamed a Cadillac Escalade in the parking lot. The SUV's fuel tank, a reservoir containing the essence of Lord knows how many dinosaurs, sends a column of greasy black smoke into the sky to mark their final return to the environment.

After a roar of triumph, the Creature from the Lime Soap Lagoon advances purposefully on a van even bigger than the Escalade (and they said it couldn't be done!). On the side of the van is blazoned EYEWITLESS NEWS.

Another burbling roar. Another blast of flame. But—disappointingly, at least to Prof. Kidder—only a small one. The news van gets scorched, but does not become as one with Nineveh and Tyre and the unmourned Escalade.

Kidder sighs. "I should have waited another minute or two. Oh, well."

For Bridezilla is undergoing another transformation—another recodification, if you will. Not from real-estate whiz and investment banker's kid to fire-breathing monster, but the reverse. To Tesla Kidder, who is thinking about Archie, going this way may be the more frightening. With a fire-breathing monster, at least, you know ahead of time what you're getting. You don't have to find out later, the hard way.

In the Northridge parking lot, Kate—yes, she's Kate again—looks vaguely confused. She doesn't remember a whole lot of what just happened. As Bridezilla, she had a brain about the size of a walnut. Most MBA candidates come with a little more cranial capacity than that.

Most reporters? It's an open question. Anyone watching the subsequent interview between the TV guy and the recently ex-dinosaur would doubt that the intelligence level of the planet's dominant species has changed much over the past 65,000,000 years.

Professor Tesla Kidder puts the long-range genetic recodifier back on the shelf. Maybe he'll need it again one of these days. "Well, Igor," he says, "what shall we work on next?"

Igor is still watching the aftermath of chaos on TV. Maybe staying in Moscow would have been better than this, or at least less wearing. But maybe not, too. That may be the scariest thought of all.

. . . .

The wedding is a great success. If everything smells a bit too strongly of lime, well, you can live with lime. After the vows, before the minister tells Archie he may kiss the bride, he beats the guy to the punch. "Kiss me, Kate!" he says, and she does. If she doesn't quite grok why he's got that kind of smile on his face while he says it, you have to remember she's only someone who's finishing an MBA.

At the reception, Kate's mother comes up to Tesla Kidder, champagne flute in hand. "Hey, listen," she says, "you didn't have anything to do with the, ah, unfortunate incident, didja?" That's what Kate's family—and their lawyers—have taken to calling the scaly, incendiary rampage through the mall.

"How could I possibly?" Professor Kidder answers. "I was in my laboratory the whole time. You can ask Igor, if you like. He was there with me."

Actually, Kate's mom *can't* ask Igor right this second. He's out on the dance floor with Stacey (who smells, defiantly, of frangipani). Kate's mother nods, as if in wisdom. "Okay," she says. "That's what I already heard, anyways." You have to remember, she's only an investment banker.

Mad scientists? They're right out of her league.

Harry Turtledove—who is often referred to as the "master of alternate history"—is the Hugo Award-winning author of more than eighty novels and a hundred short stories. His most recent books include Reincarnations, The Golden Shrine, Atlantis and Other Places, *and The War that Came Early series:* Hitler's War *and* West and East. *In addition to his SF, fantasy, and alternate history works, he's also published several straight historical novels under the name H. N. Turteltaub. Turtledove obtained a Ph.D. in Byzantine history from UCLA in 1977.*

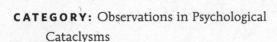

CATEGORY: Observations in Psychological Cataclysms

RULE 1304.23: Doctor, Heal Thyself

SOURCE: Professor Clarissa Garrity, behavior conditioning specialist

VIA: Seanan McGuire

Our next story takes us into the maddest of the sciences: psychology. In a future where "Schizotypal Creative Genius Personality Disorder" (SCGPD) is a bona fide psychological disorder, any bright mind is under close scrutiny. Anyone getting a Master's degree faces a battery of psych tests, and anyone continuing in scientific research can expect monthly testing for this disorder.

But a clean bill of health is no guarantee of immunity from SCGPD. In fact, as one psychologist discovers, madness is easy to induce . . . if you have the right skills.

The author says: "I find that a lot of people who study history, psychology, human behavior, or any of the other 'soft sciences' have a tendency to regard themselves as less intellectual than people who study, say, giant death lasers on the moon. I majored in folklore and mythology, and it took me a long time to stop thinking I was dumb when compared to my friend, the physicist. So this story is personal to me in the sense that it posits the soft sciences getting ready to kick your ass."

LAUGHTER AT THE ACADEMY:
A FIELD STUDY IN THE GENESIS OF SCHIZOTYPAL CREATIVE GENIUS PERSONALITY DISORDER (SCGPD)

SEANAN McGUIRE

Upon consideration, we must agree that the greatest danger of the so-called "creative genius" is its flexibility. While the stereotypes of Doctors Frankenstein and Moreau exist for good reasons, there is more to the CG-afflicted than mere biology. So much more. The time has come, ladies and gentlemen, for us to redefine what it means to be scientists . . . and what it means to be afraid.

> —from the keynote speech delivered to the 10th Annual World Conference on the Prevention of Creative Genius by Professor Elizabeth Midkiff-Cavanaugh (deceased)

0.

The world's best research has always been done in the field. Anyone who tells you different is lying, or trying to hide something. Ask anyone who's seen my work. My results speak for themselves.

IGNORANCE IS THE ONLY TRUE SIN; SUPPRESSION OF KNOWLEDGE IS THE ONLY TRUE CRIME. IGNITE THE BIOSPHERE. LET THE REVOLUTION BEGIN.

> —Graffiti found in the ruins of MIT. Author unknown.

1.

"I hope I haven't kept you waiting long, Miss—?"

"Channing. It's all right. Now it's my turn to hope that you don't mind, but I brewed a fresh pot of coffee and did those dishes that were in the sink. I know it was an imposition. I just don't know what to do with myself when I don't have anything to do with my hands."

"Mind? Why, no, I don't mind at all. Thank you. I've been meaning to do those dishes for . . . well, let's just say the dishes aren't the first chore to come to mind when I have time to tidy around here."

"No thanks needed. You shouldn't be wasting your time with things like this. Isn't that why you're advertising for an assistant? So that you'll have someone to take care of the mundane chores, and free you to handle the things that really matter? The *important* things?"

"Yes, Miss Channing. That's exactly right. If you'll come with me, I'd like to discuss the job a bit further."

"Why, Doctor Frieburg, it would be an honor."

> *Schizotypal Creative Genius Personality Disorder (SCGPD) was officially recognized in the 1930s by the Presidential commission convened following the destruction of the Washington Monument. Those brave, august men, half of whom were probably mad in their own right, decided that the label of "mad scientist" created a self-fulfilling prophecy, one which, by naming individuals as "mad," made their madness a foregone conclusion . . .*
> —excerpt from *The History of Creative Genius In America,*
> by Professor Paul Hauser (missing, presumed dead)

2.

Sunrise cast its bloody light across the ruins of the lab, illuminating the scene without judgment or mercy. There were still electrical fires burning deep inside the wreckage, forcing rescue personnel to add gas masks to their standard-issue gloves and reinforced boots. Many of them were secretly grateful for the extra protection, no matter how uncomfortable it was. It was never wise to breathe near a confirmed SCGPD outbreak site without protection, and doing it while something was on fire was just signing up for an interesting new mutation.

"Sarge, I think you should come and take a look at this."

Sergeant John Secor rose from his examination of a smoldering desk and picked his way through the shattered ceiling tiles and broken Sheetrock to his squad mate. After six years on the Mad Science Cleanup Patrol—not that anyone official would be so gauche as to use the name; they called it the Special Science Response Unit, like having a polite title would change the nature of the job—he was finally growing numb to the horrors that greeted him with every incident. Perversions of every natural law, horrific mockeries of humanity, impossible distortions of the fabric of reality . . . they were everyday occurrences, verging on the blessedly mundane.

The bodies were another matter. This one still looked human; no visible mutations or half-rejected cybernetic implants. If not for the bloodstains on his lab coat and the unnatural bend in his neck, the man sprawled on what was once the laboratory floor would have looked like any other research technician. Just one more scientist dreaming of a better world for all mankind.

"Poor bastard," muttered John, crouching down to study the visible injuries more closely. He didn't touch the remains. The scene was already compromised beyond recovery, but the risk of infection remained if one or more of the local madmen had been working with pathogens.

"We have an identity. It's Doctor Charles Frieburg."

"What was his field?"

The attending officer tapped the screen of his tablet computer. Then: "Particle physics. He was a faculty member at the local university until last year, when he received a grant to pursue private research. There are no flags on his file. He showed no signs of SCGPD."

"But this is a confirmed incident."

"Yes, sir."

"Poor bastard," John repeated, and stood. "Something drove him over the edge."

"Shall I call the medical team to remove the body?"

"Yes, and keep sifting. If he had any staff working with him, they probably didn't make it clear of the blast."

> One of the most controversial aspects of the SCGPD diagnosis lies in the conflict of nature versus nurture. Are mad scientists born, destined to crack under the pressure of their own minds? Or are they made, shaped by the world around them until they are driven to create even to the point of destruction? Can SCGPD be cured, or is it a scourge mankind is destined to suffer forever? And if it is inevitable, if the nature of this madness is part of our very genetic code, is it somehow necessary for our ongoing evolution?
>
> —from "Development of the Creative Genius:
> Nature v. Nurture," by Doctor Aubrey Powell
> (diagnosed SCGPD, trial pending). Published
> in *Psychology Journal*, volume 32, issue 8.

3.

"I am *so* sorry about the delay. I got wrapped up in my research, and, well . . ."

"There's no need to apologize, Doctor. Believe me, I understand the attraction of finishing a job before dealing with mundane things—like hiring a lab assistant."

"I admit, Miss Frieburg, I was a little surprised to receive your résumé. I don't want to keep you here under false pretenses; we're not hiring research staff right now."

"I'm not here for a research position."

"Then, if you don't mind me asking, what *are* you here for?"

"If I may be frank, Doctor, your lab is a mess. Your equipment is well maintained, but your filing is a disaster, and from the glance I took inside your refrigerator, you're keeping your existing staff in a state of constant danger from E. coli, or worse. You don't need more research staffers. You need an office manager. Someone who can take care of the mundane, while you focus on the extraordinary."

"And you think you're the appropriate person for the job?"

"Doctor Bellavia, I think that once I've been here for a little while, you won't be able to imagine operating this lab without me."

> *The number of incidents involving seemingly latent SCGPD sufferers has been rising precipitously in recent years. Many root causes have been proposed for this phenomenon, but we are no closer to identifying the trigger—if, in fact, there is a single trigger—than we were when the first incidents occurred. Whatever is causing these good men to lose their minds, we are neither positioned nor prepared to defend against it.*
> —report to the City Council by Captain Jovan Watkins
> of the Special Science Response Unit (deceased)

4.

The destruction of Doctor Rand Bellavia's lab made the news, not just in upstate New York, but throughout the country. His work in recombinant genetics had been hailed as a triumph of the stable mind for years, proving that a researcher who had not succumbed to the lure of jumper cables and evil plans could still push the frontiers of science. There had even been rumors that he might find a treatment for the biological causes of SCGPD, allowing for the rehabilitation of the hundreds of brilliant minds locked in endless war with their own inner demons. He was a poster child for science as a force for good . . . at least until the tentacles started bursting from the windows.

"Another one," muttered Sergeant Secor, staring at the photo of Doctor Bellavia's face gracing the latest issue of *Time*. The headline, "Science: Is Progress Worth the Price?" seemed unnecessarily sensationalist. Then again, when had the media ever dealt fairly with the victims of mad science? "If it bleeds, it leads" was the only commandment of the news.

This one sure as hell bled. What it didn't do was make sense. Doctor Bellavia had been a pillar of his community. He'd displayed none of the classic signs of the latent mad scientist. He'd had friends, family, a healthy social life; he'd left his lab more than once a month. He'd been tested every year for signs of SCGPD, and every test had come back clean. This should never have happened.

But it had—and Doctor Bellavia wasn't the first. John started thumbing through the incident report for what felt like the hundredth time. Everything looked normal. The shipping manifests showed the items and amounts to be expected for a medium-sized genetics lab. The staff list was up-to-date, and matched the list of casualties provided by the coroner's office perfectly.

Almost perfectly.

Frowning, John dug through the papers on his desk until he found the coroner's report. The staff list was one name longer. They'd recovered a lot of bodies from the wreckage. DNA were required to identify many of the researchers, in some cases because multiple individuals had been twisted into a single grotesquerie. The report stated that all analysis was completed, and there were no more foreign DNA strains in need of identification . . . and there was still one name missing. The office manager, Dora Frieburg.

Five minutes on the computer introduced two disturbing new facts to the case. There were no records of an individual named "Dora Frieburg" anywhere in the Special Sciences database, which meant she'd never been tested for SCGPD, and that she hadn't graduated from any known Master's program. In fact, the only hits for the name "Frieburg" came from the incident report on the destruction of Doctor Charles Frieburg's lab eight months earlier, in central Minnesota. His lab had been rather more thoroughly devastated, and they never did quite get the coroner's report and the staff lists to match . . .

And the office manager, Cathy Channing, was among the missing.

The office seemed suddenly colder. John bent over his keyboard and continued to type.

> *The only certainty we have when dealing with this insidious disease is that it will not be, and cannot be, truly defeated. It is the monster in us all, waiting for the opportunity to open the final door between the human mind and madness. Keeping that door guarded is our duty and our burden, as scientists, for to allow the lock to be broken is to lose everything that makes us moral, that keeps us honest . . . that makes us men.*
>
> —from the keynote speech delivered to the 10th Annual
> World Conference on the Prevention of Creative Genius
> by Professor Midkiff-Cavanaugh (deceased)

5.

"Professor Raymond, I have that shipment that you requested. I'm afraid the delivery man didn't leave an invoice, so I can't be sure that everything is here. Would you like me to assist with the unpacking process?"

"Yes, Miss Bellavia, that would be most appreciated. Did he say *why* he couldn't leave the shipping list?"

"No. He just dropped off the boxes and ran. I can call the office, if you'd like . . ."

"I think that would be best. But first, let's get these things put away. Some of them are perishable."

"Of course."

"I . . . Miss Bellavia, did you order this?"

"No, sir. I entered the request exactly as you gave it to me. What is it?"

"It's—it's a Jacob's ladder. A form of spark gap. They're mostly decorative, although some people say you can learn things through watching the movement of the electricity. That you can see the true nature of the universe in the ionization of the air . . ."

"Professor? Are you all right?"

"I'm sorry, Miss Bellavia. I'm fine. I just haven't seen one of these in years—not since my high school science fair. I wasn't prepared for all the memories it brought pouring back. That's all."

"Would you like me to ship it back to the distributor?"

"I don't think that will be necessary. It will be . . . nice . . . to have something around that reminds me of my past. The reasons I fell in love with science. Yes. I'll put this somewhere safe, somewhere in the lab . . . you needn't worry yourself about it, Miss Bellavia. I'll take care of everything."

"Yes, Professor."

"Are you smiling, Miss Bellavia?"

"I'm just glad to see you progressing with your work. That's all."

The question remains: If SCGPD is an incurable part of our genetic makeup, what causes its expression? Can that expression be prevented, or even controlled? Imagine a world where the forces of creative genius are harnessed, devoted only to growth, and independent of all destruction. A world where each child is free to reach his or her potential, free of the fear that one day, a casual word or an unexpected setback will trigger madness. If this paradise could be made available to the human race, would it not be our duty to pursue it?

—from "Development of the Creative Genius: Nature
v. Nurture," by Doctor Powell (diagnosed SCGPD,
trial pending). Published in *Psychology Journal*,
volume 32, issue 8.

6

"Captain, I'm telling you, the pattern is clear. You need to look at the data."

"Do you realize what you sound like, John? A mysterious lab assistant whose name changes every time she appears, somehow driving some of the nation's most brilliant minds into the grips of psychological disorder? Escaping disaster after disaster—to what end? What motive could this woman possibly have?"

"I don't know, sir." Sergeant Secor stared resolutely ahead, trying to ignore the look of disbelief on his superior's face. "The pattern is too consistent to be accidental. I combed through seven years of incidents. This anomaly is present in eighty percent of the reports. Five or ten percent, I might be able to dismiss, but eighty? Every time, she's been hired within the past four months. Every time, her surname matches that of a recently deceased scientist who fits the special handling profile. And every time, the lab is destroyed, with no survivors, but her body is never found. It can't be a coincidence, sir. It simply can't."

Captain Jovan Watkins sighed. "If you're sure about this, John . . ."

"I am, sir."

"Bring me proof. You'll need to find this mystery woman. We need a name, and a reason for anyone to be willing to do the things you claim she's doing."

"Yes, sir. I won't let you down."

"I certainly hope not, John. Dismissed."

THE SUN WAS CREATED BY A MAN WITH A SUPERNOVA WHERE
HIS HEART ONCE BURNED. EMBRACE GENIUS. IGNITE THE SKY.
—graffiti found in the ruins of MIT. Author unknown.

7.

"Professor, there's someone here to see you. He says he's with the SSRU. Should I show him in?"

"Please, Melissa. Then why don't you gather up the rest of the staff and take them out for lunch? My treat."

"Is this . . . is it time?"

"I think so. Be sure everyone takes their wallets and leaves their laptops, just in case."

"Will you be careful?"

"Oh, probably not. I never have been before, and I don't see the point in starting now. Hurry along, Melissa. It wouldn't do to keep the nice policeman waiting."

Melissa went. I didn't expect any different; she's been a good technician since the day I hired her. She was wasted in the herd environment of the psychology department. Her work with me may not have enhanced her résumé the way a more traditional fellowship would have, but what I can't offer in prestige, I've definitely provided in practical experience. I daresay her old classmates would be astonished by the things she's learned while they were watching rats run around in mazes and building Skinner boxes.

By the time she returned, a groomed, chisel-jawed specimen of *Homo officicus* trailing along behind her, I was wearing my formal lab coat—the one without the bloodstains—and seated behind my desk, a pair of reading glasses pushed to the top of my head as I pretended to study my monitor. When setting a scene, it's the details that matter; show, don't tell, as my creative-writing professor told me once, before he went mad and slew half the graduating class with an infectious poetic meme that inspired euphoria followed by suicidal depression. Professor Hagar was a wonderful teacher, and I will treasure his lessons always. They're so applicable in daily life. Consider:

A lab coat over a low-cut blouse shows a dichotomy of nature, implying that the subject is uncomfortable with her roles as both scientist and woman. Glasses propped against the forehead project vanity—a reluctance to conceal one's eyes behind a frame—coupled with vulnerability, due to presumably impaired vision, and absentmindedness, due to the potential that the glasses have been forgotten in their present location. A simple pair of glasses can be one of the most useful psychological tools available, if you know how best to position them. Dress shoes with a low heel show the desire to look feminine, and acknowledge the necessity of comfortable footwear in a lab setting. I looked, in short, like an insecure stereotype, and it was all achieved with nothing but a few props and a knowledge of human psychology.

"Professor Garrity?"

That was my cue. I looked up, meeting Melissa's question with a genial, somewhat vacant smile as I replied, "Yes, Melissa?"

"Sergeant John Secor, SSRU, here to see you."

"Oh!" I stood, extending a hand for him to shake. "Professor Clarissa Garrity. It's a pleasure to meet you, Sergeant. What can I do for you today?"

It was hard to tell whether my psychological cues were finding their mark with this man. He had a matinee hero's face, all sharp angles and brooding eyes. It was annoying. I don't require that my targets be open books, but it's best when I can see whether or not I'm getting through.

"I understand your field is human sociology," he said, giving my hand one short shake before releasing it. Matter-of-fact, then, business first; all work and no play. I could work with that.

"Yes, it is. I specialize in crowd psychology and behavioral conditioning. It's not flashy, compared to some disciplines, but I like it, and I find it to be an endlessly fascinating realm of study. Would you like to see our workspace?"

"Very much so, Professor. I've been working on a case that I think you might be able to assist me with."

"I would be delighted." He can't have hard evidence, or he'd have me in the station, rather than appearing here entirely on his own; he can't be acting with full departmental support, or he'd have backup with him, giving him the psychological upper hand. "Can you tell me anything about it, or do you have some data you need me to look at cold?"

"It's a bit of an odd case." He followed me out of my office, into the empty lab. Melissa worked fast. The staff was gone, probably ordering pizza on my tab, and she knew to keep them away for at least an hour. "Did you hear about the latest SCGPD outbreak?"

I made a show of thinking about it, reaching up to slide my glasses into place like I thought it would somehow make me smarter. Finally, I "guessed," asking, "Professor Raymond in New Hampshire?"

"Yes. He was a robotics engineer. Clean psych profiles dating all the way back to his college entrance applications. Everyone who knew him said there was no sign he was at risk."

"Oh, I see." Professor Raymond. Such a fascinating man. Such *skilled* hands. He'd been a joy to work with, and the dividends . . . my work is always rewarding, but Professor Raymond had carried it to new heights. Once he decided to open himself to the possibilities of the universe, he'd opened himself all the way.

The radiologists say Bedford won't be safe for human habitation for at least another hundred years. A fitting monument for a truly gifted man.

"It's a tragedy, but it's a fairly cut-and-dried one. He always had the potential to become symptomatic. There's just one thing that's troubling me about the situation."

"Oh?"

"He hired an office manager about three months before he went mad. She wasn't among the dead—and her name matches another low-risk scientist who became symptomatic for SCGPD about five months prior. Doctor Bellavia in New York."

Dear, sweet Rand. It's rare that I encounter a mind that brilliant. It's rarer that I get the opportunity to work on it directly. "I'm sorry, but I'm afraid I don't quite understand what you're getting at. What is it you think I can do to assist you?"

"Professor Garrity, your graduate thesis was on nonstandard manifestations of SCGPD. Scientists whose work didn't fit the standard 'mad science' model, yet had the same potential as any other genius."

The same potential, and much looser testing standards. Never mind that a mad mathematician could cripple a nation with an equation, that a mad linguist could drive a city insane with a radio ad, that a mad musical theorist could control the world with a single Billboard hit. Keeping my expression neutral, I said, "That's true. Again, what is it that you think we can do for you?"

"Professor Garrity, can you account for your whereabouts on the evening of August sixteenth?"

"Certainly. I was leaving Doctor Bellavia's lab via the back door. He'd just reached the stage of wanting to test his creations on a living human population, and I thought it would be best if I was out of the building before the mutagens made it into the ventilation system." The screams had been beautiful. They had sung me out of the parking lot like a flight of angels.

Sergeant Secor's eyes went wide. "You admit to your involvement in the triggering of Doctor Bellavia's SCGPD?"

"Naturally. It was some of my best work. But you must answer a question for me, Sergeant, before this goes any further."

His hand inched toward his sidearm. He was a clever boy, really. Not clever enough to come in with a full extraction team, but one can't have everything in this world. "What?"

"How resistant are you to transdermal sedatives? On a scale of, say, one to losing consciousness right about now."

The sound he made when he hit the floor was deeply satisfying.

One day, the world will realize that it has been at war for years. War between the past and the future; war between the visionary and the blind. One day the world will realize that human nature cannot be dictated by law. It can only be temporarily suppressed, and one day, when that suppression ends—as it inevitably must—those who have been kept in bondage will rise up, and together, they will set the skies to burn.

—from the manifesto of Professor Clarissa Garrity,
unpublished

8.

The sergeant returned to consciousness to find himself strapped to his chair. He struggled briefly before he subsided, glaring. "I am an officer of the law. Release me at once."

"I'm afraid that won't be happening for a few hours yet, Sergeant. I hope you're comfortable." I busied myself with getting the screens into position. The work would have gone faster with Melissa and the others helping me, but I needed them out of the lab, watching the door for any additional uninvited guests. "The straps aren't too tight?"

"I don't think you understand the severity of the charges you're facing here."

"In good time, I promise. Congratulations, by the way, on catching the sequential names. I really did hope that would be the first trail of bread crumbs to be successfully followed to me." I stepped back, offering him a warm smile. "Can I get you anything before we begin?"

"Begin? Begin what?" His bravado died in an instant, replaced by wariness. That was good. That showed intelligence.

"Your tests."

It took quite some time for the screams to stop.

> There is no cure. There is no hope. There is no God. There is only fire, and
> the echoes of those fools who laughed. They're always laughing . . .
> —from the suicide note of Professor Midkiff-Cavanaugh
> (deceased)

9.

I hate force conditioning a subject. It lacks subtlety, and more, it lacks *elegance*. There's an art to finding the locks buried in a person's mind and crafting the keys that will undo them, each one beautiful and unique. Sadly, time was short, and there was no other way.

"I'm so sorry, Sergeant. This was a job for a scalpel, and I've had to use a sledgehammer. I hope you can forgive me." I turned off the projector and walked toward him. He was whimpering and twitching in his chair, eyes frantically searching the corners of the room. The hot smell of urine hung in the air. He'd wet himself at least twice. That was good. That meant things were going as planned.

"How are you feeling? Do you need a drink of water?"

He giggled.

"Good." I pulled a damp washcloth from my pocket, beginning to wipe his forehead. "Let me tell you a secret, Sergeant. You're losing this war because the men who created the diagnosis for SCGPD left a few classes of genius out. They forgot that brilliance can take many forms. You, for example. You have a brilliant analytic mind. It's a shame that you were never given the opportunities that would have allowed you to hone it to its greatest potential. You were never taken seriously as a scientist of human behavior." I scowled, remembering the glares of my so-called classmates, the ones who believed that real science was found only in electrons and DNA. They never understood that the mind, and the mind alone, is where the heart of genius truly lies. "This petty world and its petty lines. One day, they'll understand. One day, they'll see that madness is the only route to sanity."

Silence.

"But you don't want to hear about all that, do you? No, you've wasted enough time. Haven't your hands been tied for long enough, Sergeant? Aren't you tired of being hobbled by artificial, useless constraints? Religion, morality, social expectations, rules and regulations and *paperwork*—you've spent so much valuable time and energy justifying yourself. That was time you could have used saving lives. Doesn't that bother you? Doesn't it just make you *burn*?"

Silence . . . but there was a new light in his eyes; a light that spoke of understanding. I was getting through to him, and that was all I needed. Sometimes a spark is all it takes.

"I'm setting you free today, Sergeant. After this, you'll never need to hesitate, never need to question yourself. Their rules won't apply anymore. It's time for you to find out what kind of man you *really* are, and I'm happy to help, because I want to know just as much as you do. That's what I do. I help people reach their full potential, and in return, they help me set the sky on fire. That's what you'll have to do. You'll have to set the sky on fire. Do you think you can do that for me? Do you think you can make them pay?"

Sergeant Secor babbled something incoherent, following it with a peal of merry laughter. I leaned forward and kissed the top of his head.

"Don't worry. You've waited long enough." I returned the washcloth to my pocket, withdrawing the first syringe. "Everyone deserves the opportunity to go mad."

> *It's all so clear now. Crime is a natural outpouring of the septic core of human nature. It can be predicted. Human response illustrates every possible violation. There's no point in waiting for those violations to occur. All we need to do is strike.*
>
> —Sergeant John Secor, SSRU, transcribed from security
> footage taken immediately prior to his shooting

9.

"Hello, Doctor Talwar."

"Why, Miss Secor. I wasn't expecting you for another hour."

"Well, you know what they say. The early bird catches the worm."

"I always wondered what that said about the early worm."

"That it's always best to be a bird, I suppose. I do hope you don't mind. I'm just so excited about the opportunity to help you with your work that I couldn't wait for the chance to get started."

"That's very industrious of you."

"I believe that everyone should have the tools they need to achieve their full potential."

"And you believe you could be one of those tools?"

"Oh, Doctor. I know that I am."

Seanan McGuire is the author of the October Daye and InCryptid urban fantasy series. Writing under the open pseudonym Mira Grant, she is the author the Newsflesh trilogy—which includes Feed, Deadline, *and* Blackout—*which she describes as "science fiction zombie political thrillers" that focus on blogging, medical technology, and the ethics of fear. A story set in that milieu appeared in John Joseph Adams's anthology* The Living Dead 2. *Her other short work has appeared in* Fantasy Magazine, Book View Café, The Edge of Propinquity, Apex Magazine, *and in the anthologies* Zombiesque *and* Tales from the Ur-Bar.

> **CATEGORY:** Vectors and Properties in Nemesis Relationships
>
> **RULE 444.4:** Every Genius Needs a Good Publicist
>
> **SOURCE:** Doctor Talon, astrophysicst and criminal genius
>
> **VIA:** David D. Levine

Brilliance comes with a hefty price tag. To understand the sciences at the level required for true mastery calls for sacrifice, hard work, and isolation. That level of commitment pulls a scientist away from ordinary life, swallows time that otherwise would go to a girlfriend, a bowling league, or poker night with the guys. But all work and no play . . . well, we all know where that leads.

But the narrator of our next tale, Doctor Talon, would argue that he's not mad at all. He simply lacks the kind of powerful friends who could tell his side of the story in a sympathetic manner. For Doctor Talon, it's not a question of a deranged mind—but simply being misunderstood.

In a world of caped superheroes and mysterious technology, it's not easy to draw the line between hero and villain. For Doctor Talon, there's only one way to redeem a life of strange science. He's got to speak up for himself.

Just when the Op-Eds were getting boring, here comes an editorial that might change your mind about a villain's job.

LETTER TO THE EDITOR

DAVID D. LEVINE

Once I was an astrophysicist. Once I struggled only with balky equipment, recalcitrant equations, obstinate administrators. Once I was well on the way to uncovering the secrets of the Universe.

But then *he* arrived. The caped and costumed alien who has occupied my days and dogged my dreams for my entire adult life.

You know him as Ultimate Man, or the Emerald Avenger, or the Champion of Humanity. You know me—if you think of me at all—only in relation to him: "Doctor Talon, Ultimate Man's constant foe and implacable adversary." Or perhaps to you I am "Doctor Talon, mad scientist" or "Doctor Talon, criminal genius." But though I do not deny that some components of my actions have been against the law, I know that history will eventually exonerate me.

Everything I have done, you see, I have done to save the world.

• • • •

In real life, the most important moments in science are not greeted by the exclamation "Eureka!" but by a puzzled frown and the words "That's funny . . ." So it was with me. I soon tracked the anomalous energy signature that had spoiled my radio observations of the Eagle Nebula to a humble dairy farm in Wisconsin, and then to a single point source. A point source that moved and grew and behaved in a most unusual way.

Intrigued, I studied the phenomenon as it developed. Despite its humanoid appearance, I soon ascertained that it was in fact an extraterrestrial energy matrix with a human shape—not even alive, in the conventional sense. More like a standing wave of solar energy.

By the time the media finally managed to notice a flying man in a gaudy green-and-gold costume zipping hither and yon over the city, over twenty years later, I had already verified, identified, and analyzed this extraterrestrial and determined that he was a threat. The rest of my career—of my life—has been devoted to this threat's amelioration.

• • • •

My personal relationship with Ultimate Man began with the famous incident in which my right hand was severed above the wrist. I won't go into details about this unfortunate episode, except to say that the primary reason it is significant to me is not simply the physical pain it caused me. Nor is it the psychological pain resulting from the cruel nickname with which I have been saddled by the media, based upon the appearance of the eminently practical prosthesis I designed to replace my missing appendage. Rather, it was the data I gathered about Ultimate Man during the incident, which proved beyond question that my hypothesis about him was in fact correct.

It was shortly after the completion of my analysis of this data that I began performing the series of actions which have been described with wearisome hyperbole as "a criminal career without precedent in history," but which, as I said above, were necessary in order to save the world.

I know that you will not believe this assertion, choosing instead to accept the conventional narrative that I have done what I have done because of an irrational, personal hatred for the alien being known as Ultimate Man (who is, by the way, an illegal immigrant—he arrived here without papers, and resides in this country under a false identity). But, as any thoughtful consumer of today's media knows, it is the frame in which the facts are considered, rather than the facts themselves, that determines their emotional content and the impression the viewer carries away. Rather than "Mad Genius Threatens Crowd with Heat Ray," for example, what would you think if you read the headline "Philanthropic Inventor Staves Off Global Destruction"?

You may scoff, but I can prove my position is well-founded.

· · · ·

Let me begin by pointing out something that you might even have noticed yourself: Ultimate Man's power is growing. Over the years, he has gone from leaping tall buildings in a single bound to outright flight; from traveling faster than a speeding bullet to exceeding the speed of light; from being so tough that nothing less than a bursting bomb could penetrate his skin to withstanding the force of an atomic blast or the interior of the sun. Additional, unrelated powers have also appeared with time, some of them quite ludicrous.

If you had been paying attention, you would have noticed that these increases in his power were most significant in the first few decades of his career, and have leveled off since then. And if you had been paying attention and were as intelligent as I, you would have realized that this was a very, very fortunate turn of events.

Why? Consider for a moment the energy required to accelerate a body the size of a human being to the transonic velocities Ultimate Man has been observed to attain. The energy required to raise the locomotives, steamships, and even entire buildings he has been observed to lift. The energy required to crush coal into diamonds, perform detailed X-ray analysis on the contents of a person's pockets at a distance, or melt steel with a glance. If you are incapable of performing the math, I hope that you will believe me when I tell you that the energy Ultimate Man expends in *a single typical day* is far in excess of the annual electrical production capacity of the entire United States.

Now consider what would occur if the energy level implied by those feats exceeded the phase space limit of an extraterrestrial humanoid standing wave.

I recognize that this last calculation depends on some unverifiable assumptions about the specific parameters of Ultimate Man's alien waveform. But my observations and my calculations have proved beyond the possibility of contradiction that such a limit must exist, and furthermore that it must be well below the energy level which would have been attained by now if his power had continued to increase at the pace of his earliest years. And if that limit should ever be exceeded, even momentarily . . . the energy would be released in a single burst.

The exact impact of such an energy release depends on its position and circumstances, but its magnitude is greater than anything seen on this planet since the formation of the solar system. If it should occur, for example, over land at an altitude of ten kilometers, the energy is certainly sufficient to crack the Earth's crust, blow half its atmosphere into space, shift its orbit, and render the planet incapable of supporting any form of life more complex than a paramecium.

So why, you might ask yourself—again, if you had been paying attention—did Ultimate Man's increase in powers level off?

Could it perhaps have been a consequence of the energy he was expending while battling the nefarious schemes of a certain master criminal?

Could those schemes, perhaps, have been carefully designed to absorb as much of his energy as possible without killing him?

Yes, I have carefully avoided killing or permanently disabling my adversary. I'm not blind, or stupid—his accomplishments during natural disasters alone, never mind the many times he has defended the Earth from extraterrestrial enemies, demonstrate to even the least perceptive observer that he must be allowed to continue in action despite the long-term threat he would pose if not controlled.

• • • •

At this point you are no doubt rolling your eyes—if indeed you are still reading at all—at my naïveté for believing that anyone would believe the assertion of a known evil genius that the Champion of Humanity is actually its greatest threat. Isn't it more likely, you may ask, that this is part of some nefarious scheme? If this threat had any basis in reality, wouldn't I have gone public long ago, to clear my name and gain allies in my long battle to keep Ultimate Man's power under control?

The two questions answer each other. I have been unable to come forward before now because no one would have believed me.

It all comes back to framing. When Ultimate Man himself believes I harbor an intense personal hatred for him, and the major media outlets are predominantly staffed by personal friends of his, any communication on my part is interpreted in terms of that frame, and is interpreted as a ruse, a hoax, or just an attempt to grab attention. The same frame has prevented my theories from being accepted by the scientific establishment.

I must assign some of the blame to myself. In the early years, uncertain of the validity of my hypothesis—and, yes, I must confess, still somewhat peeved about that early incident that deprived me of my hand—I worked tentatively, in secret, and in a way that could easily have been misinterpreted as intending deliberate harm to Ultimate Man and innocent bystanders. By the time I had confirmed my hypothesis and was prepared to announce it to the world, I had already been branded a "mad scientist."

• • • •

Which brings us to this current communication. Why, you may ask, do I think this letter to the editor will be taken seriously when my previous phone calls, broadsheets, and loudspeaker announcements from hovering dirigibles have been dismissed as the ravings of a brilliant but deranged madman?

Evidence. Incontrovertible and unbiased evidence.

At the same time this letter was released to the press, all of the data, analysis, and conclusions I have gathered on the alien known as Ultimate Man were published on the World Wide Web. You can see it right now at this URL as well as several redundant locations which can be located with a simple Google search. It includes all of the raw data, all of my steps in the development of my theory—complete with every blind alley, misstep, and error—and details of every action I have taken to test the theory and put it into practice. It is my hope that by sharing all of this information, some of it embarrassing or incriminating, I will make it as clear to you as it as been to me for decades that Ultimate Man must be continuously monitored and controlled, with frequent and serious challenges to his ever-increasing powers to keep them in check, or humanity is doomed.

My files also include pointers to physical evidence, including the exact locations of my various secret laboratories, where you will find specialized instruments and devices which I have used to both monitor and challenge Ultimate Man. I recognize that many people—including Ultimate Man himself and many of my criminal associates—will immediately attempt to take exclusive control of these devices. However, by making their locations and the data behind their creation simultaneously available to the public, I expect that any advantage gained by such control will be short-lived.

. . . .

But why am I releasing this information now, after so many decades of secrecy? The answer is that my circumstances have changed.

My occupation—this career that has been thrust upon me by circumstance—is by no means easy or safe. Even though Ultimate Man, for all that he endangers the planet by his very existence, would never voluntarily hurt me, the same cannot be said for the less sophisticated members of the law enforcement community, or for my criminal rivals, or for the unplanned side effects of my own actions. Though I have so far evaded every bomb, missile, and collapsing secret laboratory sent my way, it seems that I have failed to dodge one bullet—one too small to be seen. It turns out that long-term exposure to certain extraterrestrial radioactive materials was not as harmless to Earth life as I had thought.

To be blunt: I am afflicted with aggressive late-stage leukemia. As I write this, I will be dead within six months; if you are reading it, I am dead already. And with my death, the release of my theories and the supporting data becomes not only possible but necessary.

Naturally you will suspect a hoax. Please do visit the URL above and check out the resources there for yourself, which include several different third-party verifications of my demise. If you are reading this letter, you can be certain that my passing has been noted, confirmed, and verified by numerous automated systems and trusted colleagues, and that I am truly and irretrievably dead.

And even though death in my line of work is not always permanent, at the very least it seems to require some time to recover, and in that time Ultimate Man's power could grow to planet-shattering levels.

Therefore, now that I am gone, I ask that you—yes, you, the person reading this letter on the Internet or in any of over six hundred daily newspapers around the world—take up my tools and my cause. Challenge Ultimate Man, dissipate his power, prevent disaster.

. . . .

I know that most of my readers will not heed this request. Your daily life is already too full; you feel you lack the necessary expertise; you wish to avoid the consequences of such action. Having faced those consequences myself, I cannot impugn your reluctance. But some small percentage of those who read this will feel called to action, and will take up the challenge. Perhaps, if you are still reading, you are one of these.

My life since Ultimate Man's arrival has been a hard and lonely one. But you, with the head start provided by my files and devices, will have an easier time of it than I did. And you will have colleagues around the world, others like yourself who have heeded my call, working together on difficult challenges with dramatic and immediate real-world impact. I cannot imagine anything more exciting or satisfying: it is, in effect, the biggest and most important open-source project in history.

I have been labeled a "mad scientist." I rebelled against this label at first, then eventually learned to wear it with pride. Now I pass it along to you, to share with your peers.

You are the mad scientist now. Go forth and save the world.

David D. Levine is the Hugo Award–winning author of more than a dozen short stories. His work has appeared in Analog, Asimov's Science Fiction, Interzone, The Magazine of Fantasy & Science Fiction, Realms of Fantasy, Beneath Ceaseless Skies, Daily Science Fiction, *and in anthologies such as* The Year's Best Science Fiction, Transhuman, Gateways, All-Star Zeppelin Adventure Stories, The Mammoth Book of Extreme Fantasy, *and John Joseph Adams's* Armored. *A collection of his short work,* Space Magic, *was published in 2008. In addition to the Hugo, he has also won the Endeavour Award and the James White Award, and has been nominated for the Nebula, John W. Campbell, and Theodore Sturgeon awards.*

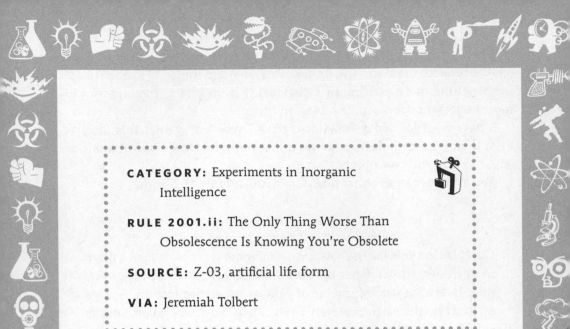

CATEGORY: Experiments in Inorganic
Intelligence

RULE 2001.ii: The Only Thing Worse Than
Obsolescence Is Knowing You're Obsolete

SOURCE: Z-03, artificial life form

VIA: Jeremiah Tolbert

No two thinkers seem to agree on The Singularity, that moment when we create a smarter-than-human intelligence. A lot of people think it will never happen. Technology is limited and so are resources, these folks say. The human brain is as smart as it gets. Some scientists and programmers, however, not only believe we can create a technology that trumps our own intelligence, but that we have a moral obligation to do so. We need bigger brains to solve the world's biggest problems.

The scientist in our next piece couldn't care less about morality or the world's difficulties. In fact, if humanity is destroyed by his creations, so much the better. He wants to create a machine smarter than himself just to prove that he can.

One of two reprints in this anthology, this story, which first appeared in the small-press anthology All Star Zeppelin Adventure Stories, paints the picture of heartless intelligence and genius fixated upon itself without concern for others—the perfect image of the archetypal mad scientist. I'd have been crazy—or perhaps I should say mad—to leave this one out.

INSTEAD OF A LOVING HEART

JEREMIAH TOLBERT

I hate it here. It is too cold for my motors, and it never stops snowing, but Dr. Octavio says that the weather is conducive to his experiments. I'm still not certain that what he is working on isn't meant to replace me. He tells me impatiently that it isn't, but I live in constant fear of it. I have nightmares that he will withhold the fuel that is my sustenance, that my parts will run down slowly until they can no longer nourish my brain while the rest of me turns to red dust. No oil can would bring me back.

It is a terrible sort of death; one that I could sit back and watch unfold in gruesome detail. I want to go quickly, when the time comes.

· · · ·

We are somewhere among the tallest mountains of the world. When we arrived, I was locked away in a cargo hold, so I don't know exactly where. Our home is a small, drafty castle and a separate laboratory. Dr. Octavio had the locals construct the lab before he tested the new death ray on their village. There's very little left there. In my little bit of spare time, I try to bury the bodies and collect anything useful to the doctor's experiment.

My primary duties consist of keeping the castle's furnace running and clearing the never-ending snow from the path between the two buildings. Sometimes, it falls too fast for my slow treads and shovel-attachment to keep up with and I find myself half-buried in the snow. It is horrible on my gears when this happens, but I use heavy-weight oil now and it helps.

It is one of the few benefits of my metal frame that I appreciate. Life in this contraption is like being wrapped in swaddling clothes. I wonder if I would feel anything if my casing caught on fire? I need to ask the doctor when he isn't in one of his moods.

I am plowing fresh snow from the path when the wind begins to blow harder than usual. I swivel my cameras and spot Lucinda's flying machine landing on the rocky field behind the castle. Dr. Octavio calls it a heliocopter. It is the perfect transportation for a jewel thief of her skill; painted black, with stylized diamonds on the sides. She calls it the *Kingfisher* because it can hover above her prey. It is faster and more agile than a zeppelin, her previous method of transportation.

I feel a twinge of happiness that she has caught up with us, even though it will send the doctor into a fit of anger. Before the Protectorate destroyed our previous laboratory, they argued and she left without telling me good-bye. Dr. Octavio grumbled the next day about money. Often, Lucinda became stingy and demanded "unreasonable results," so said the doctor.

Dr. Octavio assembled this new fortress on a very tight budget. We have no automated machine-gun turrets, or shock troops. We do not even have rabid yetis to protect the compound. There is only me and my flame-thrower attachment against whatever is out there. The death ray broke down due to the cold.

I roll up the path as fast as my treads let me. Lucinda climbs out of the *Kingfisher* wrapped in a scarlet cloak, her trademark color. Her raven hair is braided into a ponytail that flails in the wind like a dangerous snake. When she sees me, she smiles. I examine myself for a reaction. I cannot find one.

I have no heart, like the Tin Woodsman from the Baum books I read as a child. Only he was lucky enough to lose his body a piece at a time.

"Zed! What are you doing out in the cold?" she says. She uses the name Octavio gave me, Z-03. I try not to imagine what it was like for my predecessors.

"I must keep the path clear of snow for the doctor," I answer in my monotone, mechanical voice. I hate it nearly as much as the loss of my hands; I once prided myself on my ability to tell jokes. Now even the funniest punch line falls flat. "I saw you land. Come into the castle where it is warm."

She shakes her head. "I need to see Father immediately."

"He left me with orders that he is not to be disturbed."

Her smile fades. I cannot disobey Dr. Octavio's orders, she knows this. My body inflicts unbearable pain when I do.

"Fine then. Lead the way."

I plow a path around the castle to the servant's entrance into the kitchen and allow Lucinda inside while I swap my shovel attachment for my manipulators. They have pressure sensors.

Inside the kitchen, I put a kettle on the stove while Lucinda warms herself beside the radiator. "The tea will be ready in a few minutes," I say.

She doesn't answer, and I turn to see what has captured her attention. She has uncovered my easel and is looking at the latest of my failures. "Hmm? That'll be fine, Zed." She takes a seat at the small table in the corner. I re-cover the painting and roll to be opposite her. She reaches out and holds one of my manipulators in her hand. Six PSI. Six PSI.

"What's his mind like these days?" she asks. She looks at me when she speaks, unlike the doctor.

"It's fine," Dr. Octavio say, voice full of irritation, from the doorway. I hadn't noticed the gust of cold air. How could I? "What are you doing in here?" He points at me. "You're *my* servant, not hers. Get out there. I nearly broke my back on the ice, you useless heap of scrap!"

When I see the doctor, I see him in his youthful prime. He has designed me that way. Where his aged voice comes from, I see a stretched-out man with fidgeting hands and fevered blue eyes. I know that he must be decrepit by now. I do not know exactly how old he is, but he rants about the American Civil War as if he were there.

Lucinda gives me an apologetic look, and I roll outside, but stop on the opposite side of the door. I extend my microphone and maximize the gain.

"I saw the village, or what was left of it anyway. So you're a mass murderer now?" Lucinda shouts. "What did those people ever do to you?"

"They knew too much," Dr. Octavio says, raising his voice to match hers. "The Protectorate found me too easily last time. No one must know we are here. But you needn't worry. The death ray failed to function afterward," he grumbled, sounding like a child with a broken toy.

"Thank God for small miracles," she says. "I want to inspect the weapon, to be sure that you're not lying again, *Father*." It is quiet for a moment, and I fear that I might have made a sound. No one comes to the door. Finally, Lucinda continues. "What are you working on now?"

"I don't have to tell you that!" Dr. Octavio nearly shrieks. "It's not a weapon, if that's what you want to know."

"It had better not. The Germans are looking for weapons, and if I find out you have been dealing with them, you will learn the true meaning of poverty." If I could shudder, I would at the tone of Lucinda's voice. She can become as cold as this mountaintop when dealing with the subject of money.

They argue about money for an hour, and then the subject turns to Lucinda's latest heists, so I hurry away to the path.

. . . .

I still sleep, much to the doctor's dismay. Sleep is a requirement of the mind as well as the body. Mostly I have nightmares, but sometimes I have a real dream. I dream that I still have hands that can paint, that can sculpt, that can play the piano. In the dream I have six arms, and I do all at once. When I drift awake, there are only the manipulators, reporting pressure. Zero PSI. Zero PSI.

Lucinda left in the evening, and Dr. Octavio retired to his chambers. My internal clock tells me that it is six a.m. and I must wake the doctor. I take the crude elevator that he has rigged to allow me access to all the floors. His bedroom chamber is dark and baroque, full of intricately carved furniture. The set was a gift from Lucinda last Christmas, and somehow he managed to retrieve it from our previous fortress in the South Pacific.

"Dr. Octavio, it is a new day," I say tonelessly. He groans and rolls out of the bed, apparently a well-muscled man in his mid-twenties. Well-endowed. He shuffles into the bathroom and waves me away. "Go clean or something, Zed."

I obey.

. . . .

Once, Lucinda asked Dr. Octavio why he chose me, an unknown painter, to be the brain of his servant-machine. His reply is burned into my mind.

"Because he is an artist. Art serves no purpose but to distract. How does it improve the lives of men? Science is ultimately the true path of all men, even artists like him. Unfortunately, he is stubborn."

Dr. Octavio kidnapped me from my Paris studio, removed the brain from my body, and implanted it in a machine, to prove a philosophical point to no one in particular.

That is how the man's mind works.

. . . .

"Zed, I need your assistance in the laboratory," he says to me from the doorway. His words hang in the air amidst the fog of his breath. How long has it been since he last asked me to assist him?

I turn from my shoveling and join him inside the laboratory. I wait for my lenses to clear. When they do, I see his latest experiment.

Rows and rows of vacuum tubes connected with haphazard wiring line the walls, connected to more arcane machinery that I have no words to describe. Some of the machinery resembles parts of me, especially a manipulating arm that resembles mine, but significantly more advanced. I feel a deep pang of greed at the sight of it. The emotion surprises me, and I relish the sensation.

"What is your bidding, Dr. Octavio?" I ask.

He motions toward the arm. "I need you to interface with this. Come over here."

Dr. Octavio attaches me to the arm, and I flex it, checking the wiring. It seems good. It relays seven decimal pressures to my brain, far more sensitive than my own manipulators. "What would you like me to do with it?"

He shrugs, his attention already returning to a workbench crisscrossed with wiring. "I don't care. Give it a thorough testing for range of motion and dexterity."

"Can I retrieve a few things?" I ask.

"Fine, but don't be long. I have other tasks to attend to," he barks.

I collect my easel and paints from the kitchen and bring them to the laboratory. Dr. Octavio impatiently hooks me to the arm again, and I take up my brush.

An hour later, I want to weep. I haven't been able to achieve this level of technique since Paris. I call for the doctor to inspect my work.

He picks up the canvas and examines it passionlessly. He walks to the furnace and throws it inside the burner. "The quality of the arm is sufficient. You may go."

. . . .

It is spring when Lucinda returns. The snow has turned into freezing rain, and I've been using my flamethrower to clear ice from the path for a week and to clean the path before sunrise because I cannot sleep. After the Doctor caught me using the arm late one night, he has kept the lab padlocked. He shattered the sculpture with a sledgehammer.

Lucinda's helio-copter lands quietly and I watch as she leads several gray-uniformed men to the laboratory. They make short work of the lock, and I hear them breaking things inside the laboratory. Several minutes later, they leave with armfuls of equipment. Lucinda walks down the path to me.

"I'm sorry to do this to you, Zed," she says, and I can see that her face is bruised. "I owe money to some people." She stares at the castle for a moment, and then curses. "I'm sorry I'm leaving you here with him. One day I'll come back for you."

"Will you be alright?" I ask.

She forces a smile, and I almost believe her when she says yes. "There's a war breaking out in Europe. The Germans have taken Poland. It will be a good time for someone in my profession." The men come out of the helio-copter and shout down at us in German. They have guns. Lucinda walks back to the helio-copter, slipping only a little. She waves at me from the cockpit when the *Kingfisher* takes off.

. . . .

"Failed projects," Dr. Octavio says when he inspects the damage. "All junk. They damaged my masterpiece, but it will only take a week to get back up to speed." He grins and rubs his hands together. He enjoys a good setback. They give him an opportunity to refine work that his manic brain would not otherwise.

"What is this project?" I ask.

"Why should I tell you?" he says, and squints at me. "I'm not going to let you use the arm again. You'll waste its potential on worthless doodles."

"Will it replace me?" I ask.

The doctor muses for a moment. "I think that in the end, it will replace all of us."

"What is it?"

He grins again. "It is my greatest invention. A machine that will be smarter than me. A thinking machine, capable of creating machines more intelligent than itself."

"How can you create a machine that is smarter than yourself? Isn't that a . . . paradox?" I ask.

Dr. Octavio laughs. "No, it is not, but it is a good question. To create a mind smarter than my own, I only have to improve upon my design and give it a desire to further improve upon itself. By eliminating the flaws in my own mind, it will be superior. Then from its heightened perspective, it will analyze itself and continue to improve, all much faster at thinking than even the Human Adding Machine." He taps his head. "It will be the Supreme Intellect, my ultimate achievement, and the ultimate achievement of science!"

"So the arm is for creating?" I ask, fear growing in me. I can sense my brain sending signals to a nonexistent body. Run. Do something. The body does not obey these primitive signals.

"It will create others in its own image. I suspect humanity will become extinct in a century at the most." He says. "I have more vacuum tubes being air-dropped this afternoon. Go wait for them, and bring them straight to me when they arrive."

I obey.

. . . .

There is no doubt in my mind that these machines will have no use for me. They will create themselves to be capable of serving all their needs. They won't need assistants. Nor will they need artists.

I roll down the unused road to the old village, keeping an eye on the sky for the airdrop. I maximize the gain on my microphone, listening for the hiss of radio static.

. . . .

I awake from my nightmares to the sound of explosions. The castle shudders beneath me. Outside, it is raining in the darkness. There are voices inside the castle, speaking in British accents. I can hear Dr. Octavio calling for me above it all—he is using the radio commander. "Come quickly! Kill all who stand in your way!"

I attach my flamethrower as quickly as my manipulators allow and then I roll out into the hallway. British commandos spill through a break in the wall. They ignite like cheap wax candles and flail around uselessly. I press past them toward the elevator.

Dr. Octavio has fallen silent, and I suspect he has been captured. When I arrive at the highest floor of the castle, a commando opens fire with a machine gun. Bullets ricochet from my armor-plating and kill him.

Allen Stone, leader of the Protectorate, has Dr. Octavio handcuffed to a chair. "Tell us where the superweapon is, Octavio!"

"What superweapon?" The doctor asks. His eyes search around him wildly. Blood trickles from a cut in his upper lip. He sees me. "Zed, tell them I am not making a weapon!"

I roll from the shadows. Stone and his men train their weapons on me. I can barely make the words. "It is in the laboratoryyy . . ." My mechanical voice shuts down.

As my body shuts itself down, piece by piece, the world seems to speed up.

Dr. Octavio lurches forward in his chair, roaring. One of the commandos spins and pulls the trigger. The gunshot deafens me, overriding all sound from my microphone. "Destroy everything down there," Stone says on his radio. My microphone shuts down.

Then the cameras. I am in darkness.

• • • •

It starts as a buzzing sound. Someone is speaking to me. My cameras come back online and focus sluggishly.

"He can hear me now?" Stone asks the balding technician in a white parka. The technician nods and backs away.

"Stone," I say.

"Good. It's time to leave," Stone asks, cigar clenched between his teeth. We stand on the open field beneath his zeppelin. The laboratory billows smoke below us. Nothing will have escaped the fire.

"I am waiting for someone," I say.

He looks away uncomfortably. "That wouldn't be Octavio's daughter, would it? Infamous jewel thief Lucinda Octavio, aka 'The Ghost'?"

"Yes," I say. I feel something familiar rising from the depths of my reptilian brain. Fear—I have almost missed you.

"I guess you have no way of knowing, living out here . . ." His voice trails off. I stare at him. If he doesn't say something soon, I will set him ablaze with the remaining fuel in my thrower.

"She's been captured by the Nazis." He pauses, considering his words. He stares at me with a perplexed expression, one I recognize as the result of searching me for outward signs of emotion. I feel sorry for him. "Seems she tried to steal from Hitler's private stash. They've been trumpeting it in their papers and on the radio. Truth is, we've been afraid she would lead them to Octavio. That's why we moved so quickly when you radioed us."

I try to pretend that I don't feel anything. I don't have a heart.

"Look, mate," Stone says, "come with us and you can make a difference in this topsy-turvy world. I can't promise you anything, but maybe you can rescue her. British Intelligence has a lot of questions for her. What do you say, Zed?"

"My name is not Zed," I say. "But yes. I will come with you."

"What is your name then?"

"Call me Tin Man."

Stone shrugs and walks up the ramp into the gondola hanging a few feet above the ground. I turn my cameras to watch the smoke from the laboratory for a few more minutes, until I can be sure that I will never doubt that every last bit of Octavio's last experiment is gone.

Jeremiah Tolbert's fiction has appeared in Fantasy Magazine, Interzone, Ideomancer, Polyphony 4, *and* Shimmer, *as well as in John Joseph Adams's anthologies* Federations, Seeds of Change, *and* Brave New Worlds. *He's also been featured several times on the* Escape Pod *and* Podcastle *podcasts. In addition to being a writer, he is a Web designer, photographer, and graphic artist—and he shows off each of those skills in his Dr. Roundbottom project, located at www.clockpunk.com. He lives in Colorado, with his wife and cats.*

CATEGORY: Experiments in Inorganic
Intelligence

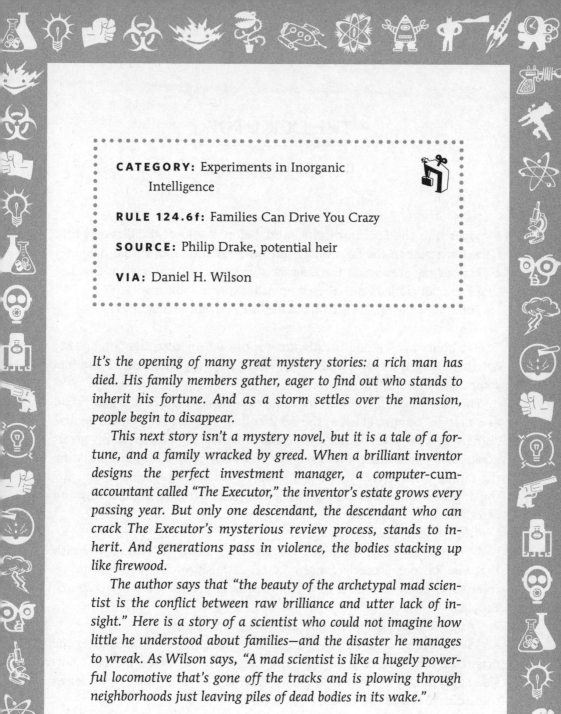

RULE 124.6f: Families Can Drive You Crazy

SOURCE: Philip Drake, potential heir

VIA: Daniel H. Wilson

It's the opening of many great mystery stories: a rich man has died. His family members gather, eager to find out who stands to inherit his fortune. And as a storm settles over the mansion, people begin to disappear.

This next story isn't a mystery novel, but it is a tale of a fortune, and a family wracked by greed. When a brilliant inventor designs the perfect investment manager, a computer-cum-accountant called "The Executor," the inventor's estate grows every passing year. But only one descendant, the descendant who can crack The Executor's mysterious review process, stands to inherit. And generations pass in violence, the bodies stacking up like firewood.

The author says that "the beauty of the archetypal mad scientist is the conflict between raw brilliance and utter lack of insight." Here is a story of a scientist who could not imagine how little he understood about families—and the disaster he manages to wreak. As Wilson says, "A mad scientist is like a hugely powerful locomotive that's gone off the tracks and is plowing through neighborhoods just leaving piles of dead bodies in its wake."

THE EXECUTOR

DANIEL H. WILSON

I stagger into the Executor's office just before my joint-stabilization field fails. I crumble to the floor and I can hear my nine-month-old daughter crying but my eyes aren't working for some reason. That's when I realize that I've really failed now—there's no other way to look at it.

The rest of my family is going to die, and I'm going first.

· · · ·

Twelve hours ago I stood in this same room on my feet, like a man. My daughter Abigail was safe and sleepy, strapped to my chest. And I still had some hope that I might save her life.

The Executor. It looms over me, imperious, an expensive hologram solid as a marble column. Flush as the devil and still with a sour mug. The machine sports the trademark scowl of the scientist who created it: my great-grcat-great-grandfather. The Executor has been controlling and building the family fortune for almost two hundred years, an angry old man staring down infinity with eyes like black pinpricks. Brilliant and wealthy and utterly alone, just like my ancestor.

"How much?" I ask.

"A common enough question," responds the Executor. "Trillions. Wealth that you cannot properly conceptualize. Diversified. Off-planet mining. Interworld currency exchanges. Hard mineral caches. Property. Patents. People."

"And yet your clothes are two hundred years out of date."

"Some things even I can't change, Mr. Drake. I am modeled after the original Dr. Arkady. As such, I am not allowed to . . . let's say, evolve, outside of certain constraints. My goal is to amass wealth. And my strategies toward that end are quite, ah, contemporary."

True enough. The Arkady Ransom is the largest concentration of loot on the planet. In his infamous will, Arkady made a promise that, one day, a descendant would claim the Ransom. That promise turned out to be a bucket of blood in the water. It broke my family into splinter dynasties. Sent the splinters borrowing from syndicates to pay for the Internecine War.

Arkady's promise destroyed my family.

"Lot of greenbacks," I muse. "And nobody to enjoy them."

"I certainly don't. I require no wages, Mr. Drake. No air and no light, either, for that matter. As stated in the original will and testament, *ab initio,* the profit from Dr. Arkady's investments—amassed over the last two centuries—shall be held in trust in perpetuity for the descendant who is able to claim it. So far, none has."

"A couple might have tried," I quip.

"Hundreds have tried, Mr. Drake. All have failed. Are you here to stake your claim?"

I adjust Abigail in her carrier. "For the kid," I say. "She needs a doctor. The kind that a guy like me can't even pay to consult."

"Drop her off at any state-run orphanage and they will provide for her."

"Kid's got meta-Parkinson's, like me. The state will throw her into a wheelchair and forget about her. But the disease is degenerative. It'll kill her sooner or later, unless she gets a fledgling exo-rig to build up her strength. If she can learn to walk, she could use a hybrid stepper until she's grown. Then a full-blown joint-stabilization field, just like her old man. It's real simple, Executor: I don't have enough money to save my daughter's life. You do."

The Executor looks at me, expressionless. It's tough to tell how smart it is. Those muddy eyes. The light sort of disappears into them.

"So what next?" I ask.

"The details of the review process are confidential. Touch the speaking stone to initiate."

I notice a flattish block of red sandstone on the ground.

"What else?" I ask.

"Nothing. The process begins when a legal descendant touches the stone. Once activated, the review process cannot be repeated. My decision will be final."

I cradle my daughter to my chest. She breathes in soft gasps, warm against me. My joint stabilizers whine as I kneel to touch the rock; they're army-issued and falling apart.

"Review process initiated," says the machine. "Answer the following question: What is inside you and all around you; created you and is created by you; and is you but not you?"

"It's a riddle?"

"You have five seconds to respond."

Five. Four. Three. Two. One.

As the seconds burn like match heads, my baby daughter squirms and coos. She rubs her balled-up fists over her cheeks and flashes those baby blues. I focus on her and try not to think about her future. A frown flickers across the Executor's face.

Zero.

"Review process complete," says the machine. "Your claim is denied, Mr. Drake."

. . . .

I take four steps toward the curb when I feel the nose of a gun jabbing into my ribs. There's nobody around, just a busy avenue buzzing with trolling auto-cars. These days, the city moves too fast for human reflexes. The streets have a numb life of their own. In turn, the citizens have become hard and precise and cold—a functioning part of the city-machine.

No drivers. No witnesses. And I've got the kid strapped to my chest.

I show my palms to the street. A slender hand clamps down on my right forearm and spins me around. A woman stares me in the face. She has a cheap-looking black polymer Beretta clutched in one gloved hand. She pauses, registers the kid sleeping against me. While her eyes are on vacation I shove the lady off balance and slap the pea-shooter out of her hand with a stabilizer-enhanced swipe. The lump of plastic hits the elasticrete sidewalk and I make sure it tumbles a safe distance away.

When I look up the lady has a retractable knife in her fist, coming off a tight swing. My right arm is grazed, jacket torn at the shoulder. The blade is too close to my daughter for comfort. I slow the situation down, relax my body, put my hands by my sides.

The woman's eyes shine with malice.

"Think I won't?" she asks.

"What do you need?" I ask.

"Just to give you some friendly advice, Drake," she says, motioning toward the Executor's ornate front door with the knife. "There's nothing in there for you. So don't worry about going back."

"No problem. I didn't make it through the review process anyway."

"You tried?"

"Sure I did. I'm an heir to the Arkady Ransom, aren't I?"

"Sure you did."

"That Executor is no softie. He failed me quick and didn't budge an inch. The machine's got no heartstrings to play."

She eyeballs the kid again. "Either way, it'd a real bad idea to make a return visit. Honest, it'd be a crying shame if you got hurt. Or if somebody in your *family* got hurt—"

I've got her by the wrist before she can finish the sentence. I dig in with my thumb, stabilizers engaging, crushing the median nerve. Her knife drops into my other hand real neat. It's an expensive pig-sticker. High-grade nano-carbon. A steep buy, out of place on her hip.

"Say what you want to me, I got thick skin, and besides, it's probably true. But don't threaten the kid," I say.

"Bastard," she says.

"Give me the sheath and we'll forget about it."

"You'll pay for this," she says through gritted teeth. My thumb digs in. The stabilizer is rock hard and I can hear her wrist bones grinding together. She reaches back with her other hand and takes the sheath off her hip. Hands it over.

What an excellent actress. Whoever put her up to this wanted that knife to draw my attention. Well, they got what they wanted. I let go of her, sheathe the knife, and slide it into my coat pocket. Abigail lets out a little mewling whine; she's starting to wake up.

The thug glares at me, rubbing her wrist. "Think you're real smart, don't you? Well I've seen smarter guys than you get dead. And then what use will you be to her?"

"Sounds like a threat. I'll bet the cops would be interested in that kind of behavior from one of their fine citizens."

The woman steps back, puffs her chest out, and laughs once. Hard.

"You don't have a clue, do you, junior? Listen, take my advice and stay far away from here," she says, glancing at the kid. "For everybody's sake."

* * * *

I head home and cram some food in the kid and change her and put her down for a nap. I make myself some lunch, eat it, clean up the sink, and then sit down at the kitchen table. I stare at the wall and listen to the auto-cars headed down to forever up on the expressway. The carbon knife sits on the table in its sheath. I pull it out and look at it: light as a feather and sharper than sunlight in space. It's got an interesting insignia pressed into it. A coat of arms.

Why'd the thug laugh when I mentioned the cops?

I sit for a while with the wooden slats of the chair pressing dents into my back, feeling the heat of the afternoon close in around me like carbon monoxide. I rub my aching right forearm stabilizer while it charges and wish I was just a little bit smarter so I could give this kid a life.

A warning. I got a warning. The lady was probably a low-level gun for hire without any solid affiliations. Could be working for anybody. Probably not the law.

I snap a pic of the coat of arms with my phone. Call it in for an image diagnostic. The ID comes back—the coat of arms reps an obscure Arkady splinter dynasty. It belongs to somebody in my family.

The Internecines have been raging since before I was born. Most people have distant cousins they run into every now and then. I have quasi-military factions of my family that routinely wipe each other out. And all the carnage is funded by speculative investing syndicates hoping to cash in on the goldenest goose of all—the Arkady Ransom.

It makes sense that the dynasties don't want me staking a claim. The day the Arkady Ransom goes tits up will be the day the syndicates put out their hands, palms up and hungry for four generations' worth of dough. But the obvious answer doesn't feel right. That dull silver knife with its gaudy coat of arms: it screams for attention. Could it be that the dynasty wants to make sure I know who I'm talking to? Or the knife's a plant and this is a frame-up job.

One thing is clear: Somebody doesn't want me to figure out the Executor's riddle. But there's a soft warm lump asleep in her crib next to the kitchen window. Every troubled breath she takes is the world's best argument for figuring out the riddle. It is what it is. There's no bravery in my decision to go back. No determination or noble auspice. I've got to save my daughter for the same reason a gun has to spit bullets.

I'm a citizen of the human machine.

The phone rings and I grab it fast before it can wake up Abigail. I say hello before I realize it's a machine talking. "Attention. This is an auto-summons issued to Philip Drake." I'm to report to the police captain of the local precinct at my earliest convenience. As long as the next hour or two is convenient. Final notice.

I pick up the knife and the kid and I strap them both on.

Outside, it's one of those searing bright afternoons where the sunlight pounds into your shoulders and then comes boiling back up off the elasti-crete to catch you under the chin. I hail the first auto that cruises past my house and tell it to head downtown. The air isn't working right in the vehicle so I figure out the voice command to roll down the window. I hang my arm out and curse as the red-hot door scalds me raw.

There's a bad feeling in my stomach and it's growing there like a tumor. As we pull up to the curb across from police headquarters I see a sleek black auto switchblade into traffic.

Something doesn't feel right.

I tap a new address into my ride's keypad because I don't want to be over-heard saying it out loud. Ten minutes later, we stop at a drive-thru every-thing store. I buy some diapers and a one-size-fits-all clip of baby food and an expensive Guardian plasma padlock.

During the drive, I play with Abigail a little. Give her my half-grin and let her paw at the dimple in my cheek. It only comes out for her, now that her mother is gone.

When we reach the capsule daycare, I pick the cleanest coffin they've got and poke my head inside to make sure the lights and electrical are in order. It's a good one—most of the padding is still left on the baby-handling arm. I load the food and diaper applicators and set the entertainment to Abigail's favorite show. I give her a kiss on the face and push her inside the coffin and say good-bye. After I pay and press the door closed, it locks and seals.

Then I put the Guardian padlock on the outside, just to be sure. I kiss my fingers and press them against the glass before it goes dark for privacy.

• • • •

A fist catches me in the stomach two steps into the captain's office. I get the feeling that the fist has been waiting here for me—maybe for hours, maybe for days. The knuckles are smooth and round and made of metal, attached to the assistive gripper arm of a walkchair.

The greeting isn't entirely unexpected, but it still knocks the breath out.

Captain Bales, a gruff, bald bullet of a man, gives me a sharp nod and a nasty grin. He's a lump of muscle confined to a beat-up walkchair that crouches on four stubby legs just inside the office door. The legged chair is brand new and black and stripped of all branding—squat and powerful as a linebacker.

"Got your attention?" Bales asks.

He turns his back on me. The chair carries him behind a sweeping steel-top desk docked in the middle of the room like an ocean liner. Bale's broad meaty shoulders sway and tremble with each scratching step of the walk-chair.

I'm glad it was the chair that hit me and not the man.

"Pleasure to meet you, too," I wheeze, holding my stomach.

"Take a seat," he says, and I collapse into a metal slug of chair. Bales drops those meat hooks on his desk and leans forward, shoulders rising like mountains. Behind him, a wall of books looms to the ceiling, up to where only a guy with a telescoping walkchair arm could reach.

"You got a problem, son," he says. "You made somebody very mad."

"Been known to happen," I say.

"Are you aware that the place you visited this morning is owned by a dynasty family? You were trespassing and they're not happy about it."

"Pushing it a little, aren't you?"

Bales gets very still. His brow drops and the next words come out slow and precise. "What are you talking about, Drake?"

"The dynasties don't own the Executor's office. Sure, they bought up the whole block and everything around it. But the Executor owns its own corridor and the speaking room. It's history. First time an A.I. ever bought property. Maybe you ought to dust off a book or two."

"Listen, you puke, it doesn't matter who owns the corridor. You walked into the building and that whole block's owned. We got you on video breaking the law."

"This isn't about the dynasties. Who's behind it?"

"You don't ask the questions, bub. That friendly pat got you all confused."

"Fine. I'll paste in my own answers. I think it's somebody rich. Powerful. Got to be if you're here wasting your batteries bullying me. An influential somebody is worried that I'm going to hit the big score. Figure out the Ransom. Why would that be?"

"You're way off, pal."

"This isn't the first day of school for either one of us, so let's say we stop playing patty-cake like a couple of little girls."

Bales grunts at me, leans back, and crosses his arms.

"The dynasties are a bunch of cutthroats," I say. "Criminals. They're locked in a fight that's never made an inch of progress and never will. All they do is borrow money from the syndicates and stake their failed claims and run around in tight little circles with guns. This is bigger. No planted knife is going to fool me."

Bales' face is blank. But the absence of information is plenty informational.

"Let me fill in that dull expression on your face, Captain. The Arkady Ransom is the biggest fund on the planet. The most stable and profitable investment that's ever existed. And for one reason: it's not run by a man. It's run by a machine. A dependable, immortal, predictably successful machine. Who cares if that machine was designed by a half-crazy scientist a couple centuries ahead of his time? Who cares if I happen to be related to that man? What matters is that I've got the potential to claim the money and ruin the best investment in history. Destabilize the world economy. That's why I've got a feeling that the toes I'm stepping on belong to a government or a multinational or somebody with enough swagger to buy you a prototype McLaren walkchair."

Bales readjusts his bulk in the legged chair.

"Great," he says. "So you're getting your little brain wrapped around it. Don't change a thing. Whoever you're dealing with, a dynasty or just a somebody, is over your head, Drake. Backing off is your only option. I could threaten you. Rough you up. God knows you think you're harder than you are. With this chair I could twist you into a goddamned pretzel and soak you in the cooler for a week. But I'm going to skip it. You're just a man and we've all got the right to wad up our lives like tissue paper and throw 'em away. My job today is just to make sure you know exactly what will happen if you go near the Executor again. You'll be throwing your life away, Drake. Walk down that road again, pal, you won't be coming back."

I stand up to leave.

"Thanks for the warning, captain. And I hate to break your heart. But you were right about one thing: I'm just a man."

. . . .

The long black auto is waiting outside. A guy who looks carved out of a rock face opens the door and motions me inside. I go because, frankly, I'm getting exhausted. Inside, the limo is as sleek and plush as the inside of a violin case—the sort you'd keep a Stradivarius in. It's also empty.

The rear wall of the limo is a curve of dark polished glass. It smells like ozone, purified air. I notice a few pin-head cameras and assume there are plenty more I can't see. The bar is all glass and light—pirate treasure glimmering just under Caribbean waves. I grab a crystal tumbler, pour myself a drink of an amber-something that could pay my rent for a month, and salute the nearest camera with it.

At that, the glass wall flickers to life and I'm looking into a three-dimensional drawing room. A man sits in a wingback chair, staring at me with expressionless gray eyes. He's middle-aged and built slightly, but decked out in a flamboyant old-school tartan smoking jacket. No technology of any kind is visible in the room, not even a lighter. The more money a person has, the more stuff he owns that's made of real wood. And I'm guessing this fella deals in the billions. The chair he sits in, the room around him, hell, even the jacket he wears are ribbed out in exquisite patterns. It's the sort of luxurious detail that slaps you in the face with the fact that your own life is nasty, brutish, and oh so disposable. I scan the scene and sigh and then pour myself three months' rent.

Off my lack of reaction, the man finally decides to speak.

"I'll get straight to the point, Drake. You're interfering. You wouldn't listen to Bales, so I'm going to see to it that you cease. Personally."

I take a drink and savor it, feeling the buzz creeping in around the corners of my vision. The man in the glass launches two shotgun slugs of gray stare my way. My response is careful: "I'd love to take some credit for interfering, friend, but I don't know who you are."

And I'm not sure I want to.

"My name is Holland Masterson and I'll tell you who I'm not. I am not your friend. I am not your family. I am Zeus on the mountaintop. You needn't concern yourself about me except inasmuch as you should avoid incurring my wrath."

I think this over a second.

"Well, I'm glad to hear we're not related. It's families like mine that keep the calluses on gravediggers' hands."

"You refer to the Internecines. Pathetic. A broken family borrowing money and making promises to strangers so they can arm themselves to murder each other. The late Dr. Arkady had amazing prescience to build the Executor. He knew the calculating avarice of so-called family and he sought to avoid it."

A trace of anger ripples over the man's face. It's like spotting a shark fin out of the corner of your eye. Something's hidden under the surface here. Something with teeth.

"I take it you're not a family man?"

"I am not, Mr. Drake. I believe achievement is the only measure of a man. And each man will be measured on his own before the eyes of god. Everything I have accomplished was achieved on my own merits. Only *I* taste the fruit of those labors."

"So what do you leave behind when you're gone?"

"A legacy of triumph. And preferably, as small a gang of squabbling vultures as is possible. Think of the pharaohs, Mr. Drake. They left behind pyramids to shine brightly through the ages. Their descendants fell into madness and despair long before time could ravage the beauty of those monuments."

"Sounds lonely as hell in there."

Masterson shoots those gray bullets at me again. Then the padded shoulders slump. "You are not an achiever and thus you cannot understand. You are only capable of taking commands. Very well, do not approach the Executor. Do not ask why. And do not interfere with me again or you will learn what pain feels like."

The screen fades back to dark polished glass and I notice the auto isn't moving anymore. For a second, I'm staring into my own flat, faded reflection. My face looks wooden and blank—a goddamned toy soldier on the march, drink in hand.

Then a shadow falls across the window and the driver yanks open the door with a *thunk*. Blinking at the sudden blazing sunlight, I step out of perfumed ozone and into hot reality. I don't hear the driver slam the door shut. I'm busy grasping the fact that I'm standing in front of the capsule daycare—the word *pain* still ringing in my ears.

. . . .

The Guardian plasma lock is sliced, laying on the ground next to the capsule. I pick it up and the dribble of melted metal is still warm from whatever industrial torch ate through it. With shaking fingers, I drop the privacy screen and unlock the capsule.

Inside, Abigail is laying on her back, watching the vidscreen with one eye and working on putting her foot into her mouth. She's fine and dandy—a cog in this efficient coffin-shaped machine. I exhale and then take a deep breath, realizing that I've been gut-punched since I saw the lock on the ground. Message received, Mr. Masterson.

But some things you can't change.

• • • •

I sit on the curb outside the capsule care with Abigail on my lap and watch the street for an older-model auto. The old ones are made of metal instead of plastic, and they cost less. I hail the first likely suspect and direct it to stop off at a Japanophile store. There, I drop some cash on a portable impact shell. The hot pink pod is hard outside and padded inside: gyro-stabilized and designed to keep an infant safe at ultra-high speeds. Hard to believe that in some places there's no stigma attached to taking your baby on a turbo-bike.

I shrug the shell onto my chest and slide Abigail into it. She's like a chubby pearl inside a clam. The glistening hull is rated for everything from impact to puncture to temperature and pressure fluctuations. With a couple of sharp yanks I secure the impact shell to my chest, straps cutting into my shoulders. Then I close the breather lid on top and listen for the gyros to engage. A soothing blue light spreads across the top of the shell, forming a happy face. Very Japanese.

The auto waits for us patiently, like a dog. An upgrade job, it has a vestigial driver compartment with a steering wheel and everything. The auto is doing its part in this clockwork city. All of us are doing our part. Not because we want to or even because we have to, but because it's the only way there is. You don't pick where the highway goes, you just keep one eye on the horizon and hope you're headed someplace nice.

I peek into the driver's-side window and notice a layer of dust on the front seat. The hunk of metal isn't designed for this but we've all of us have got to adapt. I drum my fingers on the roof and sigh then grab the door handle and yank it open. I crawl inside the doomed auto and buckle myself in and roll down the windows so the glass won't cut me when it shatters.

• • • •

There are more suits outside the offices than I expected. I catch at least one with the first jump over the curb. He has a confused look on his face and a gun in his hand for a split second. Then he is gone. Under the auto somewhere or maybe he dove out of the way.

Nobody ever drives an auto on manual anymore—surprise.

The rest of the lookouts scatter as a ton of screeching metal gallops over the curb and plows into the front door of the Executor's office. The safety belt catches me hard, dislocating my shoulder. A spray of red light slashes my face and the impact shell emits a warning shriek. The front door of the building explodes, spraying splinters into the dark corridor leading to the Executor's office.

It's quiet for an ear-ringing five seconds after impact. Dust from the pulverized office door floats in my open windows. I glance down at my chest and see a bright red sad face on top of the impact shell, fading back to a safe blue.

Breathing in ragged gasps, I try to unclip my safety belt and hiss in pain. I wrap my good arm around my hurt shoulder, hold my breath, and ram the auto door a couple times. The joint pops back into the socket and I'm underwater for a second with my pain. Tires screech and men shout as other autos arrive.

"It's Drake!" shouts somebody.

I kick the dented door open and clamber over the hood of the auto, stepping through the splintered door frame into the dark corridor. At the end of the hallway, I draw my piece and aim it at the crashed auto wedged into a rectangle of fading evening light. A dark face peeks in but disappears quick when it sees me coiled up in the shadows like a viper.

One hand over my baby, I squeeze the trigger until I see a ball of fire.

. . . .

I stagger just inside the door to the Executor's office before my joint-stabilization field fails. I crumble to the floor and I can hear Abigail crying but my eyes aren't working for some reason. I try to hug the impact shell tight against me but my arms won't listen to my brain.

An explosion rocks the hallway on the other side of the door.

I realize that I've really failed now. It was always a long shot. Strong out of the gate but faded on the stretch. In the end, no threat.

Then, the shell gives off a soft blue glow.

My eyes still work. It must be dark because they've cut the power to the building. My joint stabilizers failed, but now they've flipped to local batteries instead of leeching the ambient power supply. The stabilizers quiver—they're having trouble pulling out a pattern to offset the noise coming from my diseased nervous system.

I'm able to drag myself into a sitting position and flip the lid on the impact shell. Abigail is inside, angry and fussing but not hurt. And of course, looming over me, watching without expression, is the Executor. The ghost of the old man himself, standing in the blue-tinged darkness.

"Why didn't you listen to Mr. Masterson?" asks the machine.

"Who?" I ask. "The spook?"

That gives the Executor a pause.

"To what are you referring?" it asks.

I drag myself onto my feet, using the wall. "I'm referring to the fact that Holland Masterson was nothing but a hologram, cooked up by another hologram. The only one I know. You."

I make sure the door is locked. As secure as it's going to get.

"And what made you aware of this fact?"

"Choice of subject, pal. A legacy of triumph? I'm no genius. But that's a conversation I could have had with old man Arkady two hundred years ago. That and the décor in Masterson's little drawing room. Out of date. Some things even you can't change, right?"

"Correct."

"How long have you been doing this, Executor? Playing my family off each other?"

"Why, ever since I was created, I suppose."

"You tried too hard. That's what gave it away. If you weren't worried, you wouldn't have tried so hard. And I figured out why."

"Please enlighten me," says the machine, eyes half-lidded, confident. A distant thud rocks the building. I figure this means they've reparked my auto. Won't be long before this room is flooded with very angry men.

I don't say anything to the Executor. Favoring my busted shoulder, I pull Abigail out of the impact shell. She is small and warm and squirming in her pajamas. She's been crying. I wipe her face with my shirtsleeve and set her gently down on the speaking stone. The Executor drops the confident act and stares, eyes glittering like beetles.

"When a legal descendant touches the stone," I say, "the process begins."

With that reminder, the Executor's automatic behavior kicks in like the last second of a magic trick. "Review process initiated," it says. "Answer the following question: What is inside you and all around you; created you and is created by you; is you but not you?"

"Your answer is sitting right here," I say.

On all fours, Abigail cranes her neck to look up at me. She gives me a slobbery grin and tries to reach for me. I give her back half a smile and my index finger and then I throw a glance at the Executor.

"Family," I say. "The answer to your riddle is *family*. Old man Arkady never had one, really. Maybe that's why he booby-trapped the lives of everyone who came after him. Started the Internecines by creating you and keeping his wealth around forever, like poisoned bait. He was brilliant and maybe more machine than man and he didn't realize what was important until it was too late. You were the closest thing the old man ever had to family, sad and pathetic and wrong as that may be. Family is what he feared most. Family is what he always wanted but never had."

The Executor is silent for few seconds.

"Claim approved," it says. "Until Miss Abigail Drake is of age, the Arkady estate will be held in abeyance. Upon her aetatis suae eighteen, all goods and chattels shall be conveyed to her as sole inheritor. However, at this time you have no claim to the monies—"

"I'm not after your money, pal."

"Very well, then—"

"But I've got one more thing to say to you. So listen close."

The Executor stands very still, watching me like a predator.

"As her guardian," I say, "*you're* part of her family now. And if you are called upon, my friend, you will give her a life not imaginable to a person like me. A life of wealth and travel. Knowledge. You'll protect her. You'll bend every twisted circuit of your will to guide her, to help make her a strong and good and just woman. And in due time, she will become the matriarch of our line and your successor. When that day comes you will step down, Executor. And Abigail Drake will carry on our family name in peace. Understand?"

"Yes, Mr. Drake. I understand."

"Good," I say, ignoring a foreboding rumbling coming from the hallway. "Now I've got to go out there and settle this before they come in here and settle it for us."

"Are you sure that's safe?"

"It's as safe as anything."

"I'm afraid they've cut off my communications. I'm not able to cancel my previous orders. However, the police will arrive in less than four minutes—"

The machine is cut off as something big and loud happens just outside. But I'm not watching the machine. I'm putting Abigail back inside the impact shell. I tuck her in and set the shell on the speaking stone with the lid open.

"We don't have four minutes. If they get in here they'll shoot everything that moves."

"I'll simply talk to them, order them to stop."

"I don't think that's going to help much, friend. I made a messy entrance. They're understandably upset."

I check my revolver and holster it under my left arm. The knife I secure in the waistband of my pants, in the small of my back. I juice my stabilizers to full power, until my arms and legs hum with strength. Should last about ten minutes. Plenty long enough.

Only then do I allow myself one last look. The pink shell rests on the stone. Inside it, the world's wealthiest individual is blowing spit bubbles at me. I press my sagging holster against my chest so the gun won't bump her and lean down and kiss Abigail on her forehead. I close my eyes for a second, just a blink, and inhale her smell. Her skin is soft as rose petals on my stubbled chin and I remind myself to try and remember this detail for later—for when things get bad.

Somehow, later is always closer than you think.

I close the impact shell and stride over to the quivering door. With one hand I check the knife again to make sure I can draw it fast. I give the machine a stern look but the Executor knows the score.

I grab hold of the doorknob and put my head down. Take a breath. Flex my arms until the joint stabilizers are singing.

"You're a good father," says the Executor.

I hear the thugs in the hall outside, shuffling past each other, body armor clinking. I feel a cold spot on my chest where my daughter is missing. I know that each of us has to do our part in this city, like clockwork.

"No, I'm not," I say to the Executor. "But you better be."

And I step through the door.

Daniel H. Wilson is the author of the pop-science books How to Survive a Robot Uprising, Where's My Jetpack, How to Build a Robot Army, Bro-Jitsu: The Martial Art of Sibling Smackdown, *and* The Mad Scientist Hall of Fame *(with Anna C. Long). His first two novels—*A Boy and His Bot *and* Robopocalypse—*came out in 2011. He is the "Resident Roboticist" for* Popular Mechanics, *and was the host of the History Channel show* The Works; *he has also appeared on the TV show* Modern Marvels, *and the documentary* Countdown to Doomsday. *His short fiction has previously appeared on Tor.com and in John Joseph Adams's anthology* Armored. *His latest novel is called* Amped.

CATEGORY: Vectors and Properties in
Nemesis Relationships

RULE 1113.2: Everybody Needs Help with Their Evil
Monologue

SOURCE: Angie, career counselor

VIA: Heather Lindsley

*Entering the workforce is hard enough, but landing—and keeping—
your dream job can sometimes feel impossible. This is the reason
why career counseling and vocational psychology is a growth industry, even in a recession. Sometimes people just need a little help
launching their careers.*

*In our next piece, one enterprising career counselor has identi-
fied a niche market: counseling would-be supervillains. After all,
in a field that lacks clear entry-level requirements, it's hard to
know just how to get started. There are no degree programs that
can give someone the skills needed to thrive as bad guy. There are
few, if any, mentorships to apply for. And as for fellowships and
residencies, well, that's a laugh! You're on your own when you
start out as a supervillain.*

*But with a career counselor like Angie, you're better off than
the average ne'er-do-well. She's got just the right advice, whether
her client needs help designing the perfect costume, crafting the
successful evil plot, or writing a really clever monologue. In fact,
some people might think she's a little too good at her job. . . .*

THE ANGEL OF DEATH HAS A BUSINESS PLAN

HEATHER LINDSLEY

Carl has a pair of purple knee-length boots in one hand and a black PVC codpiece in the other. "Sorry, Angie, I'm running late," he says. "I just need to get changed."

"We can do it in street clothes, Carl."

"No, no—it's not the same without the costume. I'll be quick, I promise."

Carl is a regular client, and one of my first, so I cut him some slack. I should have been able to help him years ago, but I keep coming because he seems to get closer every week. Or maybe that's just what I tell myself. Living in Megapolis is damn expensive, and a little steady income doesn't hurt.

I take a seat on Carl's couch, clearing away a stack of Commander Justice comics first. He says he'll be quick, but I've seen him struggle in and out of those boots too many times to believe him.

The comic on the top of the stack catches my eye. *Is this the end for Commander Justice?* I wish, but of course it isn't. I flip through the first few pages before tossing the candy-colored propaganda aside.

"You really shouldn't read this crap," I tell Carl when he finally comes back into the room. "It can't be doing anything for your confidence."

"I need to keep up with his latest crime-fighting techniques."

"No, you don't. You need to shoot him in the face."

Carl winces. "That sounds so unsporting."

"Exactly. You can be sporting, or you destroy your archnemesis and rule this city with an iron fist. What's it gonna be?"

"Destroy my archnemesis."

"Say it like you mean it, Carl."

Carl takes a deep breath, checks to make sure his Master Catastrophe logo is centered on his chest, and booms out, "I WILL BRING THIS CITY TO ITS KNEES!"

"There ya go. Now let's get started."

. . . .

At the end of the session Carl is sweaty and a little wild eyed. If I had the time I'd run him through one more focus exercise, but his hour's up.

"Good job with your confidence levels, Carl—lots of improvement. But you need to work on your concentration. You've got to be confident *and* focused when you take on Commander Justice."

"Thanks, Angie. But you know, I really think I could do it if you were with me. We'd make a great team . . ."

"Come on, Carl, you know that's not what I do."

"But it could be! We could be partners. Master Catastrophe and Mayhem Girl!"

"Mayhem Girl?"

"Mayhem Woman."

"Say it with me, Carl."

" 'Evil geniuses work alone.' "

"That's right. And there's a damn good reason for it."

"But Angie—"

"I don't do sidekick."

"I know, it's just that—"

"Carl."

"Okay."

"So how do you feel? What are you going to do when you see Commander Justice?"

"Ready, aim, fire."

"That's right. Even if he asks you a question. *Especially* if he asks you a question. Confidence, and no distractions. Ready, aim, fire—that's all."

"Thanks, Angie."

"No problem, Carl. Good luck."

. . . .

Every week after Carl's session I go straight back to my place and do the accounts. Villainy coaching and superhero surrogacy provide a steady revenue stream, but it's not enough to get out of this tiny basement apartment. It kills me that what I'm paying in Megapolis would buy a massive lair in the sticks, but until you're a big name you've got to be in the big city if you want to be taken seriously in this game.

I fire up the pirated copy of BadBooks I got from the Green Shade, and I'm not surprised that the latest figures show yet another week of high turnover and slim margins. My operating costs are ridiculous—insurance alone ate up half my income last month. There's just enough left over for a few more square inches of stabilized technetium plating for my Angel of Death costume, though I should be saving up for another shipment of weapons-grade plutonium.

At this rate it will take years to execute my business plan. I must admit I was hoping for more from the villains in this town. Some spark of genius. Some inspiration.

A quick e-mail check shows mostly the usual: a report from one of my insurance agents in Fiji, heated but familiar debates in various online villainy group digests, spam for penis-enlargement pills. There's also a message from a potential new client who calls himself Burn Rate. I don't recognize the handle, so I'll have to do some research before I get back to him. Probably a newbie with a flashy fire-themed costume and a half-finished death ray.

The idea hits too close to home, and I decide to use last month's surplus on boring old plutonium. Weapons first, costume second, though it pains me that in its incomplete state my Angel of Death outfit looks like it belongs in one of those four-color hero propaganda mags. It'll stay in the closet until the protective plating covers all my vital organs.

I put on a pot of coffee and move from my cramped, messy desk to my cramped, messy lab. I've been tinkering with disintegration, preferably something that leaves an on-theme sandy or dusty residue, but at my current rate of progress my own villainous schemes look more like a hobby than a profession.

It's going to be a long night.

. . . .

New client today, though The Puzzler isn't new to the game—he's been ineffectually pestering Civetman for years.

The session isn't going well. We're still standing in the foyer of The Puzzler's penthouse apartment.

"I didn't realize your agency would be sending a woman," he says.

I let him think there's an agency. "Is that a problem?"

"Well, uh, it's just that my nemesis is Civetman."

"And?"

"Civet*man*."

"Look, you hired a superhero surrogate. You know how this works, right?"

"Yes. No. I mean, I was thinking you'd be more of a stand-in. Like an actor. Civetman is taller, and he has these huge muscles, and—"

"I don't need huge muscles to listen to your monologue."

"But if it's not a convincing scenario, how will I know it's completely out of my system?"

"Okay." I hitch my bag up higher on my shoulder. "I can do captured girlfriend. Will that work for you?"

"Huh. Yeah. Yeah, okay, let's do that."

"Fine. It'll be an extra ten thousand."

"You're kidding? Why?"

Asshole tax. "Ten grand extra for captured girlfriend, or I walk away with your deposit. Or you can dial down your *Civetman* obsession and let me do my job."

"I'm not paying extra, but since you're already here how about you use the time you were supposed to be listening to my monologue doing something useful. You could clean my bathroom."

I take the detonator out of my pocket. He looks surprised. What kind of idiot is surprised to see a detonator in this situation? "Or I could blow up your bathroom and every other room in your alternate secret lair in Fiji. You just finished a big remodel, right? Laser targeting systems, Viking range in the kitchen, malachite bathtub with gold taps?" Seriously, gold taps. Tacky as hell.

"You wouldn't. I'd sue you for damages."

He'd sue me. Some supervillain. "'Clause 27.1.5: The Supplier retains the right to destroy as needed in either self-defense or in execution of the services noted herein any property of the Client's owned for the purposes of committing villainy, super- or otherwise.'"

"The lair—*house*—in Fiji is a vacation home."

"With six-megawatt lasers."

"Home security."

"Nice try." I raise the detonator. "So, what's it gonna be?"

· · · ·

I leave ten grand further ahead and thinking I should have made it twenty. The Puzzler's monologue was predictable, his plan for global domination was doomed to failure, and his weapons were the kind of junk you can get from the back room of an Army Surplus store if you know who to ask.

It's some consolation to know I won't have to worry about his repeat business, and at least I have some punching to look forward to this afternoon.

I'm on my way to Master Adisa's studio and about a hundred yards from the subway when a massive steel tentacle bursts the pavement in front of me. Another tentacle wraps itself around my waist and lifts me thirty feet into the air. A dozen squad cars come tearing around the corner. A guy with a bullhorn says, "Let the hostage go, Squidinator!"

I don't have time for this—I have a private lesson today and I'm sure as hell not letting some big dumb stunt blow my chance to learn the Pincer of Death.

I've still got my shoulder bag, so I squirm around in the grip of the tentacle to reach inside. The squirming probably looks good for the crowd. I hope a publicity-minded villain like the Squidinator appreciates it.

"Hey!" I shout, thrusting my business card toward the skinny guy in the giant mecha harness. "Do you mind?"

He lifts me right up to the harness and squints at the card.

"Oh, shit. I'm really sorry. I didn't realize. My friend DoomDaddy saw you last month. He said you were great, really helped him cut back on his monologuing."

"Glad to hear it. So you gonna put me down now, or what?"

"Um, I'm sort of in the middle of a thing here . . ."

"Here's a thought—I can manage a little hysterical screaming, but I've got an appointment in twenty minutes so I'm gonna need you to drop me off at Concord and 87th."

"Concord and 87th?" He frowns. "That's, like, all the way across town . . ."

"Weren't you planning a rampage?"

"Yeah, but . . ."

"So rampage toward Concord and 87th."

"Okay, but that screaming is going to have to be really good."

"How's this?" I say, and let him have it.

"Nice shriek," the Squidinator says. "Sounds really panicked."

"Thanks. I'm just imagining what'll happen if I'm late for my appointment."

"Ah, yes, the Method," he says, missing the point. Scratch a supervillain and half the time there's a failed actor underneath.

Since he seems so pleased with the performance I consider asking him to throw in one of the bags of cash he's obviously pulled out of the smashed-up bank around the corner, but the dye packs have already gone off, bloodlike red dripping from a couple of tentacles. It's a nice effect. Sure it makes the bank robbery pointless from an income perspective, but the Squidinator will score some priceless publicity.

I let loose another round of dramatic screams while the Squidinator hitches up his tentacles and lumbers uptown.

• • • •

It's only when I'm back home that I discover just how much publicity the Squidinator's stunt got him after he dropped me off.

Arachnoboy finally turned up, late to the scene as usual. I'm pretty sure what happened was an accident, given the expression on the Squidinator's face afterward. In the news footage it looks like his tentacles were just flailing wildly when one of them clipped a bit of Arachnoboy's web and slung him headfirst into a building. Not much control, but a hell of a lot of velocity.

The tabloid headlines were right—there was only one way to describe it. Arachnoboy got squashed.

The Squidinator went into hiding. I don't know whether he was relieved or disappointed when he got pushed out of the news cycle only a day later by the explosion in front of Order Corps HQ. He might have held his own if there were no casualties, but the explosion took out the Blue Streak and both Marvel Twins.

A masked duo calling themselves Mistress Mine and the Malignant Mole released a video claiming credit. I didn't recognize the Malignant Mole, but I knew Mistress Mine when she called herself the Scarlet Woman. We only had a few sessions together, mostly working on her discomfort with direct confrontation. When she stopped booking appointments and dropped off the scene I thought she decided I wasn't helping and gave up supervillainy. I'm glad to see she's still in the game. I wouldn't have gone with the duo approach, but I wish her luck.

Two major heroes and a couple of sidekicks killed over the same weekend doesn't look good. The surviving members of the Order Corps held a press conference on Sunday night, and for a change they didn't seem smug and righteous while they told us all how safe they were making our fair city. They just looked really, really pissed off.

· · · ·

In spite of the drama over the weekend I head over to Carl's for our usual session. I'm feeling more optimistic that I can help him defeat Commander Justice, though I hope he can lie low for a while without losing the inspiration.

Lying low doesn't seem to be an option: Commander Justice is waiting on the landing in front of Carl's third-floor walk-up. Waiting for me, apparently.

"Angie, isn't it?" He's blocking the door.

"Yes."

"You come to visit old Carl every week, don't you?"

"Well, yes—I'm his massage therapist." I wonder what, if anything, Carl ever said about me during one of his rambling monologues. All I can wish is that I'd been better at my job.

"Really? Where's your table?"

"We use Carl's."

"Master Catastrophe has his own massage table?"

"I'm sorry, who?"

He indulges me. "Carl."

"Carl has back trouble. He needs a lot of work."

"I'll bet." He hasn't budged. Up close I can see lines around his eyes that they never draw in the comic. He's been in the game for as long as I can remember.

"Look," I say, trying for flirty, "you're not going to be unchivalrous and make me admit I'm not that kind of massage therapist, are you?"

His smile is grim. "I know your therapy has nothing to do with massage,

Angel. How are you doing, by the way? That must have been an awfully traumatic experience, being held hostage by the Squidinator."

Of course. All that footage, every shot, every bit of cell-phone video getting even more scrutiny with Arachnoboy's death. I should have been lying low myself.

"It was . . . being grabbed off the street like that at random."

"I'm sure. I hope it didn't throw off your lesson. I hear Master Adisa isn't very forgiving of distracted students, no matter how good the excuse."

He takes a step closer, backing me up against the rickety banister. "The superhero community has suffered some serious losses. It's completely unprecedented, and frankly some of us are considering a more . . . proactive approach to fighting crime."

I'm just about to try darting away when Carl steps out of his apartment. He's wearing his costume without the boots, and his Master Catastrophe logo is crooked. He's not carrying his death ray. He has his father's old .45 service pistol.

His voice isn't much above a whisper when he says, standing there in his grubby white athletic socks, "I will bring this city to its knees."

"Oh, please," Commander Justice says as he steps away from me and heads toward Carl. "A gun? Don't you want to wave that piece-of-shit death ray at me first? Don't you want to monologue?"

Carl takes a deep breath. "Ready, aim, fire."

Commander Justice doesn't have superspeed, and he isn't bulletproof. In the end the corpse with the large and messy hole in his head was just a guy who spent a lot of time at the gym and had some good gadgets, a trust fund, and the unholy confidence to enforce his vision of morality while wearing his underwear on the outside.

"I did it," Carl says in shock. A fleeting look of triumph follows. "I finally did it." He stares at his permanently defeated nemesis. "What do I do now?" He sits down on the floor.

I sit down next to him and put my arm around his shoulders. "Hey," I say. "You know who's a total asshole? Civetman."

"Yeah," he says with a little smile, "I've heard that."

. . . .

I go back home, taking a different route. I bolt the door. I do the accounts, but not financial ones.

Half the Order Corps is gone. If even a few of my clients take the initiative, it could tip this city's balance in favor of supervillainy for good.

I consider joining the fray myself, but my doomsday device is nowhere near ready and my half-finished costume makes me look like the worst kind of badly drawn T&A cliché. It's just not time for the world to meet the Angel of Death.

It won't be long before another member of the Order Corps follows Commander Justice's lead, so I'm about to hastily pack a bag when I notice I've got new voice mail.

It's the kid who calls himself Burn Rate.

Look, the message says, *I know you usually work with established villains, but I've had a breakthrough in the lab . . . I mean, something really big, and I want to launch it next week, but I can feel the urge to monologue, I mean, I know it's going to be irresistible, and I don't want to muff this. I just . . . I think talking to someone would help.* There's a cough and a pause. *Anyway, I did a test run the other day. It hasn't made the news, of course it wouldn't, what with the Squidinator and what happened at Order Corps HQ. But you can find it on YouTube, just search for Burn Rate.*

I call him and set an appointment for this evening. Maybe the kid has talent. It's a long shot, but my only other option is early retirement.

. . . .

Burn Rate's lair is in a discreet brownstone in a quiet neighborhood. I didn't have time for the usual insurance, but I watched his YouTube videos and did some basic research. Burn Rate turned up about six months ago, apparently funding his villainy with cash his civilian persona made selling a lucrative startup. Since then he's pulled off a couple of impressive heists. He showed style, and his weapons looked good: elegant, efficient. He has promise.

Or so I thought until he started his monologue.

"Struggle all you like, Human Tornado! You'll never escape my Electrostatic Cage!"

Not another Electrostatic Cage. Even superheroes carry enough loose change in their rubber-soled boots to discharge the damn things.

"Ah ha ha ha!" Burn Rate says before he breaks character and whispers to me, "It's not really electrostatic . . . I just want to see the look on his face when it vaporizes the quarter he tries to flip through it."

"Vaporize?"

"Yeah." He grins and gets back into character. "Nice try, Human Tornado, but you'll never save this city from my Demoleculator!"

Whoa, whoa, whoa—this is new. "You've got a Demoleculator? A *working* Demoleculator?"

"Yep, that's why I need your help. How do you not monologue about the world's first fully functional Demoleculator?"

"But no one's ever been able to stabilize the parakinetic matrix long enough to produce a reliable quantic field."

"I have," Burn Rate says.

"How'd you do that?"

"Buckyballs," he says with genuine and utterly charming enthusiasm.

"But what about Brock particle phase shift?"

"Now, see, that's the cool part. The fullerenic properties reinforce the icosohedral substrate, creating a completely stable crystalline structure."

"Ingenious."

"I know, huh?" Is he actually blushing? "Ask me about my orbiting death ray."

"You've got an orbiting death ray?"

"With targeting precision at about plus or minus three feet, but I'm working on that. I was tempted to do a demo during my last heist, but I thought it might be overkill."

"Yeah, you want to save a device like that for serious world domination action."

"Exactly. Look, I know you're only getting paid to hear the monologue, but are you interested in taking a look? I've got a pretty nice lab in the basement. I don't mean to show off, but you really seem to know your death rays, and it's just so damn cool."

His grin is as infectious as a well-designed bioweapon. "I'd love to," I say.

. . . .

His lab isn't pretty nice—it's stunning. And it isn't so much in the basement as part of an underground lair so vast you'd need a map to navigate: this way to the lab, this way to the firing range, this way to the master control room, this way to more storage than most Megapolites could even imagine.

We talk shop while he gives me the tour. His enthusiasm is boundless—he's obviously in it for the science.

"Take the orbiting death ray," he says. "Next to the challenges of maintaining the power supply, you'd think ultraprecise targeting from a geosynchronous orbit would be a snap. And to be fair the current margin for error isn't that bad, but it does limit it to villainous applications."

"So there are nonvillainous uses for an orbiting death ray?"

"Well, there'd be a certain amount of rebranding involved." He looks a little sheepish. "Anyway, do you want to give it a try?"

"Seriously?"

"Of course. Go on, pick a target."

He shows me the controls. I've never seen such a clean interface. In only a moment I've got it locked on The Puzzler's 1937 Bugatti.

"Ouch," says Burn Rate.

"He painted question marks all over it. I'm putting it out of its misery."

"Fair enough," he says, and the car disappears in a cloud of parking garage debris.

"That was amazing."

"I always find it a bit distant. Now the handheld version of the Demoleculator, that's a much more immediate experience."

"Okay, I was already impressed. A *handheld?*"

"Well, it's just a prototype. Terrible battery life. Every shot means overnight on the charger." He looks shy again. "Look, I know I'm being a terrible show-off, but I just spend so much time working on this stuff by myself . . ."

"Don't worry. You have a lot to be proud of here."

"So do you want to try it?"

"Of course I do."

"You're not worried about Brock particles?"

"I trust you."

We go to the firing range. There's a wooden bowl of fruit on a pedestal about fifty yards away. When Burn Rate stands behind me, unnecessarily helping me aim the Demoleculator, a pleasant sensation runs up and down my spine.

I fire.

I walk over to the pile of dirty-looking sand that used to be the bowl, the fruit, and the pedestal.

"The handheld version leaves more residue," he says apologetically. "It just doesn't have enough power to properly vaporize."

"Is it safe to touch?" I ask, kneeling over the pile.

"Oh, yes," he says. "It's completely inert."

I let the grains run through my fingers. "It's perfect," I say. I look up and see a strange smile on his face, probably a reflection of my own.

"So it's not particularly villainous," he says, "but do you want to check out the wine cellar?"

. . . .

"This is extraordinary." The complexity in the first sip of Château Pétrus is unlike anything I've ever tasted.

"It is nice, isn't it?" He looks a little surprised by the taste himself. "I have to admit I bought most of the cellar at an estate sale, so I can't take credit for its quality. I am learning, though. Mastering oenology was one of my New Year's resolutions."

"You do realize compulsive truth-telling is a very unhealthy quality in a supervillain, right?"

"I know," he says. "I need help."

"We never got through your monologue. I think we should give it another try."

He checks his watch and looks both embarrassed and hopeful when he says, "Can we do it in the morning?"

I swirl my wine in its crystal glass, inhaling the scent of a vintage older than either of us. My research says he's about my age, but he looks so young I can't help smiling at him.

"Okay."

A bottle of wine later he says, "Have you ever thought about working with someone? Not just on the monologuing, I mean."

"I don't do sidekick."

"I didn't mean sidekick. I meant partner."

I look at his handsome face and think about his beautiful lab, his elegant weapons, his vast storage space. I'm so lost in visions of the future I'm not really listening to him anymore, but I think he's saying, "All this could be yours."

• • • •

And now the world knows the Angel of Death very well indeed.

That wasn't the case at first. In the chaos of the early days, supervillains all over the city stopped talking and started shooting. A few turned on other heroes, or each other. A lot of them, like Carl, retired once they took out the archnemesis they'd built their lives around. Carl did go after Civetman, but he said it just wasn't the same. He has a nice garden allotment near his apartment now. He seems happy.

Most of the surviving villains knew about my insurance policies. I've heard their monologues. I've seen their weapons. I know their weaknesses.

I emerged from the mayhem with my finger on the trigger of Burn Rate's orbiting death ray and a business plan that was just waiting for the right arsenal.

I like to think I've been a benign global overlord, for the most part. Yes, some people complain about my banning cell phones on public transportation, or more specifically the fact that phones explode if they try to talk into them on a bus or a train. Or in a restaurant, or at the movies, or in any of a dozen other public places. But I think most of the population appreciates the peace and quiet.

I try to stay away from too much social engineering, though, and concentrate instead on more profitable ventures. My home dry-cleaning cabinet, licensed to Whirlpool, has been quite a little moneymaker. And of course it's terrible for the planet, so it's in keeping with my villainous brand. Image is so important in this business.

The giant statue of me with my boot on the actual White House might be a bit much, but I stand by adding my head to Mount Rushmore—it's about time there was a woman's face in that granite boys' club.

After a challenging year things are ticking over nicely now. I'm still running the whole show from Burn Rate's lair. It has everything I ever wished for while I was trapped in my crappy basement apartment.

I did make one change—I installed my dream desk in the master control room. It's huge, and glossy black. Retractable compartments across its glorious broad surface let me indulge my love of paper and my love of order at the same time.

The only item I never clear off my desk at the end of the day is a dull metal cylinder about the size of a beer can. It holds Burn Rate's grainy remains. The recharged Demoleculator worked beautifully.

I keep it there to remind me of the first rule of this business, the one the poor kid forgot: evil geniuses work alone.

———————

Heather Lindsley's work has appeared several times in The Magazine of Fantasy & Science Fiction, *as well in the magazines* Asimov's Science Fiction, Strange Horizons, Escape Pod, *and* Greatest Uncommon Denominator. *Her fiction has also appeared in John Joseph Adams's dystopian anthology* Brave New Worlds, *in* Year's Best SF 12, *edited by David G. Hartwell and Kathryn Cramer, and in* Talking Back, *edited by L. Timmel Duchamp. She is a graduate of the Clarion West Writers Workshop and currently lives in London.*

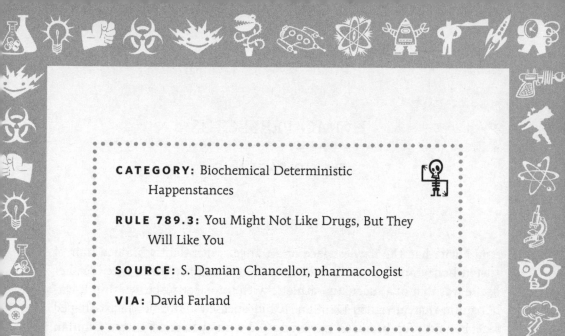

CATEGORY: Biochemical Deterministic Happenstances

RULE 789.3: You Might Not Like Drugs, But They Will Like You

SOURCE: S. Damian Chancellor, pharmacologist

VIA: David Farland

In the modern world, pharmaceuticals rule. Drug companies influence Congress, buy ads on prime-time TV, and wine-and-dine doctors' associations, all for the promise of health. After all, pills help roll back aging, fight disease, even combat depression. But can the drug manufacturers really be trusted, or do they have their own agenda?

Our next author, who was once a premed student and has retained an interest in the field, says of the drug industry, "Very often I will read stories about promising medical experiments, such as those used to boost intelligence, and then never hear a word again. It makes me wonder—are the drug companies holding out on us?"

This next story is a tale of a madman with access to all the resources of a powerful pharmaceutical company. He has chemicals to influence women's desires. He has drugs to make him stronger and smarter. Is immortality the next potion in his bottle?

Now that really would be better living through chemistry.

HOMO PERFECTUS

DAVID FARLAND

Drinks

Asia Nicita had the flawless face of an angel, with tightly braided hair of rusted honey and sea-green eyes that proclaimed her innocence. Yet her figure was that of a succubus—athletic with intoxicating curves. But it was her mind that intrigued Damian. It hid encased above her heart-shaped face, behind a forehead and cheeks dusted with opalescent glitter. Damian wondered what secrets he might pry from it.

As she folded her napkin onto her lap and scooted into the seat of the booth, Damian smiled. The club here in SoHo smelled of Thai-spiced chicken, vague perfumes, and female musk. The air throbbed with music from an Irish runic band, with electric violins and Celtic women's voices synched in stunning harmonies.

"You look wonderful tonight," Damian said softly.

"I *am* wonderful," she teased, as if she had just reached that conclusion.

Damian smiled. He knew that she found him attractive. Most women responded to his short dark curls, his gray eyes. If she didn't think him desirable now, she soon would. They were seated in a booth at the back of the restaurant. The pheromones that he had slathered on his neck would sublime into the air and then attach to the chemoreceptors at the back of her tongue. She'd be aching with desire for him within fifteen minutes.

"Have you eaten here before?" he asked.

She shook her head. "I'm new to the city."

"It's very popular with the after-theater crowd. We should leave before the place really fills up."

She pouted for a microsecond, dismayed at the thought of having to rush. "The food smells sooo fantastic!"

"Oh, don't worry. We have plenty of time. So . . . how do you like the new job at . . . the company?"

It was a casual-sounding question, as if spoken from lack of anything better to talk about, but Asia, instantly wary, fell silent. "Uh, let's not talk about work."

That was almost all that Damian *did* want to talk about, but he'd circle the subject. It was a technique gleaned from the master interrogator Hanns Scharff, whose efforts for the Luftwaffe during WWII had nearly decimated the Allied Alliance.

"Don't be worried," Damian said. "After all, I'm in the Personnel Department. I know everything . . ." he trailed off, leaving her to wonder what he really did know. The truth was, he did know everything about the company. The pheromones that he wore were a tightly controlled company secret. They were but one of many that he kept, and he longed to share some of them with Asia.

She was employed in the C Wing at Chancellor Pharmaceutical as a research chemist. She'd held the job for only a week. At twenty-four, she was young to be a Ph.D. Asia was half Greek and half Swedish. Women from such stock were often gorgeous. She had an IQ of 184, and a bust that was 34D hidden beneath a red-sequined blouse that was a bit too conservative. It concealed her beauty rather than revealed it.

On the basis of breeding alone, she was perhaps the most perfect woman he'd ever had the pleasure to meet—a fine prospect for biological upgrades.

"There is nothing wrong with talking about your job with fellow workers," Damian suggested. "You're on the Methuselah project, and you're studying toxicity levels of common contaminants—dioxin, bisphenol A, chlorine and the like—in long-lived animals."

"We're not supposed to talk about it outside the compound," she said sharply. Her voice sounded loud as the singers on stage worked a soft crooning melody to a solitary drum.

"It's all right," he said, seeking to redefine her fear. "With me, it's safe to talk about what you do; you just can't reveal what your research teaches you." He did not wait for her to agree. She had been told during her employee orientation to keep silent. But as her desire for him grew, he knew that she would begin to open her mouth. "Even *I* don't know what Chancellor Pharmaceuticals has discovered, and I have a Level Six security clearance."

That was a good line, he thought, *delivered with authority.* He needed her to see him as the authority here.

He hurried on, "Yet the implications of your research . . . hint at astonishing things. Think of it: the only reason that the company would want to know how toxicity levels affect people with life spans of a thousand years, or ten thousand years, suggests that some discovery is about to be unveiled, something monumental!"

"Is that what you think I do?" she asked coyly, struggling to change the subject.

She had to know more than she feigned, of that Damian was sure. But even with her high IQ, he doubted that she could guess what was really going on. The world was about to change. Mankind was about to change at a fundamental level. He wanted her to embrace that change.

"You have beautiful eyes," he said, suddenly wanting to possess her completely.

The waiter, a young man named Chaz, a Cuban who wore a shiny gold nose ring and spiked hair bleached white on top, came from the kitchens and asked what they would like to drink.

"I'll have the 2002 Merlot," Damian ordered, then suggested to Asia, "you really should try it."

"Perrier," she said, "in a bottle."

Smart girl. The taste of some common date-rape drugs could be masked by wine.

Damian talked for a bit on other topics—the latest earthquake, her favorite rock band. He watched until her breathing had slowed and deepened, her eyes had closed to slits, and her face had become slightly flushed. She was feeling the effects of his pheromones. He took her hand and asked, "How do you feel about casual sex?"

"I . . . can't fraternize with other employees," she said.

"No, that rule applies only to people within your own department," he quoted the employee manual. "I'm in Personnel. You're in Research. We can . . . fraternize."

She shook her head hesitantly. The drug-induced lust was fooling with her mind. "I don't believe in that. Sex isn't meant to be casual. It's more about . . . bonding than pleasure. Americans fall in love to mate, while the French mate to fall in love. In the end, everyone falls."

Damian chuckled. For a woman who still looked like a child, she showed unexpected maturity.

The waiter brought the drinks, setting one on each side of the candle that guttered in a glass container in the midst of the table. He offered to pour Asia's water over ice, but she took her bottle and said, "Excuse me."

With eyes half closed, like a lizard basking in the sun, Damian watched her get up and head for the women's room, hips swaying seductively as she dodged a waitress. She clutched her drinking water as she elbowed the restroom door open.

This girl has been rufied before, Damian surmised, as he swirled the merlot in his glass and inhaled its bouquet. Either that, or she's just very cautious. No matter, there's plenty of time. . . .

The Appetizer

When Asia returned, most of the glitter had been dabbed off of her forehead, and a few strands of her hair were wet. Her eyes had cleared.

She relaxed into her seat, but she did a poor job of maintaining her composure. She had the slightest tremor to her hands, and she stared at him as if she were breaking inside, as if she feared that she would collapse under the weight of his gaze.

"I'm sorry if I made you nervous," Damian apologized. He *was* sorry. He didn't enjoy destroying her. This wasn't his normal assignment at the company. Chancellor Pharmaceuticals could minimize the threat from corporate spyware—the recordings that others tried to make night and day. But the company had to test its employees against more subtle threats, moles that might seduce. Normally, Damien handled weightier matters. Indeed, he assigned flunkies to test the new employees. But there was something about Asia's heart-shaped face that drew Damian, something in her dossier that . . . called to him. He couldn't define exactly what he wanted from her.

Lately, since taking the age-regression therapy, he had been going through dramatic physical changes. Even in his youth, he'd never suffered from such an overpowering libido. It almost frightened him.

"It's all right," Asia said. "I suppose that we should get those kinds of questions out of the way. So if you're curious, yes, I'm healthy. Yes, I am a virgin. No, I won't sleep with you tonight. I want a . . . permanent relationship."

Damian smiled pleasantly. He could tell just how nervous she was. Good, let her be nervous.

"Well," Damian said, "I suppose I can't talk you out of being healthy, but perhaps you'll change your mind on the last two points?"

She reached down and clutched her purse, as if ready to leave the table. "Or not—" he joked. "I like a woman who can hold to a commitment. I'd feel lucky if a woman like you were committed to a man like me."

He toasted her. Her Perrier bottle clicked with his wineglass, and she relaxed into her seat.

Damian stared down at the table, affected embarrassment. "That sounded lame, didn't it? I suppose a woman like you has heard every line in the book."

"Not really," Asia said. "Men find me intimidating."

Genius, beauty, brains, overwhelming sexuality. Of course men found her intimidating.

"But . . . surely you date all of the time?"

Asia shook her head. "I'm from a small town in Colorado. I didn't date much." She retreated into her seat again. It was very subtle, as were all of her movements. Another man might have thought that she was stoic, that she did not react at all, but Damian could read her microsignals.

He apologized, "I don't mean to pry. I'm just . . . fishing for something to talk about. You don't want to talk about work. That's understandable: after all of those warning about corporate spies. I suppose that your instructor brought out the box of surveillance devices?"

He was speaking of course of the hardware they'd found in the compound over the years—voice and audio recorders, taps for phone lines, spyware for computers.

"Oh, my gosh," she said. "I couldn't believe it. Did you see that little red camera? It looked like an eye, like from that robot in *The Terminator*!"

"I think that if we took all of those parts, we could *build* a Terminator," Damian joked. "And you only saw a quarter of the collection."

"Where does it all come from?" she wondered. He was glad that she asked. Talking about sex had made her nervous, more willing to discuss more important forbidden topics.

"Mostly other pharmaceutical firms," Damian replied. "Places with dignified names like Johnson and Johnson, Roche, and GlaxoSmithKline. In an industry that sells a trillion dollars per year, the competition is fierce. But not all competitors are just companies—some are entire countries, places like North Korea and China.

"That red 'eye' you mentioned was a thermal-imaging device planted by the Russians. Every human body gives off its own heat signature, and that eye was built to see through walls. Lasers built into the same unit were aimed at the windows, so that they could measure vibrations made when people spoke. They could watch our people and record them at will."

"I suppose that we have our own corporate spies?"

"That would be safe to assume."

Chaz brought the appetizer—Thai lettuce wraps. There were heaps of spiced chicken lying beside butter lettuce, sprouts, sliced water chestnuts, sweet dipping sauce, and peanut sauce.

"I hope you don't mind," Damian told Asia. "I ordered while you were gone."

"It smells so good," she said hungrily, then began stuffing a leaf with filling. She picked up her knife and smeared some peanut sauce over it. Damian smiled.

He'd put a single drop of Rohypnol on the knife, in a liquid base.

The Main Course

Asia ate her first lettuce wrap quickly, but twelve minutes later her movements began to slow. She fixed another lettuce wrap, blinked at it stupidly.

"Eat up," Damian suggested. "They're the best in Manhattan."

She looked up at him slowly, like a drugged bird in a cage. She hunched her shoulders in, as if the booth was closing around her.

"I don't like your eyes," she said.

The drug did that to people, released their inhibitions. She was only saying what came to her mind.

"What do you mean?" Damian asked. "I've been told that my eyes are one of my finest features."

"I feel . . . I feel like I've seen you before," she said, setting her knife down. Her head swayed slightly from side to side, and her breathing was shallow.

"You mean 'before' this morning?" Damian asked. "I think I would remember a girl as lovely as you."

"It's the intelligence in your eyes, the feral brilliance," she said, as if a startling thought had occurred. "You're like all the other guys at the top echelon at the company. There's a strange . . . fierceness to you. Your eyes are like a tiger's."

Damian hissed, surprised by her observation. Many of the top execs had boosted intelligence. A few years back, in the early 2000s, Chancellor Pharmaceuticals had won a military contract that tested ways to boost memory. By creating neurons from stem cells, Chancellor's technicians learned to transfer clumps of brain cells into the cerebral cortex. Combining this treatment with the administration of growth hormones could coax hundreds of thousands of neuronal connections between each new brain cell.

Though the process had been a success, the military had ordered Chancellor Pharmaceuticals to declare the project a bust. The technology had been secreted away in some government lab. After all, if people knew what the treatment could do, everyone would want it.

But the company had duplicated the process easily enough, and now most of the company's key personnel had boosted their intelligence. It often raised one's IQ by 80 points.

Damian had availed himself of the treatment, of course, and his IQ could no longer be measured by conventional means.

"The company recruits only the best and brightest," he suggested. "We like to bind them with 'golden handcuffs,' and if those fail, we find some other means."

"Security came to my house," Asia confided dazedly, as if she'd forgotten the topic of conversation. "They swept for bugs. They said that they've found a lot of bugs lately. They think . . . it has something to do with the project I'm working on."

Damian laughed dismissively and folded his hands, then peered at her like an owl gauging a mouse. He needed to keep her talking for only a moment more. "It's not your project that they're interested in. The company is about to announce the release of a new drug, a broad-spectrum anti-inflammatory that treats everything from arthritis to allergies and diabetes, M.S., and Alzheimer's. It will be bigger than penicillin!"

She opened her mouth in feigned horror that he would speak so openly, here in a nightclub.

"Oh, there's nothing that 'the enemy' can do. The press releases go out Monday morning, and we're a decade ahead of anyone else."

Such news would indeed astonish the world, but Damian knew that it was a mere smokescreen for greater discoveries.

"I've overheard something about that," she said, "but . . . isn't there a problem with it?" Her voice fell to a whisper. "Liver toxicity?"

Damian's smile faltered, and he found himself on the defensive. "This could be the Holy Grail of pharmaceuticals."

"But the long-term effects to the liver—"

"Will be studied in the decades to come. The world needs this drug. *We* need this drug."

The company put billions into R&D every year. For each product that hit the street, dozens flopped. It cost an average of two billion dollars to bring a new treatment to market. Asia had to know the numbers. She knew the game. The company needed a cash cow. Pfizer's stock was surging, as was Murasaki's. The world needed a reminder of Chancellor Pharmaceutical's efficacy.

"Can they push this one through the FDA?" Asia asked. "Isn't it too early?"

"Half of the FDA inspectors once worked for us," Damian said dismissively. "One hand washes the other."

"There are oversight committees—"

"Run by senators and congressmen who eagerly need our company's support to get reelected," Damian pointed out. "I'm sure that our lobbyists will remind them of that."

Asia's face fell and she stared at the floor as if into the depths of hell. The girl was obviously lost. Most new employees felt this way, until their consciences faded.

Asia looked as if she was about to fall.

"Let's get you home," Damian said. "It has been a long day."

"What about the rest of dinner? What about the main course?"

"Let's skip the main course," he suggested, "and go straight to dessert."

She climbed up on wobbly legs, holding the table. Chaz came rushing up. "Is everything all right?" He studied Asia with evident alarm.

"My date isn't feeling well." Damian stuffed $300 into the waiter's hand. "Could you hail a taxi?"

Chaz hesitated, as if unsure whether to take the money or call the police. "She'll be fine," Damian assured. Chaz nodded conspiratorially and bustled out to the street.

Moments later the two hustled Asia into a cab. Soon the car crawled down the one-way streets, hampered by trucks and other vehicles. Asia leaned up against her door, half asleep, and asked, "Did you drug me?"

Damian didn't answer.

"'Cause if you drugged me, I'd kill you for it. I hate drugs. There are too damned many of them, coming too damned fast."

"Yet you work for us," he suggested.

"So," she said defiantly, counting down her fingers. "We get this on the market, we make our money, and if things start to go south, we pull the drug before too many people get hurt; and then we rush the next *miracle* drug onto the streets." By the time she was done counting, she had made a fist. Her face filled with the righteous anger that only the young and truly idealistic can feel. "This doesn't sound like mankind's salvation to me—"

"It's a prescription for success; the same one we've used for fifty years," Damian admitted. "We don't need a new plan for global domination. This one is working fine. Everyone knows about it, but no one dares shut us down. The world demands its drugs. Only we can deliver them."

She turned, head still butted against the car door, and glared at him. "Who do you think the company will sell those drugs to, the ones that make you live forever?" Rohypnol can sometimes make its victims combative, and now she sneered like an angry drunk. "Who are they going to sell them to?" she said. "I'll tell you—anyone who has the money. Mobsters and drug lords and rock stars; senators that do them dirty little favors, and greedy dictators in Africa who starve children as part of their ethnic cleansing programs? Chinese slavers who sell Thai girls as prostitutes in Malaysia, and blood mine owners. Arab princes and billionaires—that's who will get those drugs: any prick who can pay!"

"Take it easy," Damian said. "If such drugs did exist, some sort of program would be put in place, some . . . controls."

"I can tell you who won't get them—" Asia said. "Poor black women in Haiti who work their fingers to the bone trying to raise their kids. Dads who spend their time coaching basketball to teens."

"I think there would be . . . rewards," Damian said, "for lives well lived."

"Sure," Asia said. "Immortal pontiffs and TV talk-show hosts. Oprah and Jerry Springer forever!" She began to weep.

"What would you suggest?" Damian demanded. "Would you give it to welfare moms who would waste eternity watching soap operas, or derelicts that would spend their time trying to score their next high?

"Look at it this way," Damian pressed. "We'd be giving humanity hope, something to strive for. Life itself might be a gift, but immortality could be earned. For all of history, every animal on this planet has been a slave to its biology. But all of that is about to change. We're moving into an era where, through various biological processes—through drugs and genetic engineering and stem cell migrations—we'll control our own biology. We'll reinvent ourselves: eradicate diseases, make ourselves stronger, smarter, faster, more adaptable and durable. Immortal. Imagine if you remembered everything that you saw, everything you heard. Imagine if your mind grasped complex ideas beyond the ken of modern man . . . Imagine that you suddenly could envision the shapes of the proteins that bond in your genome at a molecular level, and had the tools to remake yourself into something better. Imagine all of that, and imagine that you had an eternity to implement these new processes. Who knows what shapes our children might decide to manifest themselves in? One thing is sure, they'll transform, becoming something better. By taking thought alone, a new species will emerge: *homo perfectus,* the self-perfected ones!"

She peered at him with a look of stricken horror. "And what about the people left behind?"

"With every evolutionary leap," Damian said, "only a few make it. The rest of the monkeys cling to their trees. When the first man went striding across the plains of Africa, he did so alone, and he did not gaze back longingly to the animals peering from the shadows of the bush."

She gaped at him. He could tell that she was thinking of her own single mother, the woman who had scrubbed floors in a hospital at night to put Asia through college.

She slapped him.

This wasn't going well.

Damian glanced at the driver, who glared back through the rearview mirror. Damian had more than one drug in his arsenal. Palms sweaty, he reached into his pocket and pulled out a spray bottle. He misted the phero-mones into her face, just as she gasped. In the glare of a streetlight, he saw the iris of her right eye suddenly expand and relax, and she moaned with desire.

Dessert

By the time that they reached her apartment, Asia was panting. She stumbled from the cab, and he helped her into her brownstone, opening the front door and carrying her up the stairs. Everything in her spoke of her cravings—the slack jaw, the wanton eyes, the breasts that had become so engorged that they strained at the fabric of her blouse.

The combination of drugs had left her like some animal, mindless with desire, and as Damian opened the door to her apartment, she clung to his neck and kissed him, a smothering kiss that tasted wet and sweet.

"I'm yours," she moaned. "I'm yours. Take me. I'll be anything you want."

"Even *homo perfectus?*"

She nodded seductively, but all rational thought had fled her, and Damian had a sudden insight.

Rational thought is what he'd wanted from her. He'd wanted a partner—not a sexual partner, a mate, a woman that he could love as an equal.

She planted her feet and tried to pull, leading him to her bed in a frenzy of desire. When she reached the darkened room, she ripped at her clothes, fumbling in her haste, then fell back onto the bed and lay there.

"Come on," she groaned.

Damian stood for a moment, and suddenly it seemed as if he was seeing her from afar, a pitiable little creature, like a worm, writhing on her bed.

His drugs had transformed her, left her drowsy and disoriented and twisted with desire. They'd stripped her of all rational thought, leaving her a cripple, an animal.

Seeing her like this sickened him.

• • • •

Back at the office that night, Damian passed the security desk with barely a thought and glanced up at the painting of the company's founder: eighty-year-old Sterling D. Chancellor.

In the portrait he looked stern and uncompromising. The muscles in his shoulders were wasted, the flesh of his face sagging and wrinkled. Decrepit.

That is what Sterling Damian Chancellor had looked like six weeks ago, before he'd become the first human to test the new treatment. Damian realized that Asia *had* indeed seen him before, seen his dark eyes staring at her from that portrait.

Bright girl to remember me, to see through my youthful disguise.

He'd left her with her virginity in the end, though not her dignity. Yet he realized now that her body was not what he'd wanted. As CEO, testing female employees for corporate fidelity was not part of Damian's ordinary job description. Yet he'd longed for Asia. Now he understood why.

Being the first of a new species is a lonely thing.

He'd wanted to take a companion into the future, a woman who was capable of thinking as he did.

Instead, he strode up to his office, leaving the apes of Manhattan to blink and gape from the shadows.

David Farland is the author of the bestselling Runelords series, which began with The Sum of All Men; *the eighth and latest volume,* Chaosbound, *came out in 2010. Farland, whose real name is Dave Wolverton, has also written several novels using his real name as his byline, such as* On My Way to Paradise, *and a number of Star Wars novels such as* The Courtship of Princess Leia *and* The Rising Force. *His short fiction has appeared in* Peter S. Beagle's Immortal Unicorn, David Copperfield's Tales of the Impossible, Asimov's Science Fiction, Intergalactic Medicine Show, War of the Worlds: Global Dispatches, *and in John Joseph Adams's anthology* The Way of the Wizard. *He is a Writers of the Future winner and a finalist for the Nebula Award and Philip K. Dick Award.*

One problem with writing stories about mad scientists is creating a believable character. How many of us can really identify with obsessed geniuses hell-bent on taking over the world?

Luckily, our next story gives us a mad scientist we can all understand. Sure, Ernest Lassiter is a lot smarter than most people. He's got doctoral degrees in quantum mechanics, quantum physics, and biology, and he can do crosswords in languages that have been dead for centuries. And yes, he's a little quirky, living on a diet of sprouts and veggies that he grows himself on his organic farm in a remote corner of Pennsylvania's Amish country. But under it all, Ernest is just like the rest of us: desperately yearning for love. He's been lonely a long, long time, and he's itching for some female companionship.

It's not easy to find Ms. Right when your standards are as high as Ernest's, though. With a little inspiration, and a lot of brilliance, he comes up with a way to bring the perfect woman into his world. She's hot; she's sassy; she's a dream come true.

But is he man enough for such a goddess?

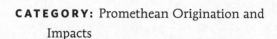

ANCIENT EQUATIONS

L. A. BANKS

Ernest Lassiter flipped over the funeral notice and drew on the back of it, sketching the symbols used in the Egyptian Book of the Dead to send a soul on to its everlasting voyage. He then added some symbols for reanimation used in Voodoo ceremonies, then the Cuneiform burial rites symbols. His years of poring over Cuneiform equations had finally begun to yield a pattern, but what was he missing that connected them all? If he could just find the key, the Akashic Records would open to him, and he'd have access to the entirety of human knowledge and the history of the cosmos.

A funeral! Did they really expect him to stop his research . . . for a *funeral?* They had to be out of their feral little minds to even bother him with something so mundane; he certainly couldn't spare time for it *now,* not when he was so close to a breakthrough.

Frustration stole his concentration. He flipped over the funeral notice again and stared at a photograph of his recently deceased uncle.

He'd tried to tell them—every single freakin' member of his family who later died of cancer or some abominable disease. Tried to explain that it was all an evil profit plot to keep people sick—because sick people made some sectors of industry gazillions of dollars . . . and this worldwide, diseased way of life was created by the food and drug cartel, who were in collusion with big pharma and the whole medical oligarchy. But, like frightened cattle, none of the family he'd once had would listen to him.

Rather than listen or do the hard thing—namely changing the bad habits forced on them by the constant battering of the alpha and beta waves in their brains by subliminal advertising—the people he loved chose to do the *harder* thing, which was to die a long and painful death due to a preventable disease.

And now they were all gone. Every single living relative that he had cared about.

His cousins were still around, but he considered them a waste of protoplasm, so they didn't count as family. All they did was eat, sleep, shit, fuck, and consume. What was their true contribution to society? Did they do anything but breed more of themselves to buy more of the crap that made other people rich?

The problem with knowing as much as Ernest did was that people thought you were a kook, a quack, or—at best—an eccentric. The problem was that people mislabel and misdiagnose you as a borderline idiot savant as a kid, until the ignorant people administering the tests realize—duh—you're a genius.

Ernest tossed aside the funeral notice with disdain and left the wide lab bench that doubled as his mail desk. He needed a cup of green tea.

He knew he could crack the code on reanimation—more important, on bringing intelligent life though the veil between worlds. It was all about energy. Nothing that was created could ever be destroyed. It had to still exist somewhere in some form—and if people created entire mythologies about superbeings, then they had to exist somewhere in some form . . . simply because thought was matter. It created matter.

So what the hell were they thinking inviting him to some dead relative's funeral?

The purpose of said events was so pedestrian. If his family grieved the man so badly, then why not spend the time to figure out how to raise him or maybe to prevent his type of unnecessary death in the first place. As far as he was concerned, people died who didn't have to because they were constantly being poisoned to death by a toxic environment for profit. He hated the hypocrisy of attending such sentimental, superstitious rubbish.

Uncle Fred's funeral was the last one he might feel obligated to attend, but in reality, he was distant enough to his uncle that a no-show would be acceptable. Sending flowers and a sympathy card was out; it was part of the death profiteering system that he couldn't abide. Uncle Fred, if he was still living, would have understood. Now that he was gone, the point of his understanding was moot. And anybody else could kiss Ernest's ass.

Off the grid was how he liked it. Ernest set his teapot on his wood-burning stove and leaned down to stoke the fire. Living this way was the only way to live, as far as he was concerned, and a primary reason he'd gone out to Lancaster County. The Amish had it right—live off the fucking grid. Solar panels on the roof, a generator in the garage, candles and lamps . . . Which is not to say he was without modern conveniences: flashlights and enough ammo to start a small war were among his concessions.

He was living proof that it was feasible to grow your own food without being held hostage to the major seed corporations that had genetically altered every goddamned plant in the land, and actually held a monopoly on *seeds*. Seeds! They cornered the market on seeds so that developing nations couldn't feed themselves without poisoning their land, because in order for the seeds to grow they had to buy special fertilizers and patented pesticides that wiped out vegetative scourges (and bee colonies right along with it) so that the evolutionary process of plant hybridization and strengthening just stopped dead in its tracks. Those motherfuckers had stopped species evolution!

Ernest held his head with both hands, threading his fingers through his dreadlocks, feeling an anxiety attack coming on. He took a deep breath and closed his eyes, and then slowly lifted one bare foot to rest against his inner thigh in the yoga tree pose.

Yes, there were ways to combat the evil system. He had to stop stressing. One could compost from organic food sources, replenish the earth, grow your own shit—literally and figuratively—and then eat food that hadn't been sprayed with pesticides. Well water—any water in the land now, truthfully—with acid rain and toxic runoff was a problem. The general public will be fucked, but not Ernest; no, he'd be fine, thanks to the mint he spent on water negative ionization systems. He'd read Dr. Masaru Emoto's work on infusing water with intentions to heal. It worked and he had bumper crops. He'd been disciplined and followed the scientific wisdom in books like *Back to Eden,* and didn't eat flesh of any kind—not even fish, and now that they screwed up the Gulf with that massive oil spill, he *definitely* wouldn't. But the water was already jacked up in the streams from strip-mining and city sludge before that even happened—no matter how pristine they looked.

And he wouldn't allow the mind-raping cartels to bore into his thoughts with the brain-rot of television. There were enough books in the world and he had all kinds of research to do, anyway. The only other partial compromise that he'd conceded to was that he had a retrofitted car that burned biofuels; still, one had to register it with the enemy state to be legal and not be hassled. Yes, he even paid taxes so the rat bastards couldn't come and take his land. He had a cell phone, just in case, but nobody had the number. It was for dialing out only; he didn't want incoming calls. Had to have a P.O. box to get his book orders, which meant submitting to at least a debit card and a small bank account, but the rest of his earnings from inventions and selling crops, he immediately transferred into gold, which went in the bomb shelter.

All of his lab equipment he'd built from scratch, and he was proud of that. The corporate and university labs he'd worked in over the years had also seen their fair share of shrinkage because of him, but it was only reparations for all they stole from the general public, he reasoned—so his karma was okay with that. Hand-pumped well water came into his sinks and tub. Human refuse went into compost the old-fashioned way: from an in-house toilet with removable slop pot beneath. He only cooked enough to eat each day and jarred extra fruits and vegetables to hold him through the harsh winter. He ate mostly raw, sprouted legumes, and root vegetables of that season, anyway . . . it was all good.

Well, lonely, but it was *mostly* all good. At least they wouldn't get him like they'd gotten everybody else he had known. He wasn't a dumb consumer buying a lot of shit he didn't need. He got everything natural or recycled.

Ernest came out of the tree pose and took his tea off the hot stove as the kettle sounded. He slowly began the process of filling another bamboo tea ball with loose green tea leaves—the authentic, organic kind he got from the Master who ran the Dojo in town.

He was no longer the geek-nerd he'd been in college. At thirty-nine, he had a body of steel. Hours of manual labor on his small farm, attention to his yoga practice, and a daily hard run in the mountains or a ten-mile ride into town on his bike to get supplies left him with a body in peak physical condition. He was proud of his personal transformation; his seed wouldn't be a waste. His body was not only purified through excellent nutrition, but his mental capacity was stellar as well; he was living proof that nature trumped steroids and cosmetic surgery any day.

In addition to reshaping his body, he'd also learned how to defend himself in hand-to-hand combat. Just like he now knew how to make ammo and bombs. (The Internet was a beautiful thing.) His property—like his body and immune system—was well fortified in the event of the apocalypse.

When Ernest had allowed himself the indulgence of watching movies, one of his favorites had been *The Fly,* with Jeff Goldblum. He could relate to the scientist in the flick, who, in his opinion, was vastly misunderstood. That kind of natural power—gene spliced from a fruit fly and added to the human DNA spiral—was an awesome concept.

That was a remaining indulgence: he gave artists credit—those that were honest with their talent, anyway. Those that were sellouts could kiss his ass just like his family, but he truly respected the ones that put in the effort to really create something noteworthy. Just like he gave other scientists (that weren't co-opted by corporations) kudos for their genius.

Revolution could happen through both science and art. All the rest was bullshit, as far as he was concerned.

Adding a little bit of raw honey to his tea, Ernest moved to the seat beside the window in the front room of his spacious log cabin and sat down watching the last of the fall leaves swirl in bright, dancing piles in the yard.

The tranquil scene was not enough to calm him, however. It still pissed him off that, even though he opted out of the system, he'd had to use money from a temporarily co-opted existence to get the freedom he needed in order to get away from the clutches of the system. And yet they still controlled what wars got fought, who lived and died, who got services and who didn't, and it was all about power—power that didn't yield itself for anyone or anything. The Bildebergers and the Illuminati still ran the entire fucking world. They were the devil, and they got regular people to buy into being blind consumers, suckered them into debt, poisoned them for profit, made them so unhappy with their lives, their looks, their bodies, their families that they had to spend money—somehow, somewhere in the food chain of greed—to make themselves feel better.

Somebody needed to do something.

Somebody really smart could fuck up their decadent Roman orgy party forever.

He was smart enough. Ernest took a sip of his tea, slurping it. He wouldn't do something that would hurt common people. No. They were already hurting enough. Thing is, he wasn't sure of how to wrest power from the powerful without hurting the innocent in the process. If he shut down the power grid, the powerful still had bunkers and access to private planes and extraction teams.

Some poor grandmother or preemie baby would die when their ventilator stopped, not some rat bastard head of state. If he created an outbreak, those same powerful people at the top would get quarantined on some lush tropical island while the rest of the world, especially the urban areas, went into apocalyptic meltdown. If he sent a message in the form of a bomb, that would only give them a reason to spin the (controlled) media to get the frightened electorate to agree to even more civil liberties transgressions and fund more military spending—which would just make their asses even richer from all the military contracts.

There was nothing wrong with his mind and he was no extremist, no matter what the psychiatrists had said. He did not have a breakdown. Thinking differently than the zombified public did not mean he'd gone around the bend. He'd had an awakening on the job, is all . . . one that brought him clarity!

Ernest again slurped his hot tea. How could a man get a Ph.D. in quantum physics, quantum mechanics, and biology, with an in-depth knowledge of chemistry, botany, and genetics, all by the age of thirty-nine if he were crazy? Didn't happen. *Couldn't* happen. Hell, he could do crossword puzzles in dead languages and had virtually taught himself ancient text translations. Think a crazy man could manage that?

So, hell no, he wasn't going to go to Philadelphia and walk past the dregs of society (that had been made dregs by the oligarchy) just to listen to some old choir hags sing "Amazing Grace" over a dead body. (And then serve dead flesh—fried chicken of all things—and act polite when they asked him if he had *a job* yet, or a *woman*. Fuck that, if that's what they called tradition. That was medieval, Dark Ages shit, if ever he heard it. He could better spend the day realigning his crystals and copper pyramids, in an attempt to establish a better connection to the Akashic Records.

The Records would tell him how to best use his mind to bring down the powerful evil that controlled the world. While he wanted that more than anything, deep down, however, what he really wished for was for the interdimensional beings who managed the Akashic Records to also send him a soul mate. It was very difficult to find a female companion with the same level of intelligence he had—and he could not countenance an ignorant woman. He'd very clearly asked them for a woman who met the following criteria: (1) She has the same commitment to living off the grid as he does; (2) She hasn't succumbed to the false traditions or superstitious religions of the zombified masses; and (3) Her body is as a fine-tuned work of art as his was. That was another issue from *The Fly* to which he could relate . . . he'd been celibate a very long time, not wanting to compromise himself with human drama, and yet his physique was functioning like a well-maintained machine. By any standard, he was a Porsche with nowhere to run on the open road.

Ernest leaned his head back against the wall and closed his eyes. Why was it so impossible sometimes to quell the urge to procreate? The Fly went though that, as well, but the gene splice made him that way. Still, there had to be a way to overcome that basic urge, just as there was a way to change one's eating habits and one's fondness for wasteful things like gas heat. That was one of the promises of meditation and yoga, that one could go outside of one's body to think away one's desires. But his body still ran regular diagnostics, giving him erections that begged for relief.

When he really thought back on it, his experiences with the opposite sex were so fleeting and so unfulfilling that he wondered why he thought of them at all. By now the subject should have been dead to him. Thinking about sex, or better stated, yearning for it, had to be some stupid DNA glitch in the medulla oblongata. The lizard brain—the reptilian center that just regulated heartbeat and other peristaltic functions. Procreation was necessarily a peristaltic function to ensure the continuation of the species. That's the only reason it remained on his mind because it sure couldn't have been from the one backseat fumbling attempt he'd had in high school when he wore Coke-bottle glasses and braces.

Fat Reenie. Damn. Even to this day he couldn't shake the image. She was his cousin's girlfriend's fat sister. She had given him his first experience groping breasts. That was as far as he got, but he remembered how they changed under his palm and how she'd actually let him slip a hand under her sweater. Remembered how her thick nipples got hard and how that made him hump her leg like a pathetic, agonized puppy until she'd said, "Get off me," and pushed him away.

But he also remembered what was going on in the front seat, and recalled how it was clear that the same thing wasn't going to happen for him that night. Sad but true, the image still excited him. His cousin had scored, while he went home with blue balls and jerked off. Then, to add insult to injury, he got ridiculed the next day for being in a "geek and fat girl" couple, so much so that poor Reenie couldn't take the pressure and decided to go get a thug to replace him.

That's when he'd learned the pecking order of the streets—a fat girl putting out could get a thug, even if the son of a bitch treated her badly. A nerd couldn't get squat, because all females run in a pack and need corroboration from the others that they'd picked a provider . . . so Neanderthal. He hated the inner city that had bred him and was so glad that he'd been smart enough to escape from it.

College didn't change that much; that was a rude awakening. Maybe the rudest of all, because they were supposed to be intelligent people at MIT. He'd been smart enough to get there on a full scholarship at sixteen. True, he was young, but he was old enough to pick up the game.

Ernest stared out the window and released a weary sigh. The jocks and guys with social savoir faire got laid. Guys in the lab didn't—unless they were going to be a medical doctor, which again linked to the female perception of what constituted a good provider down the line.

In grad school, he'd finally found another geek like him who had shown him a little mercy. After a drunken night of shots at a project completion party, he finally got some at twenty-five years old. Ernest had shut his eyes tightly; just three strokes and he was done. She'd been so drunk that she rolled over and puked afterward. The next day in lab they both apologized and agreed that what had happened wasn't really a good idea, and it would never be discussed again.

Jennifer was a very nice person, but in the cold light of day he knew it had been the alcohol. That was the last time he'd tried to press for a mate. He figured if something was meant to be, it would happen naturally.

So, where was his queen? Where was that one, hot, smart, physically unstoppable, sexually insatiable being, like him, ready to get it on rough and hard and without relent, and then take over the world?

Anger filled him as he set down his mug and let out another breath of frustration. He had to do better at controlling his thoughts. That was the problem of having an intense brain, it was so full that keeping parameters around it was nearly impossible. His idle wondering where his soul mate was had given him another early morning erection.

He stared down at the bulge in his lab scrubs, deciding. Maybe he should just break down and order a female orifice off the Internet. He could make one, he was sure, but the act of actually making one and putting so much time into that process would really be depressing—whereas if he just ordered something online, he could do that without really thinking about it again until the box arrived in the mail. But he couldn't force himself to *not think*. (And whatever they sent wouldn't be biodegradable.)

Plus, if he stopped himself from thinking that would make him just like the blind masses that consumed everything in a state of oblivion. He also didn't want to be played by the system that made money off other people's misery. Lastly, he didn't want the rat bastards that ran the world to see that they were getting to him when they traced his life through his credit-card purchase and discovered that he'd ordered a female part like a man in prison might if he could. That would give them a good laugh at his expense, and that was the last thing he'd allow.

Rage filled him, this time more intensely than he'd felt in the years since he'd had an episode—what *they* called a breakdown—in his ex-employer's lab. The only benefit of that job had been that he now received disability income from it. Regardless, he hated them all and hated that his life had been relegated to this, all because he saw the truth and refused to be quiet about what they were doing in their poison factories abroad.

He needed more tea. Needed to get back to his jigsaw puzzle of formulas on his whiteboard.

But then a quiet thought entered his mind, almost as though it had tiptoed in through the back door of his brain. Call it an insight, or perhaps it was a download from the Akashic Records, he wasn't sure. But it made him slow his process of standing up so he could pay attention to it.

What if his body-needs increasing were a sign? What if he was getting frustrated and turned on because *it was time?* What if he'd finally reached the peak of his mental, physical, and spiritual evolution, so that *now* was the time for him to find that mate?

Or, perhaps, *create* her?

All this time he'd been trying to find the answers in the ancient knowledge of kings, when the answer was—literally—right in front of him all along.

Ernest abandoned his tea and rushed out of the living room. Running as if he was being chased, he went to his lab table and began routing through his esoteric texts on female deities and intelligent species that he'd collected over the years.

What if *now,* he thought, with his intellectual acumen at full tilt, what if he could break the code on the ancient Sumerian texts or on the Cuneiform tablets that all spoke of releasing a female entity that—to his mind—sounded like a more highly evolved alien species? Powerful females that began or ended the world as humans knew it . . . As *men* knew it. What if he married the funeral rites of men, of kings, but called a female entity instead?

"Thank you for dying, Uncle Fred!" Ernest shook his head and laughed out loud. The death notice was a sign. It had to be a beautiful, gorgeous coincidence given to him by an intelligence beyond the veil.

The adjustment in the codexes would be simple. No wonder all the goddesses had been banned and removed from modern, paternalistic religious texts. *They* were the ones that could flow more easily between worlds! The information was right under his nose all along.

Ernest clutched his papers, giggling as tears formed in his eyes. This was the information that *they* wanted hidden from the general human population . . . so what better way to do that than to eradicate the goddess from all current religious thought?

His hands began to scribble a new ancient equation on the whiteboard behind his lab desk, taking careful pains to insert the feminine versus masculine in every symbol translation. The equation was a spell. He stared at it closely. It was a formula for the elements needed to raise the dead . . .

Women. It all hinged on women. The true creators and givers of life.

Every single culture spoke of them, whether as succubae, vampires, Lilith, Oshun, Kali . . . yes, like Kali—the black one, like him, Kali the goddess of annihilation, her name associated with death, but also great benevolence. In Tantric beliefs, known as "the ultimate reality." Sexual.

"Kali . . ." he murmured. The consort of Shiva, who was known as "eternal time," while Kali herself was known as *"the* time."

It was definitely *the time.*

And if Einstein was right—and there was no reason to believe that he, a genius, was not—then matter could neither be created nor destroyed. Perhaps moved into another dimension, but it would still exist, regardless. Maybe it was made temporarily inanimate—but it was still there. And it only stood to reason that if there was such a deep human story-trail of these ancient goddesses, then it was possible that there was truth to the rumors that had lasted centuries. The one thing that all modern anthropologists had learned over the years was that lies and untruths within cultures tended to die out, whereas those things that continued to be handed down from a fragment of truth tended to live on.

What if ancient cultures simply didn't have the scientific vocabulary for bringing an energy being through the dimensional fabric to manifest in our world? What if these entities occasionally *did* break through? What if angels and demons and such really *did* exist?

But one thing was for sure: all cultures generally agreed that whoever raised the deity would have power over it.

Ernest spun away from his whiteboard, opened an expensive text, and quickly turned the worn pages to the bare-breasted drawing of Kali. She was both horrible and gorgeous, with four arms and coal-black skin, long flowing hair, and a body that wouldn't stop. She could definitely be his woman, the woman that created the freakin' Kama Sutra, and could level mountains. What if an entity like that was obligated to him for bringing her through the veil to experience the seduction of the mortal world again? And her appetite for destruction could be unleashed on the powerful families and heads of corporations that were controlling (and poisoning) the world?

Oligarchies would crumble. She could blight the genetically engineered seeds and only true seeds that were natural and organic could grow. She could destroy the oil industry, making wells go dry, so as not to further damage the Earth by making it bleed black blood into the Gulf or anywhere else. That would make nations have to scramble to develop biofuels and solar and wind technology, and he wouldn't have to wait on fucking Congress to vote beyond their own personal campaign interests. She could create a plague that would just kill all the genetically altered toxic animals on their way to slaughter, something so horrible and massive that it couldn't be covered up and people would be too afraid—on their own—to eat from those diseased food sources. Then people would demand real change.

Oh, yeah, he could keep his goddess busy fucking up the world until the rich weren't rich and the poor woke up and got a clue. There would be anarchy, and she could stop armies while the masses took over the reins of their towns again and planted organic food to feed their people from small community farms, and drummed out the assholes on Wall Street that created nothing but made billions by electronic transfers of paper. She could make the trading boards go black. That wouldn't hurt people like a blackout, but it would sure tank the global bullshit market, just like what happened when someone supposedly keyed in a wrong amount for a trade and blue chip stocks went to zero for a few minutes. What if everything on the worldwide stock markets just went to zero and stayed there?

The more he thought about it, the better it sounded.

In a frenzy of hope and excitement, he ran to his library shelves and began yanking down every book he had on quantum physics and incantations.

He needed to get the science right—that was what undergirded the magic of the spell, or as he liked to refer to it, the ancient equation.

Crystals amplified interdimensional contact. Copper and gold were highly conductive metals. The full moon was a high tide mark, when the Earth's electromagnetic pull was at an apex, hence there was more cosmic juice to get the signal to the energy residing in a different dimensions.

Chants, words, had a vibrational resonance, and any idiot knew vibration was the very foundation of the universe. Everything vibrated—atoms and every subatomic particle down to a quark vibrated.

Ancient cultures used all of these elements to create a confluence of events. Drums were simply vibration, like the chants, and getting a bunch of people in a tribe to all do it together just amplified the vibe out to the other side. Face paint and juju herbs were just theater. Maybe the folks needed to get a buzz on to totally suspend disbelief and to open up their access to parts of their brains that the normal human hadn't learned to use yet? Who knew, but he'd roll a joint from the plants he grew in his lab under UV lights to be sure not to allow his overanalysis to create an intellectual block.

Short of having a tribe to get the job done, he could do it in the lab with Bose stereo amplifiers and crystals, copper wire and water, sea salt for more kick, under the light of a full moon . . .

All he had to do was follow the breakthrough equation he'd just discovered.

Tonight, he was bringing Kali stateside.

Tonight, he was gonna get laid.

Then tomorrow, together they would kick some corporate ass and rule the world.

. . . .

It took Ernest all day to bring in the right assortment of crystals and to research their proper alignment. He had to make sure he was in alignment with the galactic center, and had to break out his telescope and compass for that. Then there was the ritual part; Ernest didn't think it was necessary but he relented, and prepared fruit and drink offerings for the entity. It made some sense, he supposed, since she was coming into a physical body, she would need nourishment.

Then there was getting all the sounds right; downloading the right African drumbeats and Native-American flutes, and mixing them with Indian sitars took a bit of blending and then he found and added in some powerful Ohm chants.

By midnight, everything was ready. He'd even taken a bath and had gotten naked to stand under the copper wire pyramid mounted on the ceiling, hoping his body would be used as the battery to go along with everything else that was rigged; the human body was 80 percent water and was the perfect saline pH, so it was no wonder that the ancients used human sacrifices as human generators. Only, *he* wasn't gonna die. That was unnecessary and wasteful, especially when he had a generator the entity could tap to help bring itself through the vortex.

Human ignorance and a lack of enlightened vocabulary had been responsible for so much waste and way too many barbaric deaths. Ernest sighed.

But it was time.

He lit the end of the thick joint he'd rolled, brought it to his lips, and inhaled deeply, allowing his nostrils to flare. He watched the end of the huge blunt glow red, and then proceeded to light the incense pots and white candles around the room. He then stood inside a circle of sea salt and flipped on the stereo, then activated the device that he'd created.

Heavy percussion thrummed through his body. The joint and incense were making him heady. The music caused him to close his eyes and sway as he lent his voice to it between deep puffs of reefer. Soon he felt light and as though electric current was running over the surface of his skin—just like it had been described in the spell books. The anticipation gave him an unbearable erection, but if his efforts succeeded, Kali would be here soon. Now it was time to call her by name, he thought, with every fiber of his being believing she could come through, believing that she existed, suspending disbelief.

He spoke the words of the ancient equation in a loud and clear voice, speaking with conviction . . . invoking Kali until the veins rose in his temples and throat. Then he said it again, this time raising his arms and shouting it, giving in to the madness of the theater, wanting it so badly that he didn't care whether it was shamanic drama or not, so long as it worked. She had to come!

Despite all his work and research, he was still unprepared when the candles blew out and the bowls of water suddenly flipped against the wall. Nor was he prepared for the cutting chill that swept into the room, or the sudden, intense heat that followed, causing the air to become so hot it verged on painful.

"Who calls me?" an angry female voice demanded.

Ernest stood there for a moment, joint in hand, mouth agape, staring.

A naked woman had appeared in the room, with four arms and a serious attitude.

"I do," he whispered, as awed as the scientist who'd first seen an atom must have been.

"And your request?"

He bowed. "Kali . . . be my mate and let us destroy the evil-doers of the world together."

She folded one set of her arms over her naked breasts, while her other pair of hands went to her hips, and she shook her head. "You motherfuckers are all the same. You want some ass and then you wanna go take out the guys who used to get all the babes."

Ernest stared at her, blinking. She sounded like a ghetto princess, hardly the lofty goddess he'd expected.

"Look, when we come into this dimension, we come with all the baggage you've got in your subconscious, okaaay. This is why, if you read the religious texts, only holy men or women with a clue are supposed to call us up."

"I . . . I . . ."

"Yeah, heard it before, baby. You didn't know. Whateva." She sucked her teeth and rolled her eyes at him, and then took the thick joint from his fingers and drew on it hard. "Okay, so I'm here, and yeah, we can get busy, and yeah, I can roll some heads—but you know I'm Shiva's woman, right? You do know that when he finds out that your punk ass called me up, he's gonna go straight gansta on you, right? Just saying." She handed him back the joint and let the smoke filter out of her lovely nose. "You prepared for all of that?"

Ernest drew a slow drag on the joint, inhaling her fragrance as he looked over her body, and then nodded.

She smiled. "Okay. I'ma go easy on you, baby. I'll tell Shiva to be cool. You ain't had none in a really long time, I can tell. So, I guess that would make you lose your mind and wanna destroy the world. I'm cool wit that."

"I just want to carve out the bad and leave the good," Ernest said carefully, still awed as his mouth went dry.

Kali cocked her head to the side and studied his now wilted erection. "You do have potent seed, right?"

Ernest quickly nodded. "The best."

Kali smiled as the long gold fingernail on one of her right forefingers began to extend and widen into a menacing blade. "Good . . . because I'm definitely going to need a sacrifice in order to work with you, baby. Goes with the territory. No pain, no gain."

L. A. Banks was the bestselling author of the Vampire Huntress Legend series, which consists of twelve volumes. She was also the author of the Crimson Moon werewolf series, which includes Bad Blood, Bite the

Bullet, Undead on Arrival, Cursed to Death, Never Cry Werewolf, and Left for Undead. *Writing under the bylines Leslie Esdaile and Leslie Esdaile Banks, she has also published fiction in the romance and crime/suspense genres. In 2008, Banks was named the* Essence Magazine *Story-teller of the Year. She died at the age of fifty-one in August 2011.*

CATEGORY: Unmapped Variables in Multiple Intelligences

RULE 3227.0: Touch *Nothing* in the Secret Lab

SOURCE: Pat Gilcrease, journalist

VIA: Alan Dean Foster

Our next story takes us into the blazing heat of New Mexico. New Mexico is a unique state. It's given us the first chimpanzee astronaut, the first nuclear weapons test, and the alleged cover-up of an extraterrestrial space craft recovery. From that fertile ground, you can expect a lot of wild UFO stories and tall tales of atomic-fueled mutations.

With that kind of background, Albuquerque reporter Pat Gilcrease isn't expecting much when he gets a report of a two-headed chicken living on a remote country ranch. Maybe a hand-stitched fake. A genetic freak if he's lucky. He's certainly not prepared for what he finds.

As Gilcrease learns more, he discovers he is onto the story of his life. It's a story that proves not all brilliant scientists are created equal, and not every farmer's daughter is a brainless hick.

Brainless, no. But mad, on the other hand . . .

RURAL SINGULARITY

ALAN DEAN FOSTER

Gilcrease mopped his brow with the halfway clean rag he had scrounged from the trunk of the car. The only extant war between New Mexico and Texas was between ranchers and oilmen who each claimed that their side of the border was the one that was hottest in mid-August. Having driven all the way from Albuquerque, Gilcrease was happy to call it a tie and a plague on both their hothouses.

Not that it wasn't warm in Albuquerque this time of year, too. It was just that everything seemed hotter in the greater desolation that lay to the east of the Sacramento foothills. This was country that made the high desert terrain around Albuquerque seem positively arctic. With every passing moment he looked forward to the return drive and his nice, cool cubby in the newspaper office.

This was fool's errand for a slow day, he knew. "Human interest," these occasional excursions into the creases of an anomalous humanity were called. Just his luck to be nominated to do the follow-up on this one.

His first glimpse of the Parkers' "ranch" did not inspire confidence. Furnished in half twenty-first-, half nineteenth-century fashion, the single-story rock and wood structure scrunched back against a succession of rising rounded hillocks like a bear scratching his ass. There was a windmill that on a good day supplied water to the dwelling. Behind and off to the left side of the house was a traditional barn belted by wooden timbers intended to restrain more cattle than ever roamed this particular homestead.

When Gilcrease drove up in a cloud of dust and muttered adjectives, Walt Parker was working under the hood of that undying icon of mobile American steel known as a full-size pickup truck. With the heavy hood raised it looked as if the truck was saying "ahh." Parking nearby, the reporter took one last optimistic rag-swipe at his forehead and climbed out. The KEEP OFF THE GRASS sign posted in the dirt driveway made him smile. The only grass for many miles around was to be found high up in the mountains behind the house.

"Walter Parker? I'm Pat Gilcrease, from the *Albuquerque Journal*."

Weather-beaten and bank-battered, Parker looked ten years older than the fifty-one to which he would admit. There was more oil in the old towel he was using to clean his hands than in the dusty ground beneath his feet. Gilcrease winced slightly when the man extended a welcoming hand, but having no choice he took the greasy fingers firmly. Parker squinted up at the taller, younger man.

"You're here about the two-headed chickens, I expect."

Gilcrease nodded, then found himself frowning. "You have more than one?"

"Whole flock." The rancher shook his head. "People. You show them something you're proud of, tell them to keep it to themselves, and they promptly go and call a newspaper." He shook his head regretfully. "Well, you're here, and you've come all the way from the city, so I expect it would be impolite not to show you."

Gilcrease didn't even take out his camera as the rancher guided his visitor around the house and toward the barn. Between the two stood an enclosure fashioned from wood posts and chicken-wire fencing. Parker prepared himself for the worst. More than likely he would be shown a badly stitched and sewn fake. If he was lucky, one of the rancher's birds might have hatched an honest mutation. Enough to justify a quick snapshot or two and a short article for the People section of the paper. It really had been a slow news week.

"Here 'tis." Parker unlatched the door to the coop. As he did so, twenty or more clucking chickens came running. They were accompanied by a snowstorm of at least twice as many chicks. Gilcrease eyed them, and his jaw promptly dropped.

Every one of them had two heads. Every one. And they looked as healthy as any comparable flock of normal chickens.

Having anticipated his guest's reaction, Parker was grinning. "Didn't believe, did you, Mr. Gilcrease?"

Having finally succeeded in fumbling his camera out of his shirt pocket, the flabbergasted reporter was snapping pictures like mad. "How—I've seen pictures of two-headed animals before. But it's always only one or two individuals at a time. A two-headed snake, or a two-headed turtle. Even a two-headed sheep. But this . . ." Holding the camera in one hand he gestured with the other. "How did this happen?"

"Want to see something else interesting?" Parker raised a hand. "Wait here."

Gilcrease continued to fire off shots while his host disappeared into the long, low henhouse. When the rancher returned he was holding several eggs. Double-shelled eggs, like perfect little white dumbbells. He handed one to the dumbfounded reporter.

"That's how you get two-headed chickens. You get them to lay double eggs." Like light behind a T-shirt, pride began to show through his initial reticence. "My daughter Suzie bred them."

"Your daughter?"

Parker nodded. "She's one clever little girl. Special." His expression faded somewhat. "You know: special. Home-schooled. Has to be."

Staring at the back of his camera, Gilcrease was reviewing the pictures he had just taken. They were as real as the two-headed chicks presently *peep-peep*ing around his ankles.

"Why is that?" he asked absently, his present attention more focused on the pictures.

"She's addled. Clever, but addled. When she was a lot younger—eleven, I think she was—we took her to see a doctor in El Paso. Specialist. He examined her, did some tests. Said she was what you call an idiot savant. I was gonna punch the guy out until my wife told me what that meant. She's the smart one in the family, Mary is. Visiting her mother in Amarillo this week. She wouldn't like it if she knew there was a reporter out here asking about Suzie. But after the neighbors called your paper . . ." He shrugged. "I thought it better to come clean about the chickens to a real paper than wait for some tabloid freelancer to come snooping around."

"I'm flattered. My paper is flattered, I mean." Gilcrease pocketed his camera. He had his pictures and his article, but still . . . "Could I meet your daughter? I promise I won't take any photos without your permission and a signed release. Anything else would be an invasion of privacy."

Parker scrutinized his visitor closely. "You seem like a pretty straight guy, Pat. All right, you can say hi. But be careful what you say and how you say it. Keep things . . . you know. Simple. And don't touch anything. Especially her toys." Gilcrease nodded.

Parker led him out of the coop and into the barn. It was a spacious construction. Ranch equipment was scattered everywhere. Two of the horse stalls were occupied and one of the occupants neighed inquisitively at their approach. Seeing that both animals had only one head apiece, Gilcrease was mildly disappointed. Searching his surroundings he saw nothing out of the ordinary.

"Suzie's in back," Parker explained. "We fixed up a little playroom and workshop for her. It's where she spends most of her time, puttering around." Near the rear of the barn they halted outside a closed door and his tone darkened. "Promise now: no pictures." Gilcrease reaffirmed his earlier commitment whereupon his host opened the door.

The interior of the corner room was flooded with light from multiple double-pane windows. Surprisingly, there was also a skylight. More surprisingly, the light from both sources fell upon what looked like several folds of dark purple, foot-wide wrapping ribbon suspended in midair. At the center of the winding ribbons several yard-long coils of copper wire protruded from the top of a metal ovoid. Cables from the ovoid led to a bank of deep-cycle marine batteries. The entire setup emitted a very faint hum.

"Amplified solar generator." Parker spoke as though it was the most natural thing in the world. "Another of Suzie's putterings." He jerked a thumb toward the front of the property. "We got another one powers the whole house."

Gilcrease swallowed. His camera was burning a hole in his pocket, but he had promised. "Another one? The same size?" His host nodded. "That's a lot of wattage to come out of such a small solar array. I'd think you'd have to cover the whole building with panels to get enough juice to run a house."

"That's what I'd think, Mr. Gilcrease. But Suzie says these are 120 percent efficient."

Gilcrease frowned. "That doesn't make any sense."

His host grinned. "Neither does Suzie." He raised his voice. "Suzie! We got company! Where are you, girl?"

A figure rose from behind a heavy wooden workbench piled to overflowing with devices, instruments, bottles, beakers, and what to Gilcrease's eyes appeared to be just plain scrap. She was pudgy, overweight but not obese, with pale blue eyes and blond hair cut in a crude pageboy that suggested her mother did all the girl's styling and trimming. She looked at her father, then turned a shy stare on their visitor.

"Say hello, Suzie. This is Mr. Gilcrease. He's come from Albuquerque just to see your chickens." Parker gestured. "Come on, girl. He won't hurt you."

Slowly, reluctantly, the adolescent edged around from behind the workbench. Her downcast eyes only occasionally rose to glance fitfully at the two men. Her hands remained behind her back. She wore scruffy jeans, a lightweight flannel shirt, and—unusual for a girl of her apparent age—no makeup or jewelry. Keeping her eyes on the ground, she halted in front of her father.

"Say hello, Suzie," he prompted her gently.

An awkward silence ensued. Finally the girl stuck out one hand, keeping the other behind her and her eyes aimed downward. "Hullo," she mumbled. "I'm Suzie."

Gilcrease took the proffered fingers and squeezed gently. As soon as he let go, her hand vanished behind her back to rejoin its companion. The reporter was at once uncomfortable and fascinated.

"Hi, Suzie. If you don't mind my asking, how old are you?"

"Seventeen," she whispered. Gilcrease had to strain to hear. Looking and listening, he immediately understood and sympathized with the rancher's family circumstances. This girl might be seventeen chronologically, but socially and probably emotionally she was maybe nine. And might forever remain nine. He tailored his tone and words accordingly.

"I liked your chickens, Suzie.

A hint of a shy, withdrawn smile. "Thank you."

"Your dad said that you bred them?"

She nodded, showing a little more interest.

"Can you tell me how you did that?" Gilcrease asked softly.

For the first time, she looked up to meet his gaze. "It wasn't hard. I just had to induce the appropriate mutation and then crossbreed the relevant haploids until the desired dominant characteristic replaced the recessive. Mendel coulda done it but he didn't have the right tools for microscopic genetic manipulation." Her eyes dropped again, along with her voice. "Mom and Dad like the eggs, so I kept breeding them."

Gilcrease felt as if he had been hit with a hammer. Not knowing what else to say, he turned to indicate the apparent solar generator. "And—you made that, too?"

She nodded and her head came up again. "Had to. The power goes out a lot here and there are unpredictable surges that are bad for my computers. I hacked the inputs and the relevant software from the power company but this is better. It's cleaner power, too. Dad asked me to make him one for the house, so I did."

Gilcrease forced a smile as he struggled to stay on top of what was becoming an increasingly absurdist conversation. "Your dad says your generator's panels—I'm guessing they're those windy purple things—are 120 percent efficient." He leaned toward her and put his hands on his knees. "Now, Suzie, how can that be? How can you get more energy out of something than goes into it from the sun?"

Putting a finger in her mouth, she began chewing on the nail. "I made a photon multiplier. It works real good."

By now Gilcrease desperately wanted to take out his camera, but he held off. Promise or no promise, he was going to get some pictures here before he left. And some video. No matter how crazy this adolescent girl was, the story would play wonderfully in the paper's People section. Perhaps not flatteringly, but it would sell ads and maybe even drive a small if temporary uptick in circulation.

"Now, Suzie, I'm no scientist, but even I know you can't get more energy out of something than what goes into it."

Her voice rose in protest, almost irritably. "You can if you access the photonic flow from a second dimension."

It was at this point that Gilcrease knew he was being had. It wouldn't be the first time. Living in New Mexico, there was at least one good Roswell story to be exploited every year. Not to mention the inevitable wild tales of mutants born of the early atomic bomb tests running amok in the state forests. But this one, featuring a simple-minded teenage girl as its protagonist, was smarter by half than most. Whether she was faking her illness or not he didn't know. If not, then extra points to her clever father for figuring out how to program her pseudo-scientific responses. It was all based on getting someone to report on the two-headed chickens, of course. They were real enough. But the rest of this was an obvious con in the making. Pulling out a pad and pen, he eyed the father. If this was a scam, the old man should be ready to fill in the details about now. And ask for money, of course.

"I'm just going to make some notes, Mr. Parker. No photos. Maybe some quick sketches. Would that be okay?"

His host hesitated, eyed his daughter. "Suzie? Is it all right with you if our guest makes some drawings?"

More mumbling. "Don't care. He don't understand what he's seeing anyway."

Gilcrease was not offended. "Thank you, Suzie. I appreciate your courtesy."

She went silent, shifting back and forth from one foot to the other. After he had been writing and drawing for a couple of minutes she looked up again. "Want to see what I'm working on now?"

He didn't look up from his sketch pad. He was trying to make a decent rendition of the impossible "solar generator."

"Sure, Suzie, why not?"

"Okay." She brought her left hand around from behind her back. Intent on his work, Gilcrease almost didn't look at it. When he finally did, he dropped his pen and papers.

Hovering above her pale smooth-skinned palm was a model of the solar system. In perfect miniature it depicted the sun, the planets, the asteroid belt, and an occasional visiting comet. The proportions were not correct. They could not be. But the visual representation was astonishing. Forgetting his dropped papers and pen he bent closer, staring in fascination. Small clouds could be seen moving above the Earth. Jupiter's bands rotated. And the sun—the sun was hot to the touch. He swallowed.

"Suzie, what . . . how did you . . . you *made* this?"

She nodded proudly. "It's not to scale, of course. If it was, the sun would be too big and too hot and Pluto's orbit would be away out past where your car came in. It's just a toy. Our home system. All of it is our home. Not just the Earth." She smiled shyly. "Wanna see something neat?"

He was beyond dazed. "Neater than this?"

She nodded. She was eager now, more relaxed in his presence. With one

CATEGORY   UNMAPPED VARIABLES IN MULTIPLE INTELLIGENCES

finger she pointed at the floating Saturn. No, not at Saturn. At a smaller sphere orbiting around it.

"Titan. Smell it."

He bent close, careful not to make contact, inhaled, and then drew back sharply, his nose wrinkling.

"It smells like rotten eggs."

"Uh-huh. Methane. Pretty cool, huh?"

"How . . . ?" He was shaking his head. His previous conviction that what he was seeing was nothing but scam and fakery fled as he contemplated the far more fantastic story that was unfolding before him. An impossible story, an unimaginable story. Stars of another kind danced before his eyes. He saw a Pulitzer in his future. "Suzie, do you have any other toys that are 'neat'?"

"Oh sure." Turning, she headed for the big workbench. "Come on, I'll show you."

So she did. She showed him the antigravity projector the size of a cell phone, just like the one in her pocket that had kept the miniature solar system hovering above her palm. She showed him the homunculus Santa and elves that she only animated at Christmas. Showed him the robot cat that kept the barn free of rats and mice, and the extractor that drew water from the seemingly desiccated air, and the candy maker that spun elaborate gourmet treats out of plain sugar and simple flavorings. She showed him the small thermonuclear device.

"But I can't get enough radium or tritium out of the old watches dad buys for me at flea markets so I'm gonna try and build my own centrifuges to concentrate enough U-235 to 90 percent from the ore in the hills around here." She eyed her father. "For my next birthday dad promised me enough lead to make some shielding."

Gilcrease looked at his host. Parker shrugged. "It's harmless, I'm sure. Another one of her toys."

"Yeah," Gilcrease mumbled. "Harmless." He was eyeing the girl not just out of curiosity now, but warily. "Suzie, some of these things, some of your toys—aren't you afraid they might be a little bit dangerous?"

She pushed out her lower lip. "I know what I'm doing! I'd never make anything that would hurt people." She suddenly dropped her gaze and voice again. "Well, maybe that mini-Schwarzchild discontinuity, but I got rid of it before it swallowed anything besides the Deere, and that was junk anyway!"

Her father frowned slightly. "Wondered what happened to that old tractor. Thought some kids took it." He brightened. "That explains the hole in the ground under where it had been sitting."

"Wouldn't never hurt no one," Suzie muttered again. Her eyes suddenly met the reporter's. "You gonna write about all this, Mr. Gilcrease?"

"No, Suzie, I—was going to." There was something in her eyes he didn't like and he felt it was time for discretion. "But I'm not going to if you don't want me to."

"*Don't* want you to." She was insistent. "People would come here. Bad people. They'd want me to make toys for them. And I don't wanna." Her voice rose, her hands balled into fists at her sides, and she looked as if she was going to start bawling. "I don't *wanna!*"

Hastily stepping forward, her father put an arm around her shoulders and pulled her close. She immediately tucked her head into his chest. "Don't wanna," she mumbled more softly. Parker looked at his guest.

"I think you should go now, Mr. Gilcrease. You saw the chickens, and you can write about them if you insist. But that's all," he finished firmly.

The reporter nodded. "I know. I promised." A promise he had no intention whatsoever of keeping, Gilcrease knew. Not after this. Not after what he had seen. This was no scam. The girl was addled, all right. Borderline crazy. Or maybe not borderline. But she was also a genius of unparalleled acquaintance. This was a story that had to get out, needed to be told, and he was going to tell it. As Parker comforted his manic offspring, he was watching Gilcrease closely. Too closely for Gilcrease to get out his camera. But he could snap some long-range shots as he drove away, he knew. What was the old man going to do—chase after him? Just something visual to frame the story. And what a story it was going to be! And if not photos, he had his drawings, his sketches. They would suffice, for now. He'd be back. With a photographer and, if necessary, a sheriff's deputy or two. This was *big*.

Bending, he fumbled for the notes and sketches he had dropped, quickly gathering them up. They made an awkward sheaf in his hands. He looked around. "Mr. Parker, would you have—oh, never mind. I see one." Stepping to his right, he reached for something on top of a nearby tool chest.

Looking up, Suzie said sharply, "Better not."

Gilcrease smiled winningly at her and helped himself to the object. "It's okay, Suzie. I'll give you another one. A whole box, if you wa—"

There was a blinding flash of light.

. . . .

When Parker could see again, nothing remained of his visitor. There was, however, a blackened flare on the concrete of the workroom floor. Walking over to it, he took care to step around the splash of carbonization. Even without touching he could feel the heat radiating from the cone of air above the spot.

"What happened to him?" Putting his hands on his hips he glared disapprovingly over at his daughter. "Suzie, did you . . . ?"

She shook her head and began chewing on her finger again. "I told him not to. Told him."

Pushing back his cap, Parker scratched at his hairline. "It was just a paper clip, Suzie."

She shook her head and pushed out her lower lip again.

"*Quantum* paper clip."

Alan Dean Foster is the bestselling author of more than one hundred novels, and is perhaps most famous for his Commonwealth series, which began in 1975 with the novel Midworld. *His most recent novels include* Quofum, Flinx Transcendent, The Human Blend, *and* Body, Inc. *Foster's short fiction has appeared in numerous anthologies and in magazines such as* The Magazine of Fantasy & Science Fiction, Analog, Jim Baen's Universe, *and in John Joseph Adams's anthology* Federations. *A new collection,* Exceptions to Reality, *came out in 2008.*

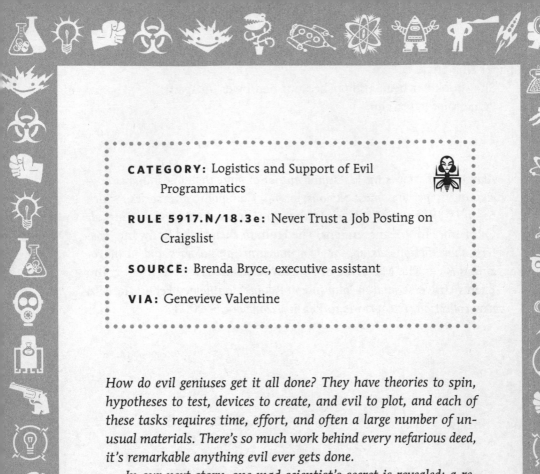

CATEGORY: Logistics and Support of Evil Programmatics

RULE 5917.N/18.3e: Never Trust a Job Posting on Craigslist

SOURCE: Brenda Bryce, executive assistant

VIA: Genevieve Valentine

How do evil geniuses get it all done? They have theories to spin, hypotheses to test, devices to create, and evil to plot, and each of these tasks requires time, effort, and often a large number of unusual materials. There's so much work behind every nefarious deed, it's remarkable anything evil ever gets done.

In our next story, one mad scientist's secret is revealed: a remarkable assistant. Someone has to be in charge of the office, and in this tale, it's Brenda. She knows just who to call to order the ignition for a doomsday device and she's got the skills it takes to edit a truly evil ransom note. She's a truly capable woman, ready for whatever her job demands—and as a mad scientist's assistant, her job will take some unusual skills.

The question is: will she survive long enough to get that well-earned raise?

CAPTAIN JUSTICE SAVES THE DAY

GENEVIEVE VALENTINE

Brenda had been working for Dr. Methuselah Mason for two years the day he mentioned strapping her to the doomsday device.

"It's a brilliant idea," he said. "Captain Justice can never resist the prospect of some helpless civilian. He'll stop to save you, and by the time he realizes the mechanism is unstoppable . . ." He sighed. "I'll be rid of him *forever*."

Brenda hit Mute on the speakerphone. "Beg pardon?"

"Don't worry," he said. "He always gets there before the timer runs out. I'll leave some clues for him like usual. You shouldn't be there long, and you don't have to really do anything."

"He said he wanted birch," came the lumberyard service rep through the speaker. "Birch isn't mothproof. He never told me the place was at risk from moths."

"Of course it's at risk from moths," snapped Dr. Mason. "It's an abandoned farmhouse lair."

Brenda said, "You told me not to tell him that. Also, he can't hear you."

"Look, I'd pay you overtime for the doomsday stuff," Dr. Mason said with a trace of disdain for time-clocking. "I don't see why we have to have a big I'm-having-feelings meeting about everything I suggest."

"I'm not giving your boss a pass on something he bought free and clear," the lumber rep said.

Dr. Mason slammed his hand on the Mute button. "You listen here, you'll give me that refund or I'll send some radioactive geese to your house at night, you lying—"

"Dave, let me call you right back," Brenda said, and hung up.

Dr. Mason shook his head. "Unbelievable! It's just impossible to get good customer service these days. The only reason Captain Justice has ever gotten anything over on me is because he has a better support team. You really need to find out who he's buying from."

"I'll make a note," Brenda said. "Now, the doomsday thing?"

"Well, I'm blacklisted at all the temp agencies," he said, "so there's nothing doing on that front. You're going to have to be a team player here. We don't have any other options."

After the first three months, she had given up mentioning the option "Don't build a doomsday device." He was disorganized enough that she'd figured it was a safe bet he'd never finish, anyway. (If she had any co-workers, she'd have just lost out big in the office pool.)

"You'll have to file preemptive worker's-comp papers with the insurance company," she said finally.

He huffed and leaned back against the wall of the farmhouse lair. "I'm so tired of that bureaucracy nonsense. That's *your* job. My last assistant wouldn't shut up about all that stuff, either. I hated it."

Brenda blinked. "What happened to her?"

He traced a figure in the air with one hand. "Went to grad school," he said vaguely, and disappeared into the lab.

Brenda dug around for information about her predecessor, but didn't find a thing. Either Enid Evans had ditched the Master's degree and gone off the grid, or this was not the first time Dr. Mason had had a brilliant idea regarding his assistant.

• • • •

4:53am
To: Brenda Bryce <bbryce@mmasonenterprises.net>
From: Dr. Methuselah Mason, Ph.D. <doctor@mmasonenterprises.net>
Subject: EMERGENCY NETWORK BREACH

Miss Bryce—I need the number of the Overlook Park office so I can bribe the officials to plant my doomsday device for me, and the address of *The Ledger* so I can send the ransom note, but something is wrong with my address book. What did you do???

• • • •

5:46am
To: Dr. Methuselah Mason, Ph.D. <doctor@mmasonenterprises.net>
From: Brenda Bryce <bbryce@mmasonenterprises.net>
Subject: EMERGENCY NETWORK BREACH

Dr. Mason,

It seems something is wrong with your address book because you erased it trying to password—protect it. I am on my way in to repopulate your address book from my computer. Please do not try to fix it until I get there.

—Brenda

• • • •

6:09am

Well, I already overrode your computer's security so I could get the numbers because you weren't getting back to me and I need to get this done, but your address book is blank, too. I don't see how that helps us.

• • • •

6:11am

Dr. Mason,

Please do not touch my computer again until I get there. I will get you the information as soon as I can call The Night Cipher for tech support and have him restore our address books.

—Brenda

• • • •

6:20am

But that's going to take forever! Don't you have a faster method to access this?

• • • •

6:27am

Brenda, do you have a faster method? I really need to start bribing ASAP.

• • • •

6:35am

Brenda, I think my e-mail's broken, too—none of my messages are getting through to you. When you get in, please address this.

• • • •

"I think this ransom note is missing something," said Dr. Mason, a few days later. He dropped it casually on her desk and folded his arms. "What do you think?"

Trick question, is what Brenda thought.

It was no secret that Dr. Mason was a big fan of flattery. The Night Cipher kept showing up for tech support even when they didn't need any, just so he could hang around the lab and kiss ass. ("You're really at the top of your field," Brenda heard from him a lot, and sometimes when he was really gunning for a favor, "Man, I would *never* have thought of this!") The praise went over swimmingly with Dr. Mason; most praise did.

On the other hand, the Night Cipher was trying to get upgraded to full member of the Dark Consortium and needed another signature on his application. Brenda was in no such predicament.

"First, it's too long," she said. "*The Ledger*'s not going to publish a ten-page ransom note."

"But I have grievances!"

Brenda flipped to the last page. "Also, it's awful. 'Unless my demands are met, we'll see where your precious Captain Justice's loyalties are at'?"

She reached for a red pen. "The conclusion needs to keep the focus on your goals and off Captain Justice," she said, making notes in the margin. "Also, you can't end sentences with prepositions."

Dr. Mason's face drained of color. Then he went beet-red from collar to hairline, and he shouted loudly enough that her pencil cup rattled, "You *presume* to tell *me* my words are *inadequate?*"

She blinked. "I'm sorry. I thought you wanted this published."

He narrowed his eyes at her. "Have you filed that insurance paperwork about the doomsday device yet?"

"You don't get to blow me up because I correct your grammar," she said. "This is what you hired me to do."

"I didn't hire you to nitpick every little thing," he muttered, and snatched it back. "We'll see what *the Ledger* has to say."

• • • •

The ten-page ransom note came back with a form rejection.

Someone had scrawled at the bottom, "Please be aware of grammar and length requirements for all Letters to the Editor submitted to the *Ledger*."

Brenda waited until late Friday and left it on Dr. Mason's desk after he was gone. Saturday he would be torn away from his dastardly doomsday experiment in order to observe Captain Justice in action; Lord Destiny III was planning an impenetrable death trap for Captain Justice and the Lawful Lass, and that would take up at least half the day.

If she was lucky, she would get all the way to Sunday without hearing from him about needing to make edits.

She was going to enjoy every minute.

• • • •

When the phone call came in (Saturday, just before dusk), she had already rewritten the ransom note.

Not that she told him. If he knew she worked weekends, she'd spend the rest of her days in that farmhouse lair.

• • • •

Her draft made it into the *Ledger*.

She knocked on the lab door to give him the good news. He was in his usual position in the far corner, making tiny adjustments to the vaguely arachnid doomsday device, which hulked fifteen feet high on knife-sharp metal legs. Brenda still didn't understand why you'd have to strap a person to it to make it seem dangerous.

When she held up the letter, he gasped, shoved his goggles back on his head, and scrambled down to see it for himself.

(Brenda's last job had been at an accounting office. You had to give *some* credit to a guy who was so excited about what he did.)

"'We will obey your demands and publish this ransom note on the front page in tomorrow's edition,'" he read with glee. He handed back the letter. "Miss Bryce, I must admit I'm impressed."

She knew better than to let an opportunity pass her by. "So, no doomsday machine?"

He frowned. "Yes. I suppose it's not ideal to risk a valued employee on a possibly risky endeavor. If you really don't want to—"

"Great," she said, and closed the door before he could change his mind.

At home, she quietly checked some job sites. There had to be admin positions that weren't quite this involving.

• • • •

The day the doomsday ransom note ran, Captain Justice held a press conference on the Town Hall steps to warn Dr. Mason and the Dark Consortium against any more civil unrest.

He was in full costume and his ceremonial-occasions-only Winged Justice helmet, but Brenda was so used to it by now that she hardly noticed the difference between him and the uniform suits of the City Hall reps.

"I am not alone," Captain Justice said, looking directly at the camera and resting a fist on the podium. "The people are with me, the Amazing League is with me, and, as always, justice is with me!"

The crowd went wild.

Dr. Mason wrinkled his nose.

"He's just so . . . *blond*," he said.

Unexpectedly, Brenda sort of knew what he meant.

• • • •

With the doomsday gauntlet officially thrown, Dr. Mason started living in the lab. Brenda eventually caved and did the same. (He offered her the bedroom infested with moths. She slept on the living-room couch.)

Sometimes, listening to his commentary on the inevitability of general municipal lesson-learning, Brenda couldn't help but feel that Enid should have left a coded warning Post-it or something two years ago.

She knocked on the door. "I have a question about the ignition switch you wanted me to order."

"Not now," he said. Behind the glasses, his eyes gleamed.

"It's time-sensitive."

"Maybe to you. You should work on budgeting your time, Miss Bryce. Oh, can I get pizza from the thin-crust place for lunch? No garlic in the sauce, though." He narrowed his eyes at the beaker in his hand. "I hate garlic."

"Pizza sauce is already made when you order," she said. "Remember you had me call the restaurant and complain for you last time?"

After a moment, the memory registered, and Mason made fists on his desk and hissed. "Those garlic-lovers! Well, find me a place that doesn't use garlic."

Fourteen phone calls later, she knocked on the lab door and stuck her head in.

"I found a place willing to make a special order. Some garlic-free pizza is coming."

Dr. Mason looked up and considered this. "Is it thin-crust? It had better be thin-crust."

There was a little silence.

Then Brenda said, "I've reconsidered the doomsday device."

. . . .

It turned out that the doomsday device was a lot taller than it seemed in the workshop, and that she was strapped awfully close to the ticking timer.

The good news was that Dr. Mason had tied her up on the scenic side, so at least she could look out over the city. It was the closest thing to a night out she'd had in a long time. There wasn't much to do after work in farmhouse-lair country.

She waited one hour, five minutes, and thirty-two seconds (according to the ticker) before Captain Justice showed.

He soared out of the sky and landed beside her with a wide-legged impact that, if the device had been motion-triggered, would have gone pretty badly. His armor, close-up, squeaked.

"Don't worry," he called, climbing across the metal legs. "This night, Captain Justice will hear your case!"

Brenda had to admit, he did seem really blond.

When he reached her, he yanked the Blade of Truth out of his belt and started slicing.

"Poor, innocent citizen. How did Dr. Mason ever steal you away to this awful fate?"

"I'm his assistant," she said.

Captain Justice's hands froze on the ropes, and he leaned back and gave her the stink eye for so long that she began to worry about the timer.

"It's overtime," she defended half-heartedly.

Captain Justice shook his head and started slicing through the ropes with the Blade of Truth again.

"You know," he said, "Enid was once where you are now, but she really grabbed the bull by the horns and pulled herself up by the bootstraps when it mattered."

"That's a mixed metaphor," Brenda said. "And does that mean Enid's the Lawful Lass?"

"Of course not," said Captain Justice. "Enid's my assistant! But that's purely administrative. The League has a rule never to recruit active members from the ranks of the enemy, unless they have superpowers." He frowned. "Does she have superpowers?"

Brenda would have shrugged if she wasn't tied up. "I wouldn't know."

"Well, if she does, I'm not supposed to leave her alone with information about the other members of the Amazing League." Captain Justice paused. "My God, she's there right now. What if she has superpowers? How could she have kept them from me all this time?"

Brenda suspected it wouldn't take much.

"Are you a good boss?" she asked.

He looked aghast. "Of course! I and my fellow crime-fighters in the League enact justice in all its forms, including workers' rights!"

"Really? Because it's eleven at night on a Saturday, and Enid's still at the office."

Captain Justice thought about that. Then he sliced off the last of the knots with significantly less gusto than he'd used on the first.

"Well," he said, "I guess you're free. You should go. I must disable this device at all costs, before the city falls to pieces under Methuselah Mason's stone-fisted despotism!"

"Don't worry," Brenda said, hopping to the ground between two of the spider legs.

"Don't worry? Listen here, you may think nothing of working for the maddest mind this city has seen in a hundred years, but some of us—"

"The ignition doesn't work."

He stopped. "What?"

"He was busy with the airborne chaos serum and wouldn't review the electronics order," she said. "I ordered the wrong switch. The ignition won't connect."

He frowned. "On purpose?"

"Well, not as far as he knows. Those things all look alike." She smiled. "Not like he could test it beforehand, right? This way everybody's safe."

His frown deepened. "You're not a very good assistant, are you?"

Brenda stared.

. . . .

When she showed up at the farmhouse lair the next morning, Dr. Mason was so surprised that he took off his goggles and blinked several times.

"I thought for sure you'd take a job with Captain Justice," he said finally. "I mean, after what happened with Enid . . ."

Brenda shrugged and sat behind her desk. "I feel my place is here," she said.

He thought that over, then nodded.

"Good thing, too," he said. "We have work to do. Captain Jerkpants beat the living daylights out of that doomsday machine."

"Sorry," said Brenda, pulling out a notebook.

"It just means we'll have to try harder on the next one," Dr. Mason said. "We'll start with some sturdier supplies, for one thing. That exoskeletal support structure could barely hold you."

He turned and slapped his goggles back on.

"So. Miss Bryce, take a note."

Genevieve Valentine's first novel, Mechanique: A Tale of the Circus Tresaulti, *was published by Prime Books in 2011 and won the Crawford Award for best fantasy debut and was a finalist for the Nebula Award. Her short fiction has appeared in the anthology* Running with the Pack *and in the magazines* Lightspeed, Strange Horizons, Futurismic, Clarkesworld, Journal of Mythic Arts, Fantasy Magazine, Escape Pod, *and more. Her work can also be found in John Joseph Adams's anthologies* Under the Moons of Mars: New Adventures on Barsoom, Armored, Federations, The Way of the Wizard, *and* The Living Dead 2. *In 2010, she was a finalist for the World Fantasy Award.*

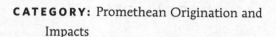

CATEGORY: Promethean Origination and
Impacts

RULE 1818: These Things Run in the Family

SOURCE: Catherine Moreau, author

VIA: Theodora Goss

*The genes we receive from our parents will shape our entire exis-
tence. Trivial details like the shapes of our fingernails or the size of
pores are spelled out in our chromosomes, as are critical inheri-
tances like our sex and our propensity for disease. When we look
in the mirror and see our father's nose or our mother's ears, it is
easy to understand how genes affect our physical bodies.*

*It's not as easy to trace the effects of genetics upon the mind.
Are traits like musical talent really passed on by our genetics—or
do prodigies simply grow up in environments that stimulate their
gifts? Do smart parents have smart children, or do they just en-
courage their kids to act more intellectual? How do genes play out
in disorders like autism and ADHD? Are our brains the product of
nature or nurture? These questions hum in the background of our
next story. With its unusual narrators, this story, which first appeared in the online magazine* Strange Horizons, *demanded to be
included. Here we meet a group of exceptional young women who
share a common bond of unusual fathers. They're all smart, interesting, and attractive. But if madness is inheritable, these ladies
are in trouble.*

THE MAD SCIENTIST'S DAUGHTER

THEODORA GOSS

In London, we formed a club. It's very exclusive. There are only six members. Five of us live on the premises. Helen, who is married, lives in Bloomsbury, but she comes to have dinner with us twice a week. We need each other. None of us has sisters, except Mary and Diana in a way, so we take the place of sisters for each other. Who else could share or sympathize with our experiences?

I. The House Near Regent's Park

Mary created a trust that holds the deed to the house. We are all listed as beneficiaries:

Miss Justine Frankenstein
Miss Catherine Moreau
Miss Beatrice Rappaccini
Miss Mary Jekyll
Miss Diana Hyde
Mrs. Arthur Meyrinck (née Helen Raymond)

But it is her house, really. Her father left it to her, along with a moderate fortune. She is the only one of us who has inherited any money. Science does not pay well; mad science pays even worse.

From that fortune, she created a fund out of which we can draw for emergencies, but we all work. Mary paints on porcelain. Justine and Beatrice embroider vestments for the church. I write potboilers for the penny press. Diana is on the music-hall stage. She can't, she says, stand the dull, ladylike sort of work the rest of us do. She must have excitement: the footlights, the greasepaint, the admirers. We don't judge. Who, indeed, are we to do so? We have all done things of which we are not proud. The club is a haven for us, a port in a particularly stormy world.

Helen does not work, of course: she has a household to run, a daughter to raise. She is also her husband's model. You might remember her as

Helen Vaughan, although she also went by Herbert or Beaumont, at the time of what the newspapers called the West End Horrors. I have seen paintings of her at the Grosvenor, as Medusa with snakes for hair, or a lamia. I envy her sometimes, living in the midst of an artistic ferment, participating in the world. But then I curl up on the sofa by the fire in the clubroom, at peace with the world and myself, and think about how lucky I am to be here, out of the tumult of life, and I am content.

II. How We Live and Work

Beatrice lives in the conservatory. We had it built especially for her, at the back of the house where the laboratory used to be. Looking in through the glass, from the garden, you would think we were growing a jungle. Vines grow up the posts of her bed, orchids and passion flowers hang down over her as she sleeps. I can see the table where she hybridizes her flowers, but only dimly, since there is always a mist on the glass. Some of the plants I recognize: jasmine, oleander, castor bean, hellebore, laburnum, all part of her poisonous pharmacopeia. And plants that she has created, plants only we have seen, and only in glimpses, since it is deadly for any of us to stay in the conservatory too long. She pollinates them herself, since insects can't live in the conservatory. She breathes in their fumes, and they give her a particular luster.

Beatrice is the only one of us other than Helen with any claim to beauty, but it is the beauty of a poisonous flower. Sometimes when she has been sitting with us in the clubroom too long, she tells us that she feels faint, and must return to the conservatory. The powders she makes and sells to the medical school supplement our income.

Apart from Beatrice, only Justine can visit the conservatory for any length of time. Nothing seems to harm her physically, although eventually, breathing those poisonous fumes, even she will begin to feel faint. But she is the most sentimental of us: the pigeons *roo-coo*ing on the roof, the first flowers on the cherry tree outside her window, a book of poetry, will all bring her to tears. Reading Wordsworth will depress her for a week. I can't help laughing sometimes, to myself of course, when I look out my window and see her sitting in the garden, sighing like a sad giantess.

Justine lives in the attic. She says that she likes to be close to the sky and the pigeons, but really I think it's the only room in the house where the ceiling is high enough for her. When you're seven feet tall, even a ten-foot ceiling feels cramped. All of her furniture had to be made to order: the long bed, the wardrobe tall enough to accommodate her dresses, the looking glass that we bought from a magician, who used it to perform tricks. We've offered to help her decorate, to paper the walls, hang lithographs. I've offered to sew her curtains. But no, she says. She prefers the spartan simplicity of whitewash, a bedstead and a single chair, sunlight streaming through the windows. A cross hanging over her bed and a miniature of her grandmother on the dresser are the only decorations. And books. Piles and piles of books. Mostly religious, but also a great deal of poetry. Too much, I think, to be entirely healthy for her.

Mary, Diana, and I live below her, on the second floor. Mary and Diana share a room. We've told them it's not necessary, that we can convert the library into a room for one of them, but they prefer to live together. I think it took so long for them to find each other, they do not want to be parted, even for a night, although they constantly disagree. Mary: tall, slender, fair, a quiet girl who is always either embroidering or reading philosophical works. Diana: short, dark as a gypsy, as temperamental as I imagine all actresses are. When we found her, she was working in a brothel. We are not entirely certain that she has given up her less respectable pursuits. When she comes home smelling of gin, it is Mary who sits with her and bathes her head while she lies on the sofa, moaning. I suspect Mary has, on more than one occasion, paid Diana's debts.

Mary's side of the room: blue wallpaper with a pattern of white flowers, blue and white checked curtains, a brass bed with white linen, a small desk on which she has put daffodils in a vase. Diana's side of the room: Indian silks in reds and pinks and oranges, like an exotic sunset. A divan covered with pillows beside a table carved to resemble an elephant. Clothes strewn all over the floor, because she is incapable of keeping anything neat. Everywhere: statues of Hindu gods, buddhas with fat bellies, an onyx dog from Africa, a collection of brass bells, dyed baskets, the detritus of Empire. A vanity inlaid with ivory and strewn with cosmetics that, Mary tells her, will eventually ruin her complexion. Mrs. Poole refuses to clean Diana's half of the room. "Let her learn to pick up after herself," she says, uncharacteristically.

What would we do without Mrs. Poole? Her father worked for the Jekylls, and his father before him. She takes care of us all, makes certain that Justine isn't starving herself on a diet of lettuce and parsley, that Diana gets up by noon so she can make her curtain call. She feeds my cats.

My room is not very interesting. I was born in Argentina and then reborn on my father's island in the South Seas. Perhaps that is why my room is as English as possible. Roses on the wallpaper, a rose chintz on the armchair. A mahogany suite: bed, dresser, wardrobe. A bookshelf filled with Jane Austen, the Brontës, George Eliot. A desk where I write my potboilers.

The Mysteries of Astarte
The Adventures of Rick Chambers

Rick Chambers and Astarte
Rick Chambers on Venus
Invasion of the Cat Women

I look down at the page in the typewriter:

"No mortal man can resist me," said Astarte, pulling back her veil. The eyes that looked at him shone like twin stars in the night sky, dark and yet luminous in her white face. The perfect mouth, with lips curved like the famous bows of the Phoenicians, laughed.

Harold fell down before her, worshiping her beauty. Even Professor Hardcastle wiped the sweat from his brow. Only Rick remained calm.

"Your beauty, Madam, is most impressive. But I am an Englishman, and I prefer justice."

That will be *The Death of Astarte*. I have already been paid for *The Resurrection of Astarte* and *Rick Chambers, Jr. in the Caverns of Doom*.

On the bed, three cats lie purring: Alpha, Omega, and Bess. I found them one morning, three ragged kittens mewing by the kitchen door. Poor things. How difficult it must be, to be a kitten in London, always running from dogs, always in danger of being run over by cartwheels. Of course we took them in. The club is a refuge for them as well, and I am particularly fond of cats.

III. What We Talk About

Sometimes we talk about our fathers.

Justine: "My father loved me. He made me from the corpse of a girl who had been a servant of the Frankenstein family. She had been hanged for a crime she did not commit, and he had preserved her body, anticipating that some day he might be able to once again give her life. He even gave me her name, to commemorate her innocence.

"I can't begin to tell you what a wonderful childhood I had! My father guided me gently through the various stages of knowledge. He taught me the words to describe the world around me: the birds, the plants, the phenomena of nature. He taught me to read, and in the evenings we would read together: *Paradise Lost, The Sorrows of Werther, Plutarch's Lives*. But he was always haunted by the memory of the creature he had created, and eventually that creature came for him. At his death, I lost my father and my only friend. Until"—she looks at us, sitting and listening to her, the firelight on our faces—"until I found you." And we look away politely, while she blows her nose into a handkerchief.

Beatrice: "For so many years I was angry at my father. I thought, he had no right to make me poisonous, to make my only playmates the plants of his garden."

Helen: "He *had* no right. Seriously, Beatrice, you're too forgiving. You need to learn to stand up for yourself."

Mary: "For goodness' sake, let her finish. You're always interrupting."

Helen: "That's because I can't stand to see any of you justifying them. I mean, seriously. They were abusive bastards, and that's all there is to it."

Catherine: "I have to agree with Helen. Abusive bastards seems, you know, fairly accurate. I mean, look at my father."

Beatrice: "I don't think you can compare my father to yours, Cat. No offense, but your father was a butcher. Mine brought me up himself, in a beautiful garden—"

Mary: "I agree that there are relative degrees of—well, although I don't like to say it, abusive bastardhood. But Bea, he never taught you anything. All that time on his hands, and he never took any of it to sit you down, teach you about your own biology. So you ended up poisoning the man you loved, basically by accident—"

Beatrice: "I should have known."

Diana: "Why in the world would you blame yourself? I'm with Helen. They were bastards, the lot of them, even Justine's sainted Papa Frankenstein. Look at me, born in a brothel. My mother died of syphilis."

Mary: "You can't generalize your story to all of us."

Diana: "Oh, right, now you're taking the other side. My story is *our* story, or have you forgotten, *sister*?"

Justine: "For goodness' sake, why are we arguing? I know perfectly well that my father wasn't perfect. But why should I remember all his faults? Why can't I remember the good times we had together, how kind he could be?"

Helen: "Because that's like lying to yourself. We've all been lied to. Do we really want to lie to ourselves as well?"

And then we are all quiet, and stare into the fire.

"My father," Helen continues, "was a scientist, like yours. He took my mother from the gutters, where she was starving, fed her, educated her, seduced her, and then experimented on her. She had a vision. She saw something she could not, or perhaps did not have the guts to, understand— the god Pan, source of all order and disorder, Alpha and Omega, to whom all things in the end will come. Nine months later I was born, daughter of the respectable Dr. Raymond and of Pan. It's not hard to understand why, as a teenager, I tried to destroy the world. Sometimes I wish I had. I mean, look at it. The other day, a man tried to steal my pocketbook. He was drunk, red-eyed and reeking of gin, and I turned and started hitting him with my umbrella. I thought, I could have destroyed you all—the beggars, the bankers, the filthy streets of London."

Catherine: "So, why didn't you?"

Helen: "Well, I married Arthur around that time, and then Leda was born. I would have had to destroy Regent's Park, and ice cream, and prams. It just didn't seem practical. Besides, I didn't want to give my father the satisfaction."

Mrs. Poole comes in. "Would any of you ladies like some tea?"

IV. A Peaceful Domestic Scene

Sometimes when Helen comes, she brings her daughter, Leda. She's a solemn child, with black hair that curls past her shoulders, genuinely hyacinthine. When she smiles, you can faintly hear the clashing of cymbals, the strings of the lyre plucked, the chanting of Bacchantes. You pause, thinking, *I must be imagining it,* and then you realize that no, you really are hearing something otherworldly. Once, I saw her in the garden, playing with a boy who had horns on his head, and the legs and hooves of a goat.

"She can't control it," says Helen. "She's too young. I couldn't control it either, at her age."

Leda is only twelve. But we can see in her, already, what we all seem to have, what I would describe as a mark, if it were not so variable.

I look in the mirror. I am, everywhere, golden brown: brown hair, brown skin, golden eyes. If you look at them too closely, you will begin to feel strange. You will realize that my pupils are slitted, except in the dark. That I do not blink as often as I ought to. And my face, although well-shaped, is seamed with scars.

We all have the mark, but in different ways. Mary, our golden-haired English girl, sits too still, is too placid for human nature. If you sit with her long enough, you will start to become nervous. Justine, willowy, elegant, is too tall for a woman, or even a man. Diana, lively and laughing, suffers from attacks of the hysteria. She will, suddenly, begin to pull out her hair, cut her arm with a dinner knife. Once, when she was younger, she almost bled to death. Beatrice, beautiful Beatrice who moves through the house like a walking calla lily, kills with her breath. When we gather together for dinner, she sits at the far end of the table. She has her own dishes and plates, which Mrs. Poole collects wearing gloves.

You could, I suppose, call us monsters. We are frightening, aren't we? Although we are, in our different ways, attractive. When we walk down the street, men look, and then look away. And then perhaps look again, and away again. Some of us don't leave the house more than we have to. The butcher delivers, and Mrs. Poole goes to the grocer's. But not even Justine can stay inside all the time. Sometimes we have to just, you know, get out. Go to the library, or the park. Personally, I'm sorry that veils are going out of fashion.

Imagine us in the evenings, sitting by the fire in the clubroom. I am reading from *The Yellow Book*. Justine is darning a sock. Mary is sketching Beatrice, who is posing by the window, which is open at the bottom despite the autumn chill.

"When will Diana return from the theater?" Beatrice asks.

"I really don't know," says Mary. "She has a new hanger-on, some sort of Viscount. I just wish she'd be more careful."

"Well," I say, "if he does anything to hurt her, we'll sic Beatrice on him."

"Or Justine," says Beatrice.

"Me?" says Justine. "You know I wouldn't hurt a fly."

"Yes," I say, "but he wouldn't know that. You look frightening enough."

"I couldn't. I mean, it would be terrible. . . ." says Justine.

"Oh, for goodness' sake," I say. "When the villagers come with pitchforks, what are you going to do? Hide in a hayloft? We should be ready to—I don't know, tear their throats out." This is London, but how far away are they ever, the villagers with pitchforks?

"Let's get back to the story," says Mary, the conciliator. "I want to know whether what's-her-name is going to have an affair with Lord-what's-his-name."

"That was the *last* story," I say. "Haven't you been listening?"

"You know I don't like that modern stuff, except your books, of course." I happen to know she never finished *Rick Chambers and Astarte*. "I just want you to stop bothering Justine. Can't you see she's upset by all this talk of violence?" She turns back to her painting. "Bea, hold your head up a little. You're drooping."

A peaceful domestic scene. An ordinary evening among monsters.

V. How I Joined the Club

I knew Justine before we joined the club. We were in the circus together, the Giantess and the Cat Girl. The manager was a good man, a Polish Jew who called himself Lorenzo the Magnificent. When I joined his Traveling Circus of Marvels and Delights, Justine had already been there for two years. She sat outside the sideshow tent, taking tickets from the patrons. She also had an act with two dwarves dressed as clowns and a pony that kicked on command.

There is an etiquette in the circus. Everyone is polite to one another, but still, the performers have a certain contempt for the sideshow, and vice versa. The performers were proud of their tricks, walking the high wire, riding bareback, being shot from a cannon. But we needed no tricks in the sideshow. We *were* the tricks. We could perform without moving a muscle.

I was Astarte, the Cat Girl from Egypt. I have no tail and my ears are almost normal, just a little pointed at the tips. But you should have seen me in my costume! Cat ears, cat tail. I certainly looked the part. I would growl with fury and show the customers my claws. I even purred for the gentlemen who paid extra to stroke me. Atlas, the Strong Man, stopped them if they went too far. I was always a respectable cat.

Atlas was in love with Justine. He even asked her to marry him.

"Why don't you?" I asked her. We had become friends, in part I think because of our similar family histories. Her father had made men out of corpses. Mine had made men out of animals. They were, in a sense, in the same profession.

"I just can't," she said.

"Is it your sainted Papa? Are you afraid that you'll never find a man with his charm, his erudition? It's true that Atlas is not exactly literate . . ."

"You're making fun of me. Please don't, Cat. No, it's something else."

I waited.

"You have to promise that you won't tell anyone."

"Who would I tell? It's not as though anyone else would understand."

"All right. The creature—the one my father made. He wanted me to be his mate. One day, he attacked me. You think I'm strong, but he was so much stronger. He had his hand around my throat . . . If he had wanted to kill me, I'm sure he would have. But that wasn't what he wanted, at least not then. I can't . . . I really can't talk about it anymore." Tears were streaming down her face.

"Oh, Justine . . ." I said.

"So you see," she said, finally blowing her nose on a handkerchief. She seemed to have an endless supply of them. "I'll never marry any man."

I put my arms around her, and we sat together on one of the packing crates, listening to the elephants trumpet.

With the circus, we toured the provinces. That was when I fell in love with England, its greenness, its freshness. That was when I created Rick Chambers, the quintessential English gentleman, Eton and Oxford and cricket and the sun never setting and all that. Astarte will never defeat the English gentleman, no matter how many times she lures him into her bed. Of course, he'll never defeat her either. It would be boring if the English gentleman ever won.

Those were happy days, more or less, with Justine, and Lola the Bearded Lady, and Harold the Wolf Boy, and the two dwarves, Pip and Squeak. The pay was low, but we were like a family. However, they were destined to end.

Lorenzo was in debt, and even the Traveling Circus of Marvels and Delights could not pay the full amount.

"If only I had the Black Widow!" he said mournfully, one evening as we were eating our supper together around a campfire. The Black Widow was a new marvel, a beautiful girl whose breath was as deadly as the deadliest poison. She was not in a circus, but at the Royal College of Surgeons. Medical men were attempting to determine what made her so toxic. It was Beatrice, of course, but Justine and I didn't know that then. We knew of her only from newspaper articles.

"Poor girl," Justine would say, reading them.

"Why? It says that even the Queen has gone to see her. Imagine the price people would pay, if she were in the sideshow."

"To kill everything you touch! I think that must be terrible."

"If you say so. Personally, I think it would come in handy sometimes."

Two days before the circus was to break up, when Justine and I were wondering what we were going to do with ourselves, a woman came to see us. She was dressed in black, and heavily veiled. When she drew back her veil, we saw a beautiful face, with an olive complexion and black eyes, obviously foreign-looking, yet it would have been difficult to tell what country she came from. She looked so completely exotic, yet at the same time so ordinary, like an English lady. Aha! I thought. If I ever write a book about Astarte, I'll make her look just like that.

"Miss Frankenstein, Miss Moreau," she said. "I'm delighted to make your acquaintance." Her voice was deep, musical, and I almost imagined that I heard the sound of lyres as she spoke. "I understand that your employment is almost over. I've been authorized to offer you membership in a very exclusive club."

VI. The Reports of our Deaths

The reports of our deaths have been greatly exaggerated.

Justine: believed dismembered, her body parts thrown into the sea.
Beatrice: believed poisoned by a toxic antidote.
Helen: believed strangled by a hangman's rope.
Catherine: believed killed by Moreau's hand.

And yet, as you see, we survive.

VII. The Stories We Tell

Mary: "People often don't know that my father had a wife. She was left out of the case history that was written shortly after his death, I suppose to protect her privacy. Poor Mother! She was only eighteen when she married, and he was in medical school. She was so proud to have married a doctor. My grandfather was a country vicar, and she had been educated at home by my grandmother, taught to sew and sing hymns and keep hens. She didn't understand when my father began refurbishing the laboratory, conducting experiments. When I was fifteen, shortly before she died, she told me, 'Your father was a good man. Never forget that, Mary. It was his science, his fatal science, that ruined him. If only it had been a woman! Read your Bible, Mary. In it you'll find everything you ever need to know. Never give in to the curiosity that killed your father.'"

Beatrice: "There's nothing wrong with science. In itself, it's neither good nor evil. It's simply a way of looking at the world."

Mrs. Poole: "Well, then why does it lead to all those nasty mad scientists, I want to know? No, Miss Beatrice, I think all that science and experimenting should be left alone, especially by young ladies like yourselves. Mrs. Jekyll was a good, upstanding woman, and she was right. Everything you need to know, you'll find in the Good Book."

Beatrice: "Science saved me, Mrs. Poole. When I recovered from Professor Baglioni's antidote, it was late afternoon. Where could I go? I loved my father, but I didn't want to return to his garden, which had been my prison for so many years, or to the lover who had so cruelly rejected me. Instead, I wandered around Padua, trying to find the university. When I finally found the front gate, I asked to see Professor Baglioni.

"He was startled to see me. I think that he had, in an indirect way, tried to kill me, absolving himself of blame because he had not been sure of the result. I told him, 'If you don't help me, I'll go to the authorities and accuse you of attempted murder. I may be a monster, but I'm also the daughter of the famous Dr. Rappaccini, who has cured many of the townspeople, including the mayor's wife. Do you think they'll ignore me?' I don't know, really, if the authorities would have listened to me, but he was already frightened and uncertain of his position, so he did what I asked.

"He took me to his villa and brought me all of his books on natural philosophy, particularly botany. When those weren't enough, he brought me books from the university library. I spent months studying them, trying to understand my own physiology. I wanted to remove the poison from my system. I think part of me still hoped I could return to my Giovanni and say, 'Look, I'm a normal woman now.' I still wanted him to love me. But I could find no way to alter my condition.

"One day, he told me of my father's death. My father had continued his studies, but without me to tend the garden for him, he had slowly been poisoned by its fumes. How I cried! All the anger I had felt toward him melted away, and I felt only an emptiness. I was now alone in the world. I left the seclusion of the villa and offered myself to the learned men of the university for study. When they could give me no answer, I went to another university, and then another. I traveled from city to city, from Padua to Milan, Geneva, Paris, and finally London, always hoping that someone would find a cure. Without that hope, sometimes I think I would have lain down on the earth and simply died. Finally, I decided that I would become a scientist myself. If I could not find an answer in books or from learned men, I would have to experiment. So I followed in my father's footsteps. I wonder if he would have been proud of me?"

Mary: "I'm certain he would have. You're doing wonderful work."

Diana: "How do you do it, Mary? You always agree with everyone. You never say anything mean or lose your temper. Honestly, I think it's creepy. Sometimes I think you're a doll that a magician brought to life and taught to behave from a good conduct book. I have no problem with Bea making potions, but we shouldn't pretend that any of us will ever be normal. Sometimes when I'm with the Viscount, all I want to do is bite him until he bleeds and lap up the blood. Cat knows what I'm talking about."

Catherine: "I often want to bite someone. The butcher looks so delicious, carrying those glorious hunks of meat!"

Diana: "Exactly. Well, you girls know my history. My mother was a whore, who didn't know she was with child until after my father died. She figured out what was what quickly enough, and Mrs. Jekyll paid though the nose—until my mother died of syphilis at twenty-one. I was sent to an orphanage run by nuns. How sick I became of their pieties! At night, when they thought all the girls were sleeping, I cut their habits to shreds and pissed in the communion cup. I rang the bells at the wrong hours. Finally, they decided the orphanage was haunted and brought in a bishop for an exorcism. But it was all me, of course. When I was old enough, I left to follow my mother's trade. Don't tell me that any science is going to make me *normal*."

VIII. The Stories We Tell, Continued

Catherine: "I killed my father. I bit him and bashed his head in. And when a ship finally came close enough to the island, I pretended to be in distress so the captain would take me aboard. He believed I was an English lady whose ship had been captured by pirates, and who had finally been left to starve on a deserted shore. That was the only way he could explain my scars, and of course I told him that I could not remember anything before my time on the island. He brought me to England, and his wife cared for me. She taught me how to dress, how to eat with a knife and fork, all the things my father had not taught me. She wanted to adopt me as her daughter—they were childless—but one day when I was sitting in the parlor, darning a sock, her little dog came by, a yapping little dog that had never liked me, and bit me on the ankle. So I bit it back. When she came in, its corpse was dangling from my jaws. She started screaming . . . I left with only the clothes on my back. I begged in the streets for months before Lorenzo asked me to join his circus."

Justine: "Those were good days with the circus, weren't they?"

Beatrice: "How did *you* join the circus, Justine?"

Justine: "Do we have to talk about it?"

Beatrice: "I'm sorry, I didn't mean to distress you. I was just curious."

Justine: "All right. But it's hard for me to talk about—I'd rather forget. The creature my father had made wanted a wife, so my father made me. But after he had completed me, he realized that he could not give me to the creature. So, he made the creature believe he was destroying me by rowing out and throwing a sack full of stones into the sea. Then, he took me to a cottage on the coast of Scotland, even more remote than our previous location had been. 'I won't give you to that monster,' he told me. 'You have the ability to reason and to appreciate the beautiful. You are not like him, and you will not belong to him.' The creature, supposing I had been destroyed, did not follow us. And so for a few years, a few happy years, we were left in peace.

"But one day, the creature found our cottage. He was determined once more to have my father make another like himself. And there, on the shore by that northern sea, he saw my father playing with me, the bride who had been meant for him. We were throwing a ball back and forth, one of my favorite games at that time—remember that although I was full-grown, I was only three years old. He was in such a rage that he ran toward my father and strangled him with his bare hands. And then he attacked me . . .

"He forced me to live with him in that cottage, to read him the books my father and I had read together, to sit by the fire with him as though we were man and wife. But one night, as he lay asleep after drinking the last of the whiskey in the house, I stuck a kitchen knife into his heart. And then I ran, sobbing, because I had killed the man who had been both brother and husband to me, the only one, as far as I knew, of my kind. I lived on berries, the bark from trees, and what I could steal from farmyards—the slop left for the pigs, the grain scattered for the hens. Once, a man tried to shoot me with a gun. Another time, boys threw stones at me. Finally I came to a town, and there was a circus. It was, of course, Lorenzo's Traveling Circus of Marvels and Delights. The tent was so bright, so cheerful, scarlet and yellow in the middle of a field. And I heard music . . . Although I was sick and starving, I walked closer to see where the music was coming from. But there, just by the tent, I fainted. When I came to again, I was in Lola's caravan, and Lorenzo was looking at me, smoothing his mustache.

Cat, you remember what a black mustache he had. We were convinced he dyed it. 'Young lady,' he said, 'I have a proposition for you.' I was terrified! I had never seen a human being before, except my father. But I accepted his offer to join the sideshow. What choice did I have? I had no way to earn my living in the world. I had only the knowledge my father had given me, and the fact that I was, you know, different."

Beatrice: "Why do we always die in the stories?"

Catherine: "Because we're not the ones who write them."

IX. The Secrets We Tell Each Other

Justine: "Once, I killed a man. I put my hands around his neck and strangled him. I didn't mean to—he threatened to shoot me with a gun."

Mary: "Once, a man tried to kiss me. He was a clerk at the attorney's office, when I went to hear the provisions of my mother's will. That was when I learned about Diana—it was my mother who had placed her in that orphanage. The front hall was narrow, and as he was handing me my coat, he suddenly leaned down . . . But then, at the last moment, he drew back. There was a look on his face, as though he had smelled something repugnant. I don't know what it is—I don't think I'm unattractive. But no man has tried to kiss me since."

Helen: "I don't know how many men I've slept with—I never kept track. They were all respectable men, the kind you meet in drawing rooms or at balls during the season. You have no idea what strange tastes some of them had . . ."

Beatrice: "Well, please don't tell us. I don't think I have any secrets. Does that make me boring?"

Diana: "I've had an abortion. And I would do it again, if I had to."

Catherine: "Some days, when I look in the mirror, I just wish I looked normal."

X. Our Plans for the Future

Helen is the only one of us who has ever been married. Arthur Meyrinck is her second husband. Her first husband committed suicide. Men have a way of doing that around Helen. But Arthur is an artist. Nothing she does can shock him. If he comes down in the morning to find that the parlor has turned into Arcadia, with naked women dancing to the sound of Pan pipes, he eats his breakfast in the kitchen.

Most men are not so tolerant. Most men do not want a wife who is stronger than they are, like Justine, or who can bite through their necks, as I can, or who, like Beatrice, can kill them with a breath.

That, I suppose, is why we rather spoil Leda, sewing her dresses, letting her borrow whatever books she likes. Mrs. Poole makes her cakes and biscuits and tarts.

Justine has said, "Why don't we make a child of our own? We would make her out of corpses, or a large dog. Or," looking at Beatrice, "some sort of shrub? Maybe a rhododendron?"

I say, "Do you really think it would be a good idea to create another one of us? Aren't there enough of us in the world already?"

I know that Justine disagrees, that she thinks there's nothing much wrong with us, that the problem is with the world, which has no place for us in it. Except here, in this house. She has the confidence that comes from having once been loved.

Helen says, "Why just one? Why not start with three—plant, animal, corpse, and see which one works best? Then go on from there. We could make any number of daughters, if we wanted. What none of you, except Diana, realizes is that we're powerful. Not just because we're strong or deadly or have sharp teeth, but because of everything we've endured. We're our father's daughters in more ways than one. We could control this society we live in, rather than hiding from it."

Ever since we joined the club, Helen has tried to convince us to take over the world.

Helen: "*Plan A*. Beatrice creates a poison that we can introduce into the water supply. We make all of London sick. We offer to release the antidote, but only if the government pays us a certain sum of money. That's if we need money."

Mary: "We always need money."

Catherine: "Bea, could you actually do that?"

Beatrice: "It wouldn't be particularly difficult, scientifically. But I wouldn't want to harm anyone."

Helen: "That's why we'd have an antidote. *Plan B*. We kidnap Queen Victoria. She shouldn't be too difficult to extract from Balmoral. Justine snaps her neck and then reanimates her in a remote location, perhaps the cottage her father used to own on the coast of Scotland. The reanimation erases her memories, creating a blank slate for us to write on. Over the course of a month, we teach her to trust us, do what we tell her to. We return her to a grateful nation, saying that we found her wandering, suffering from amnesia. And then through her, we control the government."

Justine: "How do you expect me to reanimate her? And you know how well that worked for my father—the creature he created was uncontrollable, destructive."

Beatrice: "But wasn't he made from the corpse of a criminal? I've met the Queen—she's a kind and gracious woman. I'm sure her corpse would be much more amenable to suggestion."

Mary: "For goodness' sake, don't let Mrs. Poole hear you. She has a picture of the Queen hanging over her bed. Where do you think we could get another housekeeper?"

Diana: "We know you still have your father's notebooks. They're in the bottom drawer of your dresser, under your chemises."

Justine: "I can't believe you would go through my personal things!"

Catherine: "You are talking about *Diana* here. I'm sure she's gone through all of our drawers. She doesn't take your clothes because they're too big for her, but I'm constantly missing stockings . . ."

Helen: "*Plan C.* Catherine creates an army of beast people. We use them to terrorize London."

Mary: "How would that lead to world domination?"

Helen: "Honestly, I haven't thought that far ahead. I just think it would be fun. Imagine, we could make horse people and dog people and rat people . . ."

Diana: "Well, what does Cat think?"

Catherine: "I don't know. On one hand, it would be nice to have more of us. On the other, I don't think any of you understand my and Bea's and Justine's position. At least you were *born* rather than made. Do we really want to—manufacture beings like ourselves? To create monsters, as our fathers did? Although making beast people does sound easier, scientifically, than concocting a poison and its antidote, or animating corpses. I mean, it's just sewing the parts together. Any of us could do it."

Justine: "But *why*? Would we make society any better?"

Helen: "We could, if we wanted to. We could put Mary in power. She's so orderly and logical. Imagine what sensible rules she would make. At least the trains would run on time."

Justine: "I suppose we could do it for the greater good. We could clean up the East End, especially those dreadful areas around Whitechapel. We could find homes for the children in orphanages, and employment for the women who flaunt their wares on the streets . . ."

Helen: "There, you see? I'm not saying we should spend all of our time planning to take over the world. I have other commitments myself. But I do think we should start giving it some serious consideration."

Diana: "Helen's only being practical. You know they're going to come after us eventually. They always do—scientists, other monsters, the police. So why not take control first?"

Helen: "Whether or not you agree with me now, there's going to come a day when all of you, except perhaps Mary, will want children. You'll want them to live safely in this world, and then you'll realize that it's time for us to seize power. You'll see."

Maybe she's right. I do sometimes think about how nice it would be to have a daughter of my own, not just cats.

XI. Why I Wrote This Sketch

Someday, I would like to write a book that isn't about Rick Chambers or Astarte. It would be the sort of book that George Eliot could have written, about life in a country town and the people who live there, their jealousies, their ambitions, the minutiae of their lives. How they fall in love with the wrong people, or the right people at the wrong time, or lose the mercantile business on which their fortune is built. Or misplace wills. You know, *literature*.

But I've never experienced any of those things myself. All I know is monsters.

So I decided to write about us. Just a sketch, no heroic Englishman journeying into the heart of a dark continent, no idol with rubies for eyes. No Caverns of Doom. Just us, sitting and talking. A story that George Eliot could have written.

We are as ordinary, in our own way, as the inhabitants of a country town. In the morning we rise and make our beds, except Diana. We eat breakfast (toast and eggs for Mary, steamed turnips for Justine, raw chicken for me, and for Beatrice a cup of mossy water). Then Justine and Mary take up their work, while Beatrice helps Mrs. Poole, who has found mice in the pantry. (Poor Beatrice. How she hates exterminator duty. But it's an easier death for the mice than Alpha's claws.) I curl up in the rose chintz armchair and start my chapter. In the afternoon, Mary will go around to pay the bills, Diana will rise and go to the theater, Beatrice and Justine will play a game of chess, and I will help Mrs. Poole polish the silver.

We will worry about where the money's going to come from for a summer dress, how to make a cake with only one egg in it, who left the back door open, the plumbing, whether the cherries on the tree in the back garden will ripen this year, and growing old. I think George Eliot could have made something of us, don't you?

XII. An Application for Membership

Yesterday, I received a letter. "Dear Miss Moreau," it began.

My friend Mrs. Jonathan Harker (née Mina Murray) suggested that I write to you. Until a month ago, I lived in an asylum in Wittenberg, caring for my mother, whose health and sanity had been destroyed by certain experiments in blood transfusion performed by my father, Professor Abraham Van Helsing, whose work may be familiar to you from a variety of scientific journals. My own health was affected while I was yet in the womb, for her pregnancy did not alter his research.

I suffer from an acuteness of hearing, an antipathy to light and to strong scents, and persistent anemia, as well as other medical symptoms that I can describe to you in more detail if required. After my mother's death, I could not bring myself to live with my father, so I have been staying with friends or in boardinghouses for the past month. I have no independent income, but I make a little money by giving singing and piano lessons. Mrs. Harker has described for me the club you have formed in London for the daughters of mad scientists, and I wonder if my parentage and experiences might qualify me to join you? I would certainly be grateful to have a good home and to find companionship with others in my circumstance.

> *Yours sincerely,*
> *Lucinda Van Helsing*

Justine: "Yes, of course. Write to her immediately and tell her that she can come, poor dear."

Mary: "We can turn the library into her bedroom, and put the books in the clubroom. We may also have some room for shelves in the front hall. I'll start sewing her curtains to block out the light."

Diana: "It will be nice to have some music around here. It's so deadly quiet sometimes. I wonder if the piano is still in tune?"

Mrs. Poole: "I've heard terrible things about this Professor Van Helsing. He killed a girl by driving a stake through her heart!"

Beatrice: "But that's terrible! How can society allow such things?"

Helen: "You know what I think—the more of us the better. All right, any objections? We have to be unanimous, you know." We all shake our heads. "Well, write to her then. Leda and I have to go now. We have to prepare for a Walpurgisnacht party in the studio. Artists! You can't imagine the mess they make. A troop of satyrs is nothing to it. Mrs. Poole, have you seen our umbrellas? We're going by bus, and I think it's starting to rain."

I say, "I'll write to her tomorrow. It will be nice to have a new member of the club."

Then we sit by the fire, reading or sketching or embroidering, just us monsters.

Theodora Goss's stories have appeared in magazines such as Realms of Fantasy, Strange Horizons, Clarkesworld, Fantasy Magazine, Lady Churchill's Rosebud Wristlet, *and* Apex Magazine. *Anthologies featuring her work include* Ghosts by Gaslight, Logorrhea, Other Earths, Polyphony, Year's Best Fantasy, The Year's Best Fantasy & Horror, The Apocalypse Reader, *and John Joseph Adams's* Under the Moons of Mars: New Adventures on Barsoom. *Much of her short work has been collected in* In the Forest of Forgetting. *She is also the editor of* Voices from Fairyland *and* Interfictions *(with Delia Sherman). She is a winner of the World Fantasy Award and the Rhysling Award, and has been a finalist for the Nebula, Crawford, Mythopoeic, and Tiptree awards.*

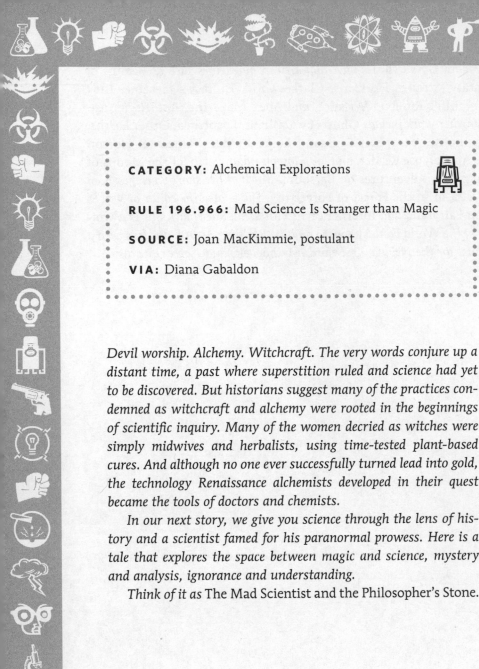

CATEGORY: Alchemical Explorations

RULE 196.966: Mad Science Is Stranger than Magic

SOURCE: Joan MacKimmie, postulant

VIA: Diana Gabaldon

Devil worship. Alchemy. Witchcraft. The very words conjure up a distant time, a past where superstition ruled and science had yet to be discovered. But historians suggest many of the practices condemned as witchcraft and alchemy were rooted in the beginnings of scientific inquiry. Many of the women decried as witches were simply midwives and herbalists, using time-tested plant-based cures. And although no one ever successfully turned lead into gold, the technology Renaissance alchemists developed in their quest became the tools of doctors and chemists.

In our next story, we give you science through the lens of history and a scientist famed for his paranormal prowess. Here is a tale that explores the space between magic and science, mystery and analysis, ignorance and understanding.

Think of it as The Mad Scientist and the Philosopher's Stone.

THE SPACE BETWEEN

DIANA GABALDON

Paris, June, 1778

He still didn't know why the frog hadn't killed him. Paul Rakoczy, Comte St. Germain, picked up the vial, pulled the cork, and sniffed cautiously for the third time, but then recorked it, still dissatisfied. Maybe. Maybe not. The scent of the dark gray powder in the vial held the ghost of something familiar—but it had been thirty years.

He sat for a moment, frowning at the array of jars, bottles, flasks, and pelicans on his workbench. It was late afternoon, and the late spring sun of Paris was like honey, warm and sticky on his face, but glowing in the rounded globes of glass, throwing pools of red and brown and green on the wood from the liquids contained therein. The only discordant note in this peaceful symphony of light was the body of a large rat, lying on its back in the middle of the workbench, a pocket-watch open beside it.

The Comte put two fingers delicately on the rat's chest and waited patiently. It didn't take so long this time; he was used to the coldness as his mind felt its way into the body. Nothing. No hint of light in his mind's eye, no warm red of a pulsing heart. He glanced at the watch: half an hour.

He took his fingers away, shaking his head.

"Mélisande, you evil bitch," he murmured, not without affection. "You didn't think I'd try anything *you* sent me on myself, would you?"

Still . . . he himself had stayed dead a great while longer than half an hour, when the frog had given him the dragon's-blood. It had been early evening when he went into Louis's Star Chamber thirty years before, heart beating with excitement at the coming confrontation—a duel of wizards, with a king's favor as the stakes—and one he'd thought he'd win. He remembered the purity of the sky, the beauty of the stars just visible, Venus bright on the horizon, and the joy of it in his blood. Everything always had a greater intensity when you knew life could cease within the next few minutes.

And an hour later, he thought his life *had* ceased, the cup falling from his numbed hand, the coldness rushing through his limbs with amazing speed, freezing the words *I've lost*, an icy core of disbelief in the center of his mind. He hadn't been looking at the frog; the last thing he had seen through darkening eyes was the woman—La Dame Blanche—her face over the cup she'd given him appalled and white as bone. But what he recalled, and recalled again now, with the same sense of astonishment and avidity, was the great flare of blue, intense as the color of the evening sky beyond Venus, that had burst from her head and shoulders as he died.

He didn't recall any feeling of regret or fear; just astonishment. This was nothing, however, to the astonishment he'd felt when he regained his senses, naked on a stone slab in a revolting subterranean chamber next to a drowned corpse. Luckily, there had been no one alive in that disgusting grotto, and he had made his way—reeling and half-blind, clothed in the drowned man's wet and stinking shirt—out into a dawn more beautiful than any twilight could ever be. So—ten to twelve hours from the moment of apparent death to revival.

He glanced at the rat, then put out a finger and lifted one of the small, neat paws. Nearly twelve hours. Limp, the rigor had already passed; it was warm up here at the top of the house. Then he turned to the counter that ran along the far wall of the laboratory, where a line of rats lay, possibly insensible, probably dead. He walked slowly along the line, prodding each body. Limp, limp, stiff. Stiff. Stiff. All dead, without doubt. Each had had a smaller dose than the last, but all had died—though he couldn't yet be positive about the latest. Wait a bit more, then, to be sure.

He needed to know. Because the Court of Miracles was talking. And they said the frog was back.

The English Channel

They did say that red hair was a sign of the Devil. Joan eyed her escort's fiery locks consideringly. The wind on deck was fierce enough to make her eyes water, and it jerked bits of Michael Murray's hair out of its binding so they did dance round his head like flames, a bit. You might expect his face to be ugly as sin if he was one of the Devil's, though, and it wasn't.

Lucky for him, he looked like his mother in the face, she thought critically. His younger brother Ian wasn't so fortunate, and that without the heathen tattoos. Michael's was just a fairly pleasant face, for all it was blotched with windburn and the lingering marks of sorrow, and no wonder, him having just lost his father, and his wife dead in France no more than a month before that.

But she wasn't braving this gale in order to watch Michael Murray, even if he might burst into tears or turn into Auld Horny on the spot. She touched her crucifix for reassurance, just in case. It was blessed by the priest and her mother'd carried it all the way to St. Ninian's Spring and dipped it in the water there, to ask the saint's protection. And it was her mother she wanted to see, as long as ever she could.

She pulled her kerchief off and waved it, keeping a tight grip lest the wind make off with it. Her mother was growing smaller on the quay, waving madly herself, Joey behind her with his arm round her waist to keep her from falling into the water.

Joan snorted a bit at sight of her new stepfather, but then thought better and touched the crucifix again, muttering a quick Act of Contrition in penance. After all, it was she herself who'd made that marriage happen, and a good thing, too. If not, she'd still be stuck to home at Balriggan, not on her way at last to be a Bride of Christ in France.

A nudge at her elbow made her glance aside, to see Michael offering her a handkerchief. Well, so. If her eyes were streaming—aye, *and* her nose—it was no wonder, the wind so fierce as it was. She took the scrap of cloth with a curt nod of thanks, scrubbed briefly at her cheeks, and waved her kerchief harder.

None of his family had come to see Michael off, not even his twin sister, Janet. But they were taken up with all there was to do in the wake of Old Ian Murray's death, and no wonder. No need to see Michael to the ship, either—Michael Murray was a wine merchant in Paris, and a wonderfully well-traveled gentleman. She took some comfort from the knowledge that he knew what to do and where to go, and had said he would see her safely delivered to the convent of the Angels, because the thought of making her way through Paris alone and the streets full of people all speaking French. . . . Though she knew French quite well, of course, she'd been studying it all the winter, and Michael's mother helping her . . . though perhaps she had better not tell the Reverend Mother about the sorts of French novels Jenny Murray had in her bookshelf, because . . .

"Voulez-vous descendre, mademoiselle?"

"Eh?" She glanced at him, to see him gesturing toward the hatchway that led downstairs. She turned back, blinking—but the quay had vanished, and her mother with it.

"No," she said. "Not just yet. I'll just . . ." She wanted to see the land so long as she could. It would be her last sight of Scotland, ever, and the thought made her wame curl into a small, tight ball. She waved a vague hand toward the hatchway. "You go, though. I'm all right by myself."

He didn't go, but came to stand beside her, gripping the rail. She turned away from him a little, so he wouldn't see her weep, but on the whole, she wasn't sorry he'd stayed.

Neither of them spoke, and the land sank slowly, as though the sea swallowed it, and there was nothing round them now but the open sea, glassy gray and rippling under a scud of clouds. The prospect made her dizzy, and she closed her eyes, swallowing.

Dear Lord Jesus, don't let me be sick!

A small shuffling noise beside her made her open her eyes, to find Michael Murray regarding her with some concern.

"Are ye all right, Miss Joan?" He smiled a little. "Or should I call ye Sister?"

"No," she said, taking a grip on her nerve and her stomach and drawing herself up. "I'm no a nun yet, am I?"

He looked her up and down in the frank way Hieland men did, and smiled more broadly.

"Have ye ever *seen* a nun?" he asked.

"I have not," she said, as starchily as she could. "I havena seen God or the Blessed Virgin, either, but I believe in them, too."

Much to her annoyance, he burst out laughing. Seeing the annoyance, though, he stopped at once, though she could see the urge still trembling there behind his assumed gravity.

"I do beg your pardon, Miss MacKimmie," he said. "I wasna questioning the existence of nuns. I've seen quite a number of the creatures with my own eyes." His lips were twitching, and she glared at him.

"Creatures, is it?"

"A figure of speech, nay more, I swear it! Forgive me, sister—I ken not what I do!" He held up a hand, cowering in mock terror. The urge to laugh herself made her that much crosser, but she contented herself with a simple, "Mmphm" of disapproval.

Curiosity got the better of her, though, and after a few moments spent inspecting the foaming wake of the ship, she asked, not looking at him, "When ye saw the nuns, then—what were they doing?"

He'd got control of himself by now, and answered her seriously.

"Well, I see the Sisters of Notre-Dame who work among the poor all the time in the streets. They always go out by twos, ken, and both nuns will be carrying great huge baskets, filled with food, I suppose—maybe medicines? They're covered, though—the baskets—so I canna say for sure what's in them. Perhaps they're smuggling brandy and lace down to the docks—" He dodged aside from her upraised hand, laughing.

"Oh, ye'll be a rare nun, Sister Joan! *Terror daemonium, solatium miserorum . . .*"

She pressed her lips tight together, not to laugh. Terror of demons, the cheek of him!

"Not Sister Joan," she said. "They'll give me a new name, likely, at the convent."

"Oh, aye?" He wiped hair out of his eyes, interested. "D'ye get to choose the name, yourself?"

"I don't know," she admitted.

"Well, though—what name would ye pick, if ye had the choosing?"

"Er . . . well . . ." She hadn't told anyone, but after all, what harm could it do? She wouldn't see Michael Murray again, once they reached Paris. "Sister Gregory," she blurted.

Rather to her relief, he didn't laugh.

"Oh, that's a good name," he said. "After Saint Gregory the Great, is it?"

"Well . . . aye. Ye don't think it's presumptuous?" she asked, a little anxious.

"Oh, no!" he said, surprised. "I mean, how many nuns are named Mary? If it's not presumptuous to be named after the Mother o' God, how can it be high-falutin' to call yourself after a mere pope?" He smiled at that, so merrily that she smiled back.

"How many nuns *are* named Mary?" she asked, out of curiosity. "It's common, is it?"

"Oh, aye, ye said ye'd not seen a nun." He'd stopped making fun of her, though, and answered seriously, "About half the nuns I've met seem to be called Sister Mary Something—ye ken, Sister Mary Polycarp, Sister Mary Joseph . . . like that."

"And ye meet a great many nuns in the course o' your business, do ye?" Michael Murray was a wine merchant, the junior partner of Fraser et Cie— and from the cut of his clothes, did well enough at it.

His mouth twitched, but he answered seriously.

"Well, I do, really. Not every day, I mean, but the sisters come round to my office quite often—or I go to them. Fraser et Cie supplies wine to most o' the monasteries and convents in Paris, and some will send a pair of nuns to place an order or to take away something special—otherwise, we deliver it, of course. And even the orders who dinna take wine themselves—and most of the Parisian houses do, they bein' French, aye?—need sacramental wine for their chapels. And the begging orders come round like clockwork to ask alms."

"Really." She was fascinated; sufficiently so as to put aside her reluctance to look ignorant. "I didna ken . . . I mean . . . so the different orders do quite different things, is that what ye're saying? What other kinds are there?"

He shot her a brief glance, but then turned back, narrowing his eyes against the wind as he thought.

"Well . . . there's the sort of nun that prays all the time—contemplative, I think they're called. I see them in the Cathedral all hours of the day and night. There's more than one order of that sort, though; one kind wears gray habits and prays in the chapel of St. Joseph, and another wears black;

ye see them mostly in the chapel of Our Lady of the Sea." He glanced at her, curious. "Will it be that sort of nun that you'll be?"

She shook her head, glad that the wind-chafing hid her blushes.

"No," she said, with some regret. "That's maybe the holiest sort of nun, but I've spent a good bit o' my life being contemplative on the moors, and I didna like it much. I think I havena got the right sort of soul to do it verra well, even in a chapel."

"Aye," he said, and wiped back flying strands of hair from his face. "I ken the moors. The wind gets into your head after a bit." He hesitated for a moment. "When my uncle Jamie—your da, I mean—ye ken he hid in a cave after Culloden?"

"For seven years," she said, a little impatient. "Aye, everyone kens that story. Why?"

He shrugged.

"Only thinking. I was no but a wee bairn at the time, but I went now and then wi' my mam, to take him food there. He'd be glad to see us, but he wouldna talk much. And it scared me to see his eyes."

Joan felt a small shiver pass down her back, nothing to do with the stiff breeze. She saw—suddenly *saw,* in her head—a thin, dirty man, the bones starting in his face, crouched in the dank, frozen shadows of the cave.

"Da?" she scoffed, to hide the shiver that crawled up her arms. "How could anyone be scairt of him? He's a dear, kind man."

Michael's wide mouth twitched at the corners.

"I suppose it would depend whether ye'd ever seen him in a fight. But—"

"Have you?" she interrupted, curious. "Seen him in a fight?"

"I have, aye. BUT—" he said, not willing to be distracted, "I didna mean *he* scared me. It was that I thought he was haunted. By the voices in the wind."

That dried up the spit in her mouth, and she worked her tongue a little, hoping it didn't show. She needn't have worried; he wasn't looking at her.

"My own da said it was because Jamie spent so much time alone, that the voices got into his head, and he couldna stop hearing them. When he'd feel safe enough to come to the house, it would take hours sometimes, before he could start to hear *us* again—Mam wouldna let us talk to him until he'd had something to eat and was warmed through." He smiled, a little ruefully. "She said he wasna human, 'til then . . . and looking back, I dinna think she meant that as a figure of speech."

"Well," she said, but stopped, not knowing how to go on. She wished fervently that she'd known this earlier. Her da and his sister were coming on to France later, but she might not see him. She could maybe have talked to Da, asked him just what the voices in his head were like—what they said. Whether they were anything like the ones she heard.

Nearly twilight, and the rats were still dead. The Comte heard the bells of Notre Dame calling Sext, and glanced at his pocket watch. The bells were two minutes before their time, and he frowned. He didn't like sloppiness. He stood up and stretched himself, groaning as his spine cracked like the ragged volley of a firing squad. No doubt about it, he *was* aging, and the thought sent a chill through him.

If. If he could find the way forward, then perhaps . . . but you never knew, that was the devil of it. For a little while, he'd thought—hoped—that traveling back in time stopped the process of aging. That initially seemed logical, like rewinding a clock. But then again, it *wasn't* logical, because he'd always gone back further than his own lifetime. Only once, he'd tried to go back only a few years, to his early twenties. *That* was a mistake, and he still shivered at the memory.

He went to the tall gabled window that looked out over the Seine.

That particular view of the river had changed barely at all in the last two hundred years; he'd seen it at several different times. He hadn't always owned this house, but it had stood in this street since 1620, and he always managed to get in briefly, if only to reestablish his own sense of reality after a passage.

Only the trees changed in his view of the river, and sometimes a strange-looking boat would be there. But the rest was always the same, and no doubt always would be: the old fishermen, catching their supper off the landing in stubborn silence, each guarding his space with outthrust elbows, the younger ones, barefoot and slump-shouldered with exhaustion, laying out their nets to dry, naked little boys diving off the quay. It gave him a soothing sense of eternity, watching the river. Perhaps it didn't matter so much if he must one day die?

"The devil it doesn't," he murmured to himself, and glanced up at the sky. Venus shone bright. He should go.

Pausing conscientiously to place his fingers on each rat's body and ensure that no spark of life remained, he passed down the line, then swept them all into a burlap bag. If he was going to the Court of Miracles, at least he wouldn't arrive empty-handed.

. . . .

Joan was still reluctant to go below, but the light was fading, the wind getting up regardless, and a particularly spiteful gust that blew her petticoats right up round her waist and grabbed her arse with a chilly hand made her yelp in a very undignified way. She smoothed her skirts hastily and made for the hatchway, followed by Michael Murray.

Seeing him cough and chafe his hands at the bottom of the ladder made her sorry; here she'd kept him freezing on deck, too polite to go below and leave her to her own devices, and her too selfish to see he was cold, the poor man. She made a hasty knot in her handkerchief, to remind her to say an extra decade of the rosary for penance, when she got to it.

He saw her to a bench, and said a few words to the woman sitting next to her, in French. Obviously, he was introducing her, she understood that much—but when the woman nodded and said something in reply, she could only sit there open-mouthed. She didn't understand a word. Not a word!

Michael evidently grasped the situation, for he said something to the woman's husband that drew her attention away from Joan, and engaged them in a conversation that let Joan sink quietly back against the wooden wall of the ship, sweating with embarrassment.

Well, she'd get into the way of it, she reassured herself. Bound to. She settled herself with determination to listen, picking out the odd word here and there in the conversation. It was easier to understand Michael; he spoke slower and didn't swallow the back half of each word.

She was trying to puzzle out the probable spelling of a word that *sounded* like "pwufgweemiarniere" but surely couldn't be, when her eye caught a slight movement from the bench opposite, and the gurgling vowels caught in her throat.

A man sat there, maybe close to her own age, which was twenty-five. He was good-looking, if a bit thin in the face, decently dressed—and he was going to die.

There was a gray shroud over him, the same as if he was wrapped in mist, so his face showed through it. She'd seen that same thing, the grayness lying on someone's face like fog, seen it twice before and knew it at once for Death's shadow. Once it had been on an elderly man, and that might have been only what anybody could see, because Angus MacWheen *was* ill, but then again, and only a few weeks after, she'd seen it on the second of Vhairi Fraser's little boys, and him a rosy-faced wee bairn with dear chubby legs.

She hadn't wanted to believe it. Either that she saw it, or what it meant. But four days later, the wean was crushed in the lane by an ox that was maddened by a hornet's sting. She'd vomited when they told her, and couldn't eat for days after, for sheer grief and terror. Because, could she have stopped it, if she'd said? And what—dear Lord, *what*—if it happened again?

Now it had, and her wame twisted. She leapt to her feet and blundered toward the companionway, cutting short some slowly worded speech from the Frenchman.

Not again, not again! she thought in agony. *Why show me such things? What can I do?*

She pawed frantically at the ladder, climbing as fast as she could, gasping for air, needing to be away from the dying man. How long might it be, dear Lord, until she reached the convent, and safety?

• • • •

The moon was rising over the Île de Notre Dame, glowing through the haze of cloud. He glanced at it, estimating the time; no point in arriving at Madame Fabienne's house before the girls had taken their hair out of curling papers and rolled on their red stockings. There were other places to go first, though; the obscure drinking-places where the professionals of the Court fortified themselves for the night ahead. One of those was where he had first heard the rumors—he'd see how far they had spread, and judge the safety of asking openly about *Maître* Raymond.

That was one advantage to hiding in the past, rather than going to Hungary or Sweden—life at this Court tended to be short, and there were not so many who knew either his face or his history, though there would still be stories. Paris held on to its *histoires*. He found the iron gate—rustier than it had been; it left red stains on his palm—and pushed it open with a creak that would alert whatever now lived at the end of the alley.

He had to *see* the frog. Not meet him, perhaps—he made a brief sign against evil—but see him. Above all else, he needed to know: had the man—if he was a man—aged?

"Certainly he's a man," he muttered to himself, impatient. "What else could he be, for heaven's sake?"

He could be something like you, was the answering thought, and a shiver ran up his spine. *Fear?* he wondered. *Anticipation of an intriguing philosophical mystery? Or possibly . . . hope?*

• • • •

"What a waste of a wonderful arse," Monsieur Brechin remarked in French, watching Joan's ascent from the far side of the cabin. "And *mon Dieu,* those legs! Imagine those wrapped around your back, eh? Would you have her keep the striped stockings on? I would."

It hadn't occurred to Michael to imagine that, but he was now having a hard time dismissing the image. He coughed into his handkerchief to hide the reddening of his face.

Madame Brechin gave her husband a sharp elbow in the ribs. He grunted, but seemed undisturbed by what was evidently a normal form of marital communication.

"Beast," she said, with no apparent heat. "Speaking so of a Bride of Christ. You will be lucky if God Himself doesn't strike you dead with a lightning bolt."

"Well, she isn't His bride yet," Monsieur protested. "And who created that arse in the first place? Surely God would be flattered to hear a little sincere appreciation of His handiwork. From one who is, after all, a connoisseur in such matters." He leered affectionately at Madame, who snorted.

A faint snigger from the young man across the cabin indicated that Monsieur was not alone in his appreciation, and Madame turned a reproving glare on the young man. Michael wiped his nose carefully, trying not to catch Monsieur's eye. His insides were quivering, and not entirely either from amusement or the shock of inadvertent lust. He felt very queer.

Monsieur sighed as Joan's striped stockings disappeared through the hatchway.

"Christ will not warm her bed," he said, shaking his head.

"Christ will not fart in her bed, either," said Madame, taking out her knitting.

"*Pardonnez-moi* . . ." Michael said in a strangled voice, and, clapping his handkerchief to his mouth, made hastily for the ladder, as though seasickness might be catching.

It wasn't *mal-de-mer* that was surging up from his belly, though. He caught sight of Joan, dim in the evening light at the rail, and turned quickly aside, going to the other side, where he gripped the rail as though it were a life raft, and let the overwhelming waves of grief wash through him. It was the only way he'd been able to manage, these last few weeks. Hold on as long as he could, keeping a cheerful face, until some small unexpected thing, some bit of emotional debris, struck him through the heart like a hunter's arrow, and then hurry to find a place to hide, curling up on himself in mindless pain until he could get a grip of himself.

This time, it was Madame's remark that had come out of the blue, and he grimaced painfully, laughing in spite of the tears that poured down his face, remembering Lillie. She'd eaten eels in garlic sauce for dinner—those always made her fart with a silent deadliness, like poison swamp gas. As the ghastly miasma had risen up round him, he'd sat bolt upright in bed, only to find her staring at him, a look of indignant horror on her face.

"How *dare* you?" she'd said, in a voice of offended majesty. "*Really*, Michel."

"You *know* it wasn't me!"

Her mouth had dropped open, outrage added to horror and distaste.

"Oh!" she gasped, gathering her small pug dog to her bosom. "You not only fart like a rotting whale, you attempt to blame it on my poor puppy! *Cochon!*" Whereupon she had begun to shake the bedsheets delicately, using her free hand to waft the noxious odors in his direction, addressing censorious remarks to Plonplon, who gave Michael a sanctimonious look before turning to lick his mistress's face with great enthusiasm.

"Oh, Jesus," he whispered, and, sinking down, pressed his face against the rail. "Oh, God, lass, I love you!"

He shook, silently, head buried in his arms, aware of sailors passing now and then behind him, but none of them took notice of him in the dark. At last the agony eased a little, and he drew breath.

All right, then. He'd be all right now, for a time. And he thanked God, belatedly, that he had Joan—or Sister Gregory, if she liked—to look after for a bit. He didn't know how he'd manage to walk through the streets of Paris to his house, alone. Go in, greet the servants—would Jared be there?—face the sorrow of the household, accept their sympathy for his father's death, order a meal, sit down . . . and all the time wanting just to throw himself on the floor of their empty bedroom and howl like a lost soul. He'd have to face it, sooner or later—but not just yet. And right now, he'd take the grace of any respite that offered.

He blew his nose with resolution, tucked away his mangled handkerchief, and went downstairs to fetch the basket his mother had sent. He couldn't swallow a thing, himself, but feeding Sister Joan would maybe keep his mind off things for that one minute more.

"That's how ye do it," his brother Ian had told him, as they leant together on the rail of their mother's sheep pen, the winter's wind cold on their faces, waiting for their Da to find his way through dying. "Ye find a way to live for just one more minute. And then another. And another." Ian had lost a wife, too, and knew.

He'd wiped his face—he could weep before Ian, while he couldn't in front of his elder brother or the girls, certainly not in front of his mother—and asked, "And it gets better after a time, is that what ye're telling me?"

His brother had looked at him straight on, the quiet in his eyes showing through the outlandish Mohawk tattoos.

"No," he'd said softly. "But after a time, ye find ye're in a different place than ye were. A different person than ye were. And then ye look about, and see what's there with ye. Ye'll maybe find a use for yourself. *That* helps."

"Aye, fine," he said, under his breath, and squared his shoulders. "We'll see, then."

• • • •

To Rakoczy's surprise, there was a familiar face behind the rough bar. If Maximilian the Great was surprised to see him, the Spanish dwarf gave no indication of it. The other drinkers—a pair of jugglers, each missing an arm (but the opposing arm), a toothless hag who smacked and muttered over her mug of arrack, and something that looked like a ten-year-old young girl but almost certainly wasn't—turned to stare at him, but seeing nothing remarkable in his shabby clothing and burlap bag, turned back to the business of getting sufficiently drunk so as to do what needed to be done tonight.

He nodded to Max and pulled up one of the splintering kegs to sit on.

"What's your pleasure, *señor?*"

Rakoczy narrowed his eyes; Max had never served anything but arrack. But times had changed; there was a stone bottle of something that might be beer, and a dark glass bottle with a chalk scrawl on it, standing next to the keg of rough brandy.

"Arrack, please, Max," he said—better the devil you know—and was surprised to see the dwarf's eyes narrow in return.

"You knew my honored father, I see, *señor,*" the dwarf said, putting the cup on the board. "It's some time since you've been in Paris?"

"*Pardonnez,*" Rakoczy said, accepting it and tossing it back. If you could afford more than one cup, you didn't let it linger on the tongue. "Your honored—late?—father, Max?"

"Maximiliano el Maximo," the dwarf corrected him firmly.

"To be sure." Rakoczy gestured for another drink. "And whom have I the honor to address?"

The Spaniard—though perhaps his accent wasn't as strong as Max's had been—drew himself up proudly. "Maxim Le Grande, monsieur, *à votre service!*"

Rakoczy saluted him gravely, and threw back the second cup, motioning for a third and with a gesture, inviting Maxim to join him.

"It has been some time since I was last here," he said. No lie there. "I wonder if another old acquaintance might be still alive—*Mâitre* Raymond, otherwise called the Frog?"

There was a tiny quiver in the air, a barely perceptible flicker of attention, gone almost as soon as he'd sensed it—somewhere behind him?

"A frog," Maxim said, meditatively pouring himself a drink. "I don't know any frogs myself, but should I hear of one, who shall I say is asking for him?"

Should he give his name? No, not yet.

"It doesn't matter," he said. "But word can be left with Madame Fabienne. You know the place? In the Rue Antoine?"

The dwarf's sketchy brows rose, and his mouth turned up at one corner. "I know it."

Doubtless he did, Rakoczy thought. "El Maximo" hadn't referred to Max's stature, and probably "Le Grande" didn't, either. God had a sense of justice, as well as a sense of humor.

"*Bon.*" He wiped his lips on his sleeve and put down a coin that would have bought the whole keg. "*Merci.*"

He stood up, the hot taste of the brandy bubbling at the back of his throat, and belched. Two more places to visit, maybe, before he went to Fabienne's. He couldn't visit more than that and stay upright; he *was* getting old.

"Good night." He bowed to the company and gingerly pushed open the cracked wooden door; it was hanging by one leather hinge, and that looked ready to give way at any moment.

"*Ribbit,*" someone said very softly, just before the door closed behind him.

. . . .

Madeleine's face lighted when she saw him, and his heart warmed. She wasn't very bright, poor creature, but she was pretty and amiable, and had been a whore long enough to be grateful for small kindnesses.

"Monsieur Rakoczy!" She flung her arms about his neck, nuzzling affectionately.

"Madeleine, my dear." He cupped her chin and kissed her gently on the lips, drawing her close so that her belly pressed against his. He held her long enough, kissing her eyelids, her forehead, her ears—so that she made high squeaks of pleasure—that he could feel his way inside her, hold the weight of her womb in his mind, evaluate her ripening.

It felt warm, the color in the heart of a dark crimson rose, the kind called "sang-de-dragon." A week before, it had felt solid, compact as a folded fist; now it had begun to soften, to hollow slightly as she readied. Three more days? He wondered. Four?

He let her go, and when she pouted prettily at him, he laughed and raised her hand to his lips, feeling the same small thrill he had felt when he first found her, as the faint blue glow rose between her fingers in response to his touch. She couldn't see it—he'd raised their linked hands to her face before and she had merely looked puzzled—but it was there.

"Go and fetch some wine, *ma belle,*" he said, squeezing her hand gently. "I need to talk to Madame."

Madame Fabienne was not a dwarf, but she was small, brown, and mottled as a toadstool—and as watchful as a toad, round yellow eyes seldom blinking, never closed.

"Monsieur le Comte," she said graciously, nodding him to a damask chair in her *salon*. The air was scented with candle wax and flesh—flesh of a far better quality than that on offer in the Court. Even so, Madame had come from that Court, and kept her connections there alive; she made no bones about that. She didn't blink at his clothes, but her nostrils flared at him, as though she picked up the scent of the dives and alleys he had come from.

"Good evening, Madame," he said, smiling at her, and lifted the burlap bag. "I brought a small present for Leopold. If he's awake?"

"Awake and cranky," she said, eyeing the bag with interest. "He's just shed his skin—you don't want to make any sudden moves."

Leopold was a remarkably handsome—and remarkably large—python; an albino, quite rare. Opinion of his origins was divided; half Madame

Fabienne's clientele held that she had been given the snake by a noble client—some said the late king himself—whom she had cured of impotence. Others said the snake had once *been* a noble client, who had refused to pay her for services rendered. Rakoczy had his own opinions on that one, but he liked Leopold, who was ordinarily tame as a cat and would sometimes come when called—as long as you had something he regarded as food in your hand when you called.

"Leopold! Monsieur le Comte has brought you a treat!" Fabienne reached across to an enormous wicker cage and flicked the door open, withdrawing her hand with sufficient speed as to indicate just what she meant by "cranky."

Almost at once, a huge yellow head poked out into the light. Snakes had transparent eyelids, but Rakoczy could swear the python blinked irritably, swaying up a coil of its monstrous body for a moment before plunging out of the cage and swarming across the floor with amazing rapidity for such a big creature, tongue flicking in and out like a seamstress's needle.

He made straight for Rakoczy, jaws yawning as he came, and Rakoczy snatched up the bag just before Leopold tried to engulf it—or Rakoczy— whole. He jerked aside, hastily seized a rat, and threw it. Leopold flung a coil of his body on top of the rat with a thud that rattled Madame's spoon in her tea-bowl, and before the company could blink, had whipped the rat into a half-hitch knot of coil.

"Hungry as well as ill-tempered, I see," Rakoczy remarked, trying for nonchalance. In fact, the hairs were prickling over his neck and arms. Normally, Leopold took his time about feeding, and the violence of the python's appetite at such close quarters had shaken him.

Fabienne was laughing, almost silently, her tiny sloping shoulders quivering beneath the green Chinese silk tunic she wore.

"I thought for an instant he'd have you," she remarked at last, wiping her eyes. "If he had, I shouldn't have had to feed him for a month!"

Rakoczy bared his teeth in an expression that might have been taken for a smile.

"We cannot let Leopold go hungry," he said. "I wish to make a special arrangement for Madeleine—it should keep the worm up to his yellow arse in rats for some time."

Fabienne put down her handkerchief and regarded him with interest.

"Leopold has two cocks, but I can't say I've ever noticed an arse. Twenty ecus a day. Plus two extra if she needs clothes."

He waved an easy hand, dismissing this.

"I had in mind something longer." He explained what he had in mind, and had the satisfaction of seeing Fabienne's face go quite blank with stupefaction. It didn't stay that way more than a few moments; by the time he had finished, she was already laying out her initial demands.

By the time they came to agreement, they had drunk half a bottle of decent wine, and Leopold had swallowed the rat. It made a small bulge in the muscular tube of the snake's body, but hadn't slowed him appreciably; the coils slithered restlessly over the painted canvas floor-cloth, glowing like gold, and Rakoczy saw the patterns of his skin like trapped clouds beneath the scales.

"He *is* beautiful, no?" Fabienne saw his admiration, and basked a little in it. "Did I ever tell you where I got him?"

"Yes, more than once. And more than one story, too." She looked startled, and he compressed his lips. He'd been patronizing her establishment for no more than a few weeks, this time. He'd known her fifteen years before—though only a couple of months, that time. He hadn't given his name then, and a madam saw so many men that there was little chance of her recalling him. On the other hand, he also thought it unlikely that she troubled to recall to whom she'd told which story, and this seemed to be the case, for she lifted one shoulder in a surprisingly graceful shrug, and laughed.

"Yes, but this one is true."

"Oh, well, then." He smiled, and reaching into the bag, tossed Leopold another rat. The snake moved more slowly this time, and didn't bother to constrict its motionless prey, merely unhinging its jaw and engulfing it in a single-minded way.

"He is an old friend, Leopold," she said, gazing affectionately at the snake. "I brought him with me from the West Indies, many years ago. He is a *Mystère*, you know."

"I didn't, no." Rakoczy drank more wine; he had sat long enough that he was beginning to feel almost sober again. "And what is that?" He was interested—not so much in the snake, but in Fabienne's mention of the West Indies. He'd forgotten that she claimed to have come from there, many years ago, long before he'd known her the first time.

The *afile* powder had been waiting in his laboratory when he'd come back; no telling how many years it had sat there—the servants couldn't recall. Mélisande's brief note—"Try this. It may be what the frog used."—had not been dated, but there was a brief scrawl at the top of the sheet, saying "Rose Hall, Jamaica." If Fabienne retained any connections in the West Indies, perhaps . . .

"Some call them *loa*"—her wrinkled lips pursed as she kissed the word—"but those are the Africans. A *Mystère* is a spirit, one who is an intermediary between the Bondye and us. Bondye is *le bon Dieu,* of course," she explained to him. "The African slaves speak very bad French. Give him another rat; he's still hungry, and it scares the girls if I let him hunt in the house."

The third rat had made another bulge; the snake was beginning to look like a fat string of pearls, and was showing an inclination to lie still, digesting. The tongue still flickered, tasting the air, but lazily now.

Rakoczy picked up the bag again, weighing the risks—but after all, if news came from the Court of Miracles, his name would soon be known in any case.

"I wonder, Madame, as you know everyone in Paris"—he gave her a small bow, which she graciously returned—"are you acquainted with a certain man known as *Maître* Raymond? Some call him the frog," he added.

She blinked, then looked amused.

"You're looking for the frog?"

"Yes. Is that funny?" He reached into the sack, fishing for a rat.

"Somewhat. I should perhaps not tell you, but since you are so accommodating"—she glanced complacently at the purse he had put beside her tea-bowl, a generous deposit on account—"*Maître Grenouille* is looking for *you.*"

He stopped dead, hand clutching a furry body.

"What? You've seen him?"

She shook her head and, sniffing distastefully at her cold tea, rang the bell for her maid.

"No, but I've heard the same from two people."

"Asking for me by name?" Rakoczy's heart beat faster.

"Monsieur le Comte St. Germain. That *is* you?" she asked with no more than mild interest; false names were common in her business.

He nodded, mouth suddenly too dry to speak, and pulled the rat from the sack. It squirmed suddenly in his hand, and a piercing pain in his thumb made him hurl the rodent away.

"*Sacrébleu!* It bit me!"

The rat, dazed by impact, staggered drunkenly across the floor toward Leopold, whose tongue began to flicker faster. Fabienne, though, uttered a sound of disgust and threw a silver-backed hairbrush at the rat. Startled by the sudden clatter, the rat leapt convulsively into the air, landed on and raced directly over the snake's astonished head, disappearing through the door into the foyer, where—by the resultant scream—it evidently encountered the maid before making its ultimate escape into the street.

"*Jésus, Marie,*" Madame Fabienne said, piously crossing herself. "A miraculous resurrection. Two months past Easter, too."

• • • •

It was a smooth passage; the shore of France came into sight just after dawn the next day. Joan saw it, a low smudge of dark green on the horizon, and felt a little thrill at the sight, in spite of her tiredness.

She hadn't slept, though she'd reluctantly gone below after nightfall, there to wrap herself in her cloak and shawl, trying not to look at the young man with the shadow on his face. She'd lain all night, listening to the snores and groans of her fellow passengers, praying doggedly and wondering in despair whether prayer was all she could do.

She often wondered whether it was because of her name. She'd been proud of her name when she was small; it was a heroic name, a saint's name, but also a warrior's name. Her mother'd told her that, often and often. She didn't think her mother had considered that the name might also be haunted.

Surely it didn't happen to everyone named Joan, though, did it? She wished she knew another Joan to ask. Because if it *did* happen to them all, the others would be keeping it quiet, just like she did.

You just didn't go round telling people that you heard voices that weren't there. Still less, that you saw things that weren't there, either. You just *didn't*.

She'd heard of a seer, of course, everyone in the Highlands had. And nearly everyone she knew at least claimed to have seen the odd fetch or had a premonition that Angus MacWheen was dead when he didn't come home that time last winter. The fact that Angus MacWheen was a filthy auld drunkard and so yellow and crazed that it was heads or tails whether he'd die on any particular day, let alone when it got cold enough that the loch froze, didn't come into it.

But she'd never *met* a seer; there was the rub. How did you get into the way of it? Did you just tell folk, "Here's a thing . . . I'm a seer," and they'd nod and say, "Oh, aye, of course, what's like to happen to me next Tuesday"? More important, though, how the devil—

"Ow!" She'd bitten her tongue fiercely as penance for the inadvertent blasphemy, and clapped a hand to her mouth.

"What is it?" said a concerned voice behind her. "Are ye hurt, Miss MacKimmie? Er . . . Sister Gregory, I mean?"

"Mm! No. No, I justh . . . bit my tongue." She turned to Michael Murray, gingerly touching the injured tongue to the roof of her mouth.

"Well, that happens when ye talk to yourself." He took the cork from a bottle he was carrying and held the bottle out to her. "Here, wash your mouth wi' that; it'll help."

She took a large mouthful and swirled it round; it burned the bitten place, but not badly, and she swallowed, as slowly as possible, to make it last.

"Jesus, Mary, and Bride," she breathed. "Is that *wine?*" The taste in her mouth bore some faint kinship with the liquid she knew as wine—just like apples bore some resemblance to horse turds.

"Aye, it *is* pretty good," he said modestly. "German. Umm . . . have a wee nip more?"

She didn't argue, and sipped happily, barely listening to his talk, telling about the wine, what it was called, how they made it in Germany, where he got it . . . on and on. Finally she came to herself enough to remember her manners, though, and reluctantly handed back the bottle, now half-empty.

"I thank ye, sir," she said primly. "'Twas kind of ye. Ye needna waste your time in bearing me company, though; I shall be well enough alone."

"Aye, well . . . it's no really for your sake," he said, and took a reasonable swallow himself. "It's mine."

She blinked against the wind. He was flushed, but not from drink or wind, she thought.

She managed a faint interrogative, "Ah . . . ?"

"Well, what I want to ask," he blurted, and looked away, cheekbones burning red. "Will ye pray for me? Sister? And my . . . my wife. The repose of . . . of—"

"Oh!" she said, mortified that she'd been so taken up with her own worries as not to have seen his distress. *Think you're a seer, dear Lord, ye dinna see what's under your neb, you're no but a fool, and a selfish fool at that.* She put her hand over his where it lay on the rail and squeezed tight, trying to channel some sense of God's goodness into his flesh.

"To be sure I will!" she said. "I'll remember ye at every Mass, I swear it!" She wondered briefly whether it was proper to swear to something like that, but after all . . . "And your poor wife's soul, of course I will! What . . . er . . . what was her name? So as I'll know what to say when I pray for her," she explained hurriedly, seeing his eyes narrow with pain.

"Lilliane," he said, so softly that she barely heard him over the wind. "I called her Lillie."

"Lilliane," she repeated carefully, trying to form the syllables like he did. It was a soft, lovely name, she thought, slipping like water over the rocks at the top of a burn. *You'll never see a burn again,* she thought with a sudden pang, but dismissed this, turning her face toward the growing shore of France. "I'll remember."

He nodded in mute thanks, and they stood for some little while, until she realized that her hand was still resting on his and drew it back with a jerk. He looked startled, and she blurted—because it was the thing on the top of her mind—"What was she like? Your wife?"

The most extraordinary mix of emotions flooded over his face. She couldn't have said what was uppermost—grief, laughter, or sheer bewilderment—and she realized suddenly just how little of his true mind she'd seen before.

"She was . . ." He shrugged, and swallowed. "She was my wife," he said, very softly. "She was my life."

She should know something comforting to say to him, but she didn't.

She's with God? That was the truth, she hoped, and yet clearly to this young man, the only thing that mattered was that his wife was not with *him*.

"What happened to her?" she asked instead, baldly, only because it seemed necessary to say something.

He took a deep breath and seemed to sway a little; he'd finished the rest of the wine, she saw, and took the empty bottle from his hand, tossing it overboard.

"The influenza. They said it was quick. Didn't seem quick to me . . . and yet, it was, I suppose it was. It took two days, and God kens well that I recall every second of those days—yet it seems that I lost her between one heart-beat and the next. And I . . . I keep lookin' for her there, in that space be-tween."

He swallowed.

"She-she was . . ." The words "with child" came so quietly that she barely heard them.

"Oh," Joan said softly, very moved. "Oh, a *chiusle.*" "Heart's blood," it meant—and what *she* meant was that his wife had been that to him—dear Lord, she hoped he hadn't thought she meant—no, he hadn't, and the tight-wound spring in her backbone relaxed a little, seeing the look of gratitude on his face. He did know what she'd meant, and seemed glad that she'd understood.

Blinking, she looked away—and caught sight of the young man with the shadow on him, leaning against the railing a little way down. The breath caught in her throat at sight of him.

The shadow was darker in the morning light. The sun was beginning to warm the deck, frail white clouds swam in the blue of clear French skies, and yet the mist seemed now to swirl and thicken, obscuring the young man's face, wrapping round his shoulders like a shawl.

Dear Lord, tell me what to do! Her body jerked, wanting to go to the young man, speak to him. But say what? *You're in danger, be careful?* He'd think she was mad. And if the danger was a thing he couldn't help, like wee Ronnie and the ox, what difference might her speaking make?

She was dimly aware of Michael staring at her, curious. He said something to her, but she wasn't listening, listening hard instead inside her head. Where were the damned voices when you bloody *needed* one?

But the voices were stubbornly silent, and she turned to Michael, the muscles of her arm jumping, she'd held so tight to the ship's rigging.

"I'm sorry," she said. "I wasna listening properly. I just . . . thought of something."

"If it's a thing I can help ye with, Sister, ye've only to ask," he said, smiling faintly. "Oh! And speak of that, I meant to say—I said to your mam, if she liked to write to you in care of Fraser et Cie, I'd see to it that ye got the letters." He shrugged, one-shouldered. "I dinna ken what the rules are at the convent, aye? About getting letters from outside."

Joan didn't know that, either, and had worried about it. She was so relieved to hear this that a huge smile split her face.

"Oh, it's that kind of ye!" she said. "And if I could . . . maybe write back . . . ?"

He smiled, the marks of grief easing in his pleasure at doing her a service.

"Anytime," he assured her. "I'll see to it. Perhaps I could—"

A ragged shriek cut through the air, and Joan glanced up, startled, thinking it one of the seabirds that had come out from shore to wheel round the ship, but it wasn't. The young man was standing on the rail, one hand on the rigging, and before she could so much as draw breath, he let go and was gone.

Paris

Michael was worried for Joan; she sat slumped in the coach, not bothering to look out of the window, until a faint waft of the spring breeze touched her face. The smell was so astonishing that it drew her out of the shell of shocked misery in which she had traveled from the docks.

"Mother o' God!" she said, clapping a hand to her nose. "What *is* that?"

Michael dug in his pocket and pulled out the grubby rag of his handkerchief, looking dubiously at it.

"It's the public cemeteries. I'm sorry, I didna think—"

"*Moran taing.*" She seized the damp cloth from him and held it over her face, not caring. "Do the French not *bury* folk in their cemeteries?" Because from the smell, a thousand corpses had been thrown out on wet ground and left to rot, and the sight of darting, squabbling flocks of black corbies in the distance did nothing to correct this impression.

"They do." Michael felt exhausted—it had been a terrible morning—but struggled to pull himself together. "It's all marshland over there, though; even coffins buried deep—and most of them aren't—work their way through the ground in a few months. When there's a flood—and there's a flood whenever it rains—what's left of the coffins falls apart, and . . ." He swallowed, just as pleased that he'd not eaten any breakfast.

"There's talk of maybe moving the bones at least, putting them in an ossuary, they call it. There are mine workings, old ones, outside the city, over there"—he pointed with his chin—"and perhaps . . . but they havena done anything about it yet," he added in a rush, pinching his nose fast to get a breath in through his mouth. It didn't matter whether you breathed through your nose or your mouth, though; the air was thick enough to taste.

She looked as ill as he felt, or maybe worse, her face the color of spoilt custard. She'd vomited when the crew had finally pulled the suicide aboard, pouring gray water and slimed with the seaweed that had wrapped round his legs and drowned him. There were still traces of sick down her front, and her dark hair was lank and damp, straggling out from under her cap. She hadn't slept at all, of course—neither had he.

He couldn't take her to the convent in this condition. The nuns maybe wouldn't mind, but she would. He stretched up and rapped on the ceiling of the carriage.

"*Monsieur?*"

"*Au château, vite!*"

He'd take her to his house, first. It wasn't much out of the way, and the convent wasn't expecting her at any particular day or hour. She could wash, have something to eat, and put herself to rights. And if it saved him from walking into his house alone, well, they did say a kind deed carried its own reward.

. . . . .

By the time they'd reached the Rue Trémoulins, Joan had forgotten—partly—her various reasons for distress, in the sheer excitement of being in Paris. She had never seen so many people in one place at the same time—and that was only the folk coming out of Mass at a parish church! While round the corner, a pavement of fitted stones stretched wider than the whole River Ness, and those stones covered from one side to the other in barrows and wagons and stalls, rioting with fruit and vegetables and flowers and fish and meat . . . she'd given Michael back his filthy handkerchief and was panting like a dog, turning her face to and fro, trying to draw all the wonderful smells into herself at once.

"Ye look a bit better," Michael said, smiling at her. He was still pale himself, but he too seemed happier. "Are ye hungry, yet?"

"I'm famished!" She cast a starved look at the edge of the market. "Could we stop, maybe, and buy an apple? I've a bit of money . . ." She fumbled for the coins in her stocking-top, but he stopped her.

"Nay, there'll be food aplenty at the house. They were expecting me this week, so everything will be ready."

She cast a brief longing look at the market, but turned obligingly in the direction he pointed, craning out the carriage window to see his house as they approached.

"That's the biggest house I've ever seen!" she exclaimed.

"Och, no," he said, laughing. "Lallybroch's bigger than that."

"Well . . . this one's *taller*," she replied. And it was—a good four stories, and a huge roof of lead slates and green-coppered seams, with what must be more than a score of glass windows set in, and . . .

She was still trying to count the windows when Michael helped her down from the carriage and offered her his arm to walk up to the door. She was goggling at the big yew trees set in brass pots and wondering how much trouble it must be to keep those polished, when she felt the arm under her hand go suddenly rigid as wood.

She glanced at Michael, startled, then looked where he was looking—toward the door of his house. The door had swung open, and three people were coming down the marble steps, smiling and waving, calling out.

"Who's that?" Joan whispered, leaning close to Michael. The one short fellow in the striped apron must be a butler; she'd read about butlers. But the other man was a gentleman, limber as a willow tree and wearing a coat and waistcoat striped in lemon and pink, with a hat decorated with . . . well, she supposed it must be a feather, but she'd pay money to see the bird it came off of. By comparison, she had hardly noticed the woman, who was dressed in black. But now she saw that Michael had eyes only for the woman.

"Li—" he began, and choked it back. "L-Léonie. Léonie is her name. My wife's sister."

She looked sharp then, because from the look of Michael Murray, he'd just seen his wife's ghost. Léonie seemed flesh and blood, however—slender and pretty, though her own face bore the same marks of sorrow as did Michael's, and her face was pale under a small, neat black tricorne with a tiny curled blue feather.

"Michel," she said, "Oh, Michel!" And with tears brimming from eyes shaped like almonds, she threw herself into his arms.

Feeling extremely superfluous, Joan stood back a little and glanced at the gentleman in the lemon-striped waistcoat—the butler had tactfully withdrawn into the house.

"Charles Pépin, mademoiselle," he said, sweeping off his hat. Taking her hand, he bowed low over it, and now she saw the band of black mourning he wore around his bright sleeve. "*À votre service.*"

"Oh," she said, a little flustered. "Um. Joan MacKimmie. *Je suis* . . . er . . . um . . ."

Tell him not to do it, said a sudden small, calm voice inside her head, and she jerked her own hand away as though he'd bitten her.

"Pleased to meet you," she gasped. "Excuse me." And turning, threw up into one of the bronze yew-pots.

Joan had been afraid it would be awkward, coming to Michael's bereaved and empty house, but had steeled herself to offer comfort and support, as became a distant kinswoman and a daughter of God. She might have been miffed, therefore, to find herself entirely supplanted in the department of comfort and support—quite relegated to the negligible position of guest, in fact, served politely and asked periodically if she wished more wine, a slice of ham, some gherkins . . . ?—but otherwise ignored. Meanwhile Michael's servants, sister-in-law, and . . . she wasn't quite sure of the position of M. Pépin, though he seemed to have something personal to do with Léonie, perhaps someone had said he was her cousin? They all swirled round Michael like perfumed bathwater, warm and buoyant, touching him, kissing him—well, all right, she'd heard of men kissing one another in France but she couldn't help staring when M. Pépin gave Michael a big wet one on both cheeks—and generally making a fuss of him.

She was more than relieved, though, not to have to make conversation in French, beyond a simple *Merci* or *S'il vous plait* from time to time. It gave her a chance to settle her nerves—and her stomach, and she would say the wine was a wonder for that—and to keep a close eye on Monsieur Charles Pépin.

"Tell him not to do it." And just what d'ye mean by that? she demanded of the voice. She didn't get an answer, which didn't surprise her. The voices weren't much for details.

She couldn't tell whether the voices were male or female; they didn't seem either one, and she wondered whether they might maybe be angels—angels didn't have a sex, and doubtless that saved them a lot of trouble. Joan of Arc's voices had had the decency to introduce themselves, but not hers, oh, no. On the other hand, if they *were* angels, and told her their names, she wouldn't recognize them anyway, so perhaps that's why they didn't bother.

Well, so. Did this particular voice mean that Charles Pépin was a villain? She squinted closely at him. He didn't look it. He had a strong, good-looking face, and Michael seemed to like him—after all, Michael must be a fair judge of character, she thought, and him in the wine business.

What was it Mr. Charles Pépin oughtn't to do, though? Did he have some wicked crime in mind? Or might he be bent on doing away with himself, like that poor wee gomerel on the boat? There was still a trace of slime on her hand, from the seaweed.

She rubbed her hand inconspicuously against the skirt of her dress, frustrated. She hoped the voices would stop in the convent. That was her nightly prayer. But if they didn't, at least she might be able to tell someone there about them without fear of being packed off to a madhouse or stoned in the street. She'd have a confessor, she knew that much. Maybe he could help her discover what God had meant, landing her with a gift like this, and no explanation what she was to do with it.

In the meantime, Monsieur Pépin would bear watching; she should maybe say something to Michael before she left. *Aye, what?* she thought, helpless.

Still, she was glad to see that Michael grew less pale as they all carried on, vying to feed him tidbits, refill his glass, tell him bits of gossip. She was also pleased to find that she mostly understood what they were saying, as she relaxed. Jared—that would be Jared Fraser, Michael's elderly cousin, who'd founded the wine company, and whose house this was—was still in Germany, they said, but was expected at any moment. He had sent a letter for Michael, too, where was it? No matter, it would turn up . . . and La Comtesse de Maurepas had had a fit, a veritable *fit* at court last Wednesday, when she came face-to-face with Mademoiselle de Perpignan wearing a confection in the particular shade of pea green that was de Maurepas's alone, and God alone knew why, because she always looked like a cheese in it, and had slapped her own maid so hard for pointing this out that the poor girl flew across the rushes and cracked her head on one of the mirrored walls—and cracked the mirror, too, very bad luck that, but no one could agree whether the bad luck was de Maurepas's, the maid's, or La Perpignan's.

Birds, Joan thought dreamily, sipping her wine. *They sound just like cheerful wee birds in a tree, all chattering away together.*

"The bad luck belongs to the seamstress who made the dress for La Perpignan," Michael said, a faint smile touching his mouth. "Once de Maurepas finds out who it is." His eye lighted on Joan, then, sitting there with a fork—an actual fork! and silver, too—in her hand, her mouth half-open in the effort of concentration required to follow the conversation.

"Sister Joan, Sister Gregory, I mean, I'm that sorry, I was forgetting. If ye've had enough to eat, will ye have a bit of a wash, maybe, before I deliver ye to the convent?"

He was already rising, reaching for a bell, and before she knew where she was, a maidservant had whisked her off upstairs, deftly undressed her, and, wrinkling her nose at the smell of the discarded garments, wrapped Joan in a robe of the most amazing green silk, light as air, and ushered her into a small stone room with a copper bath in it, then disappeared, saying something in which Joan caught the word *"eau."*

She sat on the wooden stool provided, clutching the robe about her nakedness, head spinning with more than wine. She closed her eyes and took deep breaths, trying to put herself in the way of praying. God was everywhere, she assured herself, embarrassing as it was to contemplate

Him being with her in a bathroom in Paris. She shut her eyes harder and firmly began the rosary, starting with the Joyful Mysteries.

She'd got through the Visitation before she began to feel steady again. This wasn't quite how she'd expected her first day in Paris to be. Still, she'd have something to write home to Mam about, that was for sure. If they let her write letters in the convent.

The maid came in with two enormous cans of steaming water, and upended these into the bath with a tremendous splash. Another came in on her heels, similarly equipped, and between them, they had Joan up, stripped, and stepping into the tub before she'd so much as said the first word of the Lord's Prayer for the third decade.

They said French things to her, which she didn't understand, and held out peculiar-looking instruments to her in invitation. She recognized the small pot of soap, and pointed at it, and one of them at once poured water on her head and began to wash her hair!

She had for months been bidding farewell to her hair whenever she combed it, quite resigned to its loss, for whether she must sacrifice it immediately, as a postulant, or later, as a novice, plainly it must go. The shock of knowing fingers rubbing her scalp, the sheer sensual delight of warm water coursing through her hair, the soft wet weight of it lying in ropes down over her breasts—was this God's way of asking if she'd truly thought it through? Did she know what she was giving up?

Well, she did, then. And she *had* thought about it. On the other hand . . . she couldn't make them stop, really; it wouldn't be mannerly. The warmth of the water was making the wine she'd drunk course faster through her blood, and she felt as though she were being kneaded like toffee, stretched and pulled, all glossy and falling into languid loops. She closed her eyes and gave up trying to remember how many Hail Marys she had yet to go in the third decade.

It wasn't until the maids had hauled her, pink and steaming, out of the bath and wrapped her in a most remarkable huge fuzzy kind of towel, that she emerged abruptly from her sensual trance. The cold air coalesced in her stomach, reminding her that all this luxury was indeed a lure of the devil—for lost in gluttony and sinful bathing, she'd forgot entirely about the poor young man on the ship, the poor, despairing sinner who had thrown himself into the sea.

The maids had gone for the moment. She dropped at once to her knees on the stone floor and threw off the coddling towel, exposing her bare skin to the full chill of the air in penance.

"*Mea culpa, mea culpa, mea maxima culpa,*" she breathed, knocking a fist against her bosom in a paroxysm of sorrow and regret. The sight of the drowned young man was in her mind, soft brown hair fanned across his cheek, young eyes half closed, seeing nothing—and what terrible thing was it that he'd seen before he jumped, or thought of, that he'd screamed so?

She thought briefly of Michael, the look on his face when he spoke of his poor wife . . . perhaps the young brown-haired man had lost someone dear, and couldn't face his life alone?

She should have spoken to him. That was the undeniable, terrible truth. It didn't matter that she didn't know what to say. She should have trusted God to give her words, as He had when she'd spoken to Michael.

"Forgive me, Father!" she said urgently, out loud. "Please—forgive me, give me strength!"

She'd betrayed that poor young man. And herself. *And* God, who'd given her the terrible gift of Sight for a reason. And the voices . . .

"Why did ye not tell me?" she cried. "Have ye nothing to say for yourselves?" Here she'd thought the voices those of angels, and they weren't—just drifting bits of bog-mist, getting into her head, pointless, useless . . . useless as she was, oh, Lord Jesus . . .

She didn't know how long she knelt there, naked, half drunk, and in tears. She heard the muffled squeaks of dismay from the French maids who poked their heads in, and just as quickly withdrew them, but paid no attention. She didn't know if it was right even to pray for the poor young man— for suicide was a mortal sin, and surely he'd gone straight to Hell. But she couldn't give him up; she couldn't. She felt somehow that he'd been her charge, that she'd carelessly let him fall, and surely God would not hold the young man entirely responsible, when it was she who should have been watching out for him?

And so she prayed, with all the energy of body and mind and spirit, asking mercy. Mercy for the young man, for wee Ronnie and wretched auld Angus . . . mercy for poor Michael, and for the soul of Lillie, his dear wife, and their babe unborn. And mercy for herself, this unworthy vessel of God's service.

"I'll do better!" she promised, sniffing, and wiping her nose on the fluffy towel. "Truly, I will. I'll be braver. I will."

. . . .

Michael took the candlestick from the footman, said good night, and shut the door. He hoped Sister Joan-Gregory was comfortable; he'd told the staff to put her in the main guest room. He was fairly sure she'd sleep well. He smiled wryly to himself; unaccustomed to wine, and obviously nervous in company, she'd sipped her way through most of a decanter of Jerez sherry before he noticed, and was sitting in the corner with unfocused eyes and a small inward smile that reminded him of a painting he had seen at Versailles, a thing the steward had called *La Gioconda*.

He couldn't very well deliver her to the convent in such a condition, and had gently escorted her upstairs and placed her into the hands of the chambermaids, both of whom regarded her with some wariness, as though a tipsy nun was a particularly dangerous commodity.

He'd drunk a fair amount himself in the course of the afternoon, and more at dinner. He and Charles had sat up late, talking and drinking rum punch. Not talking of anything in particular; he had just wanted not to be alone. Charles had invited him to go to the gaming rooms—Charles was an inveterate gambler—but was kind enough to accept his refusal and to simply bear him company.

The candle flame blurred briefly at thought of Charles's kindness. He blinked and shook his head, which proved a mistake; the contents shifted abruptly, and his stomach rose in protest at the sudden movement. He barely made it to the chamber pot in time and, once evacuated, lay numbly on the floor, cheek pressed to the cold boards.

It wasn't that he couldn't get up and go to bed. It was that he couldn't face the thought of the cold white sheets, the pillows round and smooth, as though Lillie's head had never dented them, the bed never known the heat of her body.

Tears ran sideways over the bridge of his nose and dripped on the floor. There was a snuffling noise, and Plonplon came squirming out from under the bed and licked his face, whining anxiously. After a little while, he sat up and, leaning against the side of the bed with the dog in one arm, reached for the decanter of port that the butler had left—by instruction—on the table beside it.

· · · ·

The smell was appalling. Rakoczy had wrapped a woolen comforter about his lower face, but the odor seeped in, putrid and cloying, clinging to the back of the throat, so that even breathing through the mouth didn't preserve you from the stench. He breathed as shallowly as he could, though, picking his way carefully past the edge of the cemetery by the narrow beam of a dark-lantern. The mine lay well beyond it, but the stench carried amazingly, when the wind lay in the east.

The chalk mine had been abandoned for years; it was rumored to be haunted. It was. Rakoczy knew what haunted it. Never religious—he was a philosopher and a natural scientist, a rationalist—he still crossed himself by reflex at the head of the ladder that led down the shaft into those spectral depths.

At least the rumors of ghosts and earth-demons and the walking dead would keep anyone from coming to investigate strange light glowing from the subterranean tunnels of the workings, if it was noticed at all. Though just in case . . . he opened the burlap bag, still redolent of rats, and fished out a bundle of pitchblende torches and the oiled-silk packet that held several lengths of cloth saturated with *salpêtre,* salts of potash, blue vitriol, verdigris, butter of antimony, and a few other interesting compounds from his laboratory.

He found the blue vitriol by smell, and wrapped the cloth tightly around the head of one torch, then—whistling under his breath—did three more, impregnated with different salts. He loved this part. It was so simple, and so astonishingly beautiful.

He paused for a minute to listen, but it was well past dark and the only sounds were those of the night itself—frogs chirping and bellowing in the distant marshes by the cemetery, wind stirring the leaves of spring. A few hovels a half mile away, only one with firelight glowing dully from a smoke-hole in the roof.

Almost a pity there's no one but me to see this. He took the little clay fire-pot from its wrappings and touched a coal to the cloth-wrapped torch. A tiny green flame flickered like a serpent's tongue, then burst into life in a brilliant globe of ghostly color.

He grinned at the sight, but there was no time to lose; the torches wouldn't last forever, and there was work to be done. He tied the bag to his belt and, with the green fire crackling softly in one hand, climbed down into darkness.

He paused at the bottom, breathing deep. The air was clear, the dust long settled. No one had been down here recently. The dull white walls glowed soft, eerie under the green light, and the passage yawned before him, black as a murderer's soul. Even knowing the place as well as he did, and with light in his hand, it gave him a qualm to walk into it.

Is that what death is like? he wondered. A black void, that you walked into with no more than a feeble glimmer of faith in your hand? His lips compressed. Well, he'd done *that* before, if less permanently. But he disliked the way that the notion of death seemed always to be lurking in the back of his mind these days.

The main tunnel was large, big enough for two men to walk side by side, and the roof was high enough above him that the roughly excavated chalk lay in shadow, barely touched by his torch. The side-tunnels were smaller, though. He counted the ones on the left, and despite himself, hurried his step a little as he passed the fourth. That was where *it* lay, down the side-tunnel, a turn to the left, another to the left—was it "widdershins" the English called it, turning against the direction of the sun? He thought that was what Mélisande had called it when she'd brought him here . . .

The sixth. His torch had begun to gutter already, and he pulled another from the bag and lit it from the remains of the first, which he dropped on the floor at the entrance to the side-tunnel, leaving it to flare and smolder behind him, the smoke catching at his throat. He knew his way, but even so, it was as well to leave landmarks, here in the realm of everlasting night. The mine had deep rooms, one far back that showed strange paintings on the wall, of animals that didn't exist, but had an astonishing vividness, as though they would leap from the wall and stampede down the passages. Sometimes—rarely—he went all the way down into the bowels of the earth, just to look at them.

The fresh torch burned with the warm light of natural fire, and the white walls took on a rosy glow. So did the painting at the end of the corridor, this one different; a crude but effective rendering of the Annunciation. He didn't know who had made the paintings that appeared unexpectedly here and there in the mines—most were of religious subjects, a few most emphatically *not*—but they were useful. There was an iron ring in the wall by the Annunciation, and he set his torch into it.

Turn back at the Annunciation, then three paces . . . he stamped his foot, listening for the faint echo, and found it. He'd brought a trowel in his bag, and it was the work of a few moments to uncover the sheet of tin that covered his cache.

The cache itself was three feet deep and three feet square—he found satisfaction in the knowledge of its perfect cubicity whenever he saw it; any alchemist was by profession a numerologist as well. It was half full, the contents wrapped in burlap or canvas; not things he wanted to carry openly through the streets. It took some prodding and unwrapping to find the pieces he wanted. Madame Fabienne had driven a hard bargain, but a fair one: two hundred ecus a month times four months, for the guaranteed exclusive use of Madeleine's services.

Four months would surely be enough, he thought, feeling a rounded shape through its wrappings. In fact, he thought one night would be enough, but his man's pride was restrained by a scientist's prudence. And even if . . . there was always some chance of early miscarriage; he wanted to be sure of the child before he undertook any more personal experiments with the space between times. If he knew that something of himself—someone with his peculiar abilities—might be left, just in case *this* time . . .

He could feel *it* there, somewhere in the smothered dark behind him. He knew he couldn't hear it now; it was silent, save on the days of solstice and equinox, or when you actually walked into it . . . but he felt the sound of it in his bones, and it made his hands tremble on the wrappings.

The gleam of silver, of gold. He chose two gold snuffboxes, a filigreed necklace, and—with some hesitation—a small silver salver. Why did the void not affect metal? he wondered, for the thousandth time. In fact, carrying gold or silver eased the passage—or at least he thought so. Mélisande had told him it did. But jewels were always destroyed by the passage, though they gave the most control and protection.

That made some sense; everyone knew that gemstones had a specific vibration that corresponded to the heavenly spheres, and the spheres themselves of course affected the earth—"As above, so below." He still had no idea exactly *how* the vibrations should affect the space, the portal . . . *it*. But thinking about it gave him a need to touch them, to reassure himself, and he moved wrapped bundles out of the way, digging down to the left-hand corner of the wood-lined cache, where pressing on a particular nailhead caused one of the boards to loosen and turn sideways, rotating smoothly on spindles. He reached into the dark space thus revealed and found the small wash-leather bag, feeling his sense of unease dissipate at once when he touched it.

He opened it and poured the contents into his palm, glittering and sparking in the dark hollow of his hand. Red and blues and greens, the brilliant white of diamonds, the lavender and violet of amethyst, and the golden glow of topaz and citrine. Enough?

Enough to travel back, certainly. Enough to steer himself with some accuracy, to choose how far he went. But enough to go forward?

He weighed the glittering handful for a moment, then poured them carefully back. Not yet. But he had time to find more; he wasn't going anywhere for at least four months. Not until he was sure that Madeleine was well and truly with child.

• • • •

"Joan." Michael put his hand on her arm, keeping her from leaping out of the carriage. "Ye're *sure*, now? I mean, if ye didna feel quite ready, ye're welcome to stay at my house until—"

"I'm ready." She didn't look at him, and her face was pale as a slab of lard. "Let me go, please."

He reluctantly let go of her arm, but insisted upon getting down with her, and ringing the bell at the gate, stating their business to the portress. All the time, though, he could feel her shaking, quivering like a blancmange. Was it fear, though, or just understandable nerves? He'd feel a bit cattywampus himself, he thought with sympathy, were he making such a shift, beginning a new life so different from what had gone before.

The portress went away to fetch the Mistress of Postulants, leaving them in the little enclosure by the gatehouse. From here, he could see across a sunny courtyard with a cloister walk on the far side, and what looked like extensive kitchen gardens to the right. To the left was the looming bulk of the hospital run by the order, and beyond that, the other buildings that belonged to the convent. It was a beautiful place, he thought—and hoped the sight of it would settle her fears.

She made an inarticulate noise, and he glanced at her, alarmed to see what looked like tears slicking her cheeks.

"Joan," he said more quietly, and handed her his fresh handkerchief. "Dinna be afraid. If ye need me, send for me, anytime; I'll come. And I meant it, about the letters."

He would have said more, but just then the portress reappeared, with Sister Eustacia, the postulant mistress, who greeted Joan with a kind motherliness that seemed to comfort her, for the girl sniffed and straightened herself, and reaching into her pocket, pulled out a little folded square, obviously kept with care through her travels.

"*J'ai une lettre,*" she said, in halting French. "*Pour Madame le . . . pour . . .* Reverend Mother?" she said, in a small voice. "Mother Hildegarde?"

"*Oui?*" Sister Eustacia took the note with the same care with which it was proffered.

"It's from . . . her," Joan said to Michael, having plainly run out of French. She still wouldn't look at him. "Da's . . . er . . . wife. You know. Claire."

"Jesus Christ!" Michael blurted, making both the portress and the postulant mistress stare reprovingly at him.

"She said she was a friend of Mother Hildegarde. And if she was still alive . . ." She stole a look at Sister Eustacia, who appeared to have followed this.

"Oh, Mother Hildegarde is certainly alive," she assured Joan, in English. "And I'm sure she will be most interested to speak with you." She tucked the note into her own capacious pocket, and held out a hand. "Now, my dear child, if you are quite ready . . ."

"*Je suis prest,*" Joan said, shaky, but dignified. And so Joan MacKimmie of Balriggan passed through the gates of the convent of Our Lady Queen of Angels, still clutching Michael Murray's clean handkerchief and smelling strongly of his dead wife's scented soap.

· · · ·

Michael had dismissed his carriage and wandered restlessly about the city after leaving Joan at the convent, not wanting to go home. He hoped they would be good to her, hoped that she'd made the right decision.

Of course, he comforted himself, she wouldn't actually be a nun for some time. He didn't know quite how long it took, from entering as a postulant to becoming a novice, to taking the final vows of poverty, chastity, and obedience, but at least a few years. There would be time for her to be sure. And at least she was in a place of safety; the look of terror and distress on her face as she'd shot through the gates of the convent still haunted him. He strolled toward the river, where the evening light glowed on the water like a bronze mirror. The deckhands were tired and the day's shouting had died away. In this light, the reflections of the boats gliding homeward seemed more substantial than the boats themselves.

He'd been surprised at the letter, and wondered whether that had any-thing to do with Joan's distress. He'd had no notion that his uncle's wife had anything to do with the convent of Les Anges—though now that he cast his mind back, he did recall Jared mentioning that Uncle Jamie had worked in Paris in the wine business for a short time, back before the Ris-ing. He supposed Claire might have met Mother Hildegarde then . . . but it was all before he himself was born.

He felt an odd warmth at the thought of Claire; he couldn't really think of her as his auntie, though she was. He'd not spent much time with her alone at Lallybroch—but he couldn't forget the moment when she'd met him, alone at the door. Greeted him briefly and embraced him in impulse. And he'd felt an instant sense of relief, as though she'd taken a heavy bur-den from his heart. Or maybe lanced a boil on his spirit, as she might one on his bum.

That thought made him smile. He didn't know what she was—the talk near Lallybroch painted her as everything from a witch to an angel, with most of the opinion hovering cautiously around "faery"—for the Auld Ones were dangerous, and you didn't talk too much about them . . . but he liked her. So did Da and Young Ian, and that counted for a lot. And Uncle Jamie, of course . . . though everyone said, very matter-of-fact, that Uncle Jamie was bewitched. He smiled wryly at that. Aye, if being mad in love with your wife was bewitchment.

If anyone outside the family kent what she'd told them—he cut that thought short. It wasn't something he'd forget, but it wasn't something he wanted to think about just yet, either. The gutters of Paris running with blood . . . he glanced down, involuntarily, but the gutters were full of the usual assortment of animal and human sewage, dead rats, and bits of rubbish too far gone to be salvaged for food even by the street beggars.

He made his way slowly through the crowded streets, past La Chapelle and Montmartre. If he walked enough, sometimes he could fall asleep without too much wine.

He sighed, elbowing his way through a group of buskers outside a tavern, turning back toward the Rue Trémoulins. Some days, his head was like a bramble patch; thorns catching at him no matter which way he turned, and no path leading out of the tangle.

Paris wasn't a large city, but it was a complicated one; there was always somewhere else to walk. He crossed the Place de la Concorde, thinking of what his uncle's wife had told them, seeing there in his mind the tall shadow of a terrible machine.

• • • •

Joan had had her dinner with Mother Hildegarde, a lady so ancient and holy that Joan had feared to breathe too heavily, lest the Reverend Mother fragment like a stale croissant and go straight off to Heaven in front of her. Mother Hildegarde had been delighted with the letter Joan had brought, though; it brought a faint flush to her face.

"From my—er . . ." Martha, Mary, and Lazarus, what was the French word for stepmother? "Ahh . . . the wife of my . . ." Fittens, she didn't know the word for stepfather, either! "The wife of my father," she ended, weakly.

"You are the daughter of my good friend Claire!" Mother had exclaimed. "And how is she?"

"Bonny, er . . . *bon,* I mean, last I saw her," said Joan, and then tried to explain, but there was a lot of French being talked very fast, and she gave up and accepted the glass of wine that Mother Hildegarde offered her. She was going to be a sot long before she took her vows, she thought, trying to hide her flushed face by bending down to pat Mother's wee dog, a fluffy, friendly creature the color of burnt sugar named Bouton.

Whether it was the wine or Mother's kindness, though, her wobbly spirit steadied. Mother had welcomed her to the community and kissed her forehead at the end of the meal, before sending her off in the charge of Sister Eustacia to see the convent.

Now she lay on her narrow cot in the dormitory, listening to the breathing of a dozen other postulants. It sounded like a byre full of cows, and had much the same warm, humid scent—bar the manure. Her eyes filled with tears, the vision of the homely stone byre at Balriggan sudden and vivid in her mind. She swallowed them back, though, pinching her lips together. A few of the girls sobbed quietly, missing home and family, but she wouldn't be one of them. She was older than most—a few were nay more than fourteen—and she'd promised God to be brave.

It hadn't been bad during the afternoon. Sister Eustacia had been very kind, taking her and a couple of other new postulants round the walled estate, showing them the big gardens where the convent grew medicinal herbs and fruit and vegetables for the table, the chapel where devotions were held six times a day, plus Mass in the mornings, the stables and kitchens, where they would take turns working—and the great Hôpital des Anges, the order's main work. They had only seen the Hôpital from the outside, though; they would see the inside tomorrow, when Sister Marie-Amadeus would explain their duties.

It was strange, of course—she still understood only half what people said to her, and was sure from the looks on their faces that they understood much less of what she tried to say to *them*—but wonderful. She loved the spiritual discipline, the hours of devotion, with the sense of peace and unity that came upon the sisters as they chanted and prayed together. Loved the simple beauty of the chapel, amazing in its clean elegance, the solid lines of granite and the grace of carved wood, a faint smell of incense in the air, like the breath of angels.

The postulants prayed with the others, but did not yet sing. They would be trained in music, such excitement! Mother Hildegarde had been a famous musician in her youth, it was rumored, and considered it one of the most important forms of devotion.

The thought of the new things she'd seen, and the new things to come, distracted her mind—a little—from thoughts of her mother's voice, the wind off the moors . . . She shoved these hastily away, and reached for her new rosary, this a substantial thing with smooth wooden beads, lovely and comforting in the fingers.

Above all, there was peace. She hadn't heard a word from the voices, hadn't seen anything peculiar or alarming. She wasn't foolish enough to think she'd escaped her dangerous gift, but at least there might be help at hand if—when—it came back.

And at least she already knew enough Latin to say her rosary properly; Da had taught her. *"Ave, Maria,"* she whispered, *"gratia plena, Dominus tecum,"* and closed her eyes, the sobs of the homesick fading in her ears as the beads moved slow and silent through her fingers.

The Next Day

Michael Murray stood in the aisle of the aging-shed, feeling puny and unreal. He'd waked with a terrible headache, the result of having drunk a great deal of mixed spirits on an empty stomach, and while the headache had receded to a dull throb at the back of his skull, it had left him feeling trampled and left for dead.

His cousin Jared, owner of Fraser et Cie, looked at him with the cold eye of long experience, shook his head, and sighed deeply, but said nothing, merely taking the list from his nerveless fingers and beginning the count on his own.

He wished Jared had rebuked him. Everyone still tiptoed round him, careful of him. And like a wet dressing on a wound, their care kept the wound of Lillie's loss open and weeping. The sight of Léonie didn't help, either—so much like Lillie to look at, so different in character. She said they must help and comfort one another, and to that end, she came to visit every other day, or so it seemed. He really wished she would . . . just go away, though the thought shamed him.

"How's the wee nun, then?" Jared's voice, dry and matter-of-fact as always, drew him out of his bruised and soggy thoughts. "Give her a good send-off to the convent?"

"Aye. Well . . . aye. More or less." Michael mustered up a feeble smile. He didn't really want to think about Sister Joan-Gregory this morning, either.

"What did ye give her?" Jared handed the checklist to Humberto, the Italian shed-master, and looked Michael over appraisingly. "I hope it wasna the new Rioja that did that to ye."

"Ah . . . no." Michael struggled to focus his attention. The heady atmosphere of the shed, thick with the fruity exhalations of the resting casks, was making him dizzy. "It was Moselle. Mostly. And a bit of rum punch."

"Oh, I see." Jared's ancient mouth quirked up on one side. "Did I never tell ye not to mix wine wi' rum?"

"Not above two hundred times, no." Jared was moving, and Michael followed him perforce down the narrow aisle, the casks in their serried ranks rising high above on either side.

"Rum's a demon. But whisky's a virtuous dram," Jared said, pausing by a rack of small, blackened casks. "So long as it's a good make, it'll never turn on ye. Speakin' of which"—He tapped the end of one cask, which gave off the resonant deep *thongk* of a full barrel—"what's this? It came up from the docks this morning."

"Oh, aye." Michael stifled a belch, and smiled painfully. "That, cousin, is the Ian Alastair Robert MacLeod Murray Memorial *uisge-baugh.* My da and Uncle Jamie made it during the winter. They thought ye might like a wee cask for your personal use."

Jared's brows rose and he gave Michael a swift sideways glance. Then he turned back to examine the cask, bending close to sniff at the seam between the lid and staves.

"I've tasted it," Michael assured him. "I dinna think it will poison ye. But ye should maybe let it age a few years."

Jared made a rude noise in his throat, and his hand curved gently over the swell of the staves. He stood thus for a moment as though in benediction, then turned suddenly and took Michael into his arms. His own breathing was hoarse, congested with sorrow. He was years older than Da and Uncle Jamie, but had known the two of them all their lives.

"I'm sorry for your faither, lad," he said, after a moment, and let go, patting Michael on the shoulder. He looked at the cask and sniffed deeply. "I can tell it will be fine." He paused, breathing slowly, then nodded once, as though making up his mind to something.

"I've a thing in mind, *a charaidh.* I'd been thinking, since ye went to Scotland—and now that we've a kinswoman in the church, so to speak . . . come back to the office with me, and I'll tell ye."

• • • •

It was chilly in the street, but the goldsmith's back room was cozy as a womb, with a porcelain stove throbbing with heat and woven wool hangings on the walls. Rakoczy hastily unwound the comforter about his neck; it didn't do to sweat indoors; the sweat chilled the instant one went out again, and next thing you knew, it would be *la grippe* at the best, pleurisy or pneumonia at the worst.

Rosenwald himself was comfortable in shirt and waistcoat, without even a wig, only a plum-colored turban to keep his polled scalp warm. The goldsmith's stubby fingers traced the curves of the octafoil salver, turned it over—and stopped dead. Rakoczy felt a tingle of warning at the base of his spine, and deliberately relaxed himself, affecting a nonchalant self-confidence.

"Where did you get this, Monsieur, if I may ask?" Rosenwald looked up at him, but there was no accusation in the goldsmith's aged face—only a wary excitement.

"It was an inheritance," Rakoczy said, glowing with earnest innocence. "An elderly aunt left it—and a few other pieces—to me. Is it worth anything more than the value of the silver?"

The goldsmith opened his mouth, then shut it, glancing at Rakoczy. *Is he honest?* Rakoczy wondered with interest. *He's already told me it's something special. Will he tell me why, in hopes of getting other pieces? Or lie, to get this one cheap?* Rosenwald had a good reputation, but he was a Jew.

"Paul de Lamerie," Rosenwald said reverently, his index finger tracing the hallmark. "This was made by Paul de Lamerie."

A shock ran up Rakoczy's backbone. *Merde!* He'd brought the wrong one!

"Really?" he said, striving for simple curiosity. "Does that mean something?"

It means I'm a fool, he thought, and wondered whether to snatch the thing back and leave instantly. The goldsmith had carried it away, though, to look at it more closely under the lamp.

"De Lamerie was one of the very best goldsmiths ever to work in London—perhaps in the world," Rosenwald said, half to himself.

"Indeed," Rakoczy said politely. He was sweating freely. *Nom d'un nom!* Wait, though—Rosenwald had said "was." De Lamerie was dead, then, thank God. Perhaps the Duke of Sandringham, from whom he'd stolen the salver, was dead, too? He began to breathe more easily.

He never sold anything identifiable within a hundred years of his acquisition of it; that was his principle. He'd taken the other salver from a rich merchant in a game of cards in the Low Countries in 1630; he'd stolen this one in 1745—much too close for comfort. Still . . .

His thoughts were interrupted by the chime of the silver bell over the door, and he turned to see a young man come in, removing his hat to reveal a startling head of dark red hair. He was dressed *à la mode,* and addressed the goldsmith in perfect Parisian French, but he didn't look French. A long-nosed face with faintly slanted eyes. There was a slight sense of familiarity about that face, yet Rakoczy was sure he'd never seen this man before.

"Please, sir, go on with your business," the young man said with a courteous bow. "I meant no interruption."

"No, no," Rakoczy said, stepping forward. He motioned the young man toward the counter. "Please, go ahead. M. Rosenwald and I are merely discussing the value of this object. It will take some thought." He snaked out an arm and seized the salver, feeling a little better with it clasped to his bosom. He wasn't sure; if he decided it was too risky to sell, he could slink out quietly while Rosenwald was busy with the red-headed young man.

The Jew looked surprised, but after a moment's hesitation, nodded and turned to the young man, who introduced himself as one Michael Murray, partner in Fraser et Cie, the wine merchants.

"I believe you are acquainted with my cousin, Jared Fraser?"

Rosenwald's round face lighted at once.

"Oh, to be sure, sir! A man of the most exquisite taste and discrimination. I made him a wine-cistern with a motif of sunflowers, not a year past!"

"I know." The young man smiled, a smile that creased his cheeks and narrowed his eyes, and that small bell of recognition rang again. But the name held no familiarity to Rakoczy—only the face, and that only vaguely. "My uncle has another commission for you, if it's agreeable?"

"I never say no to honest work, Monsieur." From the pleasure apparent on the goldsmith's rubicund face, honest work that paid very well was even more welcome.

"Well, then . . . if I may?" The young man pulled a folded paper from his pocket, but half-turned toward Rakoczy, eyebrow cocked in inquiry. Rakoczy motioned him to go on, and turned himself to examine a music box that stood on the counter—an enormous thing the size of a cow's head, crowned with a nearly naked nymph, festooned with the airiest of gold draperies and dancing on mushrooms and flowers, in company with a large frog.

"A chalice," Murray was saying, the paper laid flat on the counter. From the corner of his eye, Rakoczy could see that it held a list of names. "It's a presentation to the chapel of des Anges, to be given in memory of my late father. A young cousin of mine has just entered the convent there as a postulant," he explained. "So M. Fraser thought that the best place."

"An excellent choice." Rosenwald picked up the list. "And you wish all of these names inscribed?"

"Yes, if you can."

"Monsieur!" Rosenwald waved a hand, professionally insulted. "These are your father's children?"

"Yes, these at the bottom." Murray bent over the counter, his finger tracing the lines, speaking the outlandish names carefully. "At the top, these are my parents' names: Ian Alastair Robert MacLeod Murray, and Janet Flora Arabella Fraser Murray. Now, also, I—we, I mean—we want these two names as well: James Alexander Malcolm MacKenzie Fraser, and Claire Elizabeth Beauchamp Fraser. Those are my uncle and aunt; my uncle was very close to my father," he explained. "Almost a brother."

He went on saying something else, but Rakoczy wasn't listening. He grasped the edge of the counter, vision flickering so that the nymph seemed to leer at him.

Claire Fraser. That had been the woman's name, and her husband, James, a Highland lord from Scotland. That was who the young man resembled, though he was not so imposing as . . . but La Dame Blanche! It was her, it had to be.

And in the next instant, the goldsmith confirmed this, straightening up from the list with an abrupt air of wariness, as though one of the names might spring off the paper and bite him.

"That name—your aunt, you say? Did she and your uncle live in Paris at one time?"

"Yes," Murray said, looking mildly surprised. "Maybe thirty years ago—only for a short time, though. Did you know her?"

"Ah. Not to say I was personally acquainted," Rosenwald said, with a crooked smile. "But she was . . . known. People called her La Dame Blanche."

Murray blinked, clearly surprised to hear this.

"Really?" He looked rather appalled.

"Yes, but it was all a long time ago," Rosenwald said hastily, clearly thinking he'd said too much. He waved a hand toward his back room. "If you'll give me a moment, Monsieur, I have a chalice actually here, if you would care to see it . . . and a paten, too. We might make some accommodation of price, if you take both. They were made for a patron who died suddenly, before the chalice was finished, so there is almost no decoration—plenty of room for the names to be applied, and perhaps we might put the, um, aunt and uncle on the paten?"

Murray nodded, interested, and at Rosenwald's gesture, went round the counter and followed the old man into his back room. Rakoczy put the octafoil salver under his arm and left, as quietly as possible, head buzzing with questions.

. . . .

Jared eyed Michael over the dinner table, shook his head, and bent to his plate.

"I'm not drunk!" Michael blurted, then bent his own head, face flaming. He could feel Jared's eyes boring into the top of his head.

"Not now, ye're not." Jared's voice wasn't accusing. In fact, it was quiet, almost kindly. "But ye have been. Ye've not touched your dinner, and ye're the color of rotten wax."

"I—" The words caught in his throat, just as the food had. Eels in garlic sauce. The smell wafted up from the dish, and he stood up suddenly, lest he either vomit or burst into tears.

"I've nay appetite, cousin," he managed to say, before turning away. "Excuse me."

He would have left, but he hesitated that moment too long, not wanting to go up to the room where Lillie no longer was, but not wanting to look petulant by rushing out into the street. Jared rose and came round to him with a decided step.

"I'm nay verra hungry myself, *a charaidh*," Jared said, taking him by the arm. "Come sit wi' me for a bit and take a dram. It'll settle your wame."

He didn't much want to, but there was nothing else he could think of doing, and within a few moments, he found himself in front of a fragrant applewood fire, with a glass of his father's whisky in hand, the warmth of both easing the tightness of chest and throat. It wouldn't cure his grief, he knew, but it made it possible to breathe.

"Good stuff," Jared said, sniffing cautiously, but approvingly. "Even raw as it is. It'll be wonderful, aged a few years."

"Aye. Uncle Jamie kens what he's about; he said he'd made whisky a good many times, in America."

Jared chuckled.

"Your uncle Jamie usually kens what he's about," he said. "Not that knowing it keeps him out o' trouble." He shifted, making himself more comfortable in his worn leather chair. "Had it not been for the Rising, he'd likely have stayed here wi' me. Aye, well . . ." The old man sighed with regret and lifted his glass, examining the spirit. It was still nearly as pale as water—it hadn't been casked above a few months—but had the slightly viscous look of a fine strong spirit, like it might climb out of the glass if you took your eye off it.

"And if he had, I suppose I'd not be here myself," Michael said dryly.

Jared glanced at him, surprised.

"Och! I didna mean to say ye were but a poor substitute for Jamie, lad." He smiled crookedly, and his hooded eyes grew moist. "Not at all. Ye've been the best thing ever to come to me. You and dear wee Lillie, and . . ." He cleared his throat. "I . . . well, I canna say anything that will help, I ken that. But . . . it won't always be like this."

"Won't it?" Michael said bleakly. "Aye, I'll take your word for it."

A silence fell between them, broken only by the hissing and snap of the fire. The mention of Lillie was like an awl digging into his breastbone, and he took a deeper sip of the whisky to quell the ache. Maybe Jared was right to mention the drink to him. It helped, but not enough. And the help didn't last. He was tired of waking to grief and headache both.

Shying away from thoughts of Lillie, his mind fastened on Uncle Jamie instead. He'd lost his wife, too, and from what Michael had seen of the aftermath, it had torn his soul in two. Then she'd come back to him and he was a man transformed. But in between . . . he'd managed. He'd found a way to be.

Thinking of Auntie Claire gave him a slight feeling of comfort—as long as he didn't think too much about what she'd told the family . . . who—or what—she was, and where she'd been while she was gone those twenty years. The brothers and sisters had talked among themselves about it afterward; Young Jamie and Kitty didn't believe a word of it, Maggie and Janet weren't sure—but Young Ian believed it, and that counted for a lot with Michael. And she'd looked at him—right at him—when she said what was going to happen in Paris.

He felt the same small thrill of horror now, remembering. *The Terror. That's what it will be called, and that's what it will be. People will be arrested for no cause and beheaded in the Place de la Concorde. The streets will run with blood, and no one—no one—will be safe.*

He looked at his cousin; Jared was an old man, though still hale enough. He knew there was no way he could persuade Jared to leave Paris and his wine business. But it would be some time yet—if Auntie Claire was right. No need to think about it now. But she'd seemed so sure, like a seer, talking from a vantage point after everything had happened, from a safer time.

And yet she'd come back from that safe time, to be with Uncle Jamie again.

For a moment, he entertained the wild fantasy that Lillie wasn't dead, but only swept away into a distant time. He couldn't see or touch her, but the knowledge that she was doing things, was alive . . . maybe it was knowing that, thinking that, which had kept Uncle Jamie whole. He swallowed, hard.

"Jared," he said, clearing his own throat. "What did ye think of Auntie Claire? When she lived here?"

Jared looked surprised, but lowered his glass to his knee, pursing his lips in thought.

"She was a bonny lass, I'll tell ye that," he said. "Verra bonny. A tongue like the rough side of a rasp, if she took against something, though—and decided opinions." He nodded, twice, as though recalling a few, and grinned suddenly. "Verra decided indeed!"

"Aye? The goldsmith—Rosenwald, ye ken?—mentioned her, when I went to commission the chalice and he saw her name on the list. He called her La Dame Blanche." This last was not phrased as a question, but he gave it a slight rising inflection, and Jared nodded, his smile widening into a grin.

"Oh, aye, I mind that! 'Twas Jamie's notion. She'd find herself now and then in dangerous places without him—ken how some folk are just the sort as things happen to—so he put it about that she was La Dame Blanche. Ken what a White Lady is, do ye?"

Michael crossed himself, and Jared followed suit, nodding.

"Aye, just so. Make any wicked sod with villainy in mind think twice. A White Lady can strike ye blind or shrivel a man's balls, and likely a few more things than that, should she take the notion. And I'd be the last to say that Claire Fraser couldn't, if she'd a mind to."

Jared raised the glass absently to his lips, took a bigger sip of the raw spirit than he'd meant to and coughed, spraying droplets of memorial whisky halfway across the room. Rather to his own shock, Michael laughed.

Jared wiped his mouth, still coughing, but then sat up straight and lifted his glass, which still held a few drops.

"To your da. *Slainte mhath!*"

"*Slainte!*" Michael echoed, and drained what remained in his own glass. He set it down with finality, and rose. He'd drink nay more tonight.

"*Oidche mhath, mo brathair-athar no mathar.*"

"Good night, lad," said Jared. The fire was burning low, but still cast a warm ruddy glow on the old man's face. "Fare ye well."

The Next Night

Michael dropped his key several times before finally managing to turn it in the old-fashioned lock. It wasn't drink; he'd not had a drop since the wine at supper. Instead, he'd walked the length of the Isle de Paris and back, accompanied only by his thoughts; his whole body quivered and he felt mindless with exhaustion, but he was sure he would sleep. Jean-Baptiste had left the door unbarred, according to his orders, but one of the footmen was sprawled on a settle in the entryway, snoring. He smiled a little, though it was an effort to raise the corners of his mouth.

"Bolt the door and go to bed, Paul," he whispered, bending and shaking the man gently by the shoulder. The footman stirred and snorted, but Michael didn't wait to see whether he woke entirely. There was a tiny oil-lamp burning on the landing of the stairs; a little round glass globe in the gaudy colors of Murano. It had been there since the first day he came from Scotland to stay with Jared, years before, and the sight of it soothed him and drew his aching body up the wide, dark stair.

The house creaked and talked to itself at night; all old houses did. To-night, though, it was silent, the big copper-seamed roof gone cold and its massive timbers settled into somnolence.

He flung off his clothes and crawled naked into bed, head spinning. Tired as he was, his flesh quivered and twitched, his legs jerking like a spit-ted frog's, before he finally relaxed enough to fall headfirst into the seeth-ing cauldron of dreams that awaited him.

She was there, of course. Laughing at him, playing with her ridiculous pug. Running a hand filled with desire across his face, down his neck, eas-ing her body close, and closer. Then they were somehow in bed, with the wind blowing cool through gauzy curtains, too cool, he felt cold, but then her warmth came close, pressed against him. He felt a terrible desire, but at the same time he feared her. She felt utterly familiar, utterly strange—and the mixture thrilled him.

He reached for her, and realized that he couldn't raise his arms, couldn't move. And yet she was against him, writhing in a slow squirm of need, greedy and tantalizing. In the way of dreams, he was at the same time in front of her, behind her, touching, and seeing from a distance. Candle-glow on naked breasts, the shadowed weight of solid buttocks, falling drapes of parting white, one round, firm leg protruding, a pointed toe rooting gently between his legs. Urgency.

She was curled behind him then, kissing the back of his neck, and he reached back, groping, but his hands were heavy, drifting; they slid help-less over her. Hers on him were firm, more than firm, she had him by the cock, was working him. Working him hard, fast and hard. He bucked and heaved, suddenly released from the dream-swamp of immobility. She loosed her grip, tried to pull away, but he folded his hand round hers and rubbed their folded hands hard up and down with joyous ferocity, spilling himself convulsively, hot wet spurts against his belly, running thick over their clenched knuckles.

She made a sound of horrified disgust and his eyes flew open. A pair of huge, bugging eyes stared into his, over a gargoyle's mouth full of tiny, sharp teeth. He shrieked.

Plonplon leaped off the bed and ran to and fro, barking hysterically. There was a body behind him in bed. Michael flung himself off the bed, tangled in a winding-sheet of damp, sticky bedclothes, fell and rolled in panic.

"Jesus, Jesus, Jesus!"

On his knees, he wiped his hands on the sheet and gaped, rubbed his hands hard over his face, shook his head. Could *not* make sense of it, couldn't.

"Lillie," he gasped. "Lillie!"

But the woman in his bed, tears running down her face, wasn't Lillie;

he realized it with a wrench that made him groan, doubling up in the desolation of fresh loss.

"Oh, Jesus!"

"Michel, Michel, please, please forgive me!"

"You . . . what . . . for God's *sake* . . . !"

Léonie was weeping frantically, reaching out toward him.

"I couldn't help it. I'm so lonely, I wanted you so much!"

Plonplon had ceased barking and now came up behind Michael, nosing his bare backside with a blast of hot, moist breath.

"*Va-t'en!*"

The pug backed up and started barking again, eyes bulging with offense.

Unable to find any words suitable to the situation, he grabbed the dog and muffled it with a handful of sheet. He got unsteadily to his feet, still holding the squirming pug.

"I—" he began. "You—I mean . . . oh, Jesus Christ!" He leaned over and put the dog carefully on the bed. Plonplon instantly wriggled free of the sheet and rushed to Léonie, licking her solicitously. Michael had thought of giving her the dog after Lillie's death, but for some reason this had seemed a betrayal of the pug's former mistress, and brought Michael near to weeping.

"I can't," he said simply. "I just can't. You go to sleep now, lass. We'll talk about it later, aye?"

He went out, walking carefully, as though very drunk, and closed the door gently behind him. He got halfway down the main stair before realizing he was naked. He just stood there, his mind blank, watching the colors of the Murano lamp fade as the daylight grew outside, until Paul saw him and ran up to wrap him in a cloak and lead him off to a bed in the guest rooms.

· · · ·

Rakoczy's favorite gaming club was the Golden Cockerel, and the wall in the main salon was covered by a tapestry featuring one of these creatures, worked in gold thread, wings spread and throat swollen as it crowed in triumph at the winning hand of cards laid out before it. It was a cheerful place, catering to a mix of wealthy merchants and lesser nobility, and the air was spicy with the scents of candle wax, powder, perfume, and money.

He'd thought of going to the offices of Fraser et Cie, making some excuse to speak to Michael Murray, and maneuver his way into an inquiry about the whereabouts of the young man's aunt. Upon consideration, though, he thought such a move might make Murray wary—and possibly lead to word getting back to the woman, if she was somewhere in Paris. That was the last thing he wanted to happen.

Better, perhaps, to instigate his inquiries from a more discreet distance.

He'd learned that Murray occasionally came to the Cockerel, though he himself had never seen him there. But if he was known . . .

It took several evenings of play, wine, and conversation, before he found Charles Pépin. Pépin was a popinjay, a reckless gambler, and a man who liked to talk. And to drink. He was also a good friend of the young wine merchant's.

"Oh, the nun!" he said, when Rakoczy had—after the second bottle—mentioned having heard that Murray had a young relative who had recently entered the convent. Pépin laughed, his handsome face flushed.

"A less likely nun I've never seen—an arse that would make the Archbishop of Paris forget his vows, and he's eighty-six if he's a day. Doesn't speak any sort of French, poor thing—the girl, not the Archbishop. Not that I for one would be wanting to carry on a lot of conversation if I had her to myself, you understand . . . she's Scotch, terrible accent . . ."

"Scotch, you say." Rakoczy held a card consideringly, then put it down. "She is Murray's cousin—would she perhaps be the daughter of his uncle James?"

Pépin looked blank for a moment.

"I don't really . . . oh, yes, I do know!" He laughed heartily, and laid down his own losing hand. "Dear me. Yes, she did say her father's name was Jay-mee, the way the Scotches do, that must be James."

Rakoczy felt a ripple of anticipation go up his spine. *Yes!* This sense of triumph was instantly succeeded by a breathless realization. The girl was the daughter of La Dame Blanche.

"I see," he said casually. "And which convent did you say the girl has gone to?"

To his surprise, Pépin gave him a suddenly sharp look.

"Why do you want to know?"

Rakoczy shrugged, thinking fast.

"A wager," he said, with a grin. "If she is as luscious as you say . . . I'll bet you five hundred louis that I can get her into bed before she takes her first vows."

Pépin scoffed.

"Oh, never! She's tasty, but she doesn't know it. And she's virtuous, I'd swear it. And if you think you can seduce her inside the convent . . . !"

Rakoczy lounged back in his chair, and motioned for another bottle.

"In that case . . . what do you have to lose?"

The Next Day

She could smell the Hôpital long before the small group of new postulants reached the door. They walked two by two, practicing custody of the eyes, but she couldn't help a quick glance upward at the building, a three-story château, originally a noble house that had, rumor said, been given to Mother Hildegarde by her father, as part of her dowry when she joined the church. It had become a convent house, and then gradually been given over more and more to the care of the sick, the nuns moving to the new château built in the park.

It was a lovely old house—on the outside. The odor of sickness, of urine and shit and vomit, hung about it like a cloying veil, though, and she hoped she wouldn't vomit, too. The little postulant next to her, Sister Miséricorde de Dieu (known to all simply as Mercy), was as white as her veil, eyes fixed on the ground, but obviously not seeing it, as she stepped smack on a slug and gave a small cry of horror as it squished under her sandal.

Joan looked hastily away; she would never master custody of the eyes, she was sure. Nor yet custody of thought.

It wasn't the notion of sick people that troubled her. She'd seen sick people before, and she wouldn't be expected to do more than wash and feed them; she could manage that easily. It was fear of seeing those who were about to die—for surely there would be a great many of those in a hospital. And what might the voices tell her about *them?*

· · · ·

As it was, the voices had nothing to say. Not a word, and after a little, she began to lose her nervousness. She *could* do this, and in fact—to her surprise—quite enjoyed the sense of competence, the gratification of being able to ease someone's pain, give them at least a little attention. And if her French made them laugh (and it did), that at least took their minds off of pain and fear for a moment.

There were those who lay under the veil of death. Only a few, though, and it seemed somehow much less shocking here than when she had seen it on Vhairi's lad or the young man on the ship. Maybe it was resignation, perhaps the influence of the angels for whom the Hôpital was named . . . Joan didn't know, but she found that she wasn't afraid to speak to or touch the ones she knew were going to die. For that matter, she observed that the other sisters, even the orderlies, behaved gently toward these people, and it occurred to her that no particular Sight was needed to know that the man with the wasting sickness, whose bones poked through his skin, was not long for this world.

Touch him, said a soft voice inside her head. *Comfort him.*

"All right," she said, taking a deep breath. She had no idea how to comfort anyone, but bathed him, as gently as she could, and coaxed him to take a few spoonsful of porridge. Then she settled him in his bed, straightening his nightshirt and the thin blanket over him.

"Thank you, Sister," he said, and taking her hand, kissed it. "Thank you for your sweet touch."

She went back to the postulants' dormitory that evening feeling thoughtful, but with a strange sense of being on the verge of discovering something important.

That Night

Rakoczy lay with his head on Madeleine's bosom, eyes closed, breathing the scent of her body, feeling the whole of her between his palms, a slowly pulsing entity of light. She was a gentle gold, traced with veins of incandescent blue, her heart deep as lapis beneath his ear, a living stone. And deep inside, her soft red womb, open, soft. Refuge and succor. Promise.

Mélisande had shown him the rudiments of sexual magic, and he'd read about it with great interest in some of the older alchemical texts. He'd never tried it with a whore, though—and in fact, hadn't been trying to do it this time. And yet it had happened. Was happening. He could see the miracle unfolding slowly before him, under his hands.

How odd, he thought dreamily, watching the tiny traces of green energy spread upward through her womb, slowly but inexorably. He'd thought it happened instantly, that a man's seed found its root in the woman and there you were. But that wasn't what was happening, at all. There were *two* types of seed, he now saw. She had one; he felt it plainly, a brilliant speck of light, glowing like a fierce, tiny sun. His own—the tiny green animalculae— were being drawn toward it, bent on immolation.

"Happy, *chéri?*" she whispered, stroking his hair. "Did you have a good time?"

"Most happy, sweetheart." He wished she wouldn't talk, but an unexpected sense of tenderness toward her made him sit up and smile at her. She also began to sit up, reaching for the clean rag and douching syringe, and he put a hand on her shoulder, urging her to lie back down.

"Don't douche this time, *ma belle,*" he said. "A favor to me."

"But—" She was confused; usually he was insistent upon cleanliness. "Do you *want* me to get with child?" For he had stopped her using the wine-soaked sponge beforehand, too.

"Yes, of course," he said, surprised. "Did Madame Fabienne not tell you?"

Her mouth dropped open.

"She did *not*. What—why, for God's sake?" In agitation, she squirmed free of his restraining hand and swung her legs out of bed, reaching for her wrapper. "You aren't—what do you mean to do with it?"

"Do with it?" he said, blinking. "What do you mean, do with it?"

ALCHEMICAL EXPLORATIONS

CATEGORY

She had the wrapper on, pulled crookedly round her shoulders, and had backed up against the wall, hands plastered against her stomach, regarding him with open fear.

"You're a *magicien,* everyone knows that. You take newborn children and use their blood in your spells!"

"What?" he said, rather stupidly. He reached for his breeches, but changed his mind. He got up and went to her instead, putting his hands on her shoulders.

"No," he said, bending down to look her in the eye. "No, I do no such thing. Never." He used all the force of sincerity he could summon, pushing it into her, and felt her waver a little, still fearful, but less certain. He smiled at her. "Who told you I was a *magicien,* for heaven's sake? I am a *philosophe, chérie,* an inquirer into the mysteries of nature, no more. And I can swear to you, by my hope of heaven"—this being more or less non-existent, but why quibble?—"that I have never, not once, used anything more than the water of a man-child in any of my investigations."

"What, little boys' piss?" she said, diverted. He let his hands relax, but kept them on her shoulders.

"Certainly. It's the purest water one can find. Collecting it is something of a chore, mind you—" She smiled at that, good. "But the process does not the slightest harm to the infant, who will eject the water whether anyone has a use for it or not."

"Oh." She was beginning to relax a little, but her hands were still pressed protectively over her belly, as though she felt the imminent child already. *Not yet,* he thought, pulling her against him and feeling his way gently into her body. *But soon!* He wondered if he should remain with her until it happened; the idea of feeling it as it happened inside her—to be an intimate witness to the creation of life itself! . . . but there was no telling how long it might take. From the progress of his animalculae, it could be a day, even two.

Magic, indeed.

Why do men never think of that? he wondered. Most men—himself included—regarded the engendering of babies as a necessity, in the case of inheritance, or nuisance—but *this* . . . But then, most men would never know what he now knew, or see what he had seen.

Madeleine had begun to relax against him, her hands at last leaving her belly. He kissed her, with a real feeling of affection.

"It will be beautiful," he whispered to her. "And once you are well and truly with child, I will buy your contract from Fabienne and take you away. I will buy you a house."

"A *house?*" her eyes went round. They were green, a deep, clear emerald, and he smiled at her again, stepping back.

"Of course. Now, go and sleep, my dear. I shall come again tomorrow."

She flung her arms around him, and he had some difficulty in extracting himself, laughing, from her embraces. Normally, he left a whore's bed with no feeling save physical relief. But what he had done had made a connection with Madeleine that he had not experienced with any woman save Mélisande.

Mélisande. A sudden thought ran through him like the spark from a Leyden jar. *Mélisande.*

He looked hard at Madeleine, now crawling happily naked and white-rumped into bed, her wrapper thrown aside. That bottom . . . the eyes, the soft blond hair, the gold-white of fresh cream.

"*Chérie,*" he said, as casually as he might, pulling on his breeches. "How old are you?"

"Eighteen," she said, without hesitation. "Why, Monsieur?"

"Ah. A wonderful age to become a mother." He pulled the shirt over his head and kissed his hand to her, relieved. He had known Mélisande Robicheaux in 1744. He had not, in fact, just committed incest with his own daughter.

It was only as he passed Madame Fabienne's parlor on his way out that it occurred to him that Madeleine *might* possibly still be his granddaughter. That thought stopped him short, but he had no time to dwell on it, for Fabienne appeared in the doorway and motioned to him.

"A message, Monsieur," she said, and something in her voice touched his nape with a cold finger.

"Yes?"

"Monsieur Grenouille begs the favor of your company, at midnight tomorrow. In the square before Notre Dame de Paris."

. . . .

They didn't have to practice custody of the eyes in the market. In fact, Sister George-Mary, the stout nun who oversaw these expeditions, warned them in no uncertain terms to keep a sharp eye out for short weight and uncivil prices, to say nothing of pickpockets.

"Pickpockets, Sister?" Mercy had said, her blond eyebrows all but vanishing into her veil. "But we are nuns—more or less," she added hastily. "We have nothing to steal!"

Sister George's big red face got somewhat redder, but she kept her patience.

"Normally, that would be true," she agreed. "But we—or I, rather—have the money with which to buy our food, and once we've bought it, you will be carrying it. A pickpocket steals to eat, *n'est-ce pas?* They don't care whether you have money or food, and most of them are so depraved that they would willingly steal from God himself, let alone a couple of chick-headed postulants."

For Joan's part, she wanted to see *everything*, pickpockets included. To her delight, the market was the one she'd passed with Michael, on her first day in Paris. True, the sight of it brought back the horrors and doubts of that first day, too—but for the moment, she pushed those aside and followed Sister George into the fascinating maelstrom of color, smells, and shouting.

Filing away a particularly entertaining expression that she planned to make Sister Philomène explain to her—Sister Philomène was a little older than Joan, but painfully shy and with such delicate skin that she blushed like an apple at the least excuse—she followed Sister George and Sister Mathilde through the fishmonger's section, where Sister George bargained shrewdly for a great quantity of sand dabs, scallops, tiny gray translucent shrimp, and an enormous sea-salmon, the pale spring light shifting through its scales in colors that faded so subtly from pink to blue to silver and back that some of them had no name at all—so beautiful even in its death that it made Joan catch her breath with joy at the wonder of Creation.

"Oh, bouillabaisse tonight!" said Mercy, under her breath. *"Déliceuse!"*

"What is bouillabaisse?" Joan whispered back.

"Fish stew . . . you'll like it, I promise!" Joan had no doubt of it; brought up in the Highlands during the poverty-stricken years following the Rising, she'd been staggered by the novelty, deliciousness, and sheer abundance of the convent's food. Even on Fridays, when the community fasted during the day, supper was simple but mouthwatering, toasted sharp cheese on nutty brown bread with sliced apples.

Luckily, the salmon was so huge that Sister George arranged for the fish-seller to deliver it to the convent, along with the other briny purchases, and so they had room in their baskets for fresh vegetables and fruit, and so passed from Neptune's realm to that of Demeter. Joan hoped it wasn't sacrilegious to think of Greek gods, but she couldn't forget the book of myths that Da had read to her and Marsali when they were young, with wonderful hand-colored illustrations.

After all, she told herself, you needed to know about the Greeks, if you studied medicine. She had some trepidation at the thought of working in the hospital, but God called people to do things, and if it was His will, then—

The thought stopped short as she caught sight of a neat, dark tricorne with a curled blue feather, bobbing slowly through the tide of people. Was it . . . It was! Léonie, the sister of Michael Murray's dead wife. Moved by curiosity, Joan glanced at Sister George, who was engrossed in a huge display of fungus—dear God, people *ate* such things?—and slipped around a barrow billowing with green sallet herbs.

She'd meant to speak to Léonie, to ask her to tell Michael that she needed to talk to him. Postulants were permitted to write letters to their families only twice a year, at Christmas and Easter, but he could send a note to her mother, reassuring her that Joan was well and happy.

Surely Michael could contrive a way to visit the convent . . . but before she could get close enough, Léonie looked furtively over her shoulder, as though fearing discovery, then ducked behind a curtain that hung across the back of a small caravan.

Joan had seen gypsies before, though not often. A dark-skinned man loitered nearby, talking with a group of others; their eyes passed over her habit without pausing, and she sighed with relief. Being a nun was as good as having a cloak of invisibility in most circumstances, she thought.

She looked round for her companions, and saw that Sister Mathilde had been called into consultation regarding a big warty lump of something that looked like the excrement of a seriously diseased hog. Good, she could wait for a minute longer.

In fact, it took very little more than that, before Léonie slipped out from behind the curtain, tucking something into the small basket on her arm. For the first time, it struck Joan as unusual that someone like Léonie should be shopping without a servant to push back crowds and carry purchases—or even to be in a public market. Michael had told her about his own household during the voyage—how Madame Hortense, the cook, went to the markets at dawn, to be sure of getting the freshest things. What would a lady like Léonie be buying, alone?

Joan slithered as best she could through the rows of stalls and wagons, following the bobbing blue feather. A sudden stop allowed her to come up behind Léonie, who had paused by a flower stall, fingering a bunch of white tulips.

It occurred suddenly to Joan that she had no idea what Léonie's last name was, but she couldn't worry about politeness now.

"Ah . . . Madame?" she said tentatively. "Mademoiselle, I mean?" Léonie swung round, eyes huge and face pale. Finding herself faced with a nun, she blinked, confused.

"Er . . . it's me," Joan said, diffident, resisting the impulse to pull off her veil. "Joan MacKimmie?" It felt odd to say it, as though Joan MacKimmie was truly someone else. It took a moment for the name to register, but then Léonie's shoulders relaxed a little.

"Oh." She put a hand to her bosom, and mustered a small smile. "Michael's cousin. Of course. I didn't . . . er . . . how nice to see you!" A small frown wrinkled the skin between her brows. "Are you . . . alone?"

"No," Joan said hurriedly. "And I mustn't stop. I only saw you, and I wanted to ask—" It seemed even stupider than it had a moment ago, but no help for it. "Would you tell Monsieur Murray that I must talk to him? I have something . . . something important, that I have to tell him."

"*Soeur Gregory?*" Sister George's stentorian tones boomed through the higher-pitched racket of the market, making Joan jump. She could see the top of Sister Mathilde's head, with its great white sails, turning to and fro in vain search.

"I have to go," she said to the astonished Léonie. "Please. Please tell him!" Her heart was pounding, and not only from the sudden meeting. She'd been looking at Léonie's basket, where she caught the glint of a brown glass bottle, half hidden beneath a thick bunch of what even Joan recognized as black hellebores. Lovely, cup-shaped flowers of an eerie greenish-white—and deadly poison.

She dodged back across the market to arrive breathless and apologizing at Sister Mathilde's side, wondering if . . . She hadn't spent much time at all with Da's wife—but she *had* heard her talking with Da as she wrote down receipts in a book, and she'd mentioned black hellebore as something women used to make themselves miscarry. If Léonie were pregnant . . . Holy Mother of God, could she be with child by *Michael?* The thought struck her like a blow in the stomach.

No. No, she couldn't believe it. He was still in love with his wife, anyone could see that, and even if not, she'd swear he wasn't the sort to . . . but what did she ken about men, after all?

Well, she'd ask him when she saw him, she decided, her mouth clamping tight. And 'til then . . . Her hand went to the rosary at her waist and she said a quick, silent prayer for Léonie. Just in case.

As she was bargaining doggedly in her execrable French for six aubergines (wondering meanwhile what on earth they were for, medicine or food?), she became aware of someone standing at her elbow. A handsome man of middle age, taller than she was, in a well-cut dove-gray coat. He smiled at her and, touching one of the peculiar vegetables, said in slow, simple French, "You don't want the big ones. They're tough. Get small ones, like that." A long finger tapped an aubergine half the size of the ones the vegetable-seller had been urging on her, and the vegetable-seller burst into a tirade of abuse that made Joan step back, blinking.

Not so much because of the expressions being hurled at her—she didn't understand one word in ten—but because a voice in plain English in her head had just said clearly, *Tell him not to do it.*

She felt hot and cold at the same time.

"I . . . er . . . *je suis* . . . um . . . *Merci beaucoup, Monsieur!*" she blurted, and turning, ran, scrambling back between piles of paper narcissus bulbs and fragrant spikes of hyacinth, her shoes skidding on the slime of trodden leaves.

"*Soeur* Gregory!" Sister Mathilde loomed up so suddenly in front of her that she nearly ran into the massive nun. "What are you doing? Where is Sister Miséricorde?"

"I . . . oh." Joan swallowed, gathering her wits. "She's—over there." She spoke with relief, spotting Mercy's small head in the forefront of a crowd by the meat pie wagon. "I'll get her!" she blurted, and walked hastily off before Sister Mathilde could say more.

Tell him not to do it. That's what the voice had said about Charles Pépin. What was going on? She thought wildly. Was M. Pépin engaged in something awful with the man in the dove-gray coat?

As though thought of the man had reminded the voice, it came again.

Tell him not to do it, the voice repeated in her head, with what seemed like particular urgency. *Tell him he must not!*

"Hail Mary, full of grace, the Lord is with thee, blessed art thou among women . . ." Joan clutched at her rosary and gabbled the words, feeling the blood leave her face. There he was, the man in the dove-gray coat, looking curiously at her over a stall of Dutch tulips and sprays of yellow roses.

She couldn't feel the pavement under her feet, but was moving toward him. *I have to,* she thought. *It doesn't matter if he thinks I'm mad . . .*

"Don't do it," she blurted, coming face-to-face with the astonished gentleman. "You mustn't do it!"

And then she turned and ran, rosary in hand, apron and veil flapping like wings.

· · · ·

Rakoczy couldn't help thinking of the cathedral as an entity. An immense version of one of its own gargoyles, crouched over the city. In protection, or threat?

Notre-Dame de Paris rose black above him, solid, obliterating the light of the stars, the beauty of the night. Very appropriate. He'd always thought that the Church blocked one's sight of God. Nonetheless, the sight of the monstrous stone creature made him shiver as he passed under its shadow, despite the warm cloak.

Perhaps it was the cathedral's stones themselves that gave him the sense of menace? He stopped, paused for a heartbeat, and then strode up to the church's wall and pressed his palm flat against the cold limestone. There was no immediate sense of anything; just the cold roughness of the rock. Impulsively, he shut his eyes and tried to feel his way into the rock. At first, nothing. But he waited, pressing with his mind, a repeated question: *Are you there?*

He would have been terrified to receive an answer, and felt something that was much more relief than disappointment when he didn't. Even so, when he finally opened his eyes and took his hands away, he saw a trace of blue light, the barest trace, glow briefly between his knuckles. That frightened him, and he hurried away, hiding his hands beneath the shelter of the cloak.

Surely not, he assured himself. He'd done that before, made the light happen when he held the jewels he used for travel and said the words over them—his own version of consecration, he supposed. He didn't know if the words were necessary, but Mélisande had used them; he was afraid not to.

And yet. He had felt *something* here. The sense of something heavy, inert. Nothing resembling thought, let alone speech, thank God. By reflex, he crossed himself, then shook his head, rattled and irritated.

But *something*. Something immense, and very old. Did God have the voice of a stone? He was further unsettled by the thought. The stones there in the chalk mine, the noise they made . . . Was it after all God that he glimpsed, there in that space between?

A movement in the shadows banished all such thoughts in an instant. The frog! Rakoczy's heart clenched like a fist.

"Monsieur le Comte," said an amused, gravelly voice. "I see the years have been kind to you."

Raymond stepped into the starlight, smiling. The sight of him was disconcerting; Rakoczy had imagined this meeting for so long that the reality seemed oddly anticlimactic. Short, broad-shouldered, with long, loose hair that swept back from a massive forehead. A broad, almost lipless mouth. Raymond the frog.

"Why are you here?" Rakoczy blurted.

Mâitre Raymond's brows were black—surely they had been white, thirty years ago? One of them lifted in puzzlement.

"I was told that you were looking for me, Monsieur." He spread his hands, the gesture graceful. "I came!"

"Thank you," Rakoczy said dryly, beginning to regain some composure. "I meant, why are you in Paris?"

"Everyone has to be somewhere, don't they? They can't be in the same place." This should have sounded like badinage, but didn't. It sounded serious, like a statement of scientific principle, and Rakoczy found it unsettling.

"Did you come looking for me?" he asked boldly. He moved a little, trying to get a better look at the man. He was nearly sure that the frog looked *younger* than he had when last seen. Surely his flowing hair was darker, his step more elastic? A spurt of excitement bubbled in his chest.

"For you?" The frog looked amused for a moment, but then the look faded. "No. I'm looking for a lost daughter."

Rakoczy was surprised and disconcerted.

"Yours?"

"More or less." Raymond seemed uninterested in explaining further. He moved a little to one side, eyes narrowing as he sought to make out Rakoczy's face in the darkness. "You can hear stones, then, can you?"

"I . . . what?"

Raymond nodded at the façade of the cathedral. "They do speak. They move, too, but very slowly."

An icy chill shot up Rakoczy's spine, at thought of the grinning gargoyles perched high above him and the implication that one might at any moment choose to spread its silent wings and hurtle down upon him, teeth still bared in carnivorous hilarity. Despite himself, he looked up, over his shoulder.

"Not that fast." The note of amusement was back in the frog's voice. "You would never see them. It takes them millennia to move the slightest fraction of an inch—unless of course they are propelled or melted. But you don't want to see them do that, of course. Much too dangerous."

This kind of talk seemed frivolous, and Rakoczy was bothered by it, but for some reason, not irritated. Troubled, with a sense that there was something under it, something that he simultaneously wanted to know—and wanted very much to avoid knowing. The sensation was novel, and unpleasant.

He cast caution to the wind, and demanded boldly, "Why did you not kill me?"

Raymond grinned at him; he could see the flash of teeth, and felt yet another shock: he was sure—almost sure—that the frog had *had* no teeth when last seen.

"If I had wanted you dead, son, you wouldn't be here talking to me," he said. "I wanted you to be out of the way, that's all; you obliged me by taking the hint."

"And just why did you want me 'out of the way'?" Had he not needed to find out, Rakcozy would have taken offense at the man's tone.

The frog lifted one shoulder.

"You were something of a threat to the lady."

Sheer astonishment brought Rakoczy to his full height.

"The lady? You mean the woman—La Dame Blanche?"

"They did call her that." The frog seemed to find the notion amusing.

It was on the tip of Rakoczy's tongue to tell Raymond that La Dame Blanche still lived, but he himself hadn't lived as long as he had by blurting out everything he knew—and he didn't want Raymond thinking that he himself might be still a threat to her.

"What is the ultimate goal of an alchemist?" the frog said, very seriously.

"To transform matter," Rakoczy replied automatically.

The frog's face split in a broad amphibian grin.

"Exactly!" he said. And vanished.

He *had* vanished. No puffs of smoke, no illusionist's tricks, no smell of sulfur . . . the frog was simply gone. The square stretched empty under the starlit sky; the only thing that moved was a cat that darted mewing out of the shadows and brushed past Rakoczy's leg.

• • • •

Rakoczy was so shaken—and so excited—by the encounter that he wandered without knowing where he was going, crossed bridges without noticing, lost his way among the maze of twisting streets and *allées* on the Left Bank and did not reach his house 'till nearly dawn, footsore and exhausted, but with his mind buzzing with speculation.

Younger. He was sure of it. Raymond the frog was younger than he had been thirty years before. So it could be done—somehow.

He was convinced now that Raymond was indeed a traveler, like him. It had to be the travel: specifically, traveling forward in time. But how? He'd tried, more than once. To go back was dangerous, and the journey depleted you physically, but it was possible. If you had the right combinations of stones, you could even arrive at a certain time—more or less. But you needed also a focus; someone or something upon which to fix the mind; without that, you might still end up at some random point. And that, he thought, was the problem in going forward: it wasn't possible to focus on something you didn't know was there.

But Master Raymond had done it.

How, then, to persuade the frog to share the secret? Raymond did not seem to be hostile to him, but neither did he seem friendly; Rakoczy hardly would have expected him to be.

A lost daughter, the frog had said. And he had poisoned Rakoczy to remove him as a threat to the Fraser woman, La Dame Blanche. And the woman had glowed with blue light—because she had touched him, when handing him the cup? He couldn't remember. But she had glowed, he was positive.

So. If he was right, then she too was a traveler.

"Merveilleuse," he whispered. He had already been interested in the woman; now he was possessed. Not only did he want—need—to know what she knew; she was important to Raymond in some way, perhaps connected with the lost daughter—perhaps she was the lost daughter?

If he could but lay hands on her . . . He had made a few cautious inquiries, but no one in the Court of Miracles, or among his more respectable connections, had heard anything of Claire Fraser in the last thirty years.

Her husband had been political, had died, he thought, in Scotland. But if she had gone to Scotland with him, how did Raymond come to be searching for her in Paris?

These thoughts, and many more like them, ran round in his head like a pack of fleas, raising itching welts of curiosity.

The sky had begun to lighten, though the stars still burned dimly above the rooftops. The scent of fresh woodsmoke touched him, and a whiff of yeast: the boulangeries firing their ovens for the day's bread. A distant clop of hooves, as the farmers' wagons came in from the country, full of vegetables, fresh meat, eggs and flowers. The city was beginning to stir.

His own house, his own bed. His mind had slowed now, and the thought of sleep was overwhelming. There was a gray cat sitting on the stoop of his house, washing its paws.

"Bonjour," he said to it, and in his drowsy, exhausted state, almost expected it to answer him. It didn't, though, and when the butler opened the door it vanished, so quickly that he wondered whether it had ever really been there.

Worn out with constant walking, Michael slept like the dead these days, without dreams or motion, and woke when the sun came up. His valet, Robert, heard him stir and came in at once, one of the *femmes de chambre* on his heels with a bowl of coffee and some pastry.

He ate slowly, suffering himself to be brushed, shaved, and tenderly tidied into fresh linen. Robert kept up a soothing murmur of the sort of conversation that doesn't require response, and smiled encouragingly when presenting the mirror. Rather to Michael's surprise, the image in the mirror looked quite normal. Hair neatly clubbed—he wore his own, without powder—and suit modest in cut but of the highest quality. Robert hadn't asked him what he required, but had dressed him for an ordinary day of business.

He supposed that was all right. What, after all, did clothes matter? It wasn't as though there was a costume *de rigueur* for calling upon the sister of one's deceased wife, who had come uninvited into one's bed in the middle of the night.

He had spent the last two days trying to think of some way never to see or speak to Léonie again, but really, there was no help for it. He'd have to see her.

But what was he to say to her? he wondered, as he made his way through the streets toward the house where Léonie lived with an aged aunt, Eugenie Galantine. He wished he could talk the situation over with Sister Joan, but that wouldn't be appropriate, even were she available.

He'd hoped that walking would give him time to come up at least with a *point d'appui,* if not an entire statement of principle, but instead, he found himself obsessively counting the flagstones of the market as he crossed it, counting the bongs of the public horloge as it struck the hour of three, and—for lack of anything else to count—counting his own footsteps as he approached her door. *Six hundred and thirty-seven, six hundred and thirty-eight . . .*

As he turned into the street, though, he stopped counting abruptly. He stopped walking, too, for an instant—then began to run. Something was wrong at the house of Madame Galantine.

He pushed his way through the crowd of neighbors and vendors clustered near the steps, and seized the butler, whom he knew, by a sleeve.

"What?" he barked. "What's happened?" The butler, a tall, cadaverous man named Hubert, was plainly agitated, but settled a bit on seeing Michael.

"I don't know, sir," he said, though a sideways slide of his eyes made it clear that he did. "Mademoiselle Léonie . . . she's ill. The doctor . . ."

He could smell the blood. Not waiting for more, he pushed Hubert aside and sprinted up the stairs, calling for Madame Eugenie, Léonie's aunt.

Madame Eugenie popped out of a bedroom, her cap and wrapper neat in spite of the uproar.

"Monsieur Michel!" she said, blocking him from entering the room. "It's all right, but you must not go in."

"Yes, I must." His heart was thundering in his ears and his hands felt cold.

"You may *not*," she said firmly. "She's ill. It isn't proper."

"Proper? A young woman tries to make away with herself and you tell me it isn't *proper*?"

A maid appeared in the doorway, a basket piled with blood-stained linen in her arms, but the look of shock on Madame Eugenie's broad face was more striking.

"Make away with herself?" The old lady's mouth hung open for a moment, then snapped shut like a turtle's. "Why would you think such a thing?" She was regarding him with considerable suspicion. "And what are you doing here, for that matter? Who told you she was ill?"

A glimpse of a man in a dark robe, who must be the doctor, decided Michael that little was to be gained by engaging further with Madame Eugenie. He took her gently but firmly by the elbows, picked her up—she uttered a small shriek of surprise—and set her aside.

He went in and shut the bedroom door behind him.

"Who are you?" The doctor looked up, surprised. He was wiping out a freshly used bleeding-bowl, and his case lay open on the boudoir's settee. Léonie's bedroom must lie beyond; the door was open, and he caught a glimpse of the foot of a bed, but could not see the bed's inhabitant.

"It doesn't matter. How is she?"

The doctor eyed him narrowly, but after a moment, nodded.

"She will live. As for the child . . ." He made an equivocal motion of the hand. "I've done my best. She took a great deal of the—"

"The *child*?" The floor shifted under his feet, and the dream of two nights before flooded him, that queer sense of something half wrong, half familiar. It was the feeling of a small, hard swelling, pressed against his bum; that's what it was. Lillie had lost their child, but he remembered all too well the feeling of a woman's body in early pregnancy.

"It's yours? I beg your pardon, I shouldn't ask." The doctor put away his bowl and fleam, and shook out his black velvet turban.

"I want . . . I need to talk to her. Now."

The doctor opened his mouth in automatic protest, but then glanced thoughtfully over his shoulder.

"Well . . . you must be careful not to—" But Michael was already inside the bedroom, standing by the bed.

She was pale. They had always been pale, Lillie and Léonie, with the soft glow of cream and marble. This was the paleness of a frog's belly, of a rotting fish, blanched on the shore.

Her eyes were ringed with black, sunk in her head. They rested on his face, flat, expressionless, as still as the ringless hands that lay limp on the coverlet.

"Who?" he said quietly. "Charles?"

"Yes." Her voice was as dull as her eyes, and he wondered whether the doctor had drugged her.

"Was it his idea . . . to try to foist the child off on me? Or yours?"

She did look away then, and her throat moved.

"His." The eyes came back to him. "I didn't want to, Michel. Not—not that I find you disgusting, not that . . ."

"*Merci,*" he muttered, but she went on, disregarding him.

"You were Lillie's husband. I didn't envy her you," she said frankly, "but I envied what you had together. It couldn't be like that between you and me, and I didn't like betraying her. But"—her lips, already pale, compressed to invisibility—"I didn't have much choice."

He was obliged to admit that she hadn't. Charles couldn't marry her. Bearing an illegitimate child was not a fatal scandal in high Court circles, but the Galantines were of the emerging bourgeoisie, where respectability counted for almost as much as money. Finding herself pregnant, she would have had two alternatives: find a complaisant husband quickly, or . . . he tried not to see that one of her hands rested lightly across the slight swell of her stomach.

The child . . . He wondered what he would have done, had she come to him and told him the truth, asked him to marry her for the sake of the child. But she hadn't. And she wasn't asking now.

It would be best—or at least easiest—were she to lose the child. And she might yet.

"I couldn't wait, you see," she said, as though continuing a conversation. "I would have tried to find someone else, but I thought she knew. She'd tell you as soon as she could manage to see you. So I had to, you see, before you found out."

"She? Who? Tell me what?"

"The nun," Léonie said, and sighed deeply, as though losing interest. "She saw me in the market, and rushed up to me. She said she had to talk to you—that she had something important to tell you. I saw her look into my basket, though, and her face . . . thought she must realize . . ."

Her eyelids were fluttering, whether from drugs or fatigue, he wasn't sure. She smiled faintly, but not at him; she seemed to be looking at something a long way off.

"So funny," she murmured. "Charles said it would solve everything, that the Comte would pay him such a lot for her, it would solve everything. But how can you solve a baby?"

Michael jerked as though her words had stabbed him.

"What? Pay for whom?"

"The nun."

He grabbed her by the shoulders.

"Sister Joan? What do you mean, pay for her? What did Charles tell you?"

She made a whiny sound of protest. Michael wanted to shake her hard enough to break her neck, but forced himself to withdraw his hands. She settled into the pillow like a bladder losing air, flattening under the bed-clothes. Her eyes were closed, but he bent close, speaking directly into her ear.

"This Comte, Léonie. What is his name? Tell me his name."

A faint frown rippled the flesh of her brow, then passed.

"St. Germain," she murmured, scarcely loud enough to be heard. "The Comte St. Germain."

• • • •

Michael went instantly to Rosenwald, and by dint of badgering and the promise of extra payment, got him to finish the engraving on the chalice at once. Michael waited impatiently while it was done, and scarcely waiting for the cup and paten to be wrapped in brown paper, flung money to the goldsmith, and made for the convent des Anges, almost running.

With great difficulty, he restrained himself while making the presentation of the chalice, and with great humility, inquired whether he might ask the great favor of seeing Sister Gregory, that he might convey a message to her from her family in the Highlands. Sister Eustacia looked surprised and somewhat disapproving—postulants were not normally permitted visits—but after all . . . in view of Monsieur Murray's and Monsieur Fraser's great generosity to the convent . . . perhaps just a few moments, in the visitor's parlor, and in the presence of Sister herself. . . .

. . . .

He turned, and blinked once, his mouth opening a little. He looked shocked. Did she look so different in her robe and veil?

"It's me," Joan said, and tried to smile reassuringly. "I mean . . . still me."

His eyes fixed on her face, and he let out a deep breath and smiled, like she'd been lost and he'd found her again.

"Aye, so it is," he said softly. "I was afraid it was Sister Gregory. I mean, the . . . er . . ." He made a sketchy, awkward gesture indicating her gray robes and white postulant's veil.

"It's only clothes," she said, and put a hand to her chest, defensive.

"Well, no," he said, looking her over carefully, "I dinna think it is, quite. It's more like a soldier's uniform, no? Ye're doing your job when ye wear it, and everybody as sees it kens what ye are and knows what ye do."

Kens what I am. I suppose I should be pleased it doesn't show, she thought, a little wildly.

"Well . . . aye, I suppose." She fingered the rosary at her belt. She coughed. "In a way, at least."

Ye've got to tell him. It wasn't one of the voices, just the voice of her own conscience, but that was demanding enough. She could feel her heart beating, so hard that she thought the bumping must show through the front of her habit.

He smiled encouragingly at her.

"Léonie told me ye wanted to see me."

"Michael . . . can I tell ye something?" she blurted. He looked surprised.

"Well, of course ye can," he said. "Whyever not?"

"Whyever not," she said, half under her breath. She glanced over his shoulder, but Sister Eustacia was on the far side of the room, talking to a very young, frightened-looked French girl and her parents.

"Well, it's like this, see," she said, in a determined voice. "I hear voices." She stole a look at him, but he didn't look shocked. Not yet.

"In my head, I mean."

"Aye?" He looked cautious. "Um . . . what do they say, then?"

She realized she was holding her breath, and let a little of it out.

"Ah . . . different things. But they now and then tell me something's going to happen. More often, they tell me I should say thus-and-so to someone."

"Thus-and-so," he repeated attentively, watching her face. "What . . . *sort* of thus-and-so?"

"I wasna expecting the Spanish Inquisition," she said, a little testily. "Does it matter?"

His mouth twitched.

"Well, I dinna ken, now, do I?" he pointed out. "It might give a clue as to who's talkin' to ye, might it not? Or do ye already know that?"

"No, I don't," she admitted, and felt a sudden lessening of tension. "I-I was worrit—a bit—that it might be demons. But it doesna really . . . well, they dinna tell me *wicked* sorts of things. Just . . . more like, when something's going to happen to a person. And sometimes it's no a good thing . . . but sometimes it is. There was wee Annie MacLaren, her wi' a big belly by the third month, and by six, lookin' as though she'd burst, and she was frightened she was goin' to die come her time, like her ain mother did, wi' a babe too big to be born . . . I mean, *really* frightened, not just like all women are. And I met her by St. Ninian's spring one day, and one of the voices said to me, 'Tell her it will be as God wills and she will be delivered safely of a son.'"

"And ye did tell her that?"

"Yes. I didna say how I knew, but I must have sounded like I *did* know, because her poor face got bright all of a sudden, and she grabbed onto my hands and said, 'Oh! From your lips to God's ear!'"

"And was she safely delivered of a son?"

"Aye . . . and a daughter, too." Joan smiled, remembering the glow on Annie's face.

Michael glanced aside at Sister Eustacia, who was bidding farewell to the new postulant's family. The girl was white-faced and tears ran down her cheeks, but she clung to Sister Eustacia's sleeve as though it were a lifeline.

"I see," he said slowly, and looked back at Joan. "Is that why . . . is it the voices told ye to be a nun, then?"

She blinked, surprised by his apparent acceptance of what she'd told him, but more so by the question.

"Well . . . no. They never did. Ye'd think they would have, wouldn't ye?"

He smiled a little.

"Maybe so." He coughed, then looked up, a little shyly. "It's no my business, but what *did* make ye want to be a nun?"

She hesitated, but why not? She'd already told him the hardest bit.

"Because of the voices. I thought maybe . . . maybe I wouldna hear them in here. Or . . . if I still did, maybe somebody—a priest, maybe?—could tell me what they were, and what I should do about them."

Sister Eustacia was comforting the new girl, half-sunk on one knee to bring her big, homely, sweet face close to the girl's. Michael glanced at them, then back at Joan, one eyebrow raised.

"I'm guessing ye havena told anyone yet," he said. "Did ye reckon ye'd practice on me, first?"

Her own mouth twitched.

"Maybe." His eyes were dark, but had a sort of warmth to them, like they drew it from the heat of his hair. She looked down; her hands were pleating the edge of her blouse, which had come untucked. "It's no just that, though."

He made the sort of noise in his throat that meant, "Aye, then, go on." Why didn't French people do like that? she wondered. So much easier. But she pushed the thought aside; she'd made up her mind to tell him, and now was the time to do it.

"I told ye because . . . your friend," she blurted. "The one I met at your house. Monsieur Pépin," she added impatiently, when he looked blank.

"Aye?" He sounded as baffled as he looked.

"Aye. When I met him, a voice said, *Tell him not to do it.* And I didn't—I was frightened."

"I would ha' been a bit disturbed myself," he assured her. "It didna say what he oughtn't to do, though?"

She bit her lip.

"No, it didn't. And then, two days ago, I saw the man—the comte, Sister Mercy said he was, the Comte St. Germain—in the market, and the voice said the same thing, only a good bit more urgent. *Tell him not to do it. Tell him he must not do it!*"

"It did?"

"Aye, and it was verra firm about it. I mean . . . they are, usually. It's no just an opinion, take it or leave it. But this one truly meant it." She spread her hands, helpless to explain the feeling of dread and urgency.

Michael's thick red eyebrows drew together.

"D'ye think it's the same thing they're not supposed to do?" He sounded startled. "I didna ken they even knew each other."

"Well, I don't know, now, do I?" she said, a little exasperated. "The voices didn't say. But I saw that the man on the ship was going to die, and I didna say anything, because I couldn't think what to say. And then he *did* die, and maybe he wouldn't, if I'd spoken . . . so I—well, I thought I'd best say something to someone, and at least ye ken Monsieur Pépin."

He thought about that for a moment, then nodded uncertainly.

"Aye. All right. I'll . . . well, I dinna ken what to do about it either, to be honest. But I'll talk to them both and I'll have that in my mind, so maybe I'll think of something. D'ye want me to tell them, 'Don't do it'?"

She grimaced, and looked at Sister Eustacia. There wasn't much time.

"I already told the Comte. Just . . . maybe. If ye think it might help. Now—" Her hand darted under her apron and she passed him the slip of paper, fast. "We're only allowed to write to our families twice a year," she said, lowering her voice. "But I wanted Mam to know I was all right. Could ye see she gets that, please? And—and maybe tell her a bit, yourself, that I'm weel and—and happy. Tell her I'm happy," she repeated, more firmly.

Sister Eustacia had come back, and was standing by the door, emanating an intent to come and tell them it was time for Michael to leave.

"I will," he said. He couldn't touch her, he knew that, so bowed instead, and bowed deeply to Sister Eustacia, who came toward them, looking benevolent.

"I'll come to Mass at the chapel on Sundays, how's that?" he said rapidly. "If I've a letter from your mam, or ye have to speak to me, gie me a wee roll of the eyes or something—I'll figure something out."

    . . . .

Twenty-four hours later, Sister Joan-Gregory, postulant of Our Lady Queen of Angels, regarded the bum of a large cow. The cow in question was named Mirabeau, and was of uncertain temper, as evidenced by the nervously lashing tail.

"She's kicked three of us this week," said Sister Anne-Joseph, eyeing the cow resentfully. "*And* spilt the milk twice. Sister Jeanne-Marie was most upset."

"Well, we canna have that now, can we?" Joan murmured in English. "*N' inquiétez-vous pas*," she added in French, hoping that was at least somewhat grammatical. "Let me do it."

"Better you than me," Sister Anne-Joseph said, crossing herself, and vanished before Sister Joan might think better of the offer.

A week spent working in the cowshed was intended as punishment for her flighty behavior in the marketplace, but Joan was grateful for it. There was nothing better for steadying the nerves than cows.

Granted, the convent's cows were not quite like her mother's sweet-tempered, shaggy red Hieland coos, but if you came right down to it, a cow was a cow, and even a French-speaking wee besom like the present Mirabeau was no match for Joan MacKimmie, who'd driven kine to and from the shielings for years, and fed her mother's kine in the byre beside the house with sweet hay and the leavings from supper.

With that in mind, she circled Mirabeau thoughtfully, eyeing the steadily champing jaws and the long slick of blackish-green drool that hung down from slack pink lips. She nodded once, slipped out of the cowshed, and made her way down the allee behind it, picking what she could find. Mirabeau, presented with a bouquet of fresh grasses, tiny daisies, and—delicacy of all delicacies—fresh sorrel, bulged her eyes half out of her head, opened her massive jaw, and inhaled the sweet stuff. The ominous tail ceased its lashing and the massive creature stood as if turned to stone, aside from the ecstatically grinding jaws.

Joan sighed in satisfaction, sat down, and, resting her head on Mirabeau's monstrous flank, got down to business. Her mind, released, took up the next worry of the day.

Had Michael spoken to his friend Pépin? And if so, had he told him what she'd said, or just asked whether he kent the Comte St. Germain? Because if *Tell him not to do it* referred to the same thing, then plainly the two men must be acquent with each other.

She had got thus far in her own ruminations, when Mirabeau's tail began to switch again. She hurriedly stripped the last of the milk from Mirabeau's teats and snatched the bucket out of the way, standing up in a hurry. Then she saw what had disturbed the cow.

The man in the dove-gray coat was standing in the door to the shed, watching her. She hadn't noticed before, in the market, but he had a handsome dark face, though rather hard about the eyes, and with a chin that brooked no opposition. He smiled pleasantly at her, though, and bowed.

"Mademoiselle. I must ask you, please, to come with me."

• • • •

Michael was in the warehouse, stripped to his shirtsleeves and sweating in the hot, wine-heady atmosphere, when Jared appeared, looking disturbed.

"What is it, cousin?" Michael wiped his face on a towel, leaving black streaks; the crew were clearing the racks on the southeast wall, and there were years of filth and cobwebs behind the most ancient casks.

"Ye haven't got that wee nun in your bed, have ye, Michael?" Jared lifted a beetling gray brow at him.

"Have I what?"

"I've just had a message from the Mother Superior of the Convent des Anges, saying that one Sister Gregory appears to have been abducted from their cowshed, and wanting to know whether you might possibly have anything to do with the matter."

Michael stared at his cousin for a moment, unable to take this in.

"Abducted?" he said stupidly. "Who would be kidnapping a nun? What for?"

"Well, now, there ye have me." Jared was carrying Michael's coat over his arm, and at this point, handed it to him. "But maybe best ye go to the convent and find out."

• • • •

"Forgive me, Mother," Michael said carefully. Mother Hildegarde looked fragile and transparent, as though a breath would make her disintegrate. "Did ye think . . . is it possible that Sister J . . . Sister Gregory might have . . . left of her own accord?"

The old nun gave him a look that revised his opinion of her state of health instantly.

"We did," she said. "It happens. However—" she raised one sticklike finger. "One: there were signs of a considerable struggle in the cowshed. A full bucket of milk not merely spilt, but apparently *thrown* at something, the manger overturned, the door left open and two of the cows escaped into the herb garden." Another finger. "Two: Had Sister Gregory experienced doubt regarding her vocation, she was quite free to leave the convent after speaking with me, and she knew that."

One more finger, and the old nun's black eyes bored into his. "And three: Had she felt it necessary to leave suddenly and without informing us, where would she go? To you, Monsieur Murray. She knows no one else in Paris, does she?"

"I . . . well, no, not really." He was flustered, almost stammering, confusion and a burgeoning alarm for Joan making it difficult to think.

"But you have not seen her since you brought us the chalice and paten—and I thank you and your cousin with the deepest sentiments of gratitude, Monsieur—that would be two days ago?"

"No." He shook his head, trying to clear it. "No, Mother."

Mother Hildegarde nodded, her lips nearly invisible, pressed together amid the lines of her face.

"Did she say anything to you on that occasion? Anything that might assist us in discovering her?"

"I . . . well . . ." Jesus, should he tell her what Joan had said about the voices she heard? It couldn't have anything to do with this, surely, and it wasna his secret to share. On the other hand, Joan *had* said she meant to tell Mother Hildegarde about them . . .

"You'd better tell me, my son." The Mother Superior's voice was somewhere between resignation and command. "I see she told you *something*."

"Well, she did, then, Mother," he said, rubbing a hand over his face in distraction. "But I canna see how it has anything to do—she hears voices," he blurted, seeing Mother Hildegarde's eyes narrow dangerously.

The eyes went round.

"She what?"

"Voices," he said helplessly. "They come and say things to her. She thinks maybe they're angels, but she doesn't know. And she can see when folk are going to die. Sometimes," he added dubiously. "I don't know whether she can always say."

"Par le sang sacré de Jésus-Christ," the old nun said, sitting up straight as an oak sapling. "Why did she not . . . well, never mind about that. Does anyone else know this?"

He shook his head.

"She was afraid to tell anyone. That's why—well, one reason why—she came to the convent. She thought you might believe her."

"I might," Mother Hildegarde said dryly. She shook her head rapidly, making her veil flap. *"Nom de nom!* Why did her mother not tell me this?"

"Her mother?" Michael said stupidly.

"Yes! She brought me a letter from her mother, very kind, asking after my health and recommending Joan to me—but surely her mother would have known!"

"I don't think she . . . wait." He remembered Joan fishing out the carefully folded note from her pocket. "The letter she brought—it was from Claire Fraser. That's the one you mean?"

"Of course!"

He took a deep breath, a dozen disconnected pieces falling suddenly into a pattern. He cleared his throat, and raised a tentative finger.

"One, Mother: Claire Fraser is the wife of Joan's stepfather. But she's not Joan's mother."

The sharp black eyes blinked once.

"And two: My cousin Jared tells me that Claire Fraser was known as a—a White Lady, when she lived in Paris many years ago."

Mother Hildegarde clicked her tongue angrily.

"She was no such thing. Stuff! But it is true that there was a common rumor to that effect," she admitted grudgingly. She drummed her fingers on the desk; they were knobbed with age, but surprisingly nimble, and he remembered that Mother Hildegarde had been a famous musician in her youth.

"Mother . . ."

"Yes?"

"I don't know if it has anything to do . . . Do you know of a man called the Comte St. Germain?"

The old nun was already the color of parchment; at this, she went white as bone and her fingers gripped the edge of the desk.

"I do," she said. "Tell me—and quickly—what he has to do with Sister Gregory."

. . . .

Joan gave the very solid door one last kick, for appearances' sake, then turned and collapsed with her back against it, panting. The room was huge, extending across the entire top floor of the house, though pillars and joists here and there showed where walls had been knocked down. It smelled peculiar, and looked even more peculiar.

"A Dhia, cuidich mi," she whispered to herself, reverting to the Gaelic in her agitation. There was a very fancy bed in one corner, piled with feather pillows and bolsters, with writhing corner-posts and heavy swags and curtains of cloth embroidered in what looked like gold and silver thread. Did the Comte—he'd told her his name, or at least his title, when she'd asked—haul young women up here for wicked ends on a regular basis? For surely he hadn't set up this establishment solely in anticipation of her arrival . . . the area near the bed was equipped with all kinds of solid, shiny furniture with marble tops and alarming gilt feet that looked like they'd come off some kind of beast or bird with great curving claws.

He'd told her in the most matter-of-fact way that he was a sorcerer, too, and not to touch anything. She crossed herself, and averted her gaze from the table with the nastiest-looking feet; maybe he'd charmed the furniture, and it came to life and walked round after dark. The thought made her move hastily off to the farther end of the room, rosary clutched tight in one hand.

This side of the room was scarcely less alarming, but at least it didn't look as though any of the big colored glass balls and jars and tubes could move on their own. It *was* where the worst smells were coming from, though; something that smelled like burnt hair and treacle, and something else very sharp that curled the hairs in your nose, like it did when someone dug out a jakes for the saltpeter. But there *was* a window near the long table where all this sinister stuff was laid out, and she went to this at once.

The big river—the Seine, Michael had called it—was right there, and the sight of boats and people made her feel a bit steadier. She put a hand on the table to lean closer, but set it on something sticky and jerked it back. She swallowed, and leaned in more gingerly. The window was barred on the inside. Glancing round, she saw that all the others were, too.

What in the name of the Blessed Virgin did that man expect would try to get in? Gooseflesh raced right up the curve of her spine and spread down her arms, her imagination instantly conjuring a vision of flying demons hovering over the street in the night, beating leathery wings against the window. *Or—dear Lord in heaven!—was it to keep the furniture from getting out?*

There was a fairly normal-looking stool; she sank down on this, and closing her eyes, prayed with great fervor. After a bit, she remembered to breathe, and after a further bit, began to be able to think again, shuddering only occasionally.

He hadn't exactly threatened her. Nor had he hurt her, really; just put a hand over her mouth and his other arm round her body, and pulled her along, then boosted her into his coach with a shockingly familiar hand under her bottom, though it hadn't been done with any sense that he was wanting to interfere with her.

In the coach, he'd introduced himself, apologized briefly for the inconvenience—*inconvenience? The cheek of him*—and then had grasped both her hands in his, staring intently into her face as he clasped them tighter and tighter. He'd raised her hands to his face, so close she'd thought he meant to smell them or kiss them, but then had let go, his brow deeply furrowed.

He'd ignored all her questions and her insistence upon being returned to the convent. In fact, he almost seemed to forget she was there for a moment, leaving her huddled back in the corner of the seat while he thought intently about something, lips pursing in and out. She'd thought of jumping out—had almost got up her nerve to reach for the door handle, though the coach was rattling on at such a pace she was almost sure to be killed—but then his eyes had fastened on her again, pinning her to the seat as though he'd stabbed her through the chest with a knitting-needle.

"The frog," he'd said, intent. "You know the frog, don't you?"

"Any number of them," she'd said, thinking that if he was mad, she'd best humor him. "Green ones, mostly."

His nostrils had flared in sudden anger, and she'd shrunk back into the seat. But then he had snorted, and relapsed into a sort of brooding stare, emerging from this only to say, "The rats didn't all die," in a somewhat accusatory tone, as though it were her fault.

Her mouth was so dry that she could barely speak, but had managed to say, "Oh? Did ye try rat's-bane, then?" But she'd spoken in English, too rattled to summon any French, and he seemed not to take note. And then he had lugged her up here, told her briefly that she wouldn't be hurt, added the bit about being a sorcerer in a very offhand sort of a way, and locked her in!

She was terrified, and indignant, too. But now she'd calmed down a wee bit.

She'd believed him when he said he meant her no harm. He hadn't threatened her or tried to frighten her. But if that was true . . . what could he want of her?

He likely wants to know what ye meant by rushing up to him in the market and telling him not to do it, her common sense—lamentably absent to this point—remarked.

"Oh," she said aloud. That made some sense. Naturally, he'd be curious about that. But if so, why hadn't he asked her, instead of dragging her off? And what had he gone off to do now?

CATEGORY · ALCHEMICAL EXPLORATIONS

He had something in mind, and she didn't want to think what.

She got up again, and explored the room, thinking anyway. She couldn't tell him any more than she had, though, that was the thing. Would he believe her, about the voices? Even if so, he'd try to find out more, and there wasn't any more to find out. What then?

Don't wait about to see, advised her common sense.

Having already come to this conclusion, she didn't bother replying. She'd found a heavy marble mortar and pestle; that might do. Wrapping the mortar in her apron, she went to the window that overlooked the street. She'd break the glass, then shriek 'til she got someone's attention. Even so high up, she thought someone would hear. Pity it was a quiet street. But—

She stiffened like a bird-dog. A coach was stopped outside one of the houses opposite, and Michael Murray was getting out of it! He was just putting on his hat—no mistaking that flaming red hair.

"Michael!" she shouted at the top of her lungs. But he didn't look up; the sound wouldn't pierce glass. She swung the cloth-wrapped mortar at the window, but it bounced off the bars with a ringing *clang.* She took a deep breath and a better aim; this time, she hit one of the panes and cracked it. Encouraged, she tried again, with all the strength of muscular arms and shoulders, and was rewarded with a small crash, a shower of glass, and a rush of mud-scented air from the river.

"Michael!" But he had disappeared. A servant's face showed briefly in the open door of the house opposite, then vanished as the door closed. Through a red haze of frustration, she noticed the swag of black crepe hanging from the knob. Who was dead?

. . . .

Charles's wife, Berthe, was in the small parlor, surrounded by a huddle of women. All of them turned to see who had come, many of them lifting their handkerchiefs automatically in preparation for a fresh outbreak of tears. All of them blinked at Michael, then turned to Berthe, as though for an explanation.

Berthe's eyes were red, but dry. She looked as though she had been dried in an oven, all the moisture and color sucked out of her, her face paper-white and drawn tight over her bones. She too looked at Michael, but without much interest. He thought she was too much shocked for anything to matter much. He knew how she felt.

"Monsieur Murray," she said tonelessly, as he bowed over her hand. "How kind of you to call."

"I . . . offer my condolences, Madame, mine and my cousin's. I hadn't . . . heard. Of your grievous loss." He was almost stuttering, trying to grasp the reality of the situation. What the devil had happened to Charles?

Berthe's mouth twisted.

“Grievous loss,” she repeated. “Yes. Thank you.” Then her dull self-absorption cracked a little and she looked at him more sharply. “You hadn’t heard. You mean—you didn’t know? You came to *see* Charles?”

“Er . . . yes, Madame,” he said awkwardly. A couple of the women gasped, but Berthe was already on her feet.

“Well, you might as well see him, then,” she said, and walked out of the room, leaving him with no choice but to follow her.

“They’ve cleaned him up,” she remarked, opening the door to the large parlor across the hall. She might have been talking about a messy domestic incident in the kitchen.

Michael thought it must in fact have been very messy. Charles lay on the large dining-table, this adorned with a cloth and wreaths of greenery and flowers. A woman clad in gray was sitting by the table, weaving more wreaths from a basket of leaves and grasses; she glanced up, her eyes going from Berthe to Michael and back.

“Leave,” said Berthe with a flip of the hand, and the woman got up at once and went out. Michael saw that she’d been making a wreath of laurel leaves, and had the sudden absurd thought that she meant to crown Charles with it, in the manner of a Greek hero.

“He cut his throat,” Berthe said. “The coward.” She spoke with an eerie calmness, and Michael wondered what might happen when the shock that surrounded her began to dissipate.

He made a respectful sort of noise in his throat and, touching her arm gently, went past her to look down at his friend.

Don’t do it. That’s what Joan said the voices had told her. Was this what they’d meant?

The dead man didn’t look peaceful. There were lines of stress in his countenance that hadn’t yet smoothed out, and he appeared to be frowning. The undertaker’s people had cleaned the body and dressed him in a slightly worn suit of dark blue; Michael thought that it was probably the only thing he’d owned that was in any way appropriate in which to appear dead, and suddenly missed his friend’s frivolity with a surge that brought unexpected tears to his eyes.

Don’t do it. He hadn’t come in time. *If I’d come right away, when she told me . . . would it have stopped him?*

He could smell the blood, a rusty, sickly smell that seeped through the freshness of the flowers and leaves. The undertaker had tied a white neckcloth for Charles; he’d used an old-fashioned knot, nothing that Charles himself would have worn for a moment. The black stitches showed above it, though, the wound harsh against the dead man’s livid skin.

Michael’s own shock was beginning to fray, and stabs of guilt and anger poked through it like needles.

"Coward?" he said softly. He didn't mean it as a question, but it seemed more courteous to say it that way. Berthe snorted and looking up, he met the full charge of her eyes. No, not shocked any longer.

"You'd know, wouldn't you," she said, and it wasn't at all a question, the way she said it. "You knew about your slut of a sister-in-law, didn't you? And Babette?" Her lips curled away from the name. "His other mistress?"

"I— No. I mean . . . Léonie told me yesterday. That was why I came to talk to Charles." Well, he would certainly have mentioned Léonie. And he wasn't going anywhere near the mention of Babette, whom he'd known about for quite some time. But Jesus, what did the woman think he could have done about it?

"Coward," she said, looking down at Charles's body with contempt. "He made a mess of everything—*everything!*—and then couldn't deal with it, so he runs off and leaves me alone, with children, penniless!"

Don't do it.

Michael looked to see if this was an exaggeration, but it wasn't. She was burning now, but with fear as much as anger, her frozen calm quite vanished.

"The . . . house . . . ?" he began, with a rather vague wave around the expensive, stylish room. He knew it was her family house; she'd brought it to the marriage.

She snorted.

"He lost it in a card game last week," she said bitterly. "If I'm lucky, the new owner will let me bury him before we have to leave."

"Ah." The mention of card games jolted him back to an awareness of his reason for coming here. "I wonder, Madame, do you know an acquaintance of Charles's—the Comte St. Germain?" It was crude, but he hadn't time to think of a graceful way to come to it.

Berthe blinked, nonplussed.

"The Comte? Why do you want to know about *him?*" Her expression sharpened into eagerness. "Do you think he owes Charles money?"

"I don't know, but I'll certainly find out for you," Michael promised her. "If you can tell me where to find Monsieur le Comte."

She didn't laugh, but her mouth quirked in what might, in another mood, have been humor.

"He lives across the street." She pointed toward the window. "In that big pile of— Where are you going?"

But Michael was already through the door and into the hallway, boot-heels clattering on the parquet in his haste.

• • • •

There were footsteps coming up the stairs; Joan started away from the window, but then craned back, desperately willing the door across the street to open and let Michael out. What was he *doing* there?

That door didn't open, but a key rattled in the lock of the door to the room. In desperation, she tore the rosary from her belt and pushed it through the hole in the window, then dashed across the room and threw herself into one of the repulsive chairs.

It was the Comte. He glanced round, worried for an instant, and then his face relaxed when he saw her. He came toward her, holding out his hand.

"I'm sorry to have kept you waiting, mademoiselle," he said, very courtly. "Come, please. I have something to show you."

"I don't want to see it." She stiffened a little and tucked her feet under her, to make it harder for him to pick her up. If she could just delay him until Michael came out! But he might well not see her rosary, even if he did—or know it was hers. Why should he? All nun's rosaries looked the same!

She strained her ears, hoping to hear the sounds of departure on the other side of the street—she'd scream her lungs out. In fact . . .

The Comte sighed a little, but bent and took her by the elbows, lifting her straight up, her knees still absurdly bent. He was really very strong. She put her feet down, and there she was, her hand tucked into the crook of his elbow, being led across the room toward the door, docile as a cow on its way to be milked! She made her mind up in an instant, yanked free, and ran to the smashed window.

"HELP!" She bellowed through the broken pane. "Help me, help me! *Au secours,* I mean! *AU SECOU—*" The Comte's hand clapped across her mouth, and he said something in French that she was sure must be bad language. He scooped her up, so fast that the wind was knocked out of her, and had her through the door before she could make another sound.

· · · ·

Michael didn't pause for hat or cloak, but burst into the street, so fast that his driver started out of a doze and the horses jerked and neighed in pro-test. He didn't pause for that, either, but shot across the cobbles and pounded on the door of the house, a big bronze-coated affair that boomed under his fists.

It couldn't have been very long, but seemed an eternity. He fumed, pounded again, and, pausing for breath, caught sight of the rosary on the pavement. He ran to catch it up, scratched his hand, and saw that the ro-sary lay in a scatter of glass fragments. At once he looked up, searching, and saw the broken window just as the big door opened.

He sprang at the butler like a wildcat, seizing him by the arms.

"Where is she? Where, damn you?"

"She? But there is no she, Monsieur . . . Monsieur le Comte lives quite alone. You—"

"Where is Monsieur le Comte?" Michael's sense of urgency was so great he felt that he might strike the man. The man apparently felt he might, too, because he turned pale and, wrenching himself loose, fled into the depths of the house. With no more than an instant's hesitation, Michael pursued him.

The butler, his feet fueled by fear, flew down the hall, Michael in grim pursuit. The man burst through the door into the kitchen; Michael was dimly aware of the shocked faces of cooks and maids, and then they were out into the kitchen-garden. The butler slowed for an instant going down the steps, and Michael launched himself at the man, knocking him flat.

They rolled together on the graveled path, then Michael got on top of the smaller man, seized him by the shirtfront and, shaking him, shouted, "WHERE IS HE?"

Thoroughly undone, the butler covered his face with one arm and pointed blindly toward a gate in the wall.

Michael leapt off the supine body and ran. He could hear the rumble of coach-wheels, the rattle of hooves— He flung open the gate in time to see the back of a coach rattling down the allee, and a gaping servant, paused in the act of sliding to the doors of a carriage house. He ran, but it was clear that he'd never catch the coach on foot.

"JOAN!" he bellowed after the vanishing equipage. "I'm coming!"

He didn't waste time in questioning the servant, but ran back, pushing his way through the maids and footmen gathered round the cowering butler, and burst out of the house, startling his own coachman afresh.

"That way!" he shouted, pointing toward the distant conjunction of the Rue St. Andre and the allee, where the Comte's coach was just emerging. "Follow that coach! *Vite!!*"

• • • •

"Vite!" the Comte urged his coachman on, then sank back, letting fall the hatch in the roof. The light was fading; his errand had taken longer than he'd expected, and he wanted to be out of the city before night fell. The city streets were dangerous at night.

His captive was staring at him, her eyes enormous in the dim light. She'd lost her postulant's veil and her dark hair was loose on her shoulders. She looked charming, but very scared. He reached into the bag on the floor and pulled out a flask of brandy.

"Have a little of this, *chérie*." He removed the cork and handed it to her. She took it, but looked uncertain what to do with it, nose wrinkling at the hot smell.

"Really," he assured her. "It will make you feel better."

"That's what they all say," she said in her slow, awkward French.

"All of whom?" he asked, startled.

"The Old Ones. I don't know what you call them in French, exactly. The folk that live in the hills . . . *souterrain?*" she added doubtfully. "Underground?"

"Underground? And they give you brandy?" He smiled at her, but his heart gave a sudden thump of excitement. Perhaps she *was*. He'd doubted his instincts, when his touch failed to kindle her, but clearly she was *something*.

"They give you food and drink," she said, putting the flask down between the squab and the wall. "But if you take any, you lose time."

The spurt of excitement came again, stronger.

"Lose time?" he repeated, encouraging. "How do you mean?"

She struggled to find words, smooth brow furrowed with the effort.

"They—you . . . one who is enchanted by them . . . he, it? . . . no, he—goes into the hill and there's music and feasting and dancing. But in the morning, when he goes . . . back . . . it's two hundred years later than it was when he went to feast with the—the Folk. Everybody he knew has turned to dust."

"How interesting!" he said. It was. He also wondered, with a fresh spasm of excitement, whether the old paintings, the ones far back in the bowels of the chalk mine, might have been made by these Folk, whoever they were.

She observed him narrowly, apparently for an indication that he was a faery. He smiled at her, though his heart was now thumping audibly in his ears. *Two hundred years!* For that was what Mélisande—*"Damn her,"* he thought briefly, with a pang at the reminder of Madeleine—had told him was the usual period, when one traveled through stone. It could be changed by use of gemstones, or of blood, she said, but that was the usual. And it had been, the first time he went back.

"Don't worry," he said to the girl, hoping to reassure her. "I only want you to look at something. Then I'll take you back to the convent—assuming that you still want to go there?" He lifted an eyebrow, half teasing. It really wasn't his intent to frighten her, though he already had, and he feared that more fright was unavoidable. He wondered just what she might do, when she realized that he was in fact planning to take her underground.

• • • •

Michael knelt on the seat, his head out the window of the coach, urging it on by force of will and muscle. It was nearly full dark, and the Comte's coach was visible only as a distantly moving blot. They were out of the city, though; there were no other large vehicles on the road, nor likely to be—and there were very few turnings where such a large equipage might leave the main road.

The wind blew in his face, tugging strands of hair loose so they beat about his face. It blew the faint scent of decay, too—they'd pass the cemetery in a few minutes.

He wished passionately that he'd thought to bring a pistol, a smallsword—anything! But there was nothing in the coach with him, and he had nothing on his person save his clothes and what was in his pockets: this consisting, after a hasty inventory, of a handful of coins, a used handkerchief—the one Joan had given back to him, in fact, and he crumpled it tightly in one hand—a tinderbox, a mangled paper spill, a stub of sealing-wax, and a small stone he'd picked up in the street, pinkish with a yellow stripe—perhaps he could improvise a sling with the handkerchief, he thought wildly, and paste the Comte in the forehead with the stone, *a la* David and Goliath. And then cut off the Comte's head with the penknife he discovered in his breast pocket, he supposed.

Joan's rosary was also in that pocket; he took it out and wound it round his left hand, holding the beads for comfort—he was too distracted to pray, beyond the words he repeated silently over and over, hardly noticing what he said.

"Let me find her in time!"

· · · ·

"Tell me," the Comte asked curiously, "why did you speak to me in the market that day?"

"I wish I hadn't," Joan replied briefly. She didn't trust him an inch; still less, since he'd offered her the brandy. It hadn't struck her before that he really *might* be one of the Auld Ones. They could walk about, looking just like people. Her own mother had been convinced for years—and even some of the Murrays thought so—that Da's wife Claire was one. She herself wasn't sure; Claire had been kind to her, but no one said the Folk *couldn't* be kind if they wanted to.

Da's wife. A sudden thought paralyzed her; the memory of her first meeting with Mother Hildegarde, when she'd given the Mother Superior Claire's letter. She'd said, *"ma mere,"* unable to think of a word that might mean "stepmother." It hadn't seemed to matter; why should anyone care?

"Claire Fraser," she said aloud, watching the Comte carefully. "Do you know that name?"

His eyes widened, showing white in the gloaming. Oh, aye, he kent her, all right!

"I do," he said, leaning forward. "Your mother, is she not?"

"No!" Joan said, with great force, and repeated it in French, several times for emphasis. "No, she's not!"

But she observed, with a sinking heart, that her force had been misplaced. He didn't believe her; she could tell by the eagerness in his face. He thought she was lying to put him off. *Jesus, Lord, deliver me . . .*

"I told you what I did in the market because the voices told me to!" she blurted, desperate for anything that might distract him from the horrifying notion that she was one of the Folk. Though if *he* was one, her common sense pointed out, he ought to be able to recognize her. Oh, Jesus, Lamb of God . . . that's what he'd been trying to do, holding her hands so tight and staring into her face.

"Voices?" he said, looking rather blank. "What voices?"

"The ones in my head," she said, heaving an internal sigh of exasperation. "They tell me things now and then. About other people, I mean. You know—" she went on, encouraging him, "I'm a—a . . ." St. Jerome on a bannock, what was the *word*?!? ". . . someone who sees the future," she ended weakly. "Er . . . some of it. Sometimes. Not always."

The Comte was rubbing a finger over his upper lip; she didn't know if he was expressing doubt or trying not to laugh, but either way, it made her angry.

"So one of them told me to tell ye that, and I did!" she said, lapsing into Scots. "I dinna ken what it is ye're no supposed to do, but I'd advise ye not to do it!"

It occurred to her belatedly that perhaps killing her was the thing he wasn't supposed to do, and she was about to put this notion to him, but by the time she had disentangled enough grammar to have a go at it, the coach was slowing, bumping from side to side as it turned off the main road. A sickly smell seeped into the air, and she sat up straight, her heart in her throat.

"Mary, Joseph, and Bride," she said, her voice no more than a squeak. "Where *are* we?"

. . . .

Michael leapt from the coach almost before it had stopped moving. He daren't let them get too far ahead of him; his driver had nearly missed the turning, as it was, and the Comte's coach had come to a halt minutes before his own reached it.

"Talk to the other driver," he shouted at his own, half-visible on the box. "Find out why the Comte has come here! Find out what he's doing!"

Nothing good. He was sure of that. Though he couldn't imagine why anyone would kidnap a nun and drag her out of Paris in the dark, only to stop at the edge of a public cemetery. Unless . . . half-heard rumors of depraved men who murdered and dismembered their victims, even those who *ate* . . . his wame rose and he nearly vomited, but it wasn't possible to vomit and run at the same time, and he could see a pale splotch on the darkness that he thought—he hoped, he feared—must be Joan.

Suddenly, the night burst into flower. A huge puff of green fire bloomed in the darkness, and by its eerie glow, he saw her clearly, her hair flying in the wind.

He opened his mouth to shout, to call out to her, but he had no breath, and before he could recover it, she vanished into the ground, the Comte following her, torch in hand.

He reached the shaft moments later, and below, he saw the faintest green glow, just vanishing down a tunnel. Without an instant's hesitation, he flung himself down the ladder.

· · · ·

"Do you hear anything?" the Comte kept asking her, as they stumbled along the white-walled tunnels, he grasping her so hard by the arm that he'd surely leave bruises on her skin.

"No," she gasped. "What . . . am I listening for?"

He merely shook his head in a displeased way, but more as though he were listening for something himself than because he was angry with her for not hearing it.

She had some hopes that he'd meant what he said, and would take her back. He did mean to go back himself; he'd lit several torches and left them burning along their way. So he wasn't about to disappear into the hill altogether, taking her with him to the lighted ballroom where people danced all night with the Fine Folk, unaware that their own world slipped past beyond the stones of the hill.

The Comte stopped abruptly, hand squeezing harder round her arm.

"Be still," he said, very quietly, though she wasn't making any noise. "Listen."

She listened as hard as possible—and thought she did hear something. What she thought she heard, though, was footsteps, far in the distance. Behind them. Her heart seized up for a moment.

"What—what do *you* hear?" she thought of asking. He glanced down at her, but not as though he really saw her.

"Them," he said. "The stones. They make a buzzing sound, most of the time. If it's close to a fire-feast or a sun-feast, though, they begin to sing."

"Do they?" she said faintly. He was hearing *something*, and evidently it wasn't the footsteps she'd heard. They'd stopped now, as though whoever followed was waiting, maybe stealing along, one step at a time, careful now to make no sound.

"Yes," he said, and his face was intent. He looked at her sharply again, and this time, he saw her.

"You don't hear them," he said, with certainty, and she shook her head.

"No," she whispered. Her lips felt stiff. "I don't—I don't hear anything."

He pressed his lips tight together, but after a moment, lifted his chin, gesturing toward another tunnel, where there seemed to be something painted on the chalk.

He paused there to light another torch—this one burned a brilliant yellow, and stank of sulfur—and she saw by its light the wavering shape of the Virgin and Child. Her heart lifted at the sight, for surely faeries would have no such thing in their lair.

"Come," he said, and now took her by the hand. His own was cold.

· · · ·

Michael caught a glimpse of them as they moved into a side tunnel. The Comte had lit another torch, a red one this time—how did he do that?—and it was easy to follow its glow.

How far down in the bowels of the earth were they? He had long since lost track of the turnings, though he might be able to get back by following the torches—assuming they hadn't all burned out.

He still had no plan in mind, other than to follow them until they stopped. Then he'd make himself known, and . . . well, take Joan away, by whatever means proved necessary.

Swallowing hard, rosary still wrapped around his left hand and penknife in his right, he stepped into the shadows.

· · · ·

The chamber was round, and quite large. Big enough that the torchlight didn't reach all the edges, but it lit the pentagram inscribed into the floor in the center.

The noise was making Rakoczy's bones ache, and often as he had heard it, it never failed to make his heart race and his hands sweat. He let go of the nun's hand for a moment, to wipe his palm on the skirts of his coat, not wanting to disgust her. She looked scared, but not terrified, and if she heard it, surely she—. Her eyes widened suddenly.

"Who's *that?*" she said.

He whirled to see Raymond, standing tranquilly in the center of the pentagram.

"*Bon soir, mademoiselle,*" the frog said, bowing politely.

"Ah . . . *bon soir,*" the girl replied faintly.

"What the devil are you doing here?" Rakoczy interposed his body between Raymond and the nun.

"Very likely the same thing you are," the frog replied. "Might you introduce your *petite amie,* sir?"

Shock, anger, and sheer confusion robbed Rakoczy of speech for a moment. What was the infernal creature *doing* here? Wait—the girl! The lost daughter he'd mentioned; the nun was the daughter! *Tabernac,* had the frog sired this girl on La Dame Blanche? In any case, he'd discovered her whereabouts, and somehow had followed them to this place. He took hold of the girl's arm again, firmly.

"She is a Scotch," he said. "And as you see, a nun. No concern of yours."

The frog looked amused, cool, and unruffled. Rakoczy was sweating, the noise beating against his skin in waves. He could feel the little bag of stones in his coat, a hard lump against his heart. They seemed to be warm, warmer even than his skin.

"I doubt that she is, really," said Raymond. "Why is she a concern of yours, though?"

"That's also none of your business." He was trying to think. He couldn't lay out the stones, not with the damned frog standing there. Could he just leave with the girl? But if the frog meant him harm . . . and if the girl truly wasn't . . .

Raymond ignored the incivility, and bowed again to the girl.

"I am Master Raymond, my dear," he said. "And you?"

"Joan Mac—," she said. "Er . . . Sister Gregory, I mean." She tried to pull away from Rakoczy's grip. "Um. If I'm not the concern of either of you gentlemen . . ."

"She's my concern, gentlemen." The voice was high with nerves, but firm. Rakoczy looked round, shocked to see the young wine merchant walk into the chamber, disheveled and dirty, but eyes fixed on the girl. At his side, the nun gasped.

"Sister." The merchant bowed. He was white-faced, but not sweating. He looked as though the chill of the cavern had seeped into his bones, but put out a hand from which the beads of a wooden rosary swung. "You dropped your rosary."

. . . .

Joan thought she might faint from sheer relief. Her knees wobbled from terror and exhaustion, but she summoned enough strength to wrench free of the Comte and run, stumbling, into Michael's arms. He grabbed her and hauled her away from the Comte, half-dragging her.

The Comte made an angry sound and took a step in her direction, but Michael said, "Stop right there, ye wicked bugger!" just as the little froggy-faced man said sharply, "Stop!"

The Comte swung first toward one and then the other. He looked . . . crazed. Joan swallowed and nudged Michael, urging him toward the chamber's door, only then noticing the penknife in his hand.

"What were ye going to do wi' *that*?" she whispered. "Shave him?"

"Let the air out of him," Michael muttered. He lowered his hand, but didn't put the knife away, and kept his eyes on the two men.

"Your daughter," the Comte said hoarsely to the man who called himself Master Raymond. "You were looking for your lost daughter. I've found her for you."

Raymond's brows shot up, and he glanced at Joan.

"Mine?" he said, astonished. "She isn't one of mine. Can't you tell?"

The Comte drew a breath so deep it cracked in his throat.

"Tell? But—"

The frog looked impatient.

"Can you not see auras? The electrical fluid that surrounds people," he elucidated, waving a hand around his own head. The Comte rubbed a hand hard over his face.

"I can't—she doesn't—"

"For goodness' sake, come in here!" Raymond stepped to the edge of the star, reached across and seized the Comte's hand.

• • • •

Rakoczy stiffened at the touch. Blue light exploded from their linked hands, and he gasped, feeling a surge of energy such as he had never before experienced. It ran like water—like lightning!—through his veins. Raymond pulled hard, and he stepped across the line into the pentagram.

Silence. The buzzing had stopped. He nearly wept with the relief of it.

"I—you—" he stammered, looking at the linked hands, where the blue light now pulsed gently, with the rhythm of a beating heart. *Connection.* He felt the other. Felt him in his own blood, his bones, and astonished exaltation filled him. Another. By God, another!

"You didn't know?" Raymond looked surprised.

"That you were a—" He waved at the pentagram. "I thought you might be."

"Not that," Raymond said, almost gently. "That you were one of mine."

"Yours?" Rakoczy looked down again; the blue light was pulsing gently now, surrounding their fingers.

"Everyone has an aura of some kind," Raymond said. "But only my . . . people . . . have *this.*"

In the blessed silence, it was possible to think again. And the first thing that came to mind was the Star Chamber, the king looking on as they had faced each other over a poisoned cup. And now he knew why the frog hadn't killed him.

• • • •

His mind bubbled with questions. La Dame Blanche, blue light, Mélisande, and Madeleine . . . The thought of Madeleine and what grew in her womb nearly stopped him, but the urge to find out, to *know* at last, was too strong.

"Can you—can we—go forward?"

Raymond hesitated a moment, then nodded.

"Yes. But it's not safe. Not safe at all."

"Will you show me?"

"I mean it." The frog's grip tightened on his. "It's not a safe thing to know, let alone to do."

Rakoczy laughed, feeling all at once exhilarated, full of joy. Why should he fear knowledge? Perhaps the passage would kill him—but he had a pocket full of gems, and besides, what was the point of waiting to die slowly?

"Tell me!" he said, squeezing the other's hand. "For the sake of our shared blood!"

. . . .

Joan stood stock-still, amazed. Michael's arm was still around her, but she scarcely noticed.

"He *is*!" she whispered. "He truly is! They both are!"

"Are what?" Michael gaped at her.

"Auld Folk! Faeries!"

He looked wildly back at the scene before them. The two men stood face-to-face, hands locked together, their mouths moving in animated conversation—in total silence. It was like watching mimes, but even less interesting.

"I dinna care *what* they are. Loons, criminals, demons, angels . . . come on!" He dropped his arm and seized her hand, but she was planted solid as an oak sapling, her eyes growing wide and wider.

She gripped his hand hard enough to grind the bones and shrieked at the top of her lungs, *"Don't do it!"*

He whirled round just in time to see the front of the Comte's coat explode in sparks. And then they vanished.

. . . .

They stumbled together down the long pale passages, bathed in the flickering light of dying torches, red, yellow, blue, green, a ghastly purple that made Joan's face look drowned.

"Des feux d'artifice," Michael said. His voice sounded queer, echoing in the empty tunnels. "A conjuror's trick."

"What?" Joan looked drugged, her eyes black with shock.

"The fires. The . . . colors. Have ye never heard of fireworks?"

"No."

"Oh." It seemed too much a struggle to explain, and they went on in silence, hurrying as much as they could, to reach the shaft before the light died entirely.

At the bottom, he paused to let her go first, thinking too late that he should have gone first, she'd think he meant to look up her dress . . . he turned hastily away, face burning.

"D'ye think he was? That *they* were?" She was hanging on to the ladder, a few feet above him. Beyond her, he could see the stars, serene in a velvet sky.

"Were what?" He looked at her face, so as not to risk her modesty. She was looking better now, but very serious.

"Were they Auld Folk? Faeries?"

"I suppose they must ha' been." His mind was moving very slowly; he didn't want to have to try to think. He motioned to her to climb, and followed her up, his eyes tightly shut. If they were Auld Ones, then likely so was Auntie Claire. He truly didn't want to think about *that*.

He drew the fresh air gratefully into his lungs. The wind was toward the city now, coming off the fields, full of the resinous cool scent of pine trees and the breath of summer grass and cattle. He felt Joan breathe it in, sigh deeply, and then she turned to him, put her arms around him, and rested her forehead on his chest. He put his arms round her and they stood for some time, in peace.

Finally, she stirred and straightened up.

"Ye'd best take me back, then," she said. "The sisters will be half out o' their minds."

He was conscious of a sharp sense of disappointment, but turned obediently toward the coach, standing in the distance. Then he turned back.

"Ye're sure?" he said. "Did your voices tell ye to go back?"

She made a sound that wasn't quite a rueful laugh.

"I dinna need a voice to tell me that." She brushed a hand through her hair, smoothing it off her face. "In the Highlands, if a man's widowed, he takes another wife as soon as he can get one; he's got to have someone to mend his shirt and rear his bairns. But Sister Philomène says it's different in Paris; that a man might mourn for a year."

"He might," he said, after a short silence. Would a year be enough, he wondered, to heal the great hole where Lillie had been? He knew he would never forget—never stop looking for her—but he didn't forget what Ian had told him, either:

"*But after a time, ye find ye're in a different place than ye were. A different person than ye were. And then ye look about, and see what's there with ye. Ye'll maybe find a use for yourself.*"

Joan's face was pale and serious in the moonlight, her mouth gentle.

"It's a year before a postulant makes up her mind. Whether to stay and become a novice—or . . . or leave. It takes time. To know."

"Aye," he said softly. "Aye, it does."

He turned to go, but she stopped him, a hand on his arm.

"Michael," she said. "Kiss me, aye? I think I should maybe know *that*, before I decide."

Diana Gabaldon is the author of the award-winning, number one New York Times *bestselling Outlander novels, which include* Outlander, Dragonfly In Amber, Voyager, Drums Of Autumn, The Fiery Cross, A Breath Of Snow And Ashes, *and* An Echo In The Bone, *with twenty million copies in print worldwide. She has also written a graphic novel called* The Exile, *and a number of novels and novellas about her character, Lord John Grey, the latest of which,* The Scottish Prisoner, *came out in 2011. The eighth novel in the main series,* Written in My Own Heart's Blood, *will be published in 2013.*

CATEGORY: Unexpected Cryptozoological
Ramifications

RULE 715.2x: It's Not Easy Being Tentacled

SOURCE: Maud Charlotte Mary Victoria, Princess of
Wales

VIA: Carrie Vaughn

*There are steampunk villains, and then there are steampunk mad
scientist villains, who bring a certain panache to their evil-
doing . . . although maybe it's just the goggles and frock coats.*

*Our next story toes the waters of the steampunk subgenre,
pairing the granddaughter of Queen Victoria against the crazed
inventor of a powerful new technology. The story's roots, however, lie in the kinds of classic adventure stories Sir Arthur Conan
Doyle, Robert Louis Stevenson, and Wilkie Collins were writing
at the turn of the twentieth century.*

*Carrie Vaughn admits a love of those Victorian adventure sto-
ries, and says, "I've been wanting to tell the story of a not-so-prim
Victorian woman adventurer for a long time, and the setting here
gave me a fun way to do that. This is an alternate history—an
alien spacecraft crash landed, Roswell-like, in England in 1869,
and a vast new technology was reverse-engineered from the debris." It's the perfect setting for a little madness.*

*Here we give you a princess with a purpose, a mansion with a
secret, and a doctor with a plan. It's a madcap adventure with a
proper British accent.*

HARRY AND MARLOWE MEET THE FOUNDER OF THE AETHERIAN REVOLUTION

CARRIE VAUGHN

"We could have taken George's courier ship and arrived in a quarter of the time."

"No, we couldn't," Harry said, scowling at Marlowe, who knew very well they shouldn't be here at all, much less aboard her brother's ship. But he seemed to enjoy mentioning her brother George and reminding Harry of the impropriety of it all. It was a long-running joke, and she let him have his fun. Marlowe just smiled.

They'd taken a carriage—a regular hired coach, horse-drawn, even—from the Oxford station to the doctor's estate. The journey from London had taken most of the day, which left them facing the gatehouse on an overcast afternoon, the sunlight fading, the world growing colder.

Despite the spiked iron gate, the estate was modest. Harry could have walked the perimeter of the grounds in half an hour, though the curving gravel drive gave the impression of greater space. At the end of the curve, one could glimpse the house, a two-story gray pile with a slate roof and clay chimneys, walls fuzzed with ivy, windows brooding—all of it easily manageable, easily guarded.

The gate was the only access through a ten-foot-high wall that surrounded the house. At the top of the wall copper conductors placed every dozen feet or so guided an Aetherian charge, a crackling stream of deadly green energy: a second barrier, impassible, should someone think that they could climb the wall. The humming, flickering light traveled down the bars of the gate as well.

Impatient, Harry opened the carriage door before the driver or one of the soldiers from the gatehouse arrived to do so. However, before she could let herself out, Marlowe slipped out, let down the step, and offered his hand to her. Propriety, indeed. Remembering herself, she gathered her skirt in one hand, took his with the other, and stepped neatly out of the coach.

Four soldiers on weekly rotation from the local regiment served guard duty here. One of them—an officer by his insignia—approached. A Lieutenant Bradley commanded the unit, Harry knew. This must be him.

"I'm sorry," the lieutenant said. "I don't know what you've been told, but this area is restricted. The house isn't open—"

"I know. This is Dr. James Marlowe, and I'm Miss Mills, his secretary. We're here to see Doctor Carlisle," Harry said, drawing a folded paper from her handbag. The letter was affixed with the royal seal, confusing everyone who looked at it, but everyone who looked at it was well trained not to ask questions. They'd merely have to wonder why two unassuming travelers had the Crown Prince's approval. (They didn't, but that was beside the point.) The lieutenant opened the letter and read it over—taking his time, to his credit.

When he'd finished, he looked across the page and studied the unlikely visitors. "Very well, then. Give us a moment to open the gate. Sir. Miss." He tipped his hat at them and turned back to the house.

Marlowe tucked his portfolio under his arm and gave the driver a few coins. "Can you return for us in two hours?"

"Yes, sir." The man remounted his carriage and drove off.

Marlowe could never quite manage polish, even when he meant to be traveling as a respectable gentleman. Locks of hair escaped from under his bowler hat, his face showed pale stubble, and his tie was loose where he'd tugged on his collar. His jacket, trousers, and boots were acceptable but not outstanding. Truth be told, Harry liked him better without the polish—he looked like a man who was too busy to worry about inconsequential details like trimmed hair and neat ties.

"I hope two hours will be enough," Marlowe said, watching the driver depart.

"I fear we'll be wanting out of here much sooner than that," Harry said. "Part of me hopes this is all a waste of time."

Marlowe shook his head. "No, this is a rare opportunity: To meet the genius who created the Aetherian Revolution? Without him we'd have none of this." He gestured ahead.

The front window of the gatehouse revealed a pair of brown-uniformed soldiers at work, one hauling down on a wall-mounted lever, the other operating an unseen control panel. A metallic clang followed, the banging of steel on steel; the Aetherian hum faded, and the crackling stream of power guarding the wall vanished. Now the wall was just a wall, and the gate was just a gate.

Harry still regarded the wrought iron cautiously. "We might have been better off," she said.

"Never think so," Marlowe said. "Ernest Carlisle may be the only one who can move my work forward."

"Don't you think you'd solve the problem yourself, eventually?" Harry said.

"We don't have time for that," he said.

Of course, Harry thought. Not with the war on. It was the unspoken postscript to everything they did.

Lt. Bradley emerged from the gatehouse. "It's safe, now," he said. "I'll escort you in."

The soldiers in the gatehouse turned another set of levers, and bolts lurched open, another metallic clunk. The middle of the gate split apart, and Bradley pushed it open. Harry suppressed a flinch when the lieutenant touched the gate, but no Aetherian charge scorched him.

Marlowe offered his arm to Harry, and she took it. They walked with the lieutenant toward the manor.

The gates clanged shut and locked behind them, and Harry glanced over her shoulder, wondering how such an innocuous tone could seem so ominous, like the tolling of a church bell.

Turning back, she said, "Lieutenant, tell me about the doctor. What is his schedule like? How many servants are here at the house, and how do you supervise them?"

"He has no servants, miss. By his own request. He said the necessary restrictions on them were too great to bother. A cook from the village comes in the morning to make his meals for the day, and a cleaner comes once a week. Her work is little enough—most of the house is shut up."

"Is that so?"

"Doctor Carlisle is confined to a wheelchair, miss. He has chambers on the ground floor. I thought you would know, since you've permission to see him."

"For how long?" she said. This wasn't in any of the reports.

"Ten years, since the disaster. I'm given to understand he sustained injuries." They'd reached the house now, and Bradley nodded. "If you'll excuse me a moment, I'll let the doctor know he has visitors."

The door had a speaker box by it, which the lieutenant leaned into. Harry and Marlowe stayed back and spoke in whispers.

"Did you know Carlisle was infirm?" she asked him.

"I didn't. There were rumors of illness, but I thought it had more to do with age. Or a broken spirit."

"Why is it a secret, do you suppose?"

"Out of respect for the man's dignity, I imagine."

"As if he had any left," she said. But he did, or he would not be living like this, in a polite fiction of genteel retirement—under guard. She frowned. "What does it say about us that we're so afraid of a crippled man that we keep him locked up like this?"

"Because it's Doctor Carlisle," Marlowe said, and he was right. Carlisle certainly couldn't be allowed to go free. Neither could he be truly imprisoned, or executed, or exiled. He was the realm's great conundrum. Or rather, its second great conundrum, after the conundrum that Carlisle had made his name exploiting.

"Be careful, Marlowe. You sound as if you admire the man."

"Oh, I won't forget he's a murderer."

"Good."

"Are you sure you aren't letting your personal feelings unduly influence you?"

"Of course I am. What else are personal feelings for?" She shook her head. "He can't have turned everything over when he was arrested. A man like him—he kept something back as a bargaining chip should he ever need it. Some scrap of research, some artifact. I want to know what."

"We both do. Are you ready for this?"

"Of course I am," Harry said.

Bradley was exchanging words with the person on the other end of the speaker box. The responses were little more than incomprehensible scratching. But eventually, Bradley drew out a key and unlocked the front door.

"The doctor is ready for you," Bradley said. "I'll show you to the library."

"I very much appreciate your help, Lieutenant. I know this must disrupt your routine terribly," Harry said with a kind and practiced smile.

The soldier beamed back at her. "It's no trouble, miss."

"You're very good at that," Marlowe whispered to her after Bradley led the way inside.

"I've had a lot of practice."

"Better you than me, then."

She smiled; they did make a good team.

Bradley guided them through a tiled foyer and into a parlor.

Nothing in the house indicated the character of the man who lived in it. She might have been in any respectable gentry home: decent furniture, lightly used; unassuming still-life paintings on the wall; neat wallpaper and drapes, carpet over hardwood. All of it might have been chosen by some matron desperate not to stand out. On the other side of the parlor, Bradley opened a set of double doors and guided them into the library.

This was the doctor's room, where he spent his waking hours. Apart from walls full of books, the room had a great fireplace with a well-worn armchair in front of it, a window overlooking a patch of flowers, and many framed photographs on the walls, desks, and tables. In the middle sat two large worktables. One of them was overflowing with books—stacked, open to different pages, as if Carlisle were reading a dozen at once. The other held various crafts and hobbies: fly-tying equipment, the clockworks of antique pocket watches, a sketchbook, a set of watercolor paints . . . even toys: windups and clockworks that Carlisle seemed to be in the process of repairing. Or dissecting.

Carlisle himself sat at the table in a wheelchair, a blanket over his lap, covering his legs to his toes. He'd aged, his formerly robust form sagging on a stooped frame.

"Doctor Carlisle, here are your visitors," Lieutenant Bradley announced, then bowed himself out of the room like a good foot soldier, closing the doors behind him.

It was good that he did. Smiling, his eyes glittering, Carlisle greeted Harry, "Princess Maud. Your Highness."

She was a little surprised he recognized her and tried to act offended. "Miss Mills, today," she said, clasping her gloved hands before her.

"Ah. Of course. My apologies."

Marlowe hovered at her elbow, waiting to be protective.

"Doctor Carlisle, this is Doctor James Marlowe. He has some questions he was hoping you could answer."

"And he needed you to pull strings and finagle permission to come here? That's highly irregular."

"It's unofficial," she said.

"Doctor Marlowe? Should I have heard of you?"

"I wouldn't expect you to have, sir," Marlowe said. "I'm not affiliated with Oxbridge, though I have laboratory privileges at University College London. My interests tend to lie in fieldwork."

"No prestige in fieldwork, lad."

Marlowe's lip turned up. "Perhaps."

"You aren't an Aetherian engineer, then?" the old professor said.

"I have an interest in Aetherian mechanisms."

"Of course you do, or you would not need to come see me." Carlisle leaned back and steepled his hands. He had been kept alive and in relative comfort because no one knew more than he did on the subject. "What exactly is it that he does, my lady?"

"He solves problems," Harry said.

The photographs on the walls documented the professor's exploits—the images were monuments to his work. A history of the last two decades, even: the strange, looping coils and pocked hull of the Aetherian craft where it crashed in Surrey; the rows of canvas tents housing the hundreds of workers who built the warehouses and laboratories around the site; Ernest Carlisle directing the project, leading a team of white-coated assistants like a general commanding an army. Harry drew closer to one photograph in particular, startled by its familiarity. She had a print of the same photograph in an old scrapbook. George probably had one as well.

The event, twenty-odd years ago, was Dr. Carlisle's first public demonstration of his adapted Aetherian mechanism. He'd fitted a train engine with an Aetherian propulsion device—it would triple the power of a coal-driven steam engine, with none of the smoke and soot. The royal family had gathered to watch, bestowing their approval of the project by their presence.

The engine itself was the backdrop, its alien brass couplings and broilers projecting, an unearthly glow emanating from them like halos, visible even in black and white. On one side, apart, stood Dr. Carlisle in his prime, stretched and haughty, hand resting on a nearby strut, almost caressing it.

A space stood between him and the family: the Queen, solemn in her mourning, and her vast tangle of progeny. Harry's parents, arm in arm like they always had been when photographed or painted together, looked resigned to her eyes. And why not? The world and realm were changing before them, and this engine was proof of it. Their five young children gathered around them, as vibrant and proper a brood as any parents could hope for. The youngest, five-year-old Harry—though she hadn't acquired the nickname yet—clung to her brother George, who seemed very straight and proud at the age of nine.

A surprising number of people in the photograph had died since it was taken. Harry's father, the Crown Prince, for one. Her oldest brother Eddy, which made proud George the Crown Prince now. On the other hand, her grandmother the Queen showed no sign of fading.

Dr. Carlisle caught Harry studying the image.

"You've grown up very well, my lady. I remember you, from the day that photograph was taken. You hid every time I tried to speak to you."

The little girl in the picture wore her brown hair in tight curls, tied back with a velvet ribbon. She wore a white dress and lace-trimmed pinafore, shined shoes peeking out underneath. Chubby and shy, she gripped her brother's hand. She remembered George trying to urge her forward.

Now, she was tall and straight, a proud lift to her chin, auburn hair gathered back and bound, topped by a simple hat, secured in a corset and rose-colored silk gown, with all its fashionable layers and buttons. And she never hid.

"That was a long time ago," she said.

"Not so very long, when you've lived as long as I."

"Strange, isn't it, that you should still live when so many who were there that day have died." She dropped the hook and hoped he would bite.

Carlisle's tone was far from offended. He sounded amused. "My dear, are you implying something?"

The cheek of him. He spoke so to her because there'd be no repercussions.

She said, "If you could have continued your research, what would you have done? What further horrors would you have concocted?"

"That's a useless question," Carlisle said. "I believe I received a message from the Almighty that my research had run its course, and that to continue further was to invite disaster."

It was hard to argue with the interpretation. Disaster had already accepted the invitation.

"It seems to me," Harry said, "that once you learned everything you could from the Aetherian craft, you would next turn to the pilot. But you found more than you expected, didn't you?"

Marlowe reached a timid, placating hand. "Your Highness, this isn't why we came—"

"I want to hear him say exactly what he thought would happen," she said, brushing Marlowe away. She was repeating fables from penny dreadfuls. There was no plague, no extraplanetary conspiracy against the Empire, no Aetherian miasma that killed the Crown Prince and his eldest son and thousands of others. It had only seemed very much like it. They had died years later, her father assassinated and Eddy of flu, both unrelated to the accident at Woking.

But that accident, a horrific event borne of one man's hubris, was more than enough reason to treat Carlisle with contempt.

Carlisle frowned. "The body was thoroughly dissected. The notes published. I'm sure anyone has learned anything they're likely to learn from the beast."

"I don't believe you," Harry said.

Carlisle narrowed his gaze. "Does your grandmother know you're here?"

"I have a letter with the royal seal."

"That doesn't answer my question."

"What did you save, Doctor Carlisle? What did you learn of Aetherian biology that you didn't tell anyone?"

"My lady, I spent many days in a very uncomfortable room with men more powerful and clever than you asking me such questions. Why do you think you'll learn what they did not?"

She smiled, adding a tilt to her head that showed off the fashionable trim on her hat. "My charm."

Marlowe lay the portfolio on the table before Carlisle. "I'm terribly sorry, Doctor. When Her Highness agreed to procure permission for me to see you, it was on the condition that she accompany me. She assured me she could control herself." He threw her a glare. Playing his part.

"What's your connection to the family? Are you a schoolmate of her brother's or such?"

"Just so," Marlowe said. "My only concern here is a mechanical problem I've been attempting to solve—an air compression system for providing breathable atmosphere at high altitudes. I'm sure you know that the airships based on your designs are reaching thirty thousand feet now." He began producing pages, schematics, charts.

Carlisle still watched Harry.

"Your Highness," Marlowe said. "Perhaps you'd rather wait in the parlor."

"Yes," Carlisle added. "Perhaps you should."

Dismissed, she turned and stormed out of the room, careful to act as if she wasn't used to opening and closing doors herself.

The manor house didn't seem much altered from official accounts. The lieutenant had said most of the house was shut up, which made sense given Carlisle's condition. But it didn't mean anything. If anyone could find a way to climb stairs in a wheelchair, Carlisle would be the man. She commenced exploring.

The dining room had an air of abandonment—Carlisle took his meals elsewhere. The table was set like a museum piece, covered with a red damask runner, a vase filled with dried flowers placed in the middle. There was dust on the flowers, and the rug around the chairs was unscuffed, as though they'd never been pulled from the table.

At least the hinges on the double doors didn't squeak. She passed through a foyer, through another set of doors, and here were a set of stairs leading down. Neither the stairs nor the railing were dusty. So the cleaner paid special attention to them. Or they were used often.

As Harry descended, she retrieved the hand lantern—another Aetherian mechanism derived from Carlisle's research—from the pocket tucked into a pleat in her skirt.

The door at the base of the stairs was locked. From the opposite pocket, she drew out her lock picks and set to work. Defeating the mechanism took longer than she expected; this wasn't the door's original lock. While the rest of the house had been all but embalmed, the lock had been replaced with a complex modern version. Fortunately, her tools weren't those of a common burglar. In a few extra heartbeats, the lock clicked, and the door swung open.

The air inside smelled of alcohol and preservative.

She waited a moment, for a trap door to open under her feet, for poison darts to spring from the door frame. But nothing happened. If Carlisle really were hiding something, his traps would be more nefarious. His laboratory would be better hidden, wouldn't it? On the other hand, no one had any reason to think he ever went down here—the man couldn't walk without assistance, after all. At least, that was what they all believed. Easy enough to maintain such a fiction.

Briefly, she worried about Marlowe, alone with the man upstairs.

Perhaps Marlowe was right and she was letting her fears get the better of her.

Harry switched on the lantern and closed the door.

The glow revealed glasswork first, pale light reflecting off the smooth surfaces of beakers, flasks, slender piping secured to wooden stands with clamps, all arranged on the large table in the center of the room. This was where servants would have eaten in the house's old days. None of the equipment seemed to be in use—the glassware was all dry, a gas burner was cold. She might have made an excuse for why it was here: this was simply storage. When Carlisle had been situated in the house, his scientific equipment had been put here, locked away because he would not need it. But none of it was dusty. Not even the cupboards along the room's sides. She brought her lantern close, swept it along the table and sides of the room, studying what details revealed themselves.

The table also held a microscope, with trays of slides beside it. She drew out several, hoping the labels would give her insight, but they were only numbered. The samples on them might have been some kind of tissue—translucent pink splotches that could have been anything. A nearby cupboard contained more slides, racks and racks of them. A second cupboard held flasks of liquid, jars labeled with the names of various solvents and acids, other tools of a biologist's or chemist's trade.

This might have been all innocent hobby. He had been studying the internal structures of worms. But she didn't think so; somehow, he had access to the basement, perhaps via a secret elevator, and he was still experimenting. She didn't have the expertise to know toward what purpose the efforts were directed, but she could record this evidence and have him arrested—again. And sent to prison this time, not this polite fiction in deference to all he had done in his former life.

She would only have to explain why she'd come here at all to her brother. He could make excuses to anyone who questioned her. Likely, she wouldn't be mentioned at all.

With her small notebook and pencil in hand, she began to record an inventory. Marlowe would know what to make of it. In fact, he should probably come have a look at this himself if they could manage it.

It was the angle of light from her glowing lantern that revealed the irregularity in the wall by the cupboard full of microscope slides. A tiny gap in the paneling wavered. In full lamplight, the slight shadow would have been invisible. Perhaps this was Carlisle's hidden elevator. She had to take off her gloves and needed several moments of testing to find the catch that opened the secret panel, revealing not an elevator, but a wall of narrow shelves, filled with glassware.

The light of her Aetherian lantern glinted off of rows of two-gallon jars, dozens of them, all filled with murky liquid. The sour reek of formalin hung about them, enough to make her cover her mouth and nose with her hand. And yes, inside the jars floated preserved creatures. Her imagination tumbled. Aetherian specimens rescued from the wrecked ship perhaps? If so, Carlisle had kept them very secret.

But no . . . She'd seen photographs of the Aetherian pilot's body and the engravings diagramming the autopsy. She'd even studied some of the speculation that followed, regarding what other Aetherian creatures must be like, derived from the pilot's physiology and using Mr. Darwin's theories.

These specimens were nothing like that. They were far too familiar, in fact, despite some grotesque mutations. Pale, furless, smooth. Curved backs, large heads, arms and legs tucked in. Just small enough to cradle in her arms.

They were infants. Newborns and slightly older at the very most. Harry held the lantern closer, to study the bodies, the faces of these horrifying creatures. The mutations that distorted them weren't normal—if mutation could ever be called normal. Expected grotesqueries would include extra limbs, fused limbs, scaled skin, and so forth.

Several of these had fleshy, thorned tentacles extending from their skulls to their bellies. Some had metallic armored plates covering their heads, glinting bronze by the lamplight through the murk of preservative. Some faces had been distorted, elongated, the teeth fused and eyes bulging from sockets so that the body appeared alien. Others had limbs with too many joints that bent the wrong way. In their way, these alterations, these details that she tried to examine from a scientific, unemotional perspective, were familiar, like a certain famous photograph and set of autopsy diagrams.

These were Aetherian mutations, wrought upon human infants.

Were these accidents or experiments? And what had Carlisle been doing with them?

She had an irrational thought to drench the room in kerosene and drop a match, destroying it all, eradicating the horror. Then throw Doctor Carlisle into the inferno. An untempered response, to be sure. How much more satisfying to prosecute him in a court of law. That was the only way to learn what Carlisle was trying to do here, and where the unfortunate infants had come from. Harry wondered where their mothers were.

Marlowe needed to see this. She went back up the stairs, not bothering to close the door behind her.

No one had ever come down here. Why should they, when Carlisle could never navigate the stairs? How many dozens of officers before Bradley had declared so, confidently? Nevertheless, Carlisle had managed to find a way down the stairs.

Marlowe was still with Carlisle in the library. He'd led the old man into making sketches of some Aetherian principle or other, and they bent together over the table, studying the page before them. When she rushed through the doorway, they looked up.

For all that she was practiced at deception—putting on masks and behaving in a manner consistent with those masks—she could not face Dr. Carlisle and pretend that she had not seen what she had. Marlowe, of course, knew something was wrong the moment he saw her. Lips pressed with concern, his expression asked the question.

She felt more sure of herself, with Marlowe standing by. She could face Carlisle, her breathing steady despite her rage. But her stillness, the flush in her cheeks, gave her away. Carlisle frowned.

"Where have you been?" Dr. Carlisle asked. "Making sure I haven't stolen any of the silver?"

"I suppose I could tell you I've been in the garden like a good little girl."

"You've seen the laboratory." She nodded. "You came here at all because you guessed I was hiding something."

"We came for exactly the reason we stated," Marlowe said. "For information. We just didn't trust that you would tell us all you knew. By Her Highness' silence, can I judge you're hiding quite a lot?"

She had to swallow the lump in her throat before she could find her voice. "Marlowe, would you be so good as to have a look in the basement?"

With a last glance at Carlisle, he left the room. She followed, gesturing ahead to show him the way.

The wheels of Carlisle's chairs creaked on the floor as he pushed himself along to follow them.

"I know what you think you've found, girl. But I warrant you haven't a clue what you saw. Your unsophisticated mind cannot possibly comprehend."

She gritted her teeth and ignored him.

Marlowe stood at the top of the stairs. "Harry, how could he even get down here?"

"I don't know, but he has. Go and see."

"Doctor Marlowe, I assure you, the girl speaks nonsense." Carlisle's voice echoed after them as they descended.

"Take my lantern," she said, her hands fumbling as she handed it over at the base of the stairs.

She'd left the unholy cupboard open. It was the first thing he saw, the rows of jars, the dark eyes of the creatures within peering through translucent flesh.

"Oh, my God," he murmured.

"This is an invasion!" Carlisle shouted from the top of the stairs. "You have no right!"

"I have every right, as a loyal subject of the Crown," she called back.

Marlowe said, "I wouldn't have thought this was his doing because of the stairs, but he's all but claiming responsibility, isn't he?"

"What now?" she asked him. "What do we do? I started to write an inventory, but this . . . seems a bit beyond that."

"I want an explanation," he said, and turned to the stairs.

Which Carlisle was descending.

He'd left the wheelchair, but he wasn't walking. Slithering, perhaps. Creeping. Seeping. His legs had become something else, some kind of boneless limb that he'd kept hidden under the blanket all this time. The pseudopod stretched forward, long prehensile tendrils grasping, reaching ahead of him to pull him down the steps, balancing against the walls to either side. His torso rocked atop them, like a man learning to ride a bicycle. Carlisle held the wall for balance as he lurched toward them.

Marlowe drew his pistol from the holster hidden at his back, under his jacket. Harry stumbled away and tried to think. If the basement had a speaker box, perhaps she could call Lieutenant Bradley. But no, the guards thought the room shut up, a speaker box never would have been installed.

"It's a matter of time," Carlisle said, explaining, lecturing. "Ten years ago, I tried to do it all at once, but I've learned that it's a matter of time, careful injections, a little every day—"

"What are you saying?" Marlowe aimed the pistol at him, but Carlisle seemed not to notice.

"The promise of Aetherian biology!" Carlisle said. "Just as our machines have become more than they ever would have, so can *we*!"

"And what about them?" Harry said, pointing at the cupboard of dead children.

Carlisle filled the door, his alien limbs spreading around him like some grotesque anemone. "They are products of the first experiment."

"You mean the accident?" Harry said, disbelieving.

"Everyone thinks I was making a weapon, and that's why all those people died, but that is not it at all, I had no interest in weapons. I was trying—I was trying to *improve*."

"Improve?"

"I paid the women for their participation; it was a simple transaction."

"You mean you paid them—and took their children from them?"

"It hardly mattered, as you can see not a single one survived."

Marlowe switched on the charge of his pistol—an energy pistol, powered by the Aetherian mechanisms. "Stop there, Doctor."

One of the strange, mutated limbs whipped out and smacked Marlowe's hand. The pistol skittered away, and Marlowe fell back.

Carlisle rolled toward him, preparing to climb on top of him, to crush or strangle him. Marlowe was pinned; he struggled to find a path of escape, but Carlisle's sinuous limbs caged him. "Forget the problem of air compression. We can't bring our atmosphere with us. Instead, we will travel through Aetherian spaces ourselves! But to do that we must be like them. We must breathe like them!"

Harry realized now where all those tissue slides must have come from. No matter that he had killed thousands when his poisonous chemical bath leaked into the water supply of Woking. His crime had been more than mere neglect—mere neglect, ha. The chemical bath had been some sort of Aetherian concoction, the leak had been intentional, and he had managed to collect samples to analyze his results.

Harry looked around. To the right imagination, the laboratory was a warehouse of weaponry. She went straight to the cabinet on the opposite side of the room, containing the flasks of acid and solvent, and the hypodermic needles and syringes alongside.

When she had what she needed and approached Doctor Carlisle, he stopped her with one of those horrid limbs, fleshy, covered with thorns, like some of the embalmed infants, like the images she had seen of the Aetherian pilot. Merely placed it before her, waving the tip of it, while still harassing Marlowe.

"What are you doing, dear Princess Maud?"

"If you harm me, there will be repercussions," she said.

"Still hiding behind your brother's trousers after all?" Carlisle said, laughing.

"Harry, do you see the pistol?" Marlowe called.

"Quiet," Carlisle said and slapped him. Marlowe's head slammed against the floor and he groaned.

Harry jammed the needle into Carlisle's mutant limb and rammed home the plunger, emptying a dozen cubic centimeters of hydrochloric acid into his bloodstream, or so she hoped.

Carlisle lashed out, and the blow threw her back. She fell hard to the floor and managed to scramble away, taking shelter under the table. From there, she could see Marlowe, lying on the other side. She crawled toward him, reached for him; he grabbed her hand and squeezed.

Carlisle had fallen and lay twitching. She didn't know what she had expected—screaming, perhaps. Skin and fluids bubbling as the concentrated acid ate him from within, assuming her attack had worked. But he simply lay silent, convulsions wracking his muscles. Foam collected at his mouth and dribbled down his cheek. His horrible pseudopod flopped like worms.

"What did you put in there?" Marlowe said.

She told him, and he hissed.

"I don't know what I'm going to say to George," she said.

"It hardly matters. You were right, he was hiding something. I thought we would find a packet of notes. Not . . . not this."

"We should go tell the lieutenant," Harry said, crawling out from under the table, brushing off her gown. There was little dust; Carlisle had kept the place very clean.

Marlowe scrambled to his feet in time to offer her a hand up. She accepted and kept hold of the hand for an extra moment, for comfort.

"Give me a minute, if you don't mind," Marlowe said, and went the cabinet of equipment. He started preparing a hypodermic and syringe.

"What are you doing?"

"I just want a sample."

"Marlowe—"

"We'll tell the lieutenant. We'll tell everything, and Doctor Carlisle and all his nightmares will be studied, dissected, and locked away to keep anything like it from ever happening again. But in the meantime, I want a sample."

He knelt by the dying Doctor Carlisle, inserted the needle in one of the pseudopods, and drew back the plunger to collect a syringe full of thick, yellowish liquid.

"Marlowe!"

He glanced sharply at her with a look of pleading. Don't tell, let him have this, to continue with his own experiments. How else was Britain to win the war?

It wasn't as if this was the only secret she'd be keeping. Her entire partnership with Marlowe was nearly scandalous. And since she wanted that partnership to continue, she would keep quiet.

Marlowe secured the syringe in a tin box which he slipped in a pocket, then retrieved his pistol.

"Harry," he said, pausing at the foot of the stairs. "Are you all right?"

"I don't know." The hideous jarred infants kept staring at her. Her hands were shaking.

Marlowe reached for her. "Come. Everything'll be all right."

She chose to believe him, and, hand in hand, they went up the stairs.

Carrie Vaughn is the bestselling author of the Kitty Norville *series, which started with* Kitty and the Midnight Hour. *Her most recent books include* Kitty's Big Trouble, Voices of Dragons, Discord's Apple, Steel, and After the Golden Age. *Her short work, which has been nominated for the Hugo Award, has appeared in magazines such as* Lightspeed *and* Realms of Fantasy, *and in a number of anthologies, such as John Joseph Adams's* Armored, By Blood We Live, *and* Brave New Worlds, *as well as in* The Mammoth Book of Paranormal Romance; Fast Ships, Black Sails; *and* Warriors, *edited by George R. R. Martin and Gardner Dozois.*

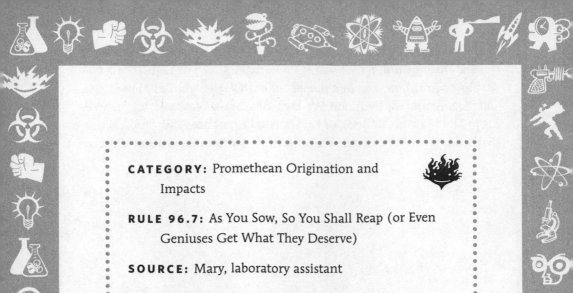

CATEGORY: Promethean Origination and Impacts

RULE 96.7: As You Sow, So You Shall Reap (or Even Geniuses Get What They Deserve)

SOURCE: Mary, laboratory assistant

VIA: Laird Barron

There is no Igor in Mary Shelley's Frankenstein.

There's also no Igor in the 1931 Universal Studios' Franken-stein, *although there is a hunchbacked assistant named Fritz (whose shoddy work as a brain-snatcher provides most of what's monstrous about the shambling monster). It's not until 1953's* House of Wax *that we get the devoted assistant with that famous moniker. Somehow, cultural memory has married the hunchback and the helper and given us the iconic gofer: Igor, dumb as a post and twice as ugly, practically enslaved by his mad employer.*

In our next story, Laird Barron gives us a whole new Igor. She's not your run-of-the-mill lab assistant and she doesn't have a hunchback. Oh, and she hates her boss. But when you've been created for your job, a career change takes more than just a new resume. It'll take . . . genius.

BLOOD & STARDUST

LAIRD BARRON

Three years later, as I hike my skirt to urinate in a dark alley in the slums of Kolkata, my arms are grasped from behind. The Doctor whispers, "So, we meet again." His face was ruined in the explosion—its severe, patrician mold is melted and crudely reformed as if an idiot child had gotten his or her stubby fingers on God's modeling clay. I can't see it from my disadvantaged perspective, but that's not necessary. I've been following him and Pelt around since our original falling-out.

Speaking of the Devil . . . Pelt slips from the shadows and drives his favorite dirk, first through my belly, then, after he smirks at the blood splattering onto our shoes, my heart. He grins as he twists the blade like he's winding a watch.

"—and this time the advantage is mine." I laugh with pure malice, and die.

. . . .

Storms unnerve me. I hate thunder and lightning—they make me jumpy, even in the Hammer Films I watch nearly every evening. Regardless of the patent cheesiness, it awakens my primitive dread. Considering the circumstances of my birth, that makes sense. Fear of the mother of elements is hardwired into me.

My nerves weren't always so frayed; once, I was too dull to fear anything but the Master's voice and his lash. I was incurious until my fifth or sixth birthday and thick as a brick physically and intellectually. Anymore, I read anything that doesn't have the covers glued shut. I devour talk radio and Oprah. Consequently, my neuroses have spread like weeds. Am I getting fat? Yes, I've got the squat frame of a Bulgarian power lifter, but at least my moles and wens usually distract the eye from my bulging trapeziuses and hairy arms.

I also dislike the dark, and wind, and being trussed hand and foot and left hanging in a closet. Dr. Kob used to give me the last as punishment; still does it now and again, needed or not, as a reminder. Perspective is extremely important in the Kob house. The whole situation is rather pathetic, because chief among his eccentric proclivities, he's an amateur storm chaser. Tornadoes and cyclones don't interest him so much as lightning and its capacity for destruction and death. Up until his recent deteriorating health, we'd bundle into the van and cruise along the coast during storm season and shoot video, and perform field tests of his arcane equipment. Happily, those days seem to be gone, and none too soon. It's rumored my predecessor, daughter *numero uno,* was blown to smithereens, and her ashes scattered upon the tides, during one of those summer outings.

• • • •

Time has come for action.

My birthday was Saturday. I'm thirty, a nice round number. By thirty, a girl should have career aspirations, picked out a man, that sort of thing. I stuck the white candle of death in a cupcake, said my prayers, and ate the damned thing with all the joy of a Catholic choking down a supersized holy wafer. Then I doused my sorrows with a bottle of Glenfiddich and watched a rerun of the late night creature-feature.

I've decided to record my deepest thoughts, although I'm young to be scribing even this outline of a memoir. Some bits I've written in spiral notebooks with ponies and unicorns on the cover.

• • • •

We live in a big Gothic mansion on a hill outside of Olympia. We being Dr. Kob, Pelt, and me. Pelt came to the United States with the Master. The old troll doesn't talk much, preferring to hole up in his backyard treehouse and drink Wild Turkey and sharpen his many, many knives. I call him Uncle, although so far as I know he's no more my uncle than the good Doctor is my father.

Dr. Kob's workshop is the converted attic in the East Wing. He's got a lordly view of everything from Olympia to Mt. Rainier. When he's in his cups, he refers to the people in the city as *villagers.* That's exactly how he says it—with a diabolical sneer. I think he reminisces about the Mother-land more than he should. His skeletons are banging on the closet door. He just keeps jamming in new ones. I wager it'll bite him in the ass one of these fine days.

The housekeeper, chef, and handyman stay in bungalows in the long shadows of the forest on the edge of the property. The gardener and his help-ers commute daily. They tend the arboretum and the vast grounds. Yet despite their indefatigable efforts to chop back the vines, the brambles, and the weeds, the estate always seems overgrown. It looks a lot like the thicket around Sleeping Beauty's castle in the classic cartoons. Some rooms in the mansion leak during rainstorms. Like the grounds crew, our handyman and his boys can't replace rotten shingles and broken windows fast enough to stay ahead of entropy that's been gathering mass since 1845. There's not enough plaster or paint in the world to cover every blister and sore blighting this once great house.

But Dr. Kob doesn't care about such trivialities. He's obsessed with his research, his experiments. Best of all, there are catacombs beneath the cellars; an extensive maze chock-full of bones. Beats digging up corpses at the graveyard in the dead of night, although he waxes nostalgic about those youthful excursions.

I'm careful in my comings and goings despite the fact Dr. Kob crushes the servants under his thumb and virtually saps their will to live. He imported most of them from places like Romania and Yugoslavia. They've united in tight-jawed dourness and palpable resentment. None speak English. They're paid to look the other way, to keep their mouths shut. They know what's good for them.

I worry anyway. I'm a busy bee, fetching and toting for the Master; coming and going, sneaking and skulking at all hours. Capturing live subjects is dangerous, especially when you're as conspicuous as I am. There can be complications. Once, I brought home three kids I'd caught smoking dope in the park. The chloroform wore off one of them, and when I popped the trunk he jumped out and ran into the woods, screaming bloody murder. Luckily, Pelt was sober enough to function, for a change, and he unleashed a pair of wolfhounds from the kennel. Mean ones. We tracked the boy down before he made it to a road. The little sucker might've escaped if I hadn't cuffed his hands behind his back.

• • • •

In unrelated events:

A circus rolled through town one week in the fall; in its wake, consternation and dismay due to a murder most foul. An article in the *Olympian* documents the spectacular and mysterious demise of Niall the Barker. The paper smoothes over the rough edges, skips most of the gruesome facts. The reporters in the know talked to the cops who know this: While hapless Niall lay upon his cot in a drunken stupor, some evildoer shoved a heavy-duty industrial-strength cattle prod up his ass and pressed the button. His internal organs liquefied. A blowhole opened in the crown of his skull, and shit, guts, and brains bubbled forth like lava from a kid's volcano exhibit at a science fair. His muscles and skin hardened and were branded with the most curious Lichtenberg Flowers.

Sometimes I go back and watch it again, just to savor the moment.

• • • •

Dr. Kob requires that we take supper together on Fridays. We sit at opposite ends of a long, Medieval-style table in the dining hall. The hall is gloomy and dusty and decorated in a fashion similar to Dracula's castle in the Bela Lugosi, Christopher Lee films. God, how I adore Christopher Lee, especially the young, B-movie incarnation. His soliloquy to carnal delights in *The Wicker Man* stands my hair on end. Dr. Kob doesn't know anything about cinema or actors. He says there's no television where he comes from, no theatre. That's likely an exaggeration—the Master is fond of hyperbole. Read a few of his interviews in the *Daily O* and you'll see what I mean.

Dr. Kob's father was an eminent scientist until some scandal swept him and his family into the shadows. After his expulsion from whatever prominent university, Kob, Sr., conducted his research in the confines of home sweet home. I think of the dungeons and oubliettes in those ancient European keeps and feel a twinge of pity for the peasants moiling in the fields beneath the Kob estate. Ripe fruit, the lot of them.

Snooping about the Master's quarters, I unearthed a musty album full of antiquated photographs of Dr. Kob and various friends and relatives. Many feature the redoubtable Pelt. Has the hunter always been Kob's henchman? Perhaps they are fraternity brothers or blood cousins. Today the good Doctor bears a strong likeness to Boris Karloff, which is also pretty much how he looks in his baby pictures.

On the other hand, the Pelt I know scarcely resembles the man posing with a pack of hounds, his curls long and golden, his bloodthirsty grin as sweet and guileless as Saint Michael's own. What a heartbreaker (and likely serial killer) he was! One of the pictures is dated 1960. Now, he slumps over his plate and goblet. His hooked nose, his sallow cheeks are gnarled as plastic that's been melted and fused. Oh, and he's pot-bellied and bald as a tumor. It's all very sad—he's like a caricature of a Grimm Brothers' illustration. Maybe this is how Rumpelstiltskin ended his days.

"Mary had a little lamb," Dr. Kob says, and titters as he downs another glass of port. That Mary business annoys me more than he can imagine. He doesn't realize I caught on to his stupid inside joke and its antecedent years ago. *I read classical literature, too, you pompous ass.* I've Melville, Dickens, and Chaucer in the bedside cupboard. And Shelley, that bitch. On the other hand, perhaps I should be grateful. He could've named me Victor or Igor.

"—Mary had a little lamb—"

"—then she had a little mutton," Pelt says in an accent so thick you'd need one of his pig-stickers to cut it. I don't think Pelt likes me, our occasional drunken coupling notwithstanding. It's not exactly easy to find a good screw in this pit. I wonder if Dr. Kob knows about Pelt and me. The Old Man is cagey—I wouldn't be surprised if Pelt reported the results of our trysts as part of some twisted experiment like the Apted documentaries that appear on PBS every seven years. Man, I'd love to get in front of a camera and monologue about some of the shit I've seen. Yeah, there's a frustrated actor in here. A frustrated nymphomaniac as well—sorry, Pelt.

PROMETHEAN ORIGINATION AND IMPACTS

CATEGORY

Midday now and I taste the ozone; my joints ache. From the parapet of the attic tower I can see way out across the water to where the horizon has shifted into black. It's coming on fast, that rolling hell.

The trees start to shake. Leaves come loose and flutter past my face. This is going to be a hummer. My hair is already frizzing. High elevations are bad places to be at times such as these. This particular roof is even worse than most because of all the lightning rods. Well, they aren't exactly lightning rods in the traditional sense. They serve other uses, primarily transferring electricity to the Doctor's lab equipment. Like a good gofer, I've come to make certain everything is shipshape—the array is rather delicate and must be aligned precisely. There's nothing more complicated about the job than jiggling a television antenna until the picture clears, but it has to be right or all hell might break loose.

I make the adjustments and then retreat inside and head for the kitchen. One of the chef's minions, a cook named Helga, fixes me cocoa and marshmallows. I'm sitting on one of the high stools, swinging my feet and sipping my hot chocolate when Dr. Kob comes around the corner, his usually slicked hair in disarray, his tie loose and shirt untucked.

"Mary," he says. "You double-checked the array, I presume?" He scarcely acknowledges my answer; his mind is already three jumps ahead, and besides, my loyalty is unquestioned. "One of my specimens expired last night—but all is not lost. My revivification project awaits!"

"Remember not to talk on the phone during the storm," I say. "I just saw an account of a woman who was fried doing dishes. Ball lightning exploded from the sink and set her on fire. It traveled through the pipes."

Dr. Kob stares at me, his beady eyes narrowed. He rubs his temples as if experiencing a migraine. "You're watching the talk shows again. You know how I frown upon that, my dear. Less daydreaming, more physical exertion. Remind me to have Pelt assign you additional duties. Idle hands and all that."

"Sure, gimme a pitchfork and I'll swamp out the stables."

"Never mention pitchforks again!"

"Or torches."

"Out! Before I lose patience for your belligerence. And tomorrow, take the rod into our lovely village for quality-assurance testing. I've altered the design. It possesses more jolt than ever."

"As you command," I say sweetly. After he wanders off, I chew my cup and swallow it piece by piece. It kind of frightens me that my Pavlovian dread of the Doctor has ebbed, replaced by an abiding irritation. This is very dangerous. He's a middle-aged megalomaniacal child—a *L'enfant Terrible*. We know what rotten children do with their toys, right?

He gave me a puppy, once. I loved her, and often imagined how she had crept into the caves of my ancestors to escape the cold and the dark. I accidentally broke the puppy's neck. It's probably a good thing he didn't hand me the little brother I always wanted.

. . . .

Some people mow the lawn, others take out the garbage, or walk the pooch. Among similar menial tasks, I kidnap and kill whomever the Doctor says to kidnap or kill. I enjoyed it during my formative years. My rudimentary self was a glutton for the endorphin rush, the ecstasy of primal release. As my brain evolved, I developed, if not a conscience, at least the semblance of ethics. The glamour has faded, alas, and now this, too, bores me to tears. Frankly, it's about as stimulating as tearing the limbs off dolls.

Usually I do the deed with this device Dr. Kob invented that's something on the order of an unimaginably powerful cattle prod. This prod is capable of emitting a charge much greater than the lethally electrified fences one might encounter surrounding a top-secret military installation. It fits in my coat pocket and telescopes with the flick of my wrist, like those baton whips cops use to pacify rowdy protesters.

There are two basic methods of killing with the rod. (Dr. Kob encourages ample experimentation.) I jumped out of a hedge and zapped the last one, a banker in a suit and tie, from a distance of six paces. He shuddered and dropped in his tracks as if shot. Sometimes the energy exits from the temple or forehead and leaves a small hole like a bullet wound. I prefer to discharge from beyond arm's reach as a safety precaution, but it's not always feasible.

The second method is rather awful. The rod is thick at the base and gradually tapers to a point the diameter of a darning needle. A few weeks back I ministered to those two pole dancers who made such a sensation when the cops discovered them. And hell no, that particular job didn't bother me a whit. I'm not altogether fond of the pretty ones, and when they're haughty little bitch queens to boot . . . well, I consider it justice served. Anyway, their housemate walked in on the proceedings. I recognized him as a bouncer from the club where the girls worked—a powerfully built guy tattooed front and back, with head-to-toe chains and piercings, and yellow, piggy eyes that burned with a love of violence. He almost got his hands on me before I stabbed him in the chest with the rod and dialed up the juice. The force hurled him end over end into the wall, where he sprawled, limbs flailing grand mal style. His eyes sizzled like egg yolks and sucked into his skull; his teeth shattered, his hair ignited, and all that miscellaneous metal reduced to slag as his skin charred and peeled. I'm no weak sister, but the greasy smoke, its stench, always gets me. I ran to the window and puked into a flower box. Then I got the hell out.

Dr. Kob wanted to hear everything, of course.

· · · ·

My lifelong fantasy about running away with the circus isn't likely to pan out. I'm okay with that. I buy tickets when a show's in town and make excuses to disappear for a few hours. Dr. Kob took me once when I was a child; for a while, he had this fascination with pretending I was his little girl. We went a lot of places during that happy period: picnics on the beach, the carnival, ice skating at the mall, and similarly nutty stuff. Nutty, because it was so damned out of character for the Doctor.

The circus is what sticks in my mind and I've continued to go long after the Doctor lost all interest in passing me off as his ugly daughter. I've even convinced Pelt to come along a couple of times, but not since he got into a row with a gang of carnies and cut off three fingers of one poor bastard. Pelt's an unpleasant drunk, to say the least.

A couple of weeks before my birthday, I'm scanning the paper and spot an advertisement for the impending arrival of the Banning Traveling Circus. Of such trivial things is treachery made . . .

This is a minor show, no Ringling Brothers extravaganza by any stretch, but it has elephants and trapeze artists and shiny women in leotards. One of the shiny women has long hair done in a single braid. A man dangles by his knees from the high swing, her hair clamped in his teeth as she spins below him with such velocity her limbs merge with her torso. The clowns zoom into the ring in their clown car, and the dancing bear wobbles in on his unicycle. Hijinks ensue. I clap, unable to contain my glee. It's all so damned simple I could cry.

After the main show I wander the grounds, a paper cup of beer in hand, a blob of pink cotton candy in the other. I resist the urge to visit the freak tent, and always fail. It's usually lame, and this collection is weaker than most. Crocodile Boy has a serious overbite, and that's it. He's from Georgia and works as a hairdresser in the off-season. No two-headed babies, no wolf men. The bearded lady is rather impressive, though. She's a brawny, Bavarian lass named Lila, who'd fit right in with the mansion staff. Her beard isn't particularly thick, yet it's immaculate and descends to her navel. Its point is waxed and gives her a sort of Mandarin vibe. She has the softest, greenest eyes.

She does her thing and it's getting dark, so the crowds trickle back to the parking lot under the pall of burnt kettle corn. Lila, Edna the tattooed lady, and I are talking and they invite me to the "after the show get-together"; a bunch of them always do. They gather under some tarps pitched between their trailers and wagons. I meet Cleo the strongman (who's definitely over the hill and suffering from chronic asthma), and Buddy Lemon and his wife, Sri Lanka, the trapeze artists, and Armand, the guy who trains the lions and elephants, although I'm informed he sucks at both by Lila, who whispers that two of the lions have mauled people and Dino stomped on a carnie, all in the last three months. Judging from how fast Armand guzzles a bottle of corn mash, I suspect she may be on to something.

They're a sweet bunch, raw and melancholy. As always, there's got to be one asshole in the crowd, though. A barker named Niall. A pigeon-chested guy with a pencil moustache and a waist like a fashion model. His crappy yellow-and-white striped suit is cut a size too small, even for him. He makes a snide remark about my "swarthy, and exceptionally stout" personage in a smarmy English accent. He tells Cleo to "watch out, mate, she appears as if she could beat you out of a job." I'm relieved and grateful when Lila glares and he slinks off to his quarters.

As the group drifts apart, Lila grabs my arm and says to come with her back to the trailer. I'm privately questioning the wisdom of this, because I've never had another woman come on to me before, and more important, there's the Doctor to consider. He keeps strange hours. There's no telling what mood he's in. I might be punished for leaving the house without permission. But I'm in a perverse mood so I follow her.

We're surrounded by farmland and it's extra dark on account of it being a moonless night, which Lila tells me is perfect for stargazing. She says the constellation she's been monitoring is tricky to capture due to its distance. Light pollution only adds to the degree of difficulty. She spends a few minutes adjusting the rig and muttering to herself, and I steady her elbow as she sways on unsteady legs.

Finally, she says, "Okay, all right, here we go. I'm getting damned good at this—you have no idea how hard it is to nail down the Serpens galaxy." She guides my eye to the viewfinder and makes adjustments as I describe what I see, which at first isn't much but black space punctuated by random lights.

Then, "Oh. It's . . . beautiful." And it is beautiful, an impossibly remote field of stars veiled in clouds of dust and gas, and at its heart, a wavering flame that illuminates from the inside out, like fire shining through a smoky glass. I know it's old, old. Older even than my ancestors who scrabbled and clawed in the earliest days on this rock.

"Have you used a telescope before?"

"No," I say, slightly embarrassed that Dr. Kob often visits the Deer Mountain Observatory just a few miles from our house and yet I've never once asked to tag along.

PROMETHEAN ORIGINATION AND IMPACTS

CATEGORY

"Don't blink," she says. "Like my Pa used to say, 'You gotta hold your jaw just right' when he taught me how to fire his deer gun. You blink, NCG 6118 will go *poof* and you might not ever find her again."

"How *do* you find her again?" I don't need Lila to explain her fascination with the constellation, her fear of losing it forever. Its austere beauty stirs something cold in my breast.

"I memorized her position. Also, I've got a chart with the coordinates and the Dreyer description. Doesn't make it easy, though."

"You wrote it down? Where?"

"It's in my stuff. In my suitcase."

"I'd love to see it," I say.

"Yeah? Why? This some kind of trick to get me cozy in my trailer?"

I wrestle my gaze from the telescope and take her small hand in mine. "Something like that."

"Man alive, I'd love to see it through a real telescope."

I think about the mega-powerful telescope owned by the Redfield Observatory and tremble. "What about your family? Couldn't your dad pull a few strings?"

"Yeah, if I hadn't left him behind for all this." She laughs. "I haven't spoken to him in . . . a while."

"Father-daughter relationships are the worst," I say.

We pack it in and meander to her trailer. She shares it with a couple of other girls, but one missed the trip, and the other stays with a boyfriend when she's in town. Nothing happens. We have a couple of Southern Comfort nightcaps. Then she falls asleep on her dumpy couch. After she's snoring, I rummage through her bags and find the astronomical charts she's gathered and stick the one I need into my pocket next to the cold, lethal smoothness of the prod. I smooch Lila's furry cheek on my way out the door.

• • • •

The storm broadsides the estate an hour or so before dark.

The Doctor has sent word that I'm to report to the laboratory at once. He requires me at the crank that revs up the dynamo. Like all his gadgets, the crank is unwieldy and impractical and nobody else is physically strong enough to make it turn with sufficient speed. The combination of my efforts and the electrical storm are crucial one-two punches in the pursuit of scientific progress. Tonight's the night he jump-starts yet another patchwork corpse, and maybe this time it'll work and he'll snag the Nobel and show his lamentably deceased dad who the *real* scientist is in the family.

At the moment, I'm on the front porch, standing beneath the awning, goggling at nature's wrath. Thin, jagged bolts of lightning splinter in whitehot strokes that repeat every fifteen to twenty seconds. Wind and rain

BLOOD & STARDUST   LAIRD BARRON

crash upon the eaves like an avalanche. By some confluence of atmospheric forces, the air dims and reddens as the grounds have been transmogrified into the soundstage of a Martian epic. I swing my hand back and forth, fascinated at how it seems to float and multiply as it drags through the bloody light. I skip from the sheltering eaves toward the middle of the driveway, feigning carefree abandon as I throw my hands skyward and tilt my face so water streams from it. The reality is, the strikes are marching ever closer and I want to get the hell clear of the house.

Pelt sits in a rocker by the rail of the third-floor balcony. He strikes a match on the sole of his cowboy boot and lights one of his nasty hand-rolled cigarettes I can smell from a hundred yards away. He eyes me with the cold intensity of a raptor studying a mouse and I wonder if his instincts are actually that damned sharp. Could he really know? The notion chills me in a way the deluge can't.

A second later none of that matters. Lightning flares directly overhead, and I feel in my bones that this is it, *this* bolt has been drawn into the array. And man, oh, man, had I screwed that over big-time earlier in the day. I clap my hand over my eyes. The blue-white flash stabs through the cracks between my fingers. The top of the house explodes and the effect is epic beyond my fondest dreams. The concussion sits me down, hard, as all the windows on this side of the building shatter. Fiery chunks of wood, glass, and stone arc upward and outward in a ring. Debris crashes to earth in the gardens, is catapulted among the waving treetops. It's glorious.

The house remains upright, although minus a substantial portion of the third story. Smoke pours down the sides of the building, thick and black, and chivvied by blasts of wind; it roils across the muddy yard and acres of lawn, lowering a hellish, apocalyptic shroud over the works. I'm on my feet again and primed for violence. Pelt will be coming for me. Except, the sly bastard's vanished—his left boot is stuck in the mud near the front steps. I hope against hope he's dead. Servants stumble through the smoke, clutching each other. Their quarters occupy the ground floor, so I doubt any got caught in the explosion. This is their lucky day. None of them glance at me as they file past, moaning and sobbing like a chain of ghosts.

I have to be sure. The rain kills the worst of the flames, snuffs them before they can create an inferno. The grand staircase is in sorry shape. Several steps are gone. I hopscotch my way onward and upward while lightning flashes through the giant hole in the ceiling. Happily, the laboratory, its various sinister machines, have been obliterated. Upon closer inspection, I spy the Doctor's mangled and gruesomely mutilated person fallen through the floor where it lies pinned beneath a shattered beam. His body is burnt and crushed. He's quite mindless in his agonies, shrieking for his dead parents and the friends he doesn't have.

Yeah, I should finish the job. That's the smart move. Alas, alack, I'm too melodramatic to take the easy way out.

· · · ·

The Doctor keeps a machine in the cellar. When I'm feeling blue I sneak down and bathe in its unearthly glow. It kicks mad-scientist old school; a mass of bulbs and monster transistors, Tesla coils, exposed circuitry, and cables as thick as pythons going every which way. At the heart of this '50s gadgetry is a bubble of glass with an upright table for a passenger. Allegedly the bubble shifts through time and space. Dr. Kob's grandfather built the prototype in 1879, powered it via lightning stored in an array of crude batteries. The new model still runs on deep cycle batteries Dr. Kob Jr. scavenged from backhoes and bulldozers.

The main reason the Master traps lightning to energize his devices is because they suck so much juice the electric bill would draw prying eyes sooner rather than later. There's a backup diesel generator gathering dust for a true emergency. The Doctor is sentimental about his methods, obsessed with the holistic nature of the process. He won't drive or fly, won't operate a computer, not even a typewriter. He scratches in his voluminous journals with quill and ink. In the mansion, every lamp runs on kerosene; the stoves and furnaces, coal; our black-and-white televisions and radios, batteries. We're like an evil alternate universe version of the Amish.

The T&S machine holds special significance for me, because that's the device of my genesis, my cradle and incubator. Dr. Kob reached back into the great dark heart of prehistory to pluck an egg from my mother's womb and fertilized it with God knows what. He effected a few cosmetic alterations to bring me marginally in line with the latest iteration of the species, dressed me up like a real girl, taught me to walk and talk and hold a spoon. He forbade my partaking in any sort of significant education—apparently he couldn't reconcile his anthropological interest with his fear that I might become too smart for his health. Indeed, I'm certain if he ever had the slightest inkling of my true intellectual capacity, he'd have sent Pelt to slit my throat in the night.

However, I learned to read, no thanks to him. Poor dearly departed Goldilocks took care of that on the sly. I was ripping through college-level lit by the tender age of fourteen. Eliza Doolittle, eat your heart out.

The procedure hasn't been without unexpected complications, however. You wouldn't believe my psychedelic dreams, and if I'm ever caught and placed on trial for crimes against humanity, I'll get an insanity pass on the descriptions alone. Genetic memory? I dunno; all I know is that in dreams I go for a ride on an astral carpet to a high desert wasteland that spreads under a wide carnivorous sky. The tribe kills with rocks and clubs; it assembles in caves and lays its feasts upon the dirt. They haven't invented fire, thus meat and skin is crushed and smeared on rocks, like fingerpaint and wet clay. The brutes, my people, see my apparition, doubtless grotesque in its familiarity, and hoot in alarm and outrage, jam-red mouths agape. Then, the large males, the killers, snarl and snatch up their clubs and their stones, and hop toward me with murder on their minds.

Nine times out of ten, I jerk into wakefulness, alone in my dingy cell with the television screen full of snow. The tenth time out of ten, I come to in a field, naked and covered in scabs of blood, with no memory but the dream memories.

· · · ·

Even the Doctor isn't quite mad enough to do what I've done. He's a lunatic, yes indeed. He's also a survivor. Better than most, he understands that one screws with the infinite at one's own peril. I'm sure the meticulously recorded results of those Victorian experiments with peasantry cooled his jets.

I, on the other hand, am a desperate sort.

Those nights the good Doctor and his toady spent drunk off their asses, I took the T&S machine for joyrides. The calibrations weren't difficult— I simply plugged in the various sequences from Doctor Kob's logs. The wild part is, the machine goes forward and back and to any physical location in the universe, provided one has the coordinates. The places I've gone, weirder and more frightening than those Technicolor nightmares.

After Doctor Kob and Pelt murder me in that squalid alley, I give them a moment to wonder at my dying words. But it's only a possible me, a shadow. Travelers exist in duplicate during collocation. It's complicated; suffice to say, each of us unique snowflakes, aren't. We exist as a plurality. That old saw about meeting yourself . . . it's only kinda true. The universe didn't unravel when I skipped ahead and met one of my future selves, an inveterate alcoholic and aimless wanderer, one bound to run afoul of Dr. Kob's plots of revenge. If she's anything like me (ha-ha!), she won't mind making the sacrifice to even the score.

Pelt knows something's wrong, but even as he turns I tap him with the prod and he's gone in a belch of gas and flame. The Doctor takes it in stride. He's a hobbled shell of a man, yet arrogant as ever. He commands me to drop the weapon and submit to my well-deserved punishment. I slug him and he falls unconscious. That feels so good, I've revisited the moment a dozen times.

This is how it ends for Daddy dearest: I strap him into the machine and send him to the land of my ancestors, and once he's evaporated into the abyss of Time I take an axe to the machine. I've gotten my kicks. That conscience I've been incubating stings like hell. Who knows what havoc I might wreak on material existence were I to keep dicking around with the timestream.

I sent the Doctor with a mint copy of *Frankenstein,* a dozen bottles of wine, and the prod with a full charge. It's the least I could do. The very least.

. . . .

I track the Banning Circus to a show in Wenatchee. The owner, the great-great-grandson of Ezra Banning, is skeptical when I apply for the strong-man job. He's got a strongman, he says, and I say I know. I also know his guy is getting long in the tooth and suffers from asthma, or emphysema, or whatever. Banning tells me to hit the bricks, he's a busy man, blah, blah. I walk over to the lion cage and tear the door off its hinges—naturally, I try to make it look casual, but the effort does me in for the day. The owner picks up his jaw. He sends one of his flunkies to break the news to poor Cleo. He doesn't even mind that it takes Armand the better part of two days and the assistance of local animal control to corral their lion and get him into his cage.

I knock on Lila's trailer door. A monster storm cloud is massing in the north and that could be good or bad. It certainly sets the scene. My hair is standing on end. Lila screams and throws her arms around me. She's crying a little and there's snot in her beard.

"Hey, this is for you," I say and give her a small wooden coffer I bought off a guy at a garage sale where I also scored some dumbbells to get in shape for my strongman—*strongperson*—audition.

"What is it?" She lifts the lid and gasps. An eerie golden light plays over her face.

"Stardust."

"Stardust?"

"I hope it's not radioactive. Maybe we should get a Geiger counter."

"You're yanking my chain."

I smile. "Never happen."

"Well . . . my God. Look at this. Where . . . ?"

I take the folded, spindled, and mutilated piece of paper with the Dreyer entry for galaxy N1168 from my pocket and give it to her. Light-ning parts the red sky like a cleaver. It reflects twin novas in her eyes. I grasp her free hand and press it against my heart.

Three, two, one. *Boom.*

———————

Laird Barron is the author many short stories, many of which appeared in The Magazine of Fantasy & Science Fiction, *and in anthologies such* as Inferno, Black Wings, Haunted Legends, Lovecraft Unbound, *and* Supernatural Noir. *Much of his short work has been collected in the volumes* The Imago Sequence *and* Occultation, *both of which won the Shirley Jackson Award for best collection. His work has also been a finalist for the World Fantasy Award, the Theodore Sturgeon Award, the International Horror Guild Award, and the Bram Stoker Award. His first novel,* The Croning, *recently came out from Night Shade Books.*

> **CATEGORY:** Power Strategies and Fact Manipulation
>
> **RULE 1776:** A Real Genius Can Fool All the People, All the Time
>
> **SOURCE:** Anonymous, advisor to William Lester, President, NAU
>
> **VIA:** L. E. Modesitt, Jr.

Madness isn't limited to the practitioners of hard science. Although the most infamous of crazed creations have sprung from the brains of scientists dabbling in physics, chemistry, or biotechnology, our next tale draws on a far more nefarious branch of intellect: political science.

Political scientists have a bit of a bad name. The lobbyists and analysts stalking the halls of the Senate and House are spurned by voters and legislators alike. Most people see them as manipulative schemers, twisting the power structure of the nation for their own benefit. For many, that scorn is probably undeserved, but the unnamed narrator of our next story lives up to that reputation and then some. He has great plans for the people of the North American continent—plans so large, they will shake the entire world.

The author says that this story was inspired by the events that led to his becoming the legislative director for a U.S. congressman and later political positions, and spending nearly twenty years in politics, government, and Washington, D.C. So he speaks from a lifetime of experience in the twisted webs of political scientists.

Which makes you wonder: Just how fictional is this story?

A MORE PERFECT UNION

L. E. MODESITT, JR.

Too many historians claim all the geniuses were mad, especially the ones who understood politics as an engineer understands structures, or a scientist under-stands his specialty. The key is to understand their genius and not fall prey to the slurs on their abilities. How do you think Hitler and Goebbels captured the heart of Germany, or Lenin Russia, or Rasputin the Czar's family, or Bush the younger and Cheney capitalist America, or Lester the North American Union or . . . ? The list is as long as history, and everyone dismisses each instance as an individual aberration, a political situation unique to that nation and time. And too many people focus on only the negative instances, unlike the positive examples, such as the American planters or development of the present-day NAU. But I digress. To understand how it all happened, it's necessary to go back a few years . . .

. . . .

I'd recently finished the last oral examinations on my dissertation from one of the very well-known universities of North America and been granted the relatively worthless Ph.D. in Political Science, despite the opposition of the most senior member of the PoliSci faculty. A "chance encounter" of a—shall we say—passionate nature he had with a young lady acquaintance of mine removed that obstacle. Shortly after that fortunate resolution I first encountered William Lester.

As part of my research, I'd become a member of the Conservative Popu-list party, and even served as a ward committee-person for Plymouth—not Massachusetts, but another Plymouth. Being the ward's titular head for the party was a position few wanted, especially when that year's elections were only for local offices and for the regional representatives to the North American Union, then far more of a coordinating body than what it later became, thanks in large part to my highly successful and unacknowledged (as well as unappreciated) efforts.

On that Tuesday night in 2067, only a few handfuls of voters attended the ward caucus to be addressed by two of the candidates for the NAU Assembly. The first candidate was Johnstone Byron III, the youngest son of the Byron family of ZipZap fame and fortune, and the second was one

William Lester, barely five years older than I was at the time, but already working on his second billion. Lester was a perfect 198 centimeters, tall enough to stand out amid the rabble, but not tall enough to be thought a less-than-intelligent athlete. His father had been a builder who'd lost almost everything in the successive American financial meltdowns in the early part of the century, and Lester could claim to be a self-made man from his foresight in purchasing northern Saskatchewan marshes and swamplands before the acceleration of global warming created a land-run. He sold out before the subsequent crash, retaining some holdings in the event of the inevitable resurgence that would come with the next wave of global warming, when the last lingering benefits—and profits—of cap-and-trade were exhausted.

Lester's voice was deep and mellifluous. His face was pleasant, with a touch of authority beyond the grown-up-boy-from-next-door image he cultivated, and his chin was just square enough to proclaim solidity, but not pigheadedness. His logic was impeccable when he addressed the thirty-odd folks with little else to do on a Tuesday night . . . and that was the problem. While he understood finance, he clearly didn't comprehend certain aspects of motivating people to tap the touchscreen next to his name in the voting booth. Part of that, I later learned, was because he'd always dealt with people who actually cared about the intricacies of systems such as politics and business, rather than, put politely, the general public.

So immediately after he finished speaking, I went out on the already half-sawed-off and spruce-beetle-killed limb. From that precarious perch, I addressed the handful of ConPoppers still in the multipurpose room of the west Plymouth Library. "My friends, we've heard from both of these fine candidates—the distinguished and noted scion of fame and fortune, the most highly educated and multiply-degreed, the honorable Johnstone Byron the Third . . . and the hard-working Bill Lester, who has made every new dollar the hard way with his own two hands. A round of applause for them both, before you make your way to the voting screens . . ."

I did have the foresight to hide Lester's Turnbull & Asser black cashmere overcoat so that he had to wait until everyone was lined up to vote—and so that no one saw it. That enabled me to lead him out to the foyer, where I offered him back his coat.

"Mr. Lester," I said, because all politicians want to be the one to tell you to be less formal, rather than having you take that initiative, "I think I can help you."

He didn't tell me "no," but he didn't agree, either. He also didn't tell me to call him "Bill." That came later.

Even with my efforts, Lester only won the ward by nineteen to ten. He did win enough wards, if only by the application of a great deal of effort and tangible financial assets and, I have to admit, his own mellifluous voice to get on the ConPopper final slate for the election of delegates to represent the old northeast USA in the NAU.

I did more research before I attended the regional NAU convention, and, before the votes were taken at the convention, I cornered William Lester while he was talking to a sandy-haired and ruddy man dressed in a cranberry-maroon Harris Tweed jacket far too loud for the tastes of most ConPoppers, and a deep solid-maroon tie that was too conservative, not that all ties weren't suspect to the bedrock ConPoppers.

Lester saw me coming, and he didn't quite roll his eyes. "Why don't you talk to Anderson, here? He's my campaign manager. He's the organization man." Lester eased away graciously and charmingly. I have to admit that he did that well.

I smiled politely at Anderson LeBrun. He'd been the staff director for Senator Claxton until the senator had lost his reelection bid after his links to the failed Northcoast Golf and Rugby Club had been revealed by his mistress. Then, it might have been that his mistress had been later revealed to be an transvestite, and Claxton had protested that he hadn't known.

"Bill said that you rounded up a few votes for him in Plymouth," offered LeBrun, "and gave a good pitch for him."

"I'd like to think so, but he's a very good speaker. I do think we could focus his speeches to be more effective." I meant that I could, of course, but you always use "we" when trying to become part of an organization, however small.

"You're one of those academic types."

"No. I use academic and other research methods to gain the maximum positive emphasis for whomever I work for, and the maximum negative exposure for his opponent. That's the polite way of putting it. Everything's aboveboard and clean in the dirtiest way possible with no fingerprints."

"Oh?" LeBrun wiggled his bushy eyebrows. "What advantage would that provide, beyond fancy language?"

"Old-fashioned results with no legal fuss."

"Why don't you explain?"

I did, and LeBrun hired me on the campaign as researcher and strategist. I didn't get paid as much as I'd made as a teaching assistant at the university, but I wasn't in it for the initial pay. The first thing I got to work on was a position piece—a Web-based info-slam or Webchure—flooding the Net and letting everyone know just how good a man William Lester was. Of course, the hidden tags about "sex," "free money," "scandal," and "reducing your utility bills"—among others—didn't hurt.

Neither did all the documentation on Wikipedia, Armsapedia, Sexapedia, Publicapedia—all of the targeted online "encyclopediae"—because all of what we posted was scrupulously true. That was to play up the lawsuit we filed when our opponents tried to claim we were electioneering on public communications systems.

By the time we were finished, Lester came out as the leading ConPopper candidate in the eastern USA—and in early 2068, he went to Ottawa as a delegate and a politician to watch, mainly because no one could figure out why he'd worked so hard and spent more than a few millions of his own funds to get elected to what amounted to being a delegate to an advisory assembly.

The NAU wasn't totally advisory, although most people thought so. It could set mandatory continental shelf fishing quotas as well as patrol the Arctic Ocean against foreign mineral-nappers, supported by the Offshore Patrol—what was left of the U.S. Coast Guard that had been transferred to the NAU, along with the less-than-adequate funding to support it. The NAU also had just completed the integrated intraborder security system between the United States and Canada, effectively erasing all border patrols there. The Congress had acquiesced in that in order to shift U.S. Homeland Security forces to the Mexican border, where they could expand their free-fire zones. Besides, since more and more U.S. citizens had migrated northward, and very few Canadians wanted to move south, there wasn't much point in the U.S. border checkpoints anyway, and the Canadians still wanted U.S. new dollars.

For the first year, Lester made speeches and attended debates, and offered high-sounding propositions—but only the ones I told him wouldn't come back to bite him. Anderson LeBrun didn't like Ottawa. That was what he told Lester, anyway, nothing about his not wanting his dalliances to come out, given his prenuptial agreement with his fourth wife—something about a different resource division if that occurred. I did counsel Anderson that leaving was probably in his best interests. I even smiled. He didn't.

Before long, Lester proposed letting the NAU Offshore Patrol take over anti-smuggling duties along the North American coastline. With the adoption of the low-cost MS integrated sonar/radar imaging systems and the RPV-towed balloon limpet mines, the Offshore Patrol effectively reduced sea-borne smuggling by 90 percent, and Lester was hailed as innovative and cost-effective.

That wasn't enough for him, but I'd known that from the beginning. Fame and adulation are far more addictive than money or sex, or even money and sex combined.

He sauntered into the staff office in Ottawa on that June fourteenth and looked at me. "I've done all I can do here. It's time to get ready to make the Senate run."

I gave him a polite smile, the one that he knew meant I had reservations.

"You don't agree. Why not?"

"You'd be better served running for vice chairman of the NAU." The popular view was that no one of any import wanted the position of vice chairman of the NAU, that is, except Charles Morgan . . . and Luis Gonsalvo, who had no chance, not when half his potential supporters had nowhere to vote. Even Lester wasn't that interested.

"It's a meaningless position in a largely ceremonial organization," he pointed out. "Why would I want to do that? I ran for the NAU Assembly to build name recognition without having to wait for years to work up through the party to run for the U.S. Senate."

I didn't tell him that running for the Senate would have been a stupid decision. "It may seem like a meaningless position, but it has national and international visibility, and you get the NAU to pay for a larger staff. Plus, since they're paid in Canadian loonies, you can get better staff while you wait for the next Senate election. You run next year, and you're against John Jacob Astor. He won with eighty percent of the vote."

"That's because he was a porn star. Besides, I've got more than enough money."

So I told him, "You might not take Astor, but you can take Morgan, and the position of vice chairman won't be ceremonial in another two years."

By then, Lester knew enough not to dispute me on things like that. "What do you see happening? What exactly do you have in mind?"

"What's the current U.S. deficit—this past year?"

"Twenty trillion."

"And what are the projections for next year?"

"You're the political scientist."

"That's true." At times, I knew he thought I was a political *mad* scientist, but I'd been right on so far as he was concerned, all the way.

"So you tell me what this has to do with me . . . and the Senate run."

"Next year's deficit will run to fifty trillion . . . if they're lucky, and the president and the Congress will have to come to the NAU to serve as an intermediary for a bailout from Canada or the Indian multinationals. They won't call it that. It'll be a restructuring of governmental assets or something like that. The Canadians will have to pony up, because they don't want the Indians getting a foothold, not after what it cost to buy off the Chinese in the second restructuring. You don't want to be the Senate to clean up that mess, but you do want to be in a visible position when that happens. Even if it doesn't happen, the visibility won't hurt your political future. In fact, visibility in a position where you can't be held accountable for the mess will be an asset."

He did nod at that, before he spoke again. "What about Morgan? Charlie's never made a mistake in his life. He's still married to his childhood sweetheart. He's not brilliant, but he's definitely not stupid. He's always hired the best and the brightest staff, and he's listened to them."

"What church does he attend?"

Lester looked puzzled. "That's not an issue. The man hasn't so much as a littering or a water-overuse citation. He's greener than the northern swamps and straighter than a hydropower spillway."

"Don't worry about it. We'll take care of it." And we did.

First, we came up with a series of Webchures—each one targeted at a different voter niche. My favorite was the one for the high-minded hypocrites. We didn't call them that, of course. They were voter group 1A-Beta: Undecided, highly educated, religiously affiliated, self-identified, self-made professionals.

The Webchure was slick. It showed Morgan in a series of images—all with members of his staff, all recognizable, and all digitally "enhanced" to highlight their attractiveness, especially that of the men, and their positions altered to bring them very close together. We also made some very subtle alterations to Morgan's expressions, so that he appeared far more interested in his companion than in the papers or the scene. And the captions were, pardon the pun, apparently straightforward.

"NAU delegate Morgan working closely with trusted aide Mark Roberts . . ."

"Morgan discussing medical issues with . . ."

"Longtime personal assistant with Delegate Morgan . . ."

The text took Morgan's own words, often from debates before the NAU in Ottawa, ostensibly setting forth his own words.

> . . . and I would like to thank the gentlewoman from London, Ontario, and she is a gentle, sensitive, and feeling woman in every sense of the word, for raising the issue of non-asset-based financial and economic interdependence, particularly as it pertains to currency stability across the NAU . . .
>
> . . . we all know what we know, but what we know is not necessarily what we think we know, especially in terms of cybertechnological-asset management interfaces . . .

The Webchures for other groups were more pointed, since most of the other niche voter groups weren't inclined to value subtlety. I particularly liked the one that went to Weapons Unlimited, which featured Lester standing beside an M-98 tank, smiling.

"Tired of tiresome U.S. regulations on the right of self-protection? Ready for a new approach? Then support Bill Lester . . ."

Then again, the one to Trees Unlimited wasn't bad, either. There, Lester was standing before a stand of Mugo pines in northern Saskatchewan and declaiming, "Reforestation is the key to a better environment and more effective government . . . I've known that for years, and that's why I was one of the first to put my own money into growing these very trees . . ."

Of course, he'd planted them years before as a backdrop for his land deals; so his claim of putting his own money out was perfectly accurate.

The one to the computer professionals was also catchy. We just provided a message that claimed it had a hidden algorithm, designed and concealed by a North American programmer, as opposed to the Microsoft techs who'd run off to India, which was why Lester favored local expertise. There wasn't any algorithm; so no one could find it, and the Microsoft attorneys filed a cease-and-desist order. We complied, and then sent another message that pointed out that Microsoft could only respond with lawyers, not programmers. They couldn't fight that, either, because it was true.

Now, an old-line news analyst of the past century might have caught a certain lack of philosophical consistency, but after the passage of the revised Freedom of Information Act of 2040 by the U.S. Congress, which affirmed the right of every citizen to the news of his or her choice, unhampered by contradictory facts, none of the 207 different news channels had a news analyst interested in such, since hiring anyone for such a position might have subjected them to civil action under the FOIA [revised].

All of the Webchures went out under the independent information provider provisions of Canadian and U.S. law, and every word in any of them was absolutely factually verifiable.

Parts of Lester's stump speech were tailored to whatever audience he was addressing, the need for ecologically sound maple tree research in Vermont, investigating sustainable and balanced cod harvests and more federal assistance for bark-beetle eradication in Maine, the need for regional communications tariff subsidies in Massachusetts, support of Tar Sands subsidies in Alberta . . . Those sorts of postures have been a political staple since Alcibiades, but since no one studies history anymore, I could adopt strategies and points from everywhere, and no one had a ready counter. But the real gut issue was belief, and that part of Lester's speech always hit certain points.

"I stand for the good, old-fashioned values of hard work . . . and the faith behind those values. There are those who condemn people of faith and belief, but what I find truly amazing is that as belief in an Almighty Deity has declined, so has this great American continent. When atheists were five percent of the population, the nations of North America were strong and proud. Today . . . almost a third of North Americans are nonbelievers. Are we as strong? Are we as dedicated to hard and honest work? I'd be the last man to tell you *how* to believe, but I'll be the first to tell you that belief is important, that trust in the Almighty and the virtues He espouses are the keys to our future . . . Would you trust any politician who puts himself above the Almighty or denies the power that created this vast universe . . . ?"

At first, Morgan didn't even understand what was happening, and by the time he did, it was far too late.

Of course, the liberals in Massachusetts, SoCal, and in what was left of flooded New York City screamed and yelled, but they did it all in newsprint, and no one but people who wouldn't have voted for Lester anyway read the handful of remaining newspapers and magazines, online or otherwise. And most of those didn't care that much who won the election.

Although it was close, even if only 10 percent of the eligible voters in Canada and the United States voted, Lester did eke out a victory over Morgan, by a good thirty-thousand votes out of forty million cast on that Sunday in September. No one paid much attention to the votes from Mexico and Central America, because there weren't all that many voters left, not after the hurricanes of the forties, and most of those who could vote, in places where there were even polling places, all voted for Gonsalvo, and he came in a distant third.

"You won," I told Lester when I walked into his small delegate's office in Ottawa on Monday morning.

"Now what?"

"Before long, Chairman Hazlett will discover he doesn't want to really run things, and you'll make yourself indispensable. . . . Just be very visible, and very charming . . . and very helpful. As always."

I could tell he wasn't happy, but I found him a new personal assistant and lined up as many speaking appearances for him as possible, just to keep him occupied until the inevitable occurred—which it did . . . just about a year later.

The United States deficit topped one hundred trillion, and the remaining Republicans and the Conservative Populists in the U.S. House of Representatives balked at increasing the marginal federal income tax on the upper middle class—those making over ten million a year—to 70 percent. The Democrats refused to consider imposing a 1 percent tax on the so-called working poor—those making less than a million. At that point, the Bank of China not only refused to buy American treasuries, but threatened to dump everything they had. Microsoft, headquartered and totally based in India since the Great Seattle Quake of 2057, stopped manufacturing replacement parts for the obsolete computers used by the American government, and the Bank of Canada foreclosed on the U.S. Federal Reserve, which had been privatized after the Collapse of 2050.

President Huston demanded that the congressional leaders work out a compromise, and they did. They impeached him. Vice President Ramirez resigned, and Speaker of the House Coulter became president. She still couldn't get the votes to break the impasse and proclaimed Martial Law under the provisions of the Patriot Act of 2051.

General Simplot, the U.S. Armed Forces Chief of Staff, threatened to release all military personnel from active duty, because none had been paid in two months.

That was the point at which I made my next suggestion to Lester. "Have Hazlett recommend that the North American Union take over government functions for the United States, using the Canadian dollar. By eliminating Congress and not funding the bureaucracies and lobbyists in Washington, the lower tax rates will cover paying the military so that Americans can feel protected by American soldiers and sailors, while finally getting real universal health care, and not the charades of 2010 and 2035. Tell everyone that the military uniforms won't change, and neither will their responsibilities, and that they'll remain right where they are, since the Canadians might get touchy, otherwise. Since you're an American, elected by Americans . . ."

It wasn't all that simple, as the massacre in Berkeley and the famine in Illinois and Indiana proved, but by the winter of 2071, the NAU was effectively governing North America. Hazlett wasn't that young, and more and more he had to rely on Lester—and his staff.

Hazlett's wife had left him because she thought he was a traitor to Canada, and fled to Buffalo Narrows, way up north. She drowned in the floods of 2072, almost instantly, when a methane belch caught fire in the permafrost and melted everything in sight. I arranged matters to provide him with some enthusiastic consolation; seven months later, he died a very happy man, and William Lester became chairman of the NAU.

Matters to the south of Ottawa weren't getting any better, especially in the United States and Central America, and the Canadians—particularly former U.S. residents who'd fled the three banking restructurings, the financial restoration surtaxes, and Buy U.S. Transport Acts—were deeply concerned that Canada had ended up funding the rebuilding of the nearly prostrate United States, despite the fact that, or perhaps because of, more than 25 percent of the U.S. population in 2050 had since emigrated to Canada.

So Lester proposed a raft of reorganization programs, among them the Regional Area Prosperity Effort, the American Financial Transformation plan, the Social Cooperation and Regional Economic Work plan, and the Financial Reconstruction and Infrastructure Grants. The most immediately effective of these was the Youth Alliance for Restoration and Progress, a regional plan for those areas of the NAU where social order was degenerating, notably those declining piles of stone south of Ottawa.

While the Union assembly had some qualms, Lester had the answers we'd prepared, particularly in his second state of the North American Union address:

"When social order begins to degenerate, the first signs are small things: loitering, littering, broken windows, lazy people using public spaces for private functions. YARP is designed to mobilize the talents of young people who would otherwise be unemployed or underemployed to combat this kind of deterioration. Those without homes will be relocated to appropriate housing elsewhere. Those who persist in unrestricted tagging or decoration or socially nonconstructive protests and objections will be detained and reeducated in socially acceptable decorative endeavors, beautifying cities and parks . . ."

The dark gray YARP uniforms were sharp, too, and . . . within a year, all sorts of crime in the old United States of America had dropped precipitously, except in Washington, D.C., where YARP was precluded by a provision requested by Acting President Coulter, and in SoCal, because the NAU had decided that the better part of valor was to wait until the various factions had determined who governed what, since the Republicans insisted on balancing local budgets with a 90 percent deficit, and the Democrats refused to cut nonexistent spending for a state workforce that no longer existed, and CrackArmy was taking over most of the urban areas.

The U.S. Army troops were, for the most part, more than happy to transfer to the NAU unified military, with their old commanders and new funding to repair their old bases, and to fuel their tanks and aircraft. They also appreciated getting regular pay and medical benefits. Not long after that, Lester returned areas of old Mexico to "local authorities," delegating all functions to the locals and surrounding such areas with remote automatic weapons. That had the effect of reducing drug deaths and related hospitalization costs, after, of course, the initial depopulation and the spate of acute withdrawal deaths, which weren't covered by NAU universal health care.

With some credit available and seaway control reestablished, Qataran LNG shipments resumed, and that allowed enough power for some air-conditioning, at least in Ottawa, and in the Toronto financial centers, and the Albertans got back full-time power, and more fertilizer was manufactured and sent to Saskatchewan, and the Tar Sands Fourth Phase really got going. Lester did have to divert money to rebuild port facilities in Victoria to replace those inundated by the rise in the Pacific Ocean.

When the time came for elections in 2073, only Johnstone Byron III filed to run against Lester. He was a good opponent, that fair-haired and wealthy do-gooder out of old New England, even if he hadn't learned much from his first contest against Lester. He got 31 percent of the vote, most of that from the provinces of Massachusetts, New York, NorCal, and Oregon.

On the other hand, turnout was light in the Old South of the United

States, but that was hardly unexpected after the 2072 hurricane that sank half of Louisiana and Mississippi, and eradicated the remains of Florida. Washington Province went heavily for Lester, since there weren't that many liberals or Democrats left after Microsoft closed down all its plants there years earlier, and the dryland farmers of Montana, the Dakotas, and lower Minnesota really didn't have anyone else to support.

Most of Alberta voted for Lester. That wasn't surprising, following the Colorado River Water Wars, since after the spruce and pine bark devastation had wiped out all the Utah mountain forests and the Great Salt Lake had become a salt flat, most of the Utah population had migrated into Alberta to follow their LDS brethren. The Temple in Salt Lake City did remain a holy place, standing in the middle of a desert—a sort of American Mecca. There was only a 30 percent turnout in Saskatchewan, because most of the voters didn't like either American candidate, although I would have thought that a few more would have supported Lester, given all the jobs his land booms had created in the northern part of the province.

Following the NAU election, it only made sense for NAU to disband the Canadian parliamentary government, and although some complained that the NAU military was overly demonstrative, particularly in Quebec, the subsequent savings certainly justified the effort, especially since bilingualism was no longer necessary in that province. And the northern relocation efforts have certainly resulted in a more equitable population distribution, and an increased labor force for the alternative minerals extraction program being pioneered by the NAU. All in all, we've created a more perfect union, and who would have thought it just a few short years ago?

. . . .

Now that the NAU has restructured North America into a far more productive and efficient nation, and all of those ills of the recent past are largely behind us, you can all set aside your fears about how a big and inefficient government will take over everything. Government is already smaller and more efficient. North Americans are keeping a greater percentage of their income because of the centralization of government and the elimination of local bureaucracies and excessive local elected bodies. With the new physical fitness initiatives, deaths from poor exercise and diet are down, as are the medical costs associated with them, after the initial readjustments, of course. The civic improvement brigades across all of NAU have lowered local infrastructure costs. With the integration of the Offshore Patrol, the former U.S. Navy, and the Canadian Naval Forces, there's absolutely no need to worry about illegal immigration, not with the wide-scale deployment of the new AI-guided limpet mines. The enactment and implementation of the Freedom of Choice Acts mean that you don't need to worry about spending your last years as a semi-sentient vegetable . . . and wasting your estate. With the reform of estate taxes and the revenues from FOCA violators, we've lowered income and property taxes, and the new educational curricula are instilling a greater reverence for the value of manual and skilled labor.

All this because of the enlightened policies of Chairman Lester . . . and a more perfect Union.

L. E. Modesitt, Jr., is the bestselling author of the Saga of Recluce, the Spellsong Cycle, the Corean Chronicles, and several other series, as well as a number of stand-alone novels, such as The Eternity Artifact and The Elysium Commission. His most recent books include Haze, Arms-Commander, Empress of Eternity, and the Imager Portfolio series. His short fiction has appeared in a number of anthologies—including John Joseph Adams's Federations—and was recently collected in Viewpoints Critical.

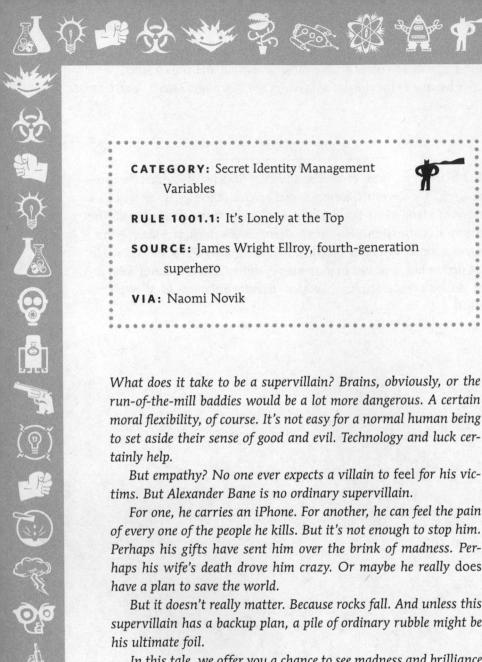

CATEGORY: Secret Identity Management
Variables

RULE 1001.1: It's Lonely at the Top

SOURCE: James Wright Ellroy, fourth-generation
superhero

VIA: Naomi Novik

What does it take to be a supervillain? Brains, obviously, or the run-of-the-mill baddies would be a lot more dangerous. A certain moral flexibility, of course. It's not easy for a normal human being to set aside their sense of good and evil. Technology and luck certainly help.

But empathy? No one ever expects a villain to feel for his victims. But Alexander Bane is no ordinary supervillain.

For one, he carries an iPhone. For another, he can feel the pain of every one of the people he kills. But it's not enough to stop him. Perhaps his gifts have sent him over the brink of madness. Perhaps his wife's death drove him crazy. Or maybe he really does have a plan to save the world.

But it doesn't really matter. Because rocks fall. And unless this supervillain has a backup plan, a pile of ordinary rubble might be his ultimate foil.

In this tale, we offer you a chance to see madness and brilliance unmasked—but no less in the dark.

ROCKS FALL

NAOMI NOVIK

"Well, that's unfortunate," he said, surveying the extremely large pile of rock.

He sat down across from me, just out of arm's length. The helmet had come off during the cave-in, and even in the sickly glow of his handheld, he didn't look much like I would've imagined. He had a nice face, pointed chin with laugh wrinkles around the eyes and mouth, and sandy blond hair. He ran a hand through it, scattering dust, and he could have been anyone: a math teacher or an optometrist or an accountant, someone not very important and not very dangerous.

"Are you in any pain?" he asked.

"I'd be better if you wouldn't mind shifting some of these boulders off me," I said.

He smiled, briefly. "No, I don't think so, but I do have some Vicodin I could toss in reach."

Alexander Bane offering me painkillers: brilliant. I wouldn't have minded something, although preferably served in a glass and out of a bottle of Macallan, but a fuzzy head didn't seem as though it would do me much good in the present circumstances. Not that the clear one was going to be particularly useful, either.

My right arm was still loose, but I couldn't reach around well enough to get hold of the big rocks pinning everything else, not with enough momentum to do anything useful. I picked one of the smaller rocks away and put it down on the cave floor and swung my fist down to crush it, more to amuse myself than anything.

"I wouldn't rely on the cave having stabilized," Bane said.

"I'm already under most of it," I said cheerily. A little anxiety wouldn't do him any harm. No one had a very clear notion of what his powers really were—there were at least fourteen different versions of his childhood records scattered about, with wildly different test results—but it was fairly settled that invulnerability wasn't one of them.

It wasn't, strictly speaking, one of mine, either, but I could hold up reasonably well under a pile of rocks, at least for a few hours.

"You might bring more of it down on whoever is digging us out," Bane said, and if I listened I could hear it, the distant rattle and scrape of shifting rubble, indistinct voices.

"Always comforting when the backup arrives only an hour late," I said, playing off my very real relief. I hadn't taken the matter seriously at first—a routine break-in at a small office building according to the incident report; nothing to merit the attention of anyone over a GS-3, except that I'd randomly been at the local precinct that morning to do a safety presentation for schoolchildren.

My call-in had been perfunctory. I recalled saying something like, "Alice, I'll look into this as long as I'm in town; send a spotter over if you have a minute, unless I'm done before they can leave. Bring you a latte on my way back!"

And then there I was, walking along an enormous room full of gray cubicles and outdated computer equipment—deserted; everyone had evacuated, for reasons about to become apparent—and out comes Alexander Bane from the corner office in his red and gold, carrying one of those old almond-colored midsize computer towers under an arm.

It was a pyrrhic comfort that he'd been equally surprised, and whatever he'd been stealing had been lost after our subsequent discussion. Along with a significant portion of the wall of the building and at least eleven million dollars' worth of structural damage to the nearest intersection. So much for my streak of six years in a row of safety-performance bonuses.

I wasn't going to regret it, if I pulled this off. The capabilities of Bane's suit were fairly well documented, barring the regular changes he made, but I hadn't reviewed his records in years. When Bane reared his shiny helmeted head, they called in the big guns: Marcus Leo, Tamisha Victoire; Calvin Washington if they could get him. Not that my gun wasn't perfectly respectable in every dimension, but there's a reason I'm a GS-12 in Maine and not a GS-15 in New York, and it's not for lack of scintillating conversation.

"I will take some of that, though, if you don't mind sharing," I said; he was drinking from a small flask.

"I'm afraid it's only Evian," he said, rolling it toward me. "You're a Macallan man, I think."

"Yes," I said, glumly. Well, that was horrifying. No reason he should ever have looked up James Wright Ellroy, twenty-eight, GS-12, Portland-based, outside his notice by any sensible standards; and it didn't matter whether he knew about my powers—he knew my drink.

I was grateful for the water anyway; the dust was settling, but my mouth was still thick with it. I capped the flask and rolled it back to him, and watched him put it away. He seemed remarkably unconcerned about the oncoming rescuers.

"Ah," he said, when I mentioned as much. "Not to make you uncomfortable, but they might be my people, actually. My suit sends an alert whenever it takes damage."

That gave the rattling and grinding outside a potentially more ominous character. "I don't suppose you can call them and find out for sure," I said, trying to listen to the voices. Would I recognize the nearest rescue crew?

"No reception," he said, raising the handheld.

"Really? No special secret network?"

"It's too annoying to keep it jailbroken," Bane said.

"Wait, what, are you actually using an iPhone?" I said.

"I like *Plants vs. Zombies*," he said, unrepentantly.

"Of course you do," I said. "So we'll just sit here until we find out who's being rescued."

"Unless you have a better idea," he said.

"None you'd like," I said, and sighed. If I could have at least worked my other arm free, or even just the shoulder, I could probably have built up enough momentum to knock myself loose, but as it was, I was stuck.

The screen on his phone went off again, and he didn't bother shaking it back to life right away. The darkness made the scraping outside—and the sound of his even breathing—seem louder. I tried not to listen to my own. I was under two tons of rock; I had every right to breathe heavily.

"I don't suppose you'd care to tell me what you were after, just to pass the time?" I asked.

"Hm? Oh, Lockheed just outsourced some of their HR department to this company," Bane said. "They made a mistake and sent over the entire company's records, including executives who should have been under top-secret clearance. They'd have caught it in the morning, so I thought it was worth picking up while I was passing by."

"So it's coincidence and bad luck all around."

I could hear the smile in his voice. "Apparently."

We sat quietly.

"Not to give you ideas," I said suddenly, "but doesn't your suit have all sorts of weaponry and things?"

"The fusion cannon does come in handy, but it's not really designed for use in a cave that might come down at any minute."

"I was thinking more about something you might use to shoot me in the head," I said.

He didn't say anything for a moment. "Pinpoint nanolaser. The beam penetrates even hyper-dense body structures," he said finally. "Fired into the medulla, it would kill you in less than a second."

"Right, comforting," I said. "And you haven't used it because . . . ?"

"There's no advantage to killing you if we're about to be picked up by a rescue squad. I'll be taken into custody anyway."

"And yet we were doing our best to kill each other fifteen minutes ago," I said.

"When I was hoping to escape without compromising my identity," he said. "I don't go around killing people for the hell of it."

"Was that an injured tone?" I said, incredulous. "You were directly responsible for ninety-three casualties last year alone!"

"One hundred and thirty-two," he said. "I'd tell you their names, but I'm feeling morbid enough at the moment."

"And do you think anything justifies that, makes it better than your being a nutter who likes to kill people? Making a billion dollars, taking over the world—"

"*Saving* the world," he said.

It stopped me. Bane's never been captured, of course, beyond five minutes here or there in theoretical custody where they didn't even get around to working off his helmet and getting photographs of his face. There aren't any prison-cell interviews, and he doesn't go in for monologuing in reality, despite the very inventive scenes in *Vengeance of Bane 1, 2,* and *3*. There aren't any records as to why he does the things he does. There aren't even good theories, really.

There are a handful of supervillains who go in for the world-saving routine. It's usually an excuse—dramatic speeches, hijacking the airwaves, self-righteousness and posturing, and it's amazing how saving the world always seems to boil down to giving them personally whatever they want. But Bane didn't do any of that. He just popped up here and there, stole something or sabotaged something else or set off a natural disaster, occasionally wrangled some top-rank superhero for a while, vanished again.

"Saving the world . . . in the environmental sense?" I said, wondering if he was in the eco-terrorism line.

"No," he said. "No. Long-term, the Earth is going to be fine. I'm more of a people-person."

"Which is why you kill substantial numbers of them."

"A few hundred people a year is trivial. You have no idea of the magnitude of—" He bit off the words. "It simply isn't meaningful on a global scale," Bane said. "Only a personal one."

"That's the one all of us *human beings* operate on, in the end."

"I know," Bane said, sounding tired. "That's the problem."

So that was encouraging, having arguably the smartest person on the planet tell you he's going around regretfully killing people to prevent something worse.

"You don't believe me," he said.

"I'm not stupid enough to think you're flat-out wrong. It's just not a good enough excuse."

"I was pretty sure you'd say that," he said, and fell silent.

"Not going to argue with me?" I said, a little suspiciously.

"No," he said. "You're a fourth-generation superhero, you grew up on the squad training grounds, you've got minor empathic abilities and your personality profile is outgoing and humanistic. There's no reasonable chance of convincing you to break with the entire framework of your life in the amount of time we have." He glanced at his phone.

"I have minor empathic abilities?" It was news to me.

"They don't show up using the standard test-evaluation methods," Bane said. "I've developed more rigorous analysis tools."

"How the hell do you get our raw results to . . . never mind. I'm sure I don't want to know."

We tried some word games on his phone after that, but it's not satisfying playing intellectual puzzles with someone with an IQ of four million or whatever, just vaguely depressing. I gave up after he managed to break five hundred points on a round of Boggle without even a piece of paper to scribble on.

"So, any holiday plans?" I threw out, half as a joke, as he picked the phone up from the ground. "Do you have people you go home to for Thanksgiving?"

"My wife's family."

"Right," I said blankly. "That's nice. Been married long?"

"We were married for two years before she died," he said. "I keep up the connection for my son."

"Oh," I said, even more stupidly. "I've got twins on the way," I added, because it was what you'd say in an ordinary conversation with an ordinary person.

"I know," he said. He looked down at the phone in his hands, greenish light flung up into his face.

It crept up slowly on me from there, while we talked—going from stilted to oddly easy, until I was telling him about the time Su Kwan had put food coloring in the coffee that none of us noticed, and we all spent a week walking around with blue teeth, not remotely confidence-inspiring; and the time Dr. Morbius had seized the capitol building and taken the governor hostage, and we'd had the entire Liberty Squad storming in to surround the place.

"Do you ever hang out with him?" I interrupted myself to ask. "Is there a social for supervillains or—"

"I've used him a few times," Bane said. "But sociopaths are inherently unreliable."

Used him like a hired hand, the single most powerful supervillain in the world; possibly the single most powerful of all of us, except for Calvin.

"Morbius isn't what you'd call a good time," he added, and that was what made me realize that Bane *was,* wholly unexpectedly and in defiance of sanity: someone I'd ask to come over and have a drink some night, and stay up late talking. Someone I'd like as a friend.

"They're all wrong, aren't they?" I said; it came out of nowhere, almost, and yet I couldn't have been more certain. "Those fourteen test profiles in the system. Everyone thinks you planted the extras to divert us from the real one, but they're all fake. Your powers don't show on the standard test. You were never classified at all."

He was silent, and it was dark; I had nothing to go on but his quiet breathing.

"You're an empath, too," I said. "Low-level . . . not enough to be projective—"

He sighed. "It's a general misconception that the degree of empathic power always correlates with the ability to project."

"You can feel people die," I said, not even needing him to confirm it. He could feel people need, also; could feel when they were interested or bored. Or in pain. Of course he was charming. Empaths almost couldn't help it. "Sorry I didn't take the Vicodin."

"Don't worry. You learn to deal with it."

He'd learned to kill, too. How would that feel, I wondered, to kill when you died along with your victim, every time? There was a reason the tests only measured projective empathy: they were looking for something that could be a weapon, not a weakness.

"It's not that hard," he said. "I feel people dying all the time."

"What's your range?"

He didn't answer. The rules said empaths and telepaths whose range went much further than their immediate vicinity went crazy before they were old enough to learn how to filter things out. A thousand voices in your head, all of them real. People all around you suffering, rejoicing. Enough to make you hate the whole world, or fall too deeply in love with it, I suppose.

There was a little daylight filtering in, through the rocks. The rescuers were getting close. "Don't you know if it's your people?" I asked.

"Anxiety fits either way," he said. "That's drowning out the details."

"Alexander?" a voice called softly from the other side, a woman's; he paused.

"Yes," he said. "I'm here."

"We'll have you out in a few minutes," she said.

"All right."

We sat in silence, while they opened the mouth enough for him to scramble out.

"I'm sorry," he said, watching the rocks disappearing out of the way, one after another.

It wasn't much comfort to know that he truly was. "You don't have to be," I said, with the desperation of the rat in the cage. I was thinking of Caro, and the twins; I'd seen them in black and white on an ultrasound screen two weeks before, one hand held up waving at me, hello. I tried to pull my arm free again, tried to kick loose; I'd been trying the whole time.

He didn't come in reach. He didn't have to.

· · · ·

Tamisha stood up silently from the body: cooling already, only the small scorch mark at the base of the neck still warm.

"The cold-hearted son of a bitch," Marcus said, low and angry. "Ellroy couldn't even chase him."

"He'd seen his face," she said. "Bane's killed for that before."

The local enforcers were huddled outside the cave looking in, hollowed-out and tear-streaked faces; he'd had a family, she understood.

"You'd better clear them away from the mountainside," Marcus said quietly. "I'll bring him out."

She nodded and brushed her hands off against her thighs before she stepped out to guide everyone away, out of the path of the landslide. The rockfall shuddered and more of the cliff face collapsed inward; Marcus lifted out of it a moment later, shrugging away boulders, bent sheltering over the body in his arms.

They found the recorder that evening before the autopsy, tucked into the pocket under Ellroy's arm; he'd had it running all the while.

Naomi Novik is the bestselling author of the Temeraire series, which consists of His Majesty's Dragon, Throne of Jade, Black Powder War, Empire of Ivory, Victory of Eagles, Tongues of Serpents, *and* Crucible of Gold. *Her short fiction has appeared in* Fantasy Magazine; The Dragon Book; Fast Ships, Black Sails; Warriors; Wings of Fire; Zombies vs. Unicorns; *and in John Joseph Adams's* The Improbable Adventures of Sherlock Holmes. *Her first manga with artist Yishan*

*Li—Liberty Vocational, Vol. 1: Will Supervillains Be on the Final?—
was published in 2011. Prior to becoming a full-time writer, Novik
worked in the video-game industry, working on* Neverwinter Nights:
Shadows of Undrentide. *She is a winner of the Compton Crook Award
and the John W. Campbell Award for best new writer, and has been a
finalist for the Hugo Award.*

CATEGORY: Mathematical Destruction
Scenarios

RULE 2000.x: Always Double-Check the Calculations

SOURCE: Fidel Dobes, computer programmer

VIA: Mary Robinette Kowal

Math is the language of geniuses with secrets. Beyond the basics of arithmetic, there are few people who really understand what to do with numbers or how calculations work. For someone with a keen mathematical mind, math is the silent weapon that few will even bother to scrutinize.

For Fidel Dobes, math is what he does best. His calculations are the starting points of his computer programs, and his programs are some of the best in the world. They are the secret programs that guide nuclear weapons systems for the U.S. government. The programs behind the big bombs.

Fidel's story is the story of one man living in the aftermath of World War II's heart-wrenching destruction. It is the Cold War. Computers run on punchcards. And America has reached a new level of paranoia. Can anyone with a conscience live with the knowledge that their work is advancing the newly massive American war machine?

We offer you the tale of a math genius who fights madness with madness. It's insanity—squared.

WE INTERRUPT THIS BROADCAST

MARY ROBINETTE KOWAL

Doubled over with another hacking cough, Fidel Dobes turned away from his 1402 punchcard reader. The last thing he needed was to cough blood onto the Beluga program source cards. Across the cramped lab, Mira raised her head and stared with concern. He hated worrying her.

Fidel's ribs ached with the force of the cough. He held a handkerchief to his mouth, waiting for the fit to pass. For a long moment, he thought he would not be able to breathe again. The panic almost closed his throat completely, but he managed a shuddering breath without coughing. Then another. He straightened slowly and pulled the cloth away from his mouth. In the glob of sputum, a bright spot of scarlet glistened.

Damn. That usually only happened in the morning. He folded the handkerchief over so it wouldn't show, turned back to the 1402 and continued loading the source cards into the sturdy machine. Its fan hummed, masking some of the ragged sound of his breathing.

Mira cleared her throat. "Would water help?"

"I'm fine." Fidel thumbed through the remaining manilla cards to make certain they were in the correct order. He had checked the serialization half a dozen times already, but anything was better than meeting Mira's worried look. "The TB won't kill me before we're finished."

Mira pursed her lips, painted a deep maroon. "I'm not worried about you finishing."

"What are—" No. He did not want the answer to that question. "Good."

She sneezed thrice, in rapid succession. On her, the sneezes sounded adorable, like a kitten.

"You still have that cold?"

She waved the question away, turning back to the 026 printer keyboard to punch a row of code into another card. Her dedication touched him. The Beluga program was huge and the verifier had tagged a score of corrupted data cards. He did not have time to send the cards back to one of the card-punch girls upstairs—as if this were even an official project—and still be ready for broadcast. He had only one chance to intercept Asteroid 29085 1952 DA before it hurtled past the Earth's orbit.

It had been a risk bringing Mira into the project, but when she asked for details he'd implied that it was classified and she left it at that. As far as the government was concerned, she had the security clearance necessary for the clerical work for which he'd *officially* employed her but then, the government didn't know about Fidel's Beluga program. They knew that he used this forgotten corner of the Pentagon's basement to do research on ways to control spacecraft through computers. The additional program that he had devised to fit into the official project was something he had managed to keep hidden from everyone. So many times he had wished for someone to confide in and had nearly told Mira. But fear kept the words inside. Despite the years that he had known her, despite the strength of her mind, he feared that if she knew what he had created, he would lose her.

Ironic, that he now kept her close to be certain she was safe.

Fidel loaded the next set of cards into the feeder and stopped. On the top card, someone had drawn a red heart. He brushed the heart with his index finger; it was a smooth and waxy maroon, like a woman's lips. The next card had an imprint of lips as if she had kissed the card. The one after that was blank.

He looked up across the lab, to Mira. She met his gaze evenly with a Mona Lisa smile.

Suddenly too warm, Fidel broke eye contact and loaded the cards, the nine edge facedown. What kind of life would he have been able to give her anyway? Not a long life together, not happily ever after. Nine months in a sanatorium had done nothing for him except give him time to read the news out of Washington and brood.

Only his correspondence with Mira had kept him sane—knowing that she had agreed with him about the outrages against humanity. And what a relief it was to know that his was not a lone voice crying out: How dare they!

He had known what the Manhattan Project was when he had worked on it, but they were only supposed to use the A-Bomb once. The threat of it was supposed to be deterrent enough, and yes, yes, he had known that it would involve a demonstration. For that, he had remorse, coupled with acceptance of his sins.

The second town. Nagasaki. That had been unnecessary. And now . . . the new project. Launching bombs into space and holding them there, ready to rain terror on any country that disagreed with the United States. As if that were a surprise coming from President Dewey, an isolationist president who defeated Truman on the strength of his reputation as a "gangbuster." His idea of foreign policy was to treat every other country like the gangs of New York. Well, no more. Fidel put the last of the cards in the 1402. "I'm ready to generate the object cards when you are."

Mira nodded and did not look up from the 026. The clacking of the machine's keys filled the room with chatter as she rekeyed Fidel's code.

Her fine black hair clung to the nape of her neck. Fidel wet his lips, watching her work. The delicate bones of her wrists peeked from the sensible long-sleeved shirt she wore. Her fingers deftly found the keys without apparent attention from her. Mira stifled another sneeze, turning her head from the machine without breaking her rhythm. His heart ached watching her. Mira must be kept safely away from D.C. "Is everything still on for our trip tomorrow?" he asked.

She laughed without looking up from her work. "This is the third time you've asked in as many days," she said. "Yes, I'm all packed."

"Good."

The punch machine clattered as she continued to work. "I'm glad you're getting away from D.C. for a few days."

"So am I. Happier that you're coming with me."

Her hands stopped on the keys and a frown creased her brow. "Fidel—"

"What?"

"Nothing. I'm just glad you're getting away. D.C. isn't good for you."

Without thinking, he laughed and plunged into a fit of coughing. His lungs burned with every breath reminding him of the gift he was leaving the world.

He had run the calculations, punching the cards over and over to check his theory against numerical fact. Blowing up Washington would get rid of the corruption and greed, but it would rekindle the tensions of the Second World War and lead to a destruction the likes of which man had never seen. An asteroid crashing into the city would seem like an Act of God. The shock waves and ash thrown up would affect the entire world. People would rally together, coming to the aid of a country shocked and devastated. It would be the dawn of a new Age of Enlightenment.

Fighting to control the coughing, Fidel pressed his handkerchief against his mouth to stifle the sound until he could breathe. "I'm okay," he said.

"I'm sorry." The distress in Mira's voice forced him upright.

He tucked the handkerchief in his pocket without looking at it. "Don't be. As you say, D.C. isn't good for me."

She twisted her fingers together. "Why don't you rest while I finish up. I can run the last compile on my own and you can check the listing for errors afterward."

"I—"

"Please, Fidel. I worry about you."

He had nothing he could say in response. She was right to worry about him and at the same time worry would do no good. His fate was sealed.

Nodding, he settled in his chair. "All right. Let me know if you need anything."

While Mira worked, Fidel let his head droop forward until his chin rested on his chest. If he could just close his eyes for a few minutes, he might be able to chase off the fatigue for a while longer.

• • • •

A hand touched his shoulder and Fidel lurched upright in his chair. Mira stood beside him, a stack of punchcards in her hand. "Sorry to wake you."

"No. It's fine." Fidel stood, trying to mask his fatigue and confusion. How long had he been asleep? The urge to check the cards one more time pulsed through him, but he'd done that enough and Mira was more than competent. "How did it go?"

"I haven't run it yet. I . . . Will you check this?" She handed him the stack of cards; a few stuck out at ninety degrees from the others as flags. "They match the listing but I don't think they're right."

He waited for enough of his drowsiness to drop away for her sentence to make sense. How could the cards be wrong if they matched his code? She was a smart girl but it was impossible that she could be critiquing his programming. Frowning, Fidel accepted the cards and sat down at his desk again. Flipping through the cards, he compared each to the lines of code he had originally written. The code handled the timing of the rocket's navigation. It was scheduled to start the takeover on March 1st, three days from today, and everything matched up. Mira hovered next to the desk, twining her fingers together.

To reassure her, he jotted the numbers on the back of an envelope and redid the calculations leading in and out of that code. "I don't see any errors here."

"What about leap day?" Mira asked.

Numb, Fidel stared at her. A blue vein beat in her neck as she stood on first one foot then the other. Leap day. Which meant that the rocket would not fire until a day late, by which point the asteroid would be gone. He shoved aside the pile of papers on his desk to uncover the ink blotter calendar there, as though Mira had made leap day up. Twenty-nine days. And he had only accounted for twenty-eight of them.

"My God." His hands shook as he picked up the cards and began to recalculate. One chance to save the world and he had almost missed it.

"Then it *is* an error." Mira nodded, pressing her lips together.

"Yes, thank you for catching that." His pencil flew over the paper. The changes were minor since the only bug in the code was how long the program lay dormant before triggering. The launch date, though, was unchanged; only the interval between had altered. Which meant that he had to make these changes quickly. "Start keying these as I hand them to you."

The lab vibrated with the sound of Mira's keypunch machine as she replaced the six cards she had flagged. As she finished them, he flipped through the deck to check the serialization one more time and nodded, grunting in satisfaction.

"Well . . ." he said. "Shall we?" Fidel winced at the banality of his own words. Perhaps he could write something in his journal that sounded more appropriate to the moment.

Straightening, Fidel let his hand drop to the 1402.

Mira ducked her head and lifted one hand to rub the base of her neck as if she were pained. "Fidel—"

He lifted his finger and waited for her to continue. She bit her lip studying the cards in the machine. He waited. "Yes?"

"Are you . . . are you sure?"

"Sure about what?" His heart sped and he glanced at his desk, but the drawer with his journal was locked and it was only there that he had recorded his thoughts. She could not know.

She touched the cards. "Sure . . . Sure that your calculations are all correct?"

"I believe so." He had gone through the cards often enough that he felt certain, and time was running out. He put his finger back on the start key. "Thanks to the error you caught."

"No . . ." she said. "I mean the other calculations. The ones about the asteroid."

His throat started to close. "Asteroid?"

Mira nodded, tears brimming in her eyes. "I read the cards."

"You read them?" He seemed only able to ask questions.

"So many people . . ." she said, trailing off as she choked back tears. "That's why we're leaving the city tomorrow, isn't it?"

He removed his hand from the key and wiped it over his face. She was never to have known. Such a soft and gentle heart should never be a party to what he was unleashing on the world. "I'm sorry. I thought I'd divided the cards up among the punchcard girls. I didn't think any of you had the whole program."

"I—I was interested in what you were doing so I printed a second copy of the listing when we ran it."

"I see." Fidel pressed his fingers against the center of his forehead, rubbing them in a circle. "Then yes, I am certain. Did you tell anyone what you read?"

"No." She grimaced. "It's just . . . This is what you faced when you worked on the Manhattan Project, isn't it?"

"Yes." He put his finger on the start key. "I had . . . I had initially planned to stay in the city when it happened. The TB, you know. I thought it would be faster this way."

A muscle pulsed in the corner of her jaw. "Why did you change your mind?"

"You. I wanted to see you safely out of the city. I wanted to know that I had not killed you."

She covered her mouth, eyes bright with tears, and turned away.

"Do you . . ." he began. All of the work he had done, all of his calculations—he would give it all up for her. "Do you want me to call it off?"

Her voice was hoarse. "No. It's just . . . all those people."

"It can't be helped. But the new world, Mira. Oh, it will be chaos and the world will suffer at first but the dawn that follows . . ."

She straightened and turned back to him, placing her soft hand over his where it rested on the keys. Compressing her mouth, she gave a small nod and pressed down on his hand.

Fidel pushed the Start key with a harsh click, and the machine began feeding the cards, whirring and clunking as it joggled the cards and then fed each piece of the program into it. From there it would get loaded into the magnetic memory tapes of the N5 rockets scheduled to launch in the morning, carrying a nuclear warhead to orbit. On March 1, his program would activate and override the rocket's programming. The rocket would appear to lose communication with ground control, but in reality it would be hurtling toward Asteroid 29085 1952 DA. Fidel's program would cause it to intercept the asteroid and redirect it to Earth and Washington.

No one else could program this. No one else would even think it was possible to hit a target so small in the vastness of space, but for Fidel, the numbers had always danced at his command.

Mira kept hold of his hand as they sat down to wait for the program to compile. He kept his focus on the machine rather than what mattered to him. She sat silently by him, shoulders hunched as though against the clatter of the card reader.

When the last one rattled through the machine and dropped into the finish tray, Fidel let out a long, careful sigh. "It is finished."

She squeezed his hand. "I thought it was just beginning?"

"More like a hard reset," he said. He held her hand, tracing the lines of her palm with his thumb, grateful that he would not have to spend his remaining months alone before the TB took him.

Mira echoed his sigh and then sneezed, daintily. A cough followed, hacking and wet. He looked at her in alarm.

Mira waved her hand to brush his concern away. "It's nothing, just a tickle in my throat."

But he knew what he had heard. "Are you certain?"

She pressed her fist against her mouth and stared at the floor for a long moment. Lifting her head, Mira looked at him with bright eyes, chin firm. "Maybe we both should stay in D.C."

Fidel gripped her other hand harder and bowed his head. In his efforts to protect her, he had killed her anyway. "Yes," he said, "perhaps we should."

Mary Robinette Kowal is the author of the novels Shades of Milk and Honey *and* Glamour in Glass. *She is a winner of the Hugo Award and the John W. Campbell Memorial Award for best new writer, and she has been a finalist for the Nebula Award. Her short fiction has appeared in* Asimov's Science Fiction, Apex Magazine, Clarkesworld, Intergalactic Medicine Show, Tor.com, Talebones, Daily Science Fiction, *and in several anthologies, such as* The Year's Best Science Fiction, Clockwork Phoenix 2, Dark Faith, *and in John Joseph Adams's* The Improbable Adventures of Sherlock Holmes. *A collection of her work,* Scenting the Dark and Other Stories, *was published in 2009. In addition to her writing, she is also a professional puppeteer and audiobook narrator.*

CATEGORY: Unexpected Cryptozoological Ramifications

RULE 1451.2b: Pick Your Supervillain Name with Care

SOURCE: Alexander Luthor, biotechnology billionaire

VIA: Marjorie M. Liu

What is "destiny"? Does it come from the stars, like the astrologists say? Is it spun out of a person's DNA, the kind of birthright monarchies claim? Is it measured out by mysterious figures, like the Greek Fates in their cave? Or could it be that a man's future determined by his name?

This is a story of a man who has allowed his name to drive his destiny. Alexander Luthor, the mind behind the multibillion-dollar LuthorTech corporation, has a talent for biotech invention—and success has brought him many government contacts. With the power and protection of the federal government behind his experiments, Alexander Luthor finds himself in a position to change the world.

As he plumbs the reaches of science, Alexander must confront the choices he's made. What is he becoming? And can he make a name for himself—one that isn't simply villainous?

THE LAST DIGNITY OF MAN

MARJORIE M. LIU

"Put on the cape," Alexander says. "Careful now. Do it slow."

He sits very still, breathless, as the young man unfolds the shining red cloth. This moment is part of an old dream, a red dream—red on blue, with gold trim, and that lovely brand upon the young man's fine, fine chest. The finest letter in the alphabet, Alexander thinks. A mighty letter, for a mighty myth.

The cape will make it perfect.

But the young man grins, ruining the effect. What was to be serious, epic, suddenly feels like the farce it is, and Alexander looks away in shame. He barely notices the young man clip the cape into place, can barely stand to hear his own voice break the quiet.

Alexander does not know the young man's real name—only the one he has been given for this evening. All part of the ruined fantasy.

"Clark," Alexander says. "Clark. You may go now."

The young man frowns. "Sir?"

Alexander shakes his head. "Just . . . get your things and go."

Puzzlement, even a little disappointment, yet the young man does as he is told. He gathers his belongings: a business suit, with tie; thick glasses. He is a beautiful creature: long of muscle and bone, with pale eyes and dark wavy hair. A lucky find, and Alexander feels a moment of regret. But no, this is not right.

The young man leaves. Alexander sits in his chair by the window and stares at the city. There is enough light to cast a reflection in the glass; like a ghost mirror, he sees his face in shadow, transparent and wry.

Alexander is bald. He thinks he looks good bald, though it is quite unnatural. The men in Alexander's family are fine bushy blonds, but when Alexander turned eighteen he shaved all the hair from his head. Shaves it still, so that his scalp gleams polished and perfect.

So. Alexander has the look. He has the money. Yet, he is still alone. Alone in his tower, his fortress of solitude.

It is a joke and Alexander knows it. His name is Alexander Luthor—Lex

Luthor—but this is not a comic book, and there is no such thing as Superman.

Still, it is an old dream.

• • • •

The research department at LuthorTech takes up an entire city block. The building squats in the center of downtown, where streets and sidewalks are a jungle during rush hour. Alexander likes the crowds; he keeps his office on the first floor so he can watch strangers pass scant yards beyond his tinted windows. He has other offices, better offices, in prettier parts of town, but he has not seen them in over five years.

Alexander's brothers do not understand this. The big picture has always eluded them, along with humility and the practical application of science and business theory. It is why Alexander's father made his youngest son the principal shareholder in LuthorTech, why his two oldest pretend to manage sales and marketing while alternating between office and golf course, why the old man rests easy at night, without fear his life's work will die. Despite their differences in lifestyle, which have crippled communication, Alexander's father knows his son is a smart man. Too eccentric, perhaps, to be acceptable—but very, very smart.

Smart enough to appreciate the backbone of the company, to dwell close within the marrow, directing firsthand the genius on his payroll. His enthusiasm helps. The employees like Alexander. They respect him, even—though he knows they make fun of his name, his appearance. Lex Luthor in the flesh, they say. Our boss, the mad scientist. Does he keep kryptonite in his shorts? Ha. Ha. Ha.

Alexander blames his mother. She insisted on his name, on the dignity of its sound. Alexander wonders if he would be a different man if she had called him George or Simon or Larry. A name without myth or power. Without expectation.

But no, he is Alexander. He is Lex. And he has lived up to that name, in more ways than one.

• • • •

"They're growing faster than we anticipated, Mr. Luthor. We'll need bigger cages soon."

The lab is poorly lit. Or rather, it is well lit according to the parameters of the experiment. Batch number 381 does not thrive under bright lights, so the scientists have installed lower energy bulbs, the kind used in photography darkrooms. Everything is cast in red, blood red, and Alexander feels as though he is in the middle of a particularly nasty horror movie. The writhing masses of glistening flesh lumped in glass tanks do not help. In fact, it looks pornographic.

Alexander steps close. The tanks are completely airtight, each one equipped with an isolated oxygen pump that filters and analyzes and recycles. There are also feeding slots—storage chambers built with a series of small airlocks and safety mechanisms, timed to release sludge when the sensors indicate that tank levels have dropped below acceptable feeding levels. The creatures like to swim through shit. It is the earthworm in them, this instinct to burrow deep.

But these pulsing undulating worms are as thick as Alexander's arm, and it is not soil they are consuming.

"Have you added mercury to the mix yet?" Alexander asks.

Dr. Reynolds, a tall woman of middle years, quirks her lips. "Mercury, toluene, and just about every other heavy metal we can think of. They eat it right up, with no visible side effects. It's incredible, Mr. Luthor. That sludge is so toxic the fumes alone could probably kill a person."

Alexander cannot tell if Dr. Reynolds is joking; the amusement in her voice does not reach her eyes. This is worrisome, because Alexander trusts her judgment.

"Kathy," he says. "What's wrong? If there's a health risk to all of you—"

"No, nothing like that." Dr. Reynolds stares at the tank. One of the worms momentarily swells, ridges flaring in response to some mysterious biological cue. Its slick bulk disappears beneath a rolling heave of supple bodies that slip sideways to strain against the sludge-packed glass. "I hate looking at these things," she finally says. "They scare me."

"Good," Alexander says. "We're playing God, Kathy. We should be afraid."

"And here I thought God was fearless."

"The only fearless God is the one who doesn't have to live with His mistakes. If that were us, I wouldn't be forced to keep more than a hundred lawyers on the company payroll."

"Yes," agrees Dr. Reynolds. "That is indeed a sign of dark times."

There is little more to discuss. Alexander ends his meeting with Dr. Reynolds. The red lights and the red worms are too much, and it will be lunch in an hour. To stay inside that lab any longer would be cruel.

So Alexander wanders, moving through each floor of his building with methodical abandon. He has a purpose, which is to make sure all the lead projects are progressing smoothly, but he does not care how he gets there. It is enough that his legs are moving. He is still thinking about worms.

It is a long-known fact that certain kinds of bacteria eat toxic waste and sewage, but such organisms are slow and require sensitive environments. More than two years ago, LuthorTech was given a government contract to develop creatures that are not so . . . sensitive. Not so slow. And now Alexander's team has succeeded. Or so he thinks.

Alexander will not lose sleep, either way. The government has paid for a genetically engineered solution to toxic spills, and that is what it shall receive. Only, there is a tiny fear in Alexander's heart. His alter ego, after all, is a wicked man. A wicked man, without any counterpart in the world to balance his darkness.

There is no Superman. Alexander must be his own moral compass.

• • • •

The wandering continues into lunch. Alexander had planned to eat in his office, but the sun is shining and his mind is still trapped in a red-lit room. He leaves the building and hits the sidewalk, carried by the crowd toward a destination unknown.

He knows why the worms frighten Dr. Reynolds. It has nothing to do with the way they look. It is enough that they are new and powerful and man-made. Evolution favors the strong, but these creatures are products of disparate evolutions. Distant biological paths, forced to collide into one body.

The government calls them Living Machines: a deceptive term, meant to soothe. There are more planned, for various purposes; the contracts and proposals are locked within Alexander's safe, awaiting his signature. The government likes to dream big and it favors LuthorTech because the company is discreet, because it gets the job done. No fuss, ever. LuthorTech does not raise moral objections. Not when the price is right.

But Alexander knows there are all kinds of prices to pay—a price for every action—and he wonders about lines and points of no return, how far he can go before he becomes the man he pretends to be; how far he can push before myth becomes reality. He wonders, not for the first time, if creating that reality will not invite another collision of coincidence. Darkness, after all, is always offset by light.

Alexander wonders what he will attract if he becomes, in truth, Lex.

The sidewalk ends; he can turn left or right, but ahead of him is a vast expanse of green, and he decides that grass might be a nice change from concrete and glass. He crosses the street, passes through the open iron gate, and enters the park. The sounds of traffic fade instantly. Alexander feels cocooned by sunlight and the scent of fresh turned soil.

The smell of grease soon overpowers the smell of nature. Alexander finds a concession stand and buys a sandwich, chips, a large soda. The surrounding benches are taken, so he wanders off the path onto thick grass, plopping down in the shade cast by a gnarled oak. He does not sit there long before he feels a presence at his back, the subtle hint of shuffling feet.

Alexander glances over his shoulder and sees a man approaching. Middle-aged, with a dusting of silver in his hair. He has a homeless sort of

THE LAST DIGNITY OF MAN

MARJORIE M. LIU

look, which has nothing to do with his somewhat scruffy clothes, his tangled beard, or the limp backpack in his hand. Alexander can tell the man is homeless because his eyes are hollow, hungry. It is a gaze of desperate despair, and Alexander feels a rush of fear to be confronted by such helpless sorrow. But then he remembers the worms and the papers in his safe, the other projects percolating in his labs, and he thinks, *I am much more frightening than this man. And he, at least, is human.*

Alexander nods at the man, who hesitates for just one moment before setting down his backpack and slumping to his knees in the grass. Alexander does not make him ask; he gives the man half his sandwich, and pushes over the drink and chips.

"Thanks," the man says. Alexander can hear the desert in that voice, which carries the dry timbre of sand. Elegant and coarse, like its owner. "My name is Richard."

"Alexander."

Richard nods. The two men say nothing more. They eat and watch joggers and mothers with strollers; children on leashes and dogs running without; teenagers slinging Frisbees, shouting obscenities at each other with adolescent affection. It is a very nice afternoon.

"Tell me about yourself," Richard finally says, finishing the last of the chips. "What kind of man are you?"

An interesting question, considering the source. Alexander studies Richard, but the man's eyes are stronger now, more full. He even looks belligerent. Defiant. Alexander smiles.

"I'm not a very nice man," he says.

Richard grunts. "So, you're an honest man."

"When it suits me."

"My statement still stands."

Alexander chuckles. This is . . . different. "What about you?"

"Ah, see, I'm a very good man."

"Liar."

"Oh, the insult." Richard slurps down the soda and wipes his mouth with the back of his hand. "What are you? Thirty, thirty-five?"

"Around there."

"You're wearing a nice suit. Armani, by the look of it. And you're sitting in the grass, getting it dirty. You must be pretty successful."

"I do all right."

"I thought you were an honest man."

"I own half this city."

Richard grins. "That's better. You earn it?"

"I plan to."

"Good enough." Richard climbs to his feet, brushing crumbs off his clothes. Alexander stands with him; he senses their conversation is over, and it leaves him awkward. Confused. He has not asked his own questions. He knows nothing about this man, who in less than a minute has managed to both surprise and disconcert.

Alexander feels like they were just getting started, but that is not right, either.

Richard holds out his hand and Alexander takes it.

"You have a good life, kid. Stay honest." Richard releases him, stoops to pick up his backpack, and begins shuffling away with a good deal more dignity than at his arrival. Alexander stares after him, heart pounding.

"Uh, wait," he calls out. "Do you . . . do you need money?"

Richard turns, fixes Alexander with a pointed stare. "I'd rather have a job."

Alexander thinks for a moment, and says, "I can do that."

• • • •

Richard will not talk about himself, who he was before losing home and livelihood. Alexander finds him work as a janitor. He is probably overqualified to clean toilets and mop floors, but that does not matter. According to Richard, the past—that life—is done. Besides, being a janitor at Luthor-Tech pays well. Alexander takes care of his employees. Keeps them from unionizing.

And Richard, in turn, takes care of Alexander. Small things, only. Words more than actions. Alexander does not have many friends—his own family rarely speaks to him—and while Richard might not count as much more than an acquaintance, Alexander enjoys talking to a man who does not ridicule him behind his back, but always, always to his face.

"You have problems," Richard says, the first time he sees Alexander's office, the poster of Superman on the wall.

"I know how to make fun of myself, that's all," Alexander says, stung.

Richard gives him a look. Alexander suddenly feels as though he has been caught in church with both hands on his dick. The most embarrassing sin, exposed.

"Kid." Richard stares at Alexander's naked scalp, still moist from a recent shave. "There's nothing fun about this."

It is the truth, the closest truth Alexander has ever heard spoken aloud, but he says nothing. To speak would acknowledge a truth that would reveal a secret, a secret too close to Alexander's heart, too entangled in his soul, to ever be breathed. Alexander has built his life around this myth. He cannot stop now—will not stop—no matter the pain.

Richard asks, "Why?"

Alexander hears himself say, "Because I believe a man can fly."

• • • •

The worms are ready.

They have passed all initial tests, and except for their size—which is startling, unusual, and somewhat disturbing—they are ready for a real-world scenario. The government has picked the time and place, and if the worms succeed within the parameters set for them, the government will take possession of the creatures and begin using them in earnest. The first of many Living Machines, created for the public good.

Which is why Alexander is encased in a rubber sleeve, standing thigh-deep in open sewage, trying not to vomit into the oxygen mask strapped over his face.

He is not the only one struggling for balance in the sludge. Dr. Reynolds and her team are present, along with scientists from the federal government. This section of the city sewer system is completely blocked off, sealed tight to prevent any of the worms from escaping into the main line. Alexander objects to the use of a public facility for this test, but the government wants to make sure the worms will thrive outside a controlled environment.

Alexander does not worry about them thriving. Quite the opposite.

These particular worms, which are waiting to be released from the plastic containers carried by Dr. Reynolds and her assistants, are young and small, fresh from the incubator. The others, the mammoths of Batch number 381, have been destroyed, their bodies conserved for study. Alexander's skin prickles, remembering those massive bodies, heavy with sludge, resting torpid at the bottom of their enlarged tanks. Still alive, still healthy, and still growing.

Alexander catches Dr. Reynolds's worried glance. They share a moment of perfect doubt. This is a lot of sludge and they are releasing a lot of worms. When the experiment is over, the government's plan is to carefully drain the remaining sludge from the system, thereby revealing—and trapping—the worms for easy collection. Alexander does not think it will be so easy, but the government scientists have insisted.

Dr. Reynolds inches close. "You really don't have to be here for this, Mr. Luthor. Once they get the instruments calibrated, all we're going to do is dump the worms into the sewage." Alexander hears an odd thumping sound. Dr. Reynolds tightens her grip on the container.

"What?" Alexander drawls, eyeing the cloudy plastic. "And miss this? You shock me, Kathy."

Dr. Reynolds snorts, but her face is pale, her eyes just a little too large beneath her mask. She has seen what the creatures become; she knows what will happen down here.

"Kathy," he says, touching her arm.

"I'm all right," she says. "I just don't know what we're doing."

"Science, Kathy. We're doing science."

"Science." She draws the word out, low and hard. "And here I thought we were playing God."

Dr. Reynolds turns away toward the other scientists. Alexander watches her go, unable to call her back. She is right, of course, and he wishes he had chosen this moment to be honest, to speak again the truth voiced in the red-lit room when he told her it was all right to be afraid because yes, what they were doing was too big for mere mortals, too much responsibility to put on human shoulders.

We're doing more than science, Alexander thinks. He watches Dr. Reynolds flip the locks on her rattling container. *We've crossed the line into something bigger.*

But we can't go back. Not now.

Dr. Reynolds opens the lid and Alexander hears a hiss that is not human, a sound that exists only because he signed a piece of paper.

The worms fall free in a tangle, smacking the sludge, writhing against the surface before sinking, sinking, out of sight. The other containers open: worms are unceremoniously dumped. Alexander imagines them working their way through the darkness, feeding, growing. He feels something brush his ankle and it takes all his strength not to shudder.

Everyone begins to clamber out of the sludge. Alexander realizes he is being left behind. It is a short climb up the ladder to the wide shelf jutting from the sewer wall. Dripping shit, Alexander is greeted by a man wearing a yellow rain slicker over a dark suit. A nameless government liaison paying his dues in a crappy assignment. His eyes are bloodshot and he keeps swallowing hard. Even better, then. A puker.

Alexander rips off his mask; he almost doubles over from the smell, but manages to maintain his composure better than the other men and women removing their facial protective gear. Amidst a symphony of gagging, Alexander forces a smile. The puker grunts, his gaze sliding sideways to the sludge below them.

"So those things really eat heavy metal and shit, huh?"

"Like the finest chocolate," Alexander says, still smiling. He wants to run, to scratch this man from his path and fight for sunlight. He hates this place.

The puker grimaces. "No kidding? So what comes out the other end?"

A stupid question. Alexander imagines the worms in their liquid heat, sucking in filth and growing large and strong. It is the bacterial strain in them, this unexpected and fortuitous ability to process sludge without creating any. Alexander would say that it defies the laws of nature, except Dr. Reynolds has assured him there is waste—only, it is processed at an extremely slow rate, released in nontoxic dribbles. Very alluring. Very practical.

Very dangerous.

The government has been given reams of paper on this subject: data and speculation, photographs and samples. Nothing has been held back, nothing, but this fool—this dangerous fool who is their liaison—remains ignorant. Alexander cannot stand it.

He steps close and it works; the man retreats, unwilling to entertain shit on his rain slicker and shoes. Alexander keeps moving, faster and faster, dangerous on this narrow path, these close quarters, his smile wider and brighter, and the puker's eyes narrow, hands fumbling for air, for a gun, for something to stop this strange, strange, man from coming too near.

The puker stumbles. He cries out. Alexander grabs his rain slicker, keeps him from falling off the ledge into the sewage with its hidden worms. He holds the puker close, smearing him with filth, and whispers, "Nothing, you idiot. Nothing comes out the other end. The worms just suck it in and keep it there, growing pregnant on the stuff. They could probably eat *you*, when they get big enough. And they will. Imagine that. Digested in a body full of shit."

Alexander releases the puker, who gasps and clings to the wall. He vomits.

Alexander does not feel compelled to apologize. No one seems to have noticed what happened. He does not worry about the puker complaining. The puker is a little man and Alexander is powerful, untouchable.

Sunlight beckons, and this time his smile is genuine.

I am not a nice person, Alexander thinks. And for the first time, he truly believes it.

· · · ·

Alexander pulls his old Superman comics out of storage and spends the evening thumbing through the varied adventures of the caped wonder, lingering over those stories that pit him against Lex Luthor. An old habit; Alexander has sought comfort in these pages since he was four years old, the age he discovered the meaning of his name, the purpose to his life.

"Ah ha!" Lex Luthor says to Superman. "I've got you now!"

If only, Alexander thinks. But that is the thing about Superman. In the comics, no one ever really has him. Not even Lois, who must share her man with every bleeding body and broken soul to cross his path. Superman is good, the best kind of man, and that means he never truly owns himself. Pure compassion cannot live in isolation. It demands the world.

And the world demands it back. The world needs more compassion. The world needs the kind of man Alexander knows he will never be.

The government proposals are still in Alexander's office safe, waiting to be signed. All of them require the creation of new life, creatures as of yet beyond the ken of man. Their desired purposes are varied, innocuous on the page. Alexander is not fooled. These organisms, should LuthorTech succeed in making them, will change the world, just as the worms—when their existence is finally, inevitably, revealed—will forever change the way people view bioengineering. It is not enough to say one supports science. The real test is to see the finished product, fat and glistening, and not flinch.

Even Alexander is incapable of that, which should be all the answer he needs, but still he keeps the papers, and still he promises the government that yes, any day now, he will sign and return them, and once again begin the process of evolutionary quilting, piecing together scraps of biology into a useful whole.

Because if he does not do this, someone else will, and while Alexander does not entirely trust himself, he has even less faith in those who would take his place. It is a strange sensation, wanting to save the world—while at the same time creating the very things that will irrevocably change it, for better or worse.

Heroes and villains. Shades of gray. Sometimes he wishes he could talk to his father about these things.

Of course, it helps that the money is good.

The next morning, he signs the papers.

• • • •

A week passes, and then two. Dr. Reynolds provides daily reports on the worms, which are along the lines of, "They're still down there." A complete and accurate statement, which tells Alexander everything he needs to know.

The worms are down there. They are eating. They are growing.

Alexander hopes the government understands what it is doing, though he himself does not fear reprisals, bad press, or protestors on his doorstep. The government provides complete anonymity to keep LuthorTech free and clear to run its experiments, safe from ecoterrorists, uneducated journalists, and public concern. It is very liberating, this lack of oversight, though Alexander still feels his moral compass with its needle swinging, and the shadow of a dream on his shoulder. The good and amoral, holding hands.

He wishes he really could hold someone's hand, just once.

Richard has been spending more time in the general vicinity of Alexander's office. Alexander knows this because he continues to pay attention to the man. Even if Richard does not care about Alexander in any special way, Alexander cares about Richard and what he has to say. Richard is not afraid of Alexander. He is not afraid of the truth.

If only Alexander's other employees were so bold, or kind.

Alexander hears them talking on a day when he wanders through the labs, peering into microscopes and poking around spreadsheets, enjoying—for once, without guilt—the simple pleasure of great thoughts applied to science.

Alexander hears them because his employees return late from lunch and do not know their boss is communing with sea slugs behind a pile of newly arrived supply crates.

"He's a freak, that's what," says a man, indignation softened by laughter.

"Freakishly *bald*, you mean," says a woman. "I go blind from the glare every time he walks by. Whoever said men sans hair are sexy needs a lobotomy."

"Ha! Ol' Lex Luthor. Sexy Lexy. Now *that* is obsession."

"Hey, he can be obsessed with sheep, for all I care. I just want him to sign my paycheck. *And* stay the hell away from me."

"You're just afraid he'll hit on you and you'll have to put out."

"Right. Who knows what kind of freak show goes on in his pants? He probably paints his balls green."

"Meteor rocks, fresh from Krypton."

This is uproariously funny. They laugh until they choke, and walk away.

Alexander does not follow them. He does not move. He stares at the sea slugs in their tank, his mind drifting, drowning, his chest growing tight and tighter. He stands there, waiting to feel better, but time passes and he knows he must leave; someone will find him eventually, and he cannot bear to face the owners of those voices.

Yes, he is the man in charge, but pain is pain, no matter the title or bank account.

Holding his breath, Alexander listens hard and carefully slips out from behind the crates. He takes one step, two, and just when he thinks he is free to run, movement catches his eye. Too late; he has been seen.

It is Richard, holding a mop and pail.

The two men stare at each other. Alexander cannot fathom Richard's expression, but his silence is confirmation enough. He has heard every word of that awful conversation.

Heat suffuses Alexander's face; he cannot meet Richard's eyes. Staring at the floor, he turns and walks quickly to the door. Richard does not stop him.

Dignity bleeding, Alexander returns to his office.

• • • •

Alexander does not dwell long on the incident. He has overheard many variations of that particular conversation, and while each one cuts raw, he recovers quickly. Life is too short to waste on insults.

CATEGORY UNEXPECTED CRYPTOZOOLOGICAL RAMIFICATIONS

Still, he wonders what Richard makes of it, what else the man has heard during his time at LuthorTech.

Alexander does not have to wonder long.

He is sitting at his desk, staring out the window at the sun-splashed rush-hour foot traffic, when Richard knocks on the door and enters. The secretary knows not to stop him. Richard is free to come and go as he pleases, though he has never been told this explicitly.

"We need to talk," he says, and Alexander nods, somewhat distracted. He is thinking about worms, wondering how big they have gotten. It is the beginning of the third week.

Richard says, "Kid, you're a mess. You're fucked up."

Alexander blinks, refocusing his entire attention on Richard. Richard places his palms on the desk and leans forward. "Yeah, you heard me. Fucked. Up."

"I can tell you've been giving this some thought," Alexander says, struggling to maintain his composure.

Richard sinks into the soft leather chair in front of Alexander's desk. "Enough to make me crazy."

Alexander does not know whether to be pleased or worried. "So. I'm making you crazy. Why is that?"

Richard shakes his head. There are shadows under his eyes, new lines around his mouth. Alexander wonders if perhaps Richard *has* been going a little crazy thinking of him.

"I don't get you," he says. "Haven't from the beginning, but that was okay. I could tell you had a good heart. And after I was here for a while and saw how you ran this place, I knew you had more than that. Real brains. Talent. One of those bright futures you hear people bragging about, but don't really deserve. Well, you deserve it, kid. You really do."

This is not what Alexander expected. Richard leans forward and drums his fingers on the desk, a harsh rough sound.

"But here's what I don't understand. You let your own employees talk shit—real abuse—and hard as I try, I just can't feel sorry for you. You know why? Because you ask for it."

"I ask for it," Alexander echoes, tasting those words.

Richard's gaze is pained. "Little things add up, kid. Like your head, the way you shave it. What, three times a day? Or the name of this place—LuthorTech, LuthorTech—not even the name it started out with. You changed it when you took over. Changed everything except *your* name."

"I like my name," Alexander says, soft.

Richard blows out his breath. "Yeah. I can tell." He points at the poster of Superman. "But that is the final straw, kid. Nothing else would matter, except for that right there. You've taken it past a hobby. You've taken it past a joke. You've taken it right into a way of life, and you're trying to be the villain."

"Because someone needs to be," Alexander says, shocked at how easy the words come to him. He wonders, Why? What has happened?

Richard frowns and says, "What's that supposed to mean?"

Alexander almost lies, but this is Richard. Richard, who has always been honest and who Alexander has always been honest with, because such is the currency between them, and it is too late, too late for anything else. The truth has become one of Alexander's worms; it exists and grows and cannot be denied. The line has been crossed.

So.

"It means," Alexander says, "that someone needs to be the villain. I want that person to be me."

Silence, and then: "You want to be Lex Luthor."

Alexander goes very still. "I think I already am."

Richard says nothing for a long time. He merely stares at Alexander, and then—to the young man's relief—turns his gaze on the window, on the hordes of nameless, nearly faceless people tramping down the sidewalk. He stares and stares, and Alexander grows light-headed from holding his breath.

Richard says, "I had a son. He died. He took drugs and it killed him. He'd be about your age now. You're not on drugs, are you?"

"No," Alexander says.

"I didn't think so." Richard glances at him. "Then why? You told me once you believe a man can fly. But men can't fly. That's a fantasy. Superman isn't real."

He's real to me, Alexander thinks, and maybe it shows on his face because Richard straightens and looks hard in Alexander's eyes. Alexander senses a fissure between them; closing or opening, he cannot tell. Just, only, that he wants to cross the distance and does not dare.

Richard stirs. "You are not Lex Luthor." A pause, then. His voice drops to a hoarse whisper, disturbed with awe. "But you believe. You believe it all."

"Yes," Alexander breathes, because to say it louder would feel coarse, like a desecration of the truth, the myth. "Yes. I've always believed."

Believed in the perfect essence of the myth, the stark lines between good and evil. How one must have the other to survive, to make whole the heart.

Perhaps Richard is psychic. Perhaps Alexander has revealed more than he thought possible: in his face, his words. Richard looks at the poster of Superman. His eyes grow dark, dark with understanding, and he says in a deep strange voice, "You're in love with him."

Shocking, to hear those words out loud. Shocking and thrilling. Alexander struggles with himself, unable to speak. The silence is confirmation enough for Richard. He presses on. His voice is cold and hard.

"I understand now. I didn't before. Not really. You're in love with Superman. The man himself, along with his ideals and all the shit wrapped up in the myth. You want him to be real so you can fuck him, and if you can't fuck him, then you want to be Lex Luthor because then at least he'll be your enemy, and you'll have him like no one else ever will."

Truth rises within Alexander, triumphant and powerful, a force within his heart beating like thunder. He leans out of his chair, steady and full and ready to speak. Someone knocks on the door.

It is Dr. Reynolds. Her face is flushed.

"There's a problem," she says.

. . . .

Richard follows them to the car. When Dr. Reynolds slips into the backseat, he places a strong hand on Alexander's shoulder, holding him still. His eyes are clear and hard.

The two men do not speak, but it is enough. Their conversation remains unfinished and neither man dares let the other out of his sight until some final word has rung. What has already been said is too strange. Like a dream, it might fade if not held tight.

Alexander steps aside and motions for Richard to precede him into the car. Dr. Reynolds looks on with some surprise, but Alexander does not explain. He is the boss and today he will take advantage of it.

They drive from downtown into a shabbier part of the city. Not so worn as to be inhospitable, but not so clean as to be frequented by anyone who might think to question the odd comings and goings of windowless utility vans, the frequent descent of uniformed men and women into the shadows below the street.

It is just the city government doing work, the locals think. Special maintenance. *Very* special.

Dr. Reynolds says, "Everything was fine on Friday. The sludge levels were getting low, but the Federal Scientists promised—those *idiots*—they *promised* me they would put more in over the weekend."

"Kathy—"

"They did it on purpose, Mr. Luthor." Her voice breaks. Alexander wonders if he will lose this woman after today's work. "They wanted to see what would happen."

Alexander closes his eyes. Richard remains silent, watching them both.

A member of Dr. Reynolds's team meets them at the site, bearing enough protective gear for two people. Alexander sends the young man back for another suit; Richard is coming with them. A bad decision, perhaps, but it is part of Alexander's reckless drive toward honesty. He cannot stop, no matter the price.

Richard asks no questions when Alexander gives the order—he says nothing at all—but his eyes are sharp, sharp, sharp.

Alexander helps Richard dress. The protective gear—suit, mask, oxygen—are tricky for the uninitiated. Alexander does not look at Richard's face as his capable hands zip and tug and button. The moment is inappropriate for words.

And what can Alexander say? Don't be afraid of my touch. Don't be afraid of me. Please, don't be afraid.

Dr. Reynolds bounces on her toes, agitated. "We don't have time for this. Please, Mr. Luthor."

"I'm done." Alexander steps back from Richard. Their eyes meet and Alexander turns away, toward the sewer entrance. "Let's go."

They descend. Down, down deep into shadow, Alexander leading the way. His mask is off, his ears keen for screams, shouts—cries of horror. Nothing. He hears nothing human.

Nothing human. Nothing coherent. Just flesh, whispering, dry and cool; the sucking of large mouths.

He smells shit. Shit, and something stronger, bitter.

Bitter, like blood.

"Fuck," Richard whispers, as they make their final descent into the sewer, stepping onto the concrete platform.

An appropriate response. Alexander would say something similar if he could, but his mouth will not work. Nothing seems to work but his eyes and mind, and how lovely—how miraculous it would be—if Alexander could somehow turn those organs off. At the moment, they are vital to nothing but nightmare.

And the nightmare is this, what the government could have prevented, what they should have known would happen: the worms have grown. Grown large and long and strong. Their sludge is gone.

And they are still hungry.

The experiments at LuthorTech, repeated time and time again, have shown that the worms have only one instinct, and that is to feed. Reproduction is asexual and infrequent, stimulated by solitude: a single worm, immersed in large amounts of sludge, will grow buds of baby worms across its body. When the worms emerge, they spill into the sludge and begin to feed.

And so the cycle goes. Feed, feed, feed—it is always feeding with them. Even when the food runs out.

Alexander watches a mouth bang against dry concrete; diverted, the orifice sucks air, seeking purchase, anything soft and wet. Flesh will do. Flesh will do just fine. It is warm, it yields to sharp lips, and just below the surface is blood, and deeper, the remnants of sludge. It is as good a meal as any, and better than death.

Alexander notices the government scientists huddled in a group, taking notes and casting surreptitious glances in his direction. Some of them look sick, but even nausea seems to take on a dispassionate quality in their faces. The worms are eating each other alive, spraying blood with each bite, tearing flesh in mighty chunks, and the scientists are doing nothing to stop it. They do not want to stop it. They will let these creatures torture each other, and simply watch.

Alexander's hands curl into fists. "Who's in charge here?"

They stare. A dark-suited figure in a rain slicker pushes clear. The puker, his black eyes small and smug. He looks as though he has been ill, but power, it seems, is a fine medicine.

"You have to stop this," Alexander says.

"I don't have to do anything," says the puker. "These creatures are government property and this is our experiment. You're a guest here, Mr. Luthor. I suggest you act like one and stay out of the way."

"A guest?" Alexander feels Richard and Dr. Reynolds close against his back. "LuthorTech designed these worms. Until the handover is official, their well-being is our business, and they are clearly *unwell*—due to *your* mismanagement, I assume."

"I won't warn you again." The puker is angry. "The government paid a high price—"

"And having paid that price, what will your superiors say when they discover there is nothing left of their experiment but a few dozen corpses? Will you impress them with a barrel full of remains? Lovely. Be my guest. *Go right ahead.*"

"Look," says a government scientist. "There was no other way to move their bodies. They're too large and the kill-gas is too slow. This way, we manage everything at once. It's not like you can't make more. That's your job, isn't it?"

"My God," Alexander hears Richard whisper. Alexander wonders if God plays such games, if He is so cruel—a disinterested observer, a scientist watching His creations in their sewer-world, watching death and malice and love and conception, waiting to see which side will win, waiting to see if there will be any side, or just clumps of blood and flesh, waiting at the very end of a failed experiment on a tiny little world in a dark little backwater of the cosmos.

No, Alexander thinks. *No, we are more than that. We must make ourselves more than worms. We must take away the hunger, or else create a hunger for better things.*

Behind the government scientists is a valve; if turned, it will release sludge into the trench below. Experiments have shown that the worms prefer sludge to flesh—bathe them in it, let them wallow in shit, and they will stop consuming each other.

Alexander strides forward. The puker does not back away. He meets Alexander with arms outstretched, blocking the path.

"Not this time," he says, as though that is enough, as though his word is law.

The government scientists are smarter; they know what is behind them and can guess what Alexander plans to do. One of them says, "He's going to stop the experiment! Don't let him near that valve."

Dr. Reynolds shouts at them. Alexander cannot understand what she says because his ears are roaring, his head buzzing with rage. The worms are writhing in blood and it is another red-lit room—red with fluid, dark and dirty—and he must stop this, he must stop this torture because the worms cannot stop it for themselves. He must play a little God and intervene.

Alexander is lean and strong. He pushes the puker aside, but the man is ready for him and has his own rage, his own bruised pride. The puker strikes Alexander hard in the gut, a sharp thrust. Alexander staggers backward.

Back into Richard, who has followed close to help.

Alexander hears a gasp, a startled cry. He turns in time to see Richard teeter on the narrow ledge, flail and swing and fall. He does not hit concrete. He hits worm.

Alexander cannot see Richard's face; he lands facedown, limbs entangled in shifting flesh. Richard tries to stand but the worms are too large. All he can do is straddle, stay on top, struggle to keep from slipping into crushing darkness.

It is the worst kind of Hell Alexander can imagine, but he does not hesitate. He jumps into the trench. Alexander lands hard but the worms cushion his fall—a grotesque trampoline made of firm flesh. He lunges forward, slithering and bouncing over thrashing bodies, thick as oaks. The worms are slippery, greased with blood and shit. Alexander swallows filth. His eyes burn.

Richard sees him. There is a moment when Alexander imagines something more than fear on the man's face—a shadow beneath the terror and disgust that looks like concern. And then a tail rises up and slams into Richard's head.

Richard disappears.

Alexander fights. His life narrows down to one thin line and he pulls his soul over this line, hand over hand, slamming fists into hard bodies, into searching mouths, razing his skin on sharp lips while his lungs fill with the hot stench of shit and blood, shit and blood in his mouth, on his tongue, gritty and slimy and metallic. He fights and fights, the worms tearing open his suit, crushing him between their surging bodies, squeezing him like a lemon. Ribs crack, but he pushes forward, slithering. He glimpses a white suit.

Alexander screams as he wrenches his torso against undulating muscle. His broken ribs shift against skin. The worms move, pull apart, and Alexander dives to the ground, scrabbling on all fours until he reaches Richard.

Richard is curled tight, his chin tucked against his chest, hands over his head. The suit around his upper thigh is ripped. Alexander sees bone.

Alexander covers Richard with his body, placing his hands against Richard's filthy hair, the bare skin of his neck. Richard turns his head just a fraction; his eyes are bloodshot, terrible.

"Get out of here," he says, and Alexander can hear the desperation in his voice, the despair.

"No," Alexander mouths, because he cannot make his lungs work past the pain in his ribs. A worm rolls over his legs and Alexander swallows a cry.

"Please," Richard begs.

Alexander says nothing. He does not have the strength to stand, to fight. Everything he had, he has given in his battle to reach Richard. All he can do now is curl around the body beneath him and hold on tight. He presses his cheek against Richard's hair. He closes his eyes.

The worms come up hard against his back, their mouths seeking flesh.

• • • •

After the accident, the government takes possession of the worms and all associated technology. It does this in a matter of days. Alexander does not fight when Dr. Reynolds gives him the news. He hopes the government has learned a lesson, that it will be more careful in the future. But hope is just that. It does not mean very much.

"When you stop being optimistic," Richard says, "the veil that hides the cruelty of things is removed."

"Then I've never been optimistic," Alexander says, and pushes down a button. The bed whirs and his upper body propels slowly forward until he can look Richard in the eyes. Richard is in a wheelchair. He wears a hospital gown that does not quite cover the thick bandages wrapped around his upper left leg. Alexander remembers bone every time he looks at that leg, but he is paying for the best regrowth technology money can buy. Richard will be able to walk again in a matter of weeks. It will take Alexander much longer. The doctors must repair his organs so he can live beyond the machines knitted into his body. They must finish destroying the last remnants of infection.

Flowers surround him: roses, lilies. They are pleasant substitutes for Alexander's parents, who have visited their son only twice since he entered the hospital. Alexander does not remember either visit. He was asleep.

"You're the most optimistic person I know," Richard tells him.

Alexander does not feel like arguing. Instead he says, "Did you see Dr. Reynolds on her way out?"

"Yes. I thanked her." Richard looks at his palms, rubs his knuckles with one finger. "I suppose she's the reason we're still alive."

"Yes," says Alexander. "I didn't know she had safety protocols in place. I thought the lockers were full of scientific equipment. Not stun rods." Stun rods powerful enough to take down an elephant. Powerful enough for the worms. Dr. Reynolds and her team, who jumped into the trench, stunned the worms long enough to drag Richard and Alexander to safety. A miracle. Alexander is very happy Dr. Reynolds has decided to remain at LuthorTech. She tells him it is good to be needed.

Richard stops looking at his hands. His gaze is clear, unwavering. "You didn't have a stun rod."

Alexander's cheeks grow warm. Before he can say anything, Richard reaches into a cloth bag attached to the side of his wheelchair and pulls out several familiar objects. Comic books. He places them on Alexander's lap. Superman shines on the covers. Alexander touches that bright face. He traces the edge of the red cape.

"You're wrong, you know," Alexander says softly, not looking at Richard. "About why I've done this to myself. I don't want to become Lex Luthor because it's all I can get. I want to be Lex Luthor because wherever he is, there's Superman. And the world needs something of Superman to exist, even if it's in the form of his very worst enemy. The world needs someone good."

I need someone good, Alexander thinks.

"Superman is a fantasy."

"He doesn't have to be." Alexander hesitates. "The laws of nature are human invention, a relationship between man and what he perceives. What there is, what man needs to keep himself going, is illusion, the dream."

Richard sits back. "A dream of better things, huh? Is that what keeps you going? Is that all Superman is to you?"

"People need to be reminded of what they can become, not what they are."

"Maybe," Richard says. "But you're still full of shit. People don't care if you're Lex Luthor or if Superman exists. *I* don't care. The only person who cares is you. And that's okay, kid. It really is. I've changed my mind. You're not fucked up. You're just fine the way you are. But"—Richard leans forward, so close Alexander can feel the heat of his breath on his face—"you didn't answer my question, and I don't think I was entirely wrong. What is Superman to you, *really*? Do you love him? Are you in love with that man on the page, that fantasy?"

Alexander swallows hard. He remembers the worms tearing off chunks of his body and wishes that he was back in that moment, because blood and pain are easier than telling the truth to this man. Alexander forces himself to look into Richard's eyes.

"Yes," he whispers. "I love him. But not just him."

Richard goes very still. Alexander listens to the slow thrum of his aching heart.

"I can't be something I'm not," Richard finally says. "I love you, kid. Just not like that."

"I know," Alexander says, and his eyes feel hot, as hot as his body, burning with shame. Richard reaches out and gently rests his hand on top of Alexander's scalp. He has not shaved since the accident. He has hair again.

"The problem with you," Richard says quietly, "is that you love too much. You love so damn much, you expect the world to do the same. And when it doesn't, when all you see is the horrible crap that goes on, day in and day out, it hurts you. It eats at you. Just like those worms, bleeding you dry. But what you're forgetting, kid, what you've let slip by, is that the world doesn't need a Lex Luthor or a Superman. The world just needs people like you. Honest, good men."

"I'm not good," Alexander says, and his voice is low, rough. He can barely speak through the lump in his throat. "I will never be that good. I cross all the lines, Richard. I make monsters. I do it for money and I ignore the consequences. I don't *care* about the consequences."

"Kid," Richard says, so gentle it makes Alexander's breath catch. "It isn't inconceivable that the same man who can make a monster, might also be the same man who risks his life to save a friend from that monster."

"I can't be both," Alexander whispers, but he wonders if such a thing is possible, if the myth can be carried on in some fashion other than desire and fantasy and desperate dream. He wonders if the world can be given its Superman and its Lex Luthor, and whether that will be enough for whatever it is Alexander believes can be made better, an answer to the need that runs deep inside his heart.

He wonders if he will ever stop loving the two men he can never have.

"I'm tired of being alone," Alexander says, throwing away the last of his dignity.

Richard takes Alexander's hand, holding it palm to palm. "Don't worry," he says, and his eyes are kind, so kind. "You're not alone."

And that is enough.

Marjorie M. Liu is the New York Times *bestselling author of the Dirk & Steele series of paranormal romances, as well as the Hunter Kiss urban fantasy series. Her short fiction has appeared in a number of anthologies, such as* Masked, Songs of Love and Death, Hotter than Hell, *and* Inked. *She also writes for Marvel Comics, penning* Black Widow, X-23, Dark Wolverine, *and* Astonishing X-Men.

CATEGORY: Observations in Psychological Cataclysms

RULE 6.022Na: If It Sounds Too Good to Be True, It's Crazy

SOURCE: George Tisdale, cashier (with aspirations)

VIA: Jeffrey Ford

The ads for them are everywhere—spread across the advertising sections at the back of magazines, shouting out of those posters you find on the back of stall doors in bar restrooms, even printed on the floor of the commuter train. Get rich quick! Learn to invest! I made one million dollars in my first year! And at the bottom of each ad, in print that's even finer than the words breaking down the costs for each seminar/book/lecture series, is the warning that your results may vary and results are not guaranteed.

Even without the fine print, most of us know better than to trust these ads. Those products are all scams by hucksters and con artists. But the man behind The Pittsburgh Technology isn't just another snake oil salesman. His program isn't another get-rich-quick scheme: it bends all the rules and writes over the top of all the fine print. Because it's utterly, utterly mad.

THE PITTSBURGH TECHNOLOGY

JEFFREY FORD

George Tisdale stepped off the bus at the corner of Merton and Pine and headed up the block toward his apartment building. As he trudged along, he considered the grim prospect of what he'd have for dinner. For a guy who worked at a grocery store, his refrigerator was always oddly empty. He pictured the frozen wasteland with its head of browning lettuce, a half stick of rancid butter, and a plastic bag holding a ball of chopped meat the color of jade.

"Same shit, different day," he mumbled to himself, and stepped aside to let a couple coming toward him arm in arm pass on the sidewalk.

"Hello," said the young woman, making eye contact with George.

He nodded and was momentarily startled by her looks—dark hair cut short, striking hazel eyes, and perfectly red valentine lips. It didn't take much to get George excited, seeing as the last date he'd had was a year earlier. He smiled. The woman's companion also said, "Hi," but George paid no attention to him. The two passed in a moment, and just as George was about to head on his way, he heard the man say, "Tis?"

George spun around at the mention of his nickname.

The fellow had turned back and was approaching. Now George noticed him. He wore a sharp, camel hair overcoat with a plaid scarf around his neck. The guy's hair was neatly cut and he was smooth shaven and handsome.

"Tisdale," the guy said, wearing a big smile. He held his hand out to George, who was certain he didn't know him.

"You must be mistaken," said George, but the guy grabbed his hand and shook it.

"It's me, Tis."

George stared and some vague sense of recognition crossed his mind, as if he might have seen the face once in a dream.

"Loopy," said the stranger. "From the grocery store."

"What?" said George, but now it became clear to him. Loopy had been the cart collector at the grocery store. The first person called upon by the managers for any kind of scut work. He was forever cleaning out the fish and deli cases, mopping up broken jars of pickles and tomato sauce, scouring the toilets. But back then, his hair was long, greasy, and straight, which earned him the name Shemp from the old women in the bakery. Otherwise, he was Loopy, the guy who everybody shit on. A sad sack who could clear the break room with a single utterance. He'd been fired for failing to punch out one night. The manager caught up with him in front of the deli counter one afternoon, and in the presence of both customers and fellow employees, proclaimed him a lost cause and told him to get out. People recounted the story in the break room and laughed for a solid month after his departure.

What George saw before him now was no less than a miracle, as if Loopy had been radically made over by a team of genius designers and beauticians. What was even more astonishing was that he had somehow traded in his dull affect for a look of—there was no other word for it—"intelligence."

"How are you doing, Tis?"

"Okay," said George, still stunned.

"I don't go by Loopy anymore," said Loopy. "I use my real name. You can call me John."

"John, good to see you," George managed to get out.

"Are you still working checkout at Bierman's?"

George nodded.

"Since I left the store, I got a new position over at the bank on Main Street. I started out as a teller, but now I'm helping customers invest their money as smartly as possible."

"That's great," said George.

"This is my partner, Cass," said Loopy, and motioned for the young woman to step up and shake George's hand. As she moved forward and lifted her arm, her coat opened and a warm, perfumed breeze wafted out. George went weak when he felt her touch.

"Do you ever think of leaving Bierman's?" Loopy asked.

"Yeah, sometimes," said George. "It's all right, though. You know, the register's the best job in the store." He tried to smile convincingly, but he saw the young woman wince at his statement.

"Well, good seeing you," said Loopy and draped his arm over Cass's shoulder and pulled her close to him. They turned and walked and George heard them laugh quietly as if they were trying not to let him hear.

"See ya," said George, who now didn't have the energy to take a step.

The couple had gone about ten yards, and then Loopy stopped, turned, and headed back toward George, leaving Cass waiting.

"Listen," he said as he approached again, "if you feel like you need a change in your life, you should check this out." He reached into his over-coat, took out his wallet, and drew a business card from it. He handed it to George. Printed on the card were the words THE PITTSBURGH TECHNOLOGY and beneath them was a phone number and an address.

"What is this?" asked George.

Loopy got close and whispered, "They told me only to give their number out to people I thought were . . . , uh, really good people. The Technology is a little expensive, but just look at that piece of ass I'm with now," he said, and gave a breathy laugh.

"What do they do to you?"

"Go check it out. Forget Bierman's. You're stuck, buddy. Go see Profes-sor Werms, and he'll free you from your ascribed fate."

"My ascribed fate?" asked George, but Loopy was again heading away from him. He caught up to Cass and put his arm around her. George slipped the card into his back pocket, and as he walked the rest of the way to his building, he thought about Loopy saying, "Really good people," and remem-bered how mean he and everyone else had been to the poor schlub. There was one time that stood out in particular. George had been in the break room, talking to the store butcher, Martone, about a football pool they were both in. Loopy walked in and sat down at their table. Before he could open his mouth, George said to him, "Beat it, retard." The Loop cowered and slunk away. Later, he felt a twinge of remorse for having been so bla-tant, but he'd never apologized.

The next evening after work, George took a different bus that went across town. He got off in an area he didn't frequent much by Gable Park. On a side street off the main thoroughfare, he found a storefront that still had a barber pole out front and a sign above the door that said CROSS-CUTS, UNISEX STYLING. But in the window there was a handmade sign, black magic marker on white oak tag. It announced, TPT, THE CHANGE OF A LIFETIME. He peered through the glass into the seemingly empty shop, but past the ini-tial bank of shadows, he saw a light in the back and could just make out the figure of a man sitting at a desk.

He opened the door and a buzzer went off somewhere in the distance. Once inside, he could see that he was right. There was a white-haired man wearing a white shirt at a desk with a gooseneck lamp, its glow dimly dis-tinguishing him from the darkness. "Hello," called George. The man looked up from his paperwork and adjusted his glasses with his middle finger. "Come forward," he said in a loud, flat tone.

George hesitated a moment and then stepped through the shadows to the desk. As he approached, the man leaned back in his chair and motioned for George to take the seat across from him. "What do you want?" he asked, folding his hands on his stomach.

George held out the business card Loopy had given him. "The Pittsburgh Technology," he said.

"You?" said the man, and laughed briefly. His features seemed chiseled from stone but still somehow conveyed a subtle expression of derision. "You don't look like you have the backbone for it," he said.

"Does it hurt?" asked George.

"Physically, you don't feel a thing. It's not you that changes, it's the universe that changes around you."

"I think I could do that."

"Answer these three questions. One, how old are you? Do you have a significant other—wife/husband/girl- or boyfriend/partner? And lastly, is your life a failure?"

"I'm thirty-two," said George.

The corners of the man's mouth turned down and he shook his head. "Where do you work?"

"I'm a cashier at a Bierman's on the other side of town."

The man sighed. "Perfectly underwhelming."

"I'm not in a relationship now."

"I suppose we can skip the last question then."

"I did go with a girl for almost a year and a half three years ago."

"Spare me the pathetic details. What's your name?"

"George."

"A child's name," said the man. "I'm Professor Werms, the inventor of The Pittsburgh Technology. I'm going to tell you about it. If it sounds like you'd like to give it a try, it will cost you four thousand dollars cash, no checks or money orders. Do you have that kind of collateral?"

"Yes."

"You, George, are a classic loser. Your kind are everywhere, trapped like flies in the web of Fate. You're not bad people basically, but you've gone about as far as you're going with the hand you've been dealt and yet there's so much more of your static life left to creep through. Think of the concept of Purgatory. Do you understand?"

George nodded, though he wasn't sure.

"Every day the same . . . or worse. The sun always setting."

"Yes."

"No doubt you've tried to change your life in the past but your efforts evaporated into nothing. That is basically the problem from a scientific standpoint. You can't change your present life because your present is contingent on your past. Your history is always chasing you and always gaining on you. Your future is set in place and it can't be deviated from because of everything that has happened to that point. No event is an island, but each reverberates outward influencing future events and states of being. Do you understand?"

"I think so," said George.

"You've sealed your Fate and as it happens your Fate turns out to be dreadfully dull. Yet, when you try to change it, because you are the product of your past, you can't affect anything. You're the problem you are trying to fix and for that you'd have to go back to the moment of your birth and begin there, or, in reality, back before it to those initial causes that co-alesced in a future to create you. Time travel is impossible, if you haven't heard, so the next best or even better thing is my Technology. What it does is sever the infernal eternal act of your past strangling your future."

George shifted in his seat and squinted. "I think I get that," he said. "What university do you teach at?"

"Are you calling me a fool?"

"No," said George and held his hands up in defense. "You said you're a professor; I was just wondering where you taught."

"The word *professor* simply means someone who professes . . . and that's what I do. I don't need some fossilized bureaucracy employing me to do so."

George quietly agreed.

"Follow me now," said Werms. "You need for something to happen in your life, an event. It could be utterly minor or something outlandish. Since everything is connected, just one event can change everything. My methods can create and insert an entirely rogue event into your closed loop of Fate and send the direction of your existence off on another heading. I've devised a way to conjure and bestow an element of explosive *chance*. We're talking random number generation. We have a machine that produces completely random numbers to six digits and then, through a complex mathematical formula, reduces them to either one, two, or three digits.

"Once this number has been determined, we consult a chart of possible events we could implement in your life. This chart was devised by me with painstaking precision. Because this event I mention is spawned outside of your history or the history of your world, no prior events having led to it, given birth to it, it will change the course of your life. Now, on the chart I spoke of, the events are number one to one hundred thirteen. We take the number ultimately calculated and produced by the generator and find its corresponding event on the chart. And then, my associates, a crack team of agents of the Technology, in a clandestine manner, produce this random event in your life. It could be that someone might sneeze at your bus stop in the morning, it could be that a woman in a crowd smiles at you, or it could be something monumental, you never know: it's random. You won't know when it happens. We are very discreet. If you were to know what it was or what it would be, you would be part of it and then the technology would be diffused."

"You have people who do things like this?" asked George.

"They're very good. You'll never see them. And the next day, you'll already be able to feel the difference in your life."

"What if my life changes, but I don't like it?"

"That's a chance you have to take. Most people make a change for the better, simply because it's original change, unsullied by a history of numerous defeats, but there have been those who've gone in the other direction. They have a tendency not to live long, and therefore, although they did not succeed in making their lives better, they did, as a consolation, make them shorter."

"So I wouldn't get my money back if things went badly?"

"Take it or leave it. Don't be a simpering turd. The Technology, I can tell you, *works*. What reason would I have to lie?"

"Why is it The *Pittsburgh* Technology?"

"Have you ever been to Pittsburgh?"

George shook his head.

"A technology does not have to denote machinery, it can also be a state-of-the-art method or process. The one I created is backed by mathematics and physics hypotheses derived from quantum investigation. That's why it's good. Why not put away the days of sorrow and those nights of hand-dancing with yourself?"

George blushed and nodded. "Okay," he said, "I'll do it."

"But first . . . ," said the professor. He opened a drawer of his desk and pulled out a sheet of paper. Setting it down so George could read it, he also passed over a pen.

I will never speak to anyone about The Pittsburgh Technology, it said, and beneath that there was a long dotted line to sign on.

George signed and handed the form to the professor, who put it back in the drawer. "Tomorrow, after you return from work, a messenger will come to your door and ask for the money. You will hand over four thousand dollars in a brown grocery bag. If this is done, the next morning, early, you will receive a call to let you know that the Technology has begun. The event that will change your life will happen on that day, although you will be unaware of it. On the following day, you'll experience the miracle of having the same past but a different future."

· · · ·

The next morning at work, George thought about how his life could be different as he scanned the endless conveyor belt of items. When he performed his little routine with each customer—*Hi, do you have a Bierman's savings card*, etc.—he was elsewhere, walking down a windy street with Cass on his arm. "We're going to the opera," he caught himself saying aloud. The woman whose bags he was packing made a sour face and shrugged. Later, someone placed a leaking gallon of milk on his conveyor, and while he cleaned it, he made the decision to leave work a little early and get to the bank before closing. He'd saved money over the years because there'd been almost no one or little else to spend it on.

He consumed a tub of microwave macaroni and cheese and two slices of buttered bread while reading his mail: a flyer from Bierman's. Just as he finished eating, he heard a knock at his apartment door. He rose nervously and went to answer it. Leaving the chain on, he peered out into the hallway. There was a small person there, wearing a Lone Ranger mask beneath a black hoody. "T.P.T.," the stranger said in a high-pitched voice. George couldn't tell if it was a woman or an adolescent boy.

"I've got it," said George. He went to the kitchen and retrieved the brown bag. When he made it back to the living room, the messenger's arm was through the door. George handed the bag over. It slipped out of sight and he heard running in the hallway. For the rest of the night, he walked around his meager apartment, looking things over as they presently existed one last time. He stood for a long while, holding a photo of his mother and father. At ten, he put it down and went to bed.

In his dream, Cass was about to pleasure him with her mouth when the phone rang and she evaporated. George came spluttering up out of sleep and grabbed the receiver next to the bed. "Yes?" he said.

"The Technology has been activated," said a computerized voice.

George hung up and lay still, stunned by the sudden prospect that whatever was going to happen could happen at any moment. Beyond his thoughts, he heard the faucet in the bathroom dripping in sets of threes. As he listened, he heard the set of three suddenly become four, and he wondered, "Was that it?" He was sure it was until he heard the faint sound of a cough come from the apartment next door. In his head he had a vision of his neighbors, Jim and Ethel, sitting in their kitchen, paying no attention to the hoodied, masked figure that leaned close to the wall and cleared its throat. Then the traffic sounded and a bird sang on the windowsill. He got out of bed and noticed the photo of his parents was turned facedown. He couldn't remember if that was the way he'd left it. The shower water was unusually cold. His deodorant stung the slightest bit more, and he smelled it to determine if they'd put something in it. Every little thing became an event fraught with possibility.

When he cracked an egg in the frying pan and discovered it had a blood spot, he grunted audibly and stepped back from the stove. He stood staring at it till the white turned to brown and the yoke hardened. Finally, he said, "Nah, that happens. I've seen that happen before a lot of times in my life." He threw out the egg and put the pan in the sink. Instead he had toast, and as he searched its dark mottling for a design, he told himself the blood spot was too obvious. Professor Werms would never stand for it.

At the bus stop that morning, a woman sneezed. A leaf came fluttering down from above and landed on an old man's hat. George glanced around to see if he could spot an agent of the Technology. As he scanned the crowd on the corner, one of the women smiled at him. Was she letting on that it was her, or was the smile itself the promised event? The cranky bus driver grudgingly nodded to the passengers as he always did, but when the woman who'd smiled got on, he said, "Morning," which had never happened before.

George sat in the last seat in the bus and watched out the back window for some sign of the conspiracy of the world. The teenagers in the front seat of an old Ford Taurus behind the bus saw him looking at them and gave him the finger. *Maybe that was it,* thought George, but when he got off at his stop, there was an abandoned soda, half empty, sitting on the curb, and the guy exiting in front of him kicked it over and whispered, "Shit." He thought he felt something vague move in his chest. He tried to decide if it was the flowering of his new life or just gas.

On his way through the store to punch in, he noticed that in the produce aisle there was one green lime mixed in with all the lemons. He went to the break room and sat down, overwhelmed with the possibilities. Taking a deep breath, he admonished himself for frantically trying to catch the agents of the Technology, to perceive the key event. *Let it happen,* he thought. *Just let it happen, or you'll ruin everything.* When he looked up he noticed that the three other people who had been at three different tables when he'd entered had immediately gotten up and left. He was too involved with the Technology to read the clue that he might be the store's new Loopy.

The grocery conveyor offered all manner of odd arrangements of items, teeming with significance. The customers said things they always said, but now their words had a covert gravity to them. The manager made an announcement over the loudspeaker for a sale on tuna fish. George finally switched to thinking about Cass and in this way was able to get through his shift. The sun was setting by the time he left Bierman's. As he walked to the bus stop, he realized the intensity of every moment of the day, on the lookout for the event, had left him exhausted. He just wanted to get home and go to sleep.

THE PITTSBURGH TECHNOLOGY

JEFFREY FORD

On the bus ride home, the young woman sitting next to him, a cute blonde with a ski cap and pink parka, out of the blue guessed his zodiac sign. "You're a Pisces," she said.

"No more," he muttered, and changed his seat. He rode the rest of the way to his stop with his hands over his ears and his eyes closed. In the darkness, he reeled at the thought of how many things were happening always and each of them, as Werms had told him, was a particle of a fate already decided.

The bus eventually stopped. He took his hands from his ears, opened his eyes, and got off without making eye contact with the blond astrologer. Only two blocks to go before he could huddle beneath the covers and wait out the night. With one block left he began to relax. Granted, a newspaper blew by with a headline, the last word of which he happened to catch—*Technology*. A child stared at him from a lit window he passed, and the exhaust of a taxi going up the street curled into a question mark before vanishing.

He managed to ignore all of it, but what he couldn't ignore was the dog, without a leash or an owner, coming toward him on the street's opposite sidewalk. It was a beautiful-looking creature, a sleek Dalmatian, whose white made it stand out in the twilight. He stopped walking when he spotted it and, as if the dog was responding to him, it stopped as well. It lifted its snout and stared directly across the street at him. He generally liked dogs, but when it started toward him, he felt slightly nervous. George couldn't take his eyes off how gracefully the dog moved, hoping it was friendly. Right when it had reached the middle of its crossing, though, a car George hadn't noticed, so intent was he on the animal, came speeding out of nowhere and plowed into the creature. There was a loud, echoing thud, the snap of bone, a gurgling yelp, and George jumped. The Dalmatian was thrown backward and skidded along the asphalt ten feet.

The driver leaped out of the car. "Is that your dog?" he yelled. George couldn't speak, but merely shook his head. In front of the car, he caught a glimpse of white with black spots dappled with gore, writhing on the blacktop. The doors of apartment buildings flew open here and there and people ran to the accident. George felt nauseous. He knew there was nothing he could do with all those people crowded around. He kept moving, made it to his apartment, and ducked inside. In the downstairs hallway, he leaned against the mailboxes and cried. The dog's slaughter, he was certain, was the event Werms had spoken of. If he'd known what was going to happen, he'd never have agreed. That's what he told himself as he tossed and turned in his bed unable to sleep. In the morning, after finally dozing off around 3 A.M., he woke groggy, late for work, and called in sick.

• • • •

Nearly a month to the day after George's induction into The Pittsburgh Technology, he stood once again in front of the shop with the barber pole. It was early on a Saturday morning. He cupped his hand above his eyes and gazed into the front window of the place. Back in the shadows, he saw the glow of the gooseneck lamp and the faint form of Werms, leaning over his paperwork. He entered TPT headquarters and the buzzer sounded.

"Step forward," said the loud, flat voice.

George walked in and took a seat, facing Werms.

"What can I do for you?" said the professor.

"Do you remember me?" asked George.

"Of course, but you were not to return here after having gone through the process, didn't I tell you that?"

"No," said George. "You didn't."

"Well, I'm telling you now," said Werms. "See yourself out."

"My life hasn't changed," said George. "Not for the better, not for the worse. And you killed a beautiful dog for nothing."

"What are you talking about, killed a dog?" said Werms.

"Don't lie to me," said George. "The Dalmatian. You had your man run it down for me."

"How grandiose you are," said Werms. "We did nothing of the sort. First, we don't harm animals in the performance of the Technology. Read the bylaws. Secondly, if we did, we wouldn't waste a dog on your sorry excuse for a life."

"The whole thing's a scam," said George.

"I might step on a cockroach for you but even that would be too much."

"I want my money back."

"You want your money back? Okay," said Werms, and opened the drawer to his desk. "Your life has not changed an iota, you're saying?"

"It's the exact same. Same days, same people, same job. Only now I have to go through it with a dead dog on my conscience."

"I'll change your life," said Werms. Instead of a roll of cash, he pulled a revolver out of the drawer and pointed it across the desk.

Geroge went limp at the sight of the gun. He couldn't speak. His legs began to tremble.

"Get up," said the professor.

George couldn't move.

"Get up or I'll shoot you where you sit. I'm mortally bored with your sniveling."

Werms cocked the trigger and stood. George managed to slowly get to his feet. The professor waved the gun. "Walk over to that door there," he said, and pointed to the left wall.

George searched the shadows off to the left and saw the dim outline of a door.

"Make it quick," said Werms. "Don't retard my life because yours is a fistula."

When George couldn't move, the professor stepped away from the desk and got behind him, nudging him forward with the barrel pressed to his spinal column. "Yes, I'll change your life," he said.

"Open the door," Werms commanded when they'd arrived.

George did as he was told, his face drenched with sweat.

Inside, there was a lit overhead bulb and a set of crude wooden steps descending into darkness.

"Get a good look," said the professor.

"What's down there?"

"Your Fate."

George let out a moan.

"One last time, for the record, do you want to report a problem with the operation and/or results of The Pittsburgh Technology?"

There was a long silence before George whispered, "No." He felt the gun pull out of his back. He heard Werms stepping away.

"What are you waiting for?" said the professor. George turned and saw the gun had been lowered.

"Now, scuttle back to your miserable existence and get on with it."

George ran like a man with a dog at his heels.

. . . .

Two months later, a package was delivered to his apartment from TPT. It held a piece of parchment decorated with intricately inscribed designs of curlicues and swirls in peacock blue. There was a gold seal on it that bore the inscription: *fatulus-fatalis*. It was a diploma for the successful completion of The Pittsburgh Technology, signed by Professor Werms. The sight of it made him ill and he cursed and said, "Four thousand dollars." He turned it facedown and left it on the table in his bedroom.

A week later he rediscovered it, and although initially deciding to throw it away, instead he bought a frame for it and hung it in the kitchen. Occasionally, before dinner, while waiting for the microwave to ding, he'd gaze at the document and wonder what the future would have been without it.

Jeffrey Ford is the author of several novels, including The Physiognomy, The Portrait of Mrs. Charbuque, The Girl in the Glass, *and* The Shadow Year. *He is a prolific author of short fiction, whose work has appeared in* The Magazine of Fantasy & Science Fiction, SCI FIC-

TION, *and in numerous anthologies, including John Joseph Adams's* The Living Dead *and* The Way of the Wizard. *Three collections of his short work have been published:* The Fantasy Writer's Assistant and Other Stories, The Empire of Ice Cream, *and* The Drowned Life. *He is a six-time winner of the World Fantasy Award, and has also won the Nebula and Edgar awards.*

CATEGORY: Vectors and Properties in Nemesis Relationships

RULE 401.k: Pick a Good Partner and an Even Better Nemesis

SOURCE: Mofongo, Gorilla of the Mind

VIA: Grady Hendrix

Human beings and gorillas share about 98 percent of the same genetic material. They are remarkably similar in biological terms: humans and gorillas are both mammals with close kin structures organizing their social groups; both species pass along learned experiences to their children; even their bodies are constructed in a fairly close fashion.

But can a gorilla be a mad scientist? Our next story gives us one.

Mofongo was once one of the great mad scientists. Not only was he a gifted inventor with a thirst for world conquest, he was also the proud possessor of a remarkable brain that could once give off rays of lethal energy. Once. Now Mofongo lives in a cage in a freak show, the prisoner of his nemesis. But as the sideshow fades in popularity, change, like the delicious smell of cotton candy, is in the air.

Here is the tale of a primate who could easily take on King Kong, with energy left to trounce Mojo Jojo in a contest of brain size. After wiping out those super-apes, what kind of challenge is humanity?

MOFONGO KNOWS

GRADY HENDRIX

Off the muddy tracks between the House of Shadows, the Freak Out, and the Gravitron, where passengers are pummeled with physics until they puke, behind the generators that push power to the Top Spin, the Zipper, and the Rainbow, back where the night air is so thick you can chew it—stale cotton candy, old dough fried in rancid oil, the ripe aroma of the IQ Zoo with its pathetic poultry who plink pianos with their beaks—here in the jumble of shooting galleries and hoopla trailers, next to Skee-Ball concessions leaning against Crystal Lil's Refreshment Emporium lies the secret heart of the fair: MOFONGO: GORILLA OF THE MIND.

The pulsating brain of the mighty ape is no longer as powerful as it once was, but even its passive presence subtly alters atoms. Read the subconscious signs. Hear the tiny fanfare. For all roads lead to Mofongo. Drop a slice of pizza, and it lands pointing toward his cage. The Wheel of Luck favors its Mofongo side. Lost children are always found in the litter-choked muck outside his tent.

On one side: the Ten-in-One. On the other: Saddam's Spider Hole featuring "The Marine who took DOWN the BUTCHER OF BAGHDAD!" In between: Mofongo. Buy a ticket. Part the canvas. Turn the corner. See his cage. This is where they come—the Scratch 'n' Win junkies, the astrology freaks, the overcompensating rednecks and their greasy-haired dates, the sullen and drunken, the viciously hip, the middle-aged losers with no more illusions, the unwed mothers broken by debt, the credit-card crucified, the ghetto schemers, twelve-year-old thug life dreamers, public housing divas, squad-car preachers, barroom philosophers, professional television watchers, expert beer-can emptiers, bastard babymakers who don't return calls, bail-bond skippers, dream destroyers, home wreckers, art-school zeroes, the angry, the humiliated, the tired, the downtrodden, the hate crazed, and all the unappreciated secret geniuses who will die still waiting for their big break . . . they all come here for his wisdom—for he is Mofongo, Gorilla of the Mind.

And Mofongo knows.

• • • •

"Mommy, the monkey is stinky."

Mofongo bows his mighty head. Yes, he knows that his jungle musk is too heady for humans.

"Mommy, the monkey smells like poop."

Mofongo's head droops lower. A soul-rattling sigh leaves his massive chest.

"Ew, Mommy, his breath smells like dog doo. He's wearing a hat."

Yes, this is his Power Turban, possessing the ability to part the veils of time and peer into the future. A spangled head wrap with an enormous jewel pinning a peacock feather to its center.

"He looks dumb and dirty like Meemaw."

Tokens rattle. Mofongo sighs and picks up one of the "Mofongo Knows" cards from the table and writes on it with a pen. Then he pushes the card through the slot and into the hand of the adult female, standing with its mate and spawn. The card reads: "Mofongo Knows . . . that you will overcome all obstacles. This is a bad month for financial decisions."

The humans snort in derision: for this they paid five tokens? For this sad ape, with his heavy brow and his matted fur, they used tokens that could have been employed in the pursuit of gravity-defying thrills over at the Hi-Flyin' Swings? This monkey would not get their gratitude, this monkey would get their backs as they walk out the door, mocking him in their high, reedy voices. The young, golden-haired child hangs back from its parents to hurl a final insult at Mofongo, hawking a loogie into its soft throat, expecting to expectorate on the great ape.

But Mofongo knows his reach, and with one leathery hand he seizes the tiny child and lifts it from the floor, pinching off its cry, pulling its red, bulging face close to the bars.

"Human," Mofongo growls, "your days are numbered. I remember your scent. I will come to your home as you sleep and break your bones and drink your blood. I will crush your kidneys. I will split you in half, human, and you will die of pain. Go, and tell your friends: Mofongo is coming."

He turns his back on the bars. The human child flees. The room is empty. Mofongo adjusts his Power Turban to better conceal his giant, pulsating brain, the enormous thinking engine that has deformed his skull, this overgrown tumorous organ swollen to the size of a beach ball.

· · · ·

A beer bottle shatters against the bars of Mofongo's cage, misting his back with glass and beer.

"You fucking touch a customer?" an angry voice slurs. "You fucking touch a customer, you jungle fuck?"

Mofongo tries to use his mind rays to kill Steve Savage, Hero of the Jungle, but these days his mind rays are weak. (Steve Savage is also weak, but Mofongo's mind rays are weaker still.) Mofongo tries to kill his old nemesis with contempt instead.

"Drunk again," he says. "How original."

"Oh, fuck you. Fuck you right between your beady eyes, you fucking hairy fuck," Steve Savage says. "What do I tell you? *Don't touch the customers.* Don't *speak* to the customers. Don't take your turban off in front of the customers. You know what would happen if I called the Feds? One phone call and they'd fucking incinerate you. They'd fucking cut out your giant fucking brain and put it in a jar and they'd stuff you in a trash incinerator and turn it up to eleven and turn you into seven hundred pounds of ape-flavored ash."

Steve Savage is a Man of Adventure, and Men of Adventure age slowly, their lives dragging on long after the actual adventures are over. Together, Mofongo and his ancient enemy are almost two hundred years old but neither of them looks a day over eighty.

Steve sways, filling himself up with Budweiser and rage. This is their fight, one that they used to perform with wondrous weapons that pushed the boundaries of science so far that they shattered. These days they have nothing left to fight with but paltry profanity. But it is a fight that never ends.

"Steve Savage," Mofongo says. "One day I will get out of this cage and on that day I will rip your head from your puny human body and wash my face in your blood."

"If you could do that, you would've by now," Steve says. "I beat your Science Army, I blew up your Danger Trees, I fucked up your Femme-Apes and Gibbon Guerillas, and I tore off Comrade Carnage's Anti-Gravity boots and beat the shit out of his Commie ass with them. So keep on threatening me, monkey!"

"You didn't defeat the Femme-Apes!" Mofongo yells, jumping up and down and shaking the bars. "You didn't defeat them! I saw photographs! You had *sex* with them!"

"They were shaved! I had a concussion!" Steve Savage screams. "You can't prove anything!"

"I can still smell their love musk on you," Mofongo cackles. "All these years later and you still stink of ape sex!"

Steve Savage climbs onstage and starts kicking the bars of the cage and Mofongo reaches out and tries to grab his legs. They slap at each other, locked in puny combat, man and gorilla, each with death in his eyes.

Then they fall back, panting, gasping, hearts pounding, on the verge of stroke. Steve throws a plastic shopping bag down, just outside the bars.

"There's your newspaper and your Dutch Masters," he says. "But no more books until you stop touching the customers."

Mofongo's muscles ache so badly that he can barely raise his arms, but with a heroic effort he manages to get them up and he shoots Steve the bird with both hands.

"That your IQ or your sperm count, cancer brain?" Steve shouts over his shoulder as he leaves the tent.

Mofongo opens the plastic bag and his enormous brain twitches painfully with humiliation. Anger, rage, hate, death. Steve knows he reads the *Wall Street Journal,* but inside the bag, beside his pack of natural wrapped cigarillos, is a copy of *USA Today.*

• • • •

"House full a got I," Barry the Backward Man says, throwing down his hand.

"Jesus, Barry, you're making Herman look bad tonight. What're you doing? Counting cards?" Gretchen the Two Ton Beauty says.

Barry laughs.

"Lucky naturally I'm," he says.

"Everyone knows you can't count cards in poker," Herman the Human Calculator grouses. "Too many variables, not enough data points."

"Everwhat," Barry says.

"What he said, but vice versa," Gretchen says. "You wanna play the next hand, Mofongo? We'll push the table over."

Mofongo presents them with his back.

"Holeass an what," Barry says.

"We come here to keep you company," Herman says. "The least you could do is act civil."

"Buy me a *Wall Street Journal,*" Mofongo says.

"This is South Carolina," Herman answers. "They don't carry the *Wall Street Journal.*"

"Then give me your copy."

"I read it online," Herman says. "And you know that Steve doesn't want you near a computer. The last time you got near a computer the space shuttle crashed."

"I forgot you humans stick together," says Mofongo.

"Oh, come on. None of us thinks you still want to take over the world," Gretchen says. "But Steve would freak."

"Stick a cake in it, Gretchen," Mofongo snarls. "This conversation is for superior intellects only."

"Hey," she says, hurt.

"Gretchen, personally it take not do," Barry says. "Business Brainiac strictly is this. Us to are they superior how themselves reminding keep to have they."

"One day, you will die," Mofongo growls.

"We're dying every day, 'fongo," Gretchen says. "But it doesn't mean we have to be rude to each other in the meantime. Besides, if you're such a superior intellect then how come we're all down here and you're up in that cage?"

· · · ·

Yes. Why is Mofongo up in that cage? The Genius Gorilla of Ghana, the Warrior of Wagadou, the Monster Who Shook the World, aka Professor Silverback, Science Ape, and Eater of Europeans—what is he doing in this cage, in a filthy, stinking, fly-specked, weary, run-down, water-stained, used-up, played-out, cheapjack funfair?

Bad luck, mostly. And hanging around with the wrong people.

When Mofongo sleeps he dreams of his glorious past, of his first desperate pilgrimage to Opar, the Hidden Jungle City, with its wondrous Atlantean geo-technology. His first Revolutionary Gorilla Army! The piezoelectric death rays! The anti-gravity granite! The neural enhancers that raised an army of thinking apes who rode antigravity platforms down the Daka River to crush the British imperialist pigs. The day they burst into the hall at Accra and turned the Big Seven into the Big Six, the head of Kwame Asanti dangling from his hand and blood dripping onto the expensive carpet.

He dreams of his first Ape Empire, its borders drawn in the blood of white men whose spines he happily ripped out and used to beat their women to death. The lady gorillas. The monkey love. His primate harem. And then the coming of Steve Savage, American adventurer and Grade-A asshole.

At first, Savage was just a jumped-up poacher with a flashy public image to peddle. Mofongo should have ignored him, but he didn't, and his attempts to kill the little twerp lent the creep legitimacy.

Over the years, it turned personal. When Mofongo had taken in the refugees of the Third Reich, Savage had been there to destroy his Diamond Dome. When Mofongo had dug the Death Mines of Yendi, Savage had appeared, and the ensuing Radar War had seen the floating Science City of If plunge into Lake Volta, its mathematics burning. The decades were a heady blur of fists connecting with jaws, ray guns melting screaming faces, the ozone tang of jet-pack exhaust, the click-whir of supercomputers calculating the unsane, the oily stink of robot death squads.

It all ended when Mofongo allied himself with the Communist freedom fighter, Comrade Carnage: half man, half clockwork terror ruled by an atomic brain. Their dreams of domination died in the nuclear fires unleashed by Steve Savage in his cowardly sneak attack. Mofongo's hover plane had risen up out of the glowing rubble of his Necro-Palace, another hairsbreadth escape, another last-minute dodge that left him at large to go on to greater and more grandiose schemes, and then the cold push of Steve

Savage's sten gun against the back of his skull, the poaching bastard having hidden in the copilot's seat until Mofongo was distracted. Mofongo knew he should have whipped around with his lightning-fast reflexes and punched Savage in the face, but he was so tired, his limbs were filled with lead, he just couldn't do it. And so, in a split second, Mofongo's days of freedom came to an end.

Trapped in a cage, Mofongo traveled with Savage, his parole officer, his warden, his captor, his keeper. He became Savage's meal ticket, the highlight of his road show. But the venues got smaller, the crowds got thinner, Savage got older, Mofongo's mental rays got weaker, and twenty-five years ago they became a single-o show, a traveling psychic ape and his owner floating from one redneck carnival to another, endlessly spinning through the southeastern United States, crossing paths and sharing midways with the same bunch of increasingly marginalized attractions as the big conglomerates took over the funfairs, pushing the sideshows further and further to the side.

There were a few years, though, when things might have gone differently. Savage had knocked up Nancy the Snake Girl and they had a daughter. Nancy was a woman of infinite practicality and limited patience for the male ego. She was in love with Steve, however, and gave him eight years to get his life in order and to give up the carnie life. While Steve was busy wasting every single one of those years, little Theresa Savage discovered Mofongo.

What little girl wouldn't want to befriend a talking gorilla? And what talking gorilla wouldn't welcome a captive audience? And when Theresa went missing and everyone assumed she was hiding near the teacups or gorging on cotton candy, it was Mofongo who used his mental rays to locate her and it was Mofongo who sent Dogtag Donald racing over to Bombo's Baby Show trailer to drag her out in the nick of time. It was Mofongo who identified that the drug in her system was nothing more than vodka, and it was Mofongo who planted a phobic aversion to children under eighteen deep inside Bombo's mind.

Not that anyone ever said "thank you."

Three months later, the eight years were over and, on the dot, Nancy Savage ditched the carnie life without a backward glance. She didn't even listen to Steve's weak protests and pathetic rationalizations. She just picked up Theresa, got her real estate license, and vanished into an alternate America where people lived in houses, went to school, and paid their taxes, leaving Steve Savage and Mofongo to return to their interminable bickering and to try to forget the eight-year interruption as best they could.

Now, every year Mofongo gets fewer visitors, and every year his mental powers fade, and every year he and Steve find new insults for old injuries, and every year he smokes his Dutch Masters and reads his paper and dreams about revenge until it is an abstraction worn smooth and feature-less by constant fantasy.

• • • •

It's been thirty years without a whiff of Theresa Savage, yet here's her smell again like a golden oldie.

"We need to talk," she says, standing outside Mofongo's cage with three men in dark suits.

"Let me guess," Mofongo says, sitting up. He is excited to have some new playmates, especially ones who wear suits. None of his visitors ever wear suits, and he hasn't seen a human being in forty hours. He can mentally dampen his hunger and thirst but his boredom knows no bounds. He points to them in order. "CIA, FBI, NSA."

"CIA, FBI, and Animal Control," the youngest suit man says to him.

"I am not an animal," Mofongo says.

"You're not exactly human, either," the man says.

Mofongo's nostrils flare.

"What is this, Theresa?" he asks. "Why did you come back?"

"Dad's dead," she says.

"What?"

"He's dead," she repeats.

"Who did it?"

"A bottle of Southern Comfort and a handful of Vicodin," she says. "Day before yesterday."

"Wrong," Mofongo says. "One of his enemies, returned for revenge."

"Mo, I appreciate that you're upset but this isn't part of you guys' soap opera. He killed himself."

"No," Mofongo says, and he feels fear because he really does not know who did it. Old allies can turn into new enemies, old friends can become new foes. Men of Adventure are no stranger to psychosis. "One of his enemies is here. I may also be in danger. You must free me so I can defend myself."

"I can't let you come to the funeral," she says, ignoring him. "People will want to know why a talking ape is there and you're kind of hard to explain."

"I don't want to go to his funeral," Mofongo snarls. "I want to defend myself!"

"I'm sorry," Theresa says. "I really am. On the plus side, we're getting you out of here."

"Yes, free to defend myself. Free to destroy my enemies."

"There's a Primate Refuge outside Austin," the Animal Control man says. "They've agreed to take you. You'll fit right in. That chimpanzee who did all those Geico ads is there."

"Chimpanzees? *Chimpanzees!* Masturbating, shit-flinging, pants-wearing attention whores! I am Mofongo: Gorilla of the Mind. I am a threat to mankind! I'm on the UN watch list!"

"You've been off that list for twenty-six years," the CIA agent says. "No one remembers you anymore."

"If men do not still feel fear," Mofongo snarls, "why do they send the CIA? Why the FBI?"

The FBI agent shrugs. "I just wanted to see a talking gorilla," he says.

The CIA agent takes a picture of Mofongo. "You're just one more thing on my to-do list."

"I'm sorry to dump all this on you at once," Theresa says. "I really am. I'll come visit you in Austin. We can catch up. I've got friends I can stay with and we can just hang out. Like we used to, right?"

"You are making a *grave* mistake," Mofongo says. "I still have my secret Science Bases hidden throughout your country. You put me in this refugee camp and I will break out and go to them and manufacture a cloned army of super-apes and together we will grind your country beneath our paws!"

"There are no more secret Science Bases," the CIA agent says. "We got them all back in '51."

"But what if I have one location locked away in my subconscious?" Mofongo says. "What if it's buried down so deep only my mental rays can find it? *What then?* Will you risk humanity's future if you're wrong?"

But Mofongo can't even convince himself.

"Mofongo," Theresa says, "you'll be out in the sun again, able to live a normal life. I'll check in on you and make sure you have everything you need."

"I should have snapped your neck when you were a child," Mofongo says.

"I'm sorry I left you alone for so long, Mo," Theresa says, then she turns and walks out of the tent with the government men.

"Don't be sorry," he shouts at her back. "Be afraid! Afraid of my wrath!"

But she is already gone.

· · · ·

It takes Mofongo all the cash hidden inside his Power Turban to convince Herman to let him out of his cage.

"If Theresa finds out I did this, I'm dead meat," Herman says.

"Pathetic," Mofongo spits. "The power of a computer in your skull and yet you tremble like a chimp."

"The power of a million brains in your skull and yet a Yale lock has kept you prisoner for thirty-some-odd years," Herman says.

"I will have my revenge," Mofongo says.

"Yeah, yeah," Herman says. "I only let you out because it's cruel to keep you locked up if some old archenemy's come back to bump you off."

Mofongo enters Steve Savage's trailer. It's dingy and stained, depressing and undersized with no room to walk around. Mofongo expected wall-to-wall photos, Steve Savage shaking the hands of presidents, Johnny Cash, Elvis Presley, scrapbooks, posters from the old movies, the radio shows. But there's nothing here except McDonald's wrappers and empty bottles.

Mofongo lets his mental rays scan the space. They strain to detect a trace of any number of old enemies and allies: The Cat, Red Charlie, The Beast with Five Thousand Fingers, Two Gun Chang, and all the rest.

Nothing.

There is no trace of murder. No hint of death. No whiff of vengeance. No deathtraps, no mantraps, no exotic poisons or mechanical ants. The only psychic residue in this trailer is despondency, despair, and the deep ache of a man who wanted to die long before he got this old.

Mofongo's nose begins to bleed and he feels a headache throb deep within his brain. He wipes the heavy black blood running from his nostrils with the back of one hairy paw.

The chair in front of the thirteen-inch TV is worn down to fit Steve's body. Mofongo sniffs it and detects something familiar. He reaches underneath and pulls out a dried leather scrap, black with age: Shaira's leather headband. Passed down the generations, it was made of the hide of a thirty-foot Mokele-mbembe lizard living on a riverbed near Boyoma Falls, a great beast that had a taste for Oparian flesh. The Third Blind Prince of Opar killed it, fashioning armor from its hide, and three thousand years later the final surviving piece was passed to Shaira, the most valuable of her possessions. It once commanded the respect of thousands, and now it is lying on the floor of Steve's trailer.

Mofongo runs his finger along it, but it crumbles at his touch and the brittle pieces fall to the linoleum. He and Steve Savage had fought a bitter war over Shaira the Jungle Empress, each of them in love with the seven-foot warrior queen who ruled the city of Opar. Their battle reduced her city to cinders, and she died in the crossfire. Mofongo hadn't thought about her in years. He always wondered which of them had loved her more, and now he knows.

There are only two of us left who remember Shaira even existed, he thinks, then corrects himself: With Steve gone, now Mofongo is the only one.

There are no enemies here, only bad memories. Let them come and put him in the primate refuge. He deserves to be with the bad monkeys now. The chimps will be his new companions and he will not speak of revolution or revenge. He will just pray each day to remember less and less until finally he dies.

Transporting a nonhuman primate over state lines is complicated business. There are protocols, procedures, shipping-container regulations, squeeze-box quarantines, OSHA guidelines, permits to be displayed, and licenses to be stamped, and the least important thing in all of this is the nonhuman primate himself. Mofongo sits, not eating, not drinking, staring off into space.

"You are a giant pain in my ass," the Animal Control agent says. "Seriously. It's going to be a relief to get you out of my hair."

He clanks out of the tractor-trailer, leaving Mofongo alone. Theresa Savage walks up the metal ramp.

"Hi, Mo," she says.

Mofongo says nothing.

"I was just with those weird collectors. They're buying all the old advertising canvases and one sheets. It's not a lot, but it'll pay for some of this, you know, getting you down to Austin and all."

A fly lands on Mofongo's nose. He doesn't notice.

"I'm glad you're not fighting or anything," Theresa says. "But would you just talk to me?"

But Mofongo will not talk to anyone anymore.

"I want you to be happy," she says. "I want you to think of this as a vacation. It's not a punishment, it's a time when you can relax. Like retirement. People really look forward to retirement. I'm already looking forward to mine! You'll have fun. You'll have a really fun time."

Mofongo does not care.

"It's pretty hot down in Texas," she says. "I really will come to visit. I want to talk to you about stuff, my dad and things. You were the only person he was close to. The only gorilla, I guess, not really person."

The air is thick and heavy.

"After we moved, I pretended you could still hear me. I'd lie under my bed and talk to you like you could still hear me through your mind rays or something. You couldn't really hear me though, right? I mean, you never actually heard me," she says. "Could you?"

It's getting hot in the tractor-trailer.

"Mom sold Dogtag Donald a split-level outside Atlanta. He's a born-again Christian now, with two little boys and everything," she says. "He told me what you did, about the baby show guy."

Mofongo will not look at her.

"You saved my life," Theresa says. "All my good memories from when I was a kid are about you."

A ten-year-old girl with an iPod jammed in her ears, pink tennis shoes, and a denim miniskirt stands at the bottom of the ramp.

350

"Mom!" she hollers. "Are we going?"

"That's Chrissy," Theresa says. "My daughter." She yells back. "Come up here and meet Mofongo."

The girl gracelessly tromps into the trailer.

"It stinks," she says.

"I didn't even notice," Theresa says. "Do you want to talk to her, Mofongo? Say 'hi' to my daughter?"

Silence.

"He used to talk all the time," Theresa says. Then, thoughtfully, "Mostly cussing."

"Mom," Chrissy says. "You're so dumb. He can't talk. He's a monkey. It was a stupid carnival trick."

"He's a gorilla," Theresa says.

Chrissy rolls her eyes. "Whatever."

"Hey," the Animal Control agent says, standing at the bottom of the ramp. "Come sign these final permits and let's get this show on the road."

Theresa turns to go.

"I'll be right back," she says, and she leaves Mofongo and Chrissy alone.

Chrissy contemplates Mofongo. She goes outside and comes back with a few small rocks. She tosses them at Mofongo. One bounces off his chest, one bounces off his forehead, then she aims one at his crotch.

"So, do you do anything?" she asks. "Or do you just sit around and smell like shit?"

She takes a step closer, and pings Mofongo on the beaner with another rock, but Mofongo doesn't notice. Because deep within Mofongo's mind a door has opened and he sees a future where everything Theresa says is true. He will have friends. He will relax. It will be like it was, and he will astonish Theresa's spawn with stories of the marvels he saw in Africa and Theresa will thank him for helping him raise her daughter, for being an inspiration, and the spirit of Mofongo will live on.

"Will you come to Austin?" he asks, throat rusty with disuse.

Chrissy stares at him. Mofongo repeats himself.

"Will. You. Come. To. Austin?"

Chrissy's high-pitched screams bring everyone running, and she crashes into them as she barrels out of the trailer, sobbing.

"Thanks, Mofongo," Theresa says, when she comes back a few minutes later and Mofongo grins. Then he realizes that she's being sarcastic and his grin fades.

"You're all signed off, sport," the Animal Control agent snarls.

Theresa is jabbing her signature on a final form. Mofongo wants to say something but he's too confused. Did he do something wrong? He doesn't think so. Theresa marches over to the bars of his cage.

"What did you say?" she snaps. "Did you say something gross? I know how you can talk. Did you say something ugly to my little girl? Because she's sitting in my car sobbing."

Mofongo can't think of an answer, his brain is so sluggish and confused and the words float to the top one at a time, like bubbles in syrup. It takes forever to put them together. Theresa's expression softens.

"Why do you have to make everything so hard, Mo?" She rests one hand on the bars. "Why won't you just talk to me?"

Mofongo wets his lips to say something, but Theresa doesn't notice. She just shakes her head and turns and walks out of the trailer. Men drop the metal ramp with a clang and slam the doors shut and Mofongo speaks too late.

"Don't go," he says.

But no one hears.

. . . .

Flat as a putting green, Arlington National Cemetery stretches out to the horizon, interrupted only by the bone white dot, dot, dot of headstones. Theresa wishes she could have a glass of wine. A thin, tinny, prerecorded version of "Taps" has just finished drilling its way into her skull and now two pimply soldiers in dress blues are folding up the American flag from her father's coffin.

They march over to her like clockwork dummies and present her with the folded flag.

"As a representative of the United States Army," one of them chants in a shrill voice that is still breaking, "it is my high privilege to present you this flag . . ."

He squeaks on and Theresa remembers how much her dad hated the military. He thought men in uniform were chumps, that's why he killed so many of them in the war. He would have died twice if he knew he'd wind up being buried with a bunch of them. Theresa uses a Kleenex to blot the sweat off her forehead.

A wild scream cuts through the hot noon air. Human blood instinctively freezes in its veins.

It is the wild scream of the great ape.

"Hoo hoo hoo!" Comes the terrifying jungle hoot. "Haa haa! Huh huh huh!"

And they look up in the sky. Hanging by one arm from the robed figure on top of the Monument to the Confederate War Dead is Mofongo. His head looks bigger than Theresa remembers, as if his brain has turned malignant. His skull looks sick and dark, like rotten fruit.

Confusion and chatter, and Mofongo shoulders some kind of rifle and one of the clockwork Marines dissolves into bones and dust. Everyone screams and scatters as a SWAT team—who were waiting for just this kind of incident—runs forward. They outnumber the mourners ten to one.

The FBI agent grabs Theresa's arm and drags her behind a round concrete memorial, where men in black are doing frantic things. The Animal Control agent is here. He says, "I'm so fired," and lights a cigarette off an eternal flame.

"I am holding you personally responsible for this travesty," the CIA agent yells at the Animal Control agent.

"I blame you people, too," the FBI agent joins in. "We've monitored this monster for almost fifty years, we turn him over to you, and he busts out of that big rig like it was nothing in less than seventy-two hours."

"He used his mind rays!" the Animal Control agent whines. "We didn't think they still worked. We thought they were supposed to be killing him!"

"Does he look dead to you?"

Mofongo leaps off the Monument to the Confederate War Dead and charges Steve Savage's freshly dug grave, tossing aside fleeing mourners like tenpins. The SWAT team sets up a skirmish line, then opens fire.

They shoot to kill. Their automatic weapons chop the still summer air. Mofongo doesn't even slow down. He barrels through them like they're a bunch of crippled children. One of the Marines in full dress makes a patriotic last stand. He locks eyes with the charging gorilla, aims his rifle at Mofongo's overflowing skull, and fires. The air around Mofongo shimmers and the bullet falls to the ground. Mofongo plucks the rifle from the soldier's hands and bashes him over the head with it.

The SWAT team fires again, but the air around Mofongo keeps shimmering and their bullets keep falling. Theresa realizes that she's relieved. She thought Mofongo was committing suicide by SWAT, trying to go out in a blaze of glory. But Mofongo is smarter than that.

More firing. More shimmering. More bullets fall.

"What the fuck is that?" the CIA agent screams.

"It's his Kinetic Suspenders," Theresa says. "He invented them a long time ago. I would tell your flamethrower guys not to bother."

A flamethrower team is trotting through the headstones, then they stop and unleash a black and orange column of fire at Mofongo. No effect.

"Kinetic Suspenders," the CIA agent moans. "That doesn't even make sense."

"Where the hell did he get them?" the FBI agent asks. "We closed down all his stupid Science Bases."

"I guess you missed one," Theresa says.

Mofongo jumps down into the grave. SWAT snipers take a few more useless shots. A CNN helicopter appears on the horizon, zooming closer.

"Listen, Savage," the CIA agent says. "We only gave your old man a plot in Arlington because he shot up a bunch of Nazis back in the day. See that helicopter? That's CNN. America is going to see this desecration of our country's most sacred site live on cable TV and you will have good, clean children throwing up into their breakfast cereal from coast to coast and it's all going to be your fault."

There's the distant sound of something breaking and pieces of plasticized wood are tossed out of the hole. Suddenly Mofongo is clambering up from the grave, and in his arms is the corpse of Steve Savage.

"Holy shit," the FBI agent says. "He's taking the body!"

"Will you people show some respect!" the CIA agent yells impotently at the CNN helicopter.

Theresa just watches.

A few more shots ring out. She flinches. Mofongo raises his middle finger at the SWAT team and then touches a control on his chest and a cloaking device clicks off, revealing a hover plane materializing behind him. He lopes over to it, climbs on board, puts Steve Savage's corpse in the co-pilot's seat and gets in. The ship lifts off.

They watch it rise into the air. It hangs there for one unnatural moment, every swooping, graceful curve of its Atom Age engineering sneering at the twenty-first century. Then it's gone, screaming for the horizon.

"Which direction is that?" shouts the CIA agent.

"East," the FBI agent says. "Toward Africa."

"Wow," Theresa says.

"Wow?" the CIA agent says. "Our nation's most hallowed resting place is vandalized by an obscene baboon and you say wow? Are you sick?"

Hearing it like that, Theresa wonders if she *is* sick.

"I just wanted to protect people from dangerous animals," the Animal Control agent moans. "I'm going to lose my job. What am I going to tell my family?"

"Come on, people," the CIA agent says. "Let's find out where they're going and shoot them down. Anyone know where they're going?"

But no one knows, because suddenly the hover plane vanishes off the radar. Expensive satellites blink in amazement. Where did Mofongo go? No one knows.

Tight-lipped, agents of the United States government stuff Theresa into the back of an armored SUV and question her severely. They want her to know just how angry they are, and so they take turns sitting backward in the front seat, yelling questions at her. Where did Mofongo go? Why did he steal her father's body? Did Mofongo have contact with Islamic fundamentalists or with members of Al Qaeda? What does she know and when did she know it?

What can she tell them? She doesn't know anything. She doesn't even know where Mofongo has taken her father. A Viking funeral in Antarctica? A memorial on the moon? A secret base buried deep beneath Saharan sands? In a way, it feels more natural to *not* know where her father is. He was out there, somewhere, the way he'd been out there somewhere all her life. No known phone number. No known address. Maybe in the Himalayas, maybe in a bar, but as long as she never knew for sure, he could be anywhere.

She smiles again, and they ask her, What's so funny? Why is she smiling? She doesn't answer them.

But Mofongo knows.

• • • •

In the hover plane, Mofongo wipes more blood from his face and feels his ultrabrain collapsing into mush. He was still smarter than five thousand men, but that number was falling fast. His push to escape the tractor-trailer, his push to locate his last science base, his push to open its doors—three pushes too far.

"Feels like old times," Mofongo says to Steve's dead body. "Except I'm not punching you in the face."

Then he turns around and punches Steve's corpse in the face.

"That's better," he says, and smiles.

Mofongo flies, finally free. America is behind him, shrinking with every second, and Africa is up ahead, getting bigger all the time.

Grady Hendrix is the author of the novel Satan Loves You, *and his short fiction has appeared in* Lightspeed Magazine, Strange Horizons, Pseudopod, *and* 365 Tomorrows. *He is one of the founders of the New York Asian Film Festival and his nonfiction writing has appeared in* Variety, Slate, Playboy, Time Out New York, *the* New York Sun, *and the* Village Voice. *He attended the Clarion Science Fiction and Fantasy Writers' Workshop in 2009.*

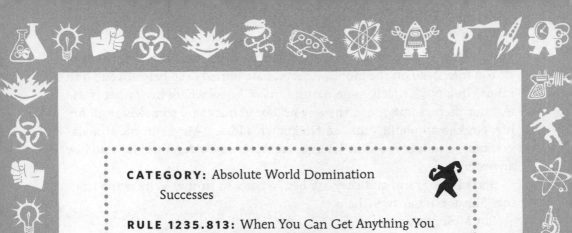

> **CATEGORY:** Absolute World Domination
> Successes
>
> **RULE 1235.813:** When You Can Get Anything You
> Want, Be Careful What You Wish For
>
> **SOURCE:** C., Despot of Earth
>
> **VIA:** Ben H. Winters

Evil and genius are not bound together. Insanity is no guarantee of evil, either—madness can bend a great mind to kindness just as easily as it can send it spiraling into cruelty. But there can be brilliance in acts of evil; there can be a mastery of despair and torment. History is dotted with great (or infamous) men who have learned these secrets.

Our final story is the story of a man gifted in these dark arts of domination. His remarkable mind has found a way to bend the world to his liking, and his methods are both cruel and hard. He's spent a lifetime bringing his boot down on the neck of the world, and now at the pinnacle of his success, he can only wonder what is left for him to conquer, what is left for him to achieve.

One of the things that inspired Winters to write this story was the contemplation of the empty lives of dictators and despots. He realized that there is a cruel paradox to have everything and yet to lead a life so hollow.

THE FOOD TASTER'S BOY

BEN H. WINTERS

I: Melancholy

Periodically, C. toured the lands.

He traveled by boat, by truck, by revolving-bladed copter, by viperclaw, by rattling rail and in massive, battered silver air-frigates, swooping in over the villages, his smoke-black contrail drawing a thick, choking curtain across the land. On tour, C. would congregate the people of a village, inspect the teeth of the children, run his fingers along the lintels of the cottages and gaze down into wells. Sometimes, unspeaking, he left the villagers as they were when he came. Sometimes, he would command the strongest man to his knees, have him lashed to senselessness; burn a factory; dissolve a marriage; elevate an idiot pauper to some administrative post.

He undertook them at irregular intervals, these traveling displays of his all-encompassing authority. Sometimes months would pass from one to the next, sometimes years. Sometimes he would return almost immediately, doubling back to reinspect the lands by a different route, to catch his subjects unawares.

But always he found the people as he left them: miserable where they lay in their meager homesteads, exhausted from their labors, reliant on his munificence, destitute of possibility and hope.

Again and again he returned, for C.'s power lay in presence. He was there, or had just been there, or was about to be there again, at any time, at all times. Any thought of insurrection, any conspiracy would then be caught out before the barest quiver of an idea could develop into action. His presence was reminder that any rebellion, any *thought* of rebellion, would earn the famous consequences: the controlled fires; the slow deaths of the children; the caloric restriction; the rains of poison and the blackened sky.

C. was leader of his Earth and God of it.

He toured the land so belief in the presence of God would not wane.

· · · ·

But it was fast approaching the second decade since the last of the Wars, and there had been no insurrection, no whiff of insurrection. Two decades, and he lorded over a grim and broken people, minds dulled by labor, hearts hushed by fear.

As C. had envisioned it, so had it come to pass.

There appeared around this time—or it might be said that around this time there emerged, within C.—a new enemy, of a kind he had not previously encountered or imagined.

One afternoon, the clouds foul smears against a gray-blue sky, C. returned by revolving-bladed copter from his latest tour of inspection. He felt the thrust of the motors in descent and then the jolt of the forward wheels biting into the landing strip. He stepped out and his boot heel crunched on the graveled roof of Glory One, that sheer gleaming black giant, the last of the tall buildings. His home, and what he called, with a dark humor only he was free to enjoy, "the seat of government."

He stood outside the craft. The engine churned down to silence, and the pilot and his guards stood in a respectful semicircle around C., waiting to proceed in his wake to the stairhead. But C. stayed still and silent. He tilted back his head, feeling in his gut a queer dark ache, a sensation of emptiness so sudden and so vivid that he shut his eyes against it and moaned, rocking slightly backward on his heels.

C. opened his eyes to the north, to the sloping hillside littered with impoverished villages, to the parched hollow below it, dotted with factories.

His villages. His factories. His world.

"What then?" C. murmured, and took a step closer to the lip of the building and said it again, his voice a low, whispering rattle. "What then?"

"Commander?" ventured the pilot, and C. rushed at him, seized him by the collar of his flight suit, kept rushing, forced the surprised, thrashing body of the pilot past the others, to the southern lip of the roof, and with a grunting burst of speed and strength hurled the man screeching over the side.

C. watched the body drop, saw it bang against the glass wall of Glory One, pinwheel out, grow smaller and smaller, until it was an insignificant speck slipping soundlessly into the water.

And still he felt it.

"What then?"

II: Epiphany

C. was not a stupid man.

The problem was not in figuring out what it was—this dark growth that had taken root in him (and which he could not thereafter shake free of)—it was melancholy, thick and clotted, belaboring his limbs, slowing the motion of his pen at his long desk, pooling behind his eyes as he tried to focus on the screen-bed, undertaking the administration of his world.

Neither did it take great effort to discover the wellspring of this foul humor. C.'s had been a life built on carnage: He had fed on the violence of his age as a beast on meat, from his squalid birth in a camp for the displaced to his days rampaging on horseback as a militia commander, the terror of all enemies, a legend of force and savagery. He had turned from each victory to the next struggle, emerging victorious from that struggle in its turn. Laying waste to challengers, building his empire, closing his fist around the universe.

But now the guns had been long silent, and every corner of the world was his and his alone. Knowledge of victory was the seed of his misery.

There was no violence but that which he ordered, no savagery that did not begin and end at his command.

Which left only silence. The cold, mocking silence of triumph.

· · · · ·

C. tried to dissipate his newfound despondency in the various decadences that his power and position afforded him. He stayed up for a week on artificial stimulants, his eyes twitching, studying the ersatz combat known as chess. He sank himself into elaborate, daylong feasts of food and drink. He ordered elaborate displays of dancing girls and acrobatics, commanded the construction of great amphitheaters in the lower depths of Glory One, sat staring with his thick arms crossed at increasingly fantastical performances and stagecraft.

All was futile, as he had known it would be. Every performance was spoiled by the trembling fear of the performers, visible just below the glittering surface. Acrobats missed their grips. The dancing girls stumbled. Their beauty was a joke; they stank with terror. The great chefs sweated into the food.

A trembling old man, a chess "grand master" from the old days, was brought to Glory One in shackles. Told that he was to play C. in the morning, and ordered to play to the best of his ability, the grand master spent the night in his cell swallowing pieces one by one, until they ruptured his intestines and he died.

This was always the story. C.'s very presence proved the spoiler to these extravagances designed to elevate his humor. He could not command the world to bring him joy. The very fruit of his victory now disgusted him, and his disgust deepened his sadness.

On C.'s next inspection tour, he lingered in the village squares, peering into the eyes of his slack-mouthed subjects, subjecting to lengthy interviews people who clearly knew nothing, understood nothing. He cracked open ancient trunks that once might have contained munitions, and were now empty, dust-blown, ransacked by rats and moles. He did not find that which he barely knew he was looking for: in some debased subject, a spark of anger; in some squalid corner, a cache of arms.

Flying home, C. stared unblinking from the shaded window of the air-frigate, tasting bitter, paradoxical truth. True pleasure in his unquestioned power required the existence of a contrary authority.

· · · ·

C. returned to Glory One and descended in the rattlebox to the forty-sixth floor. He walked down the long steel floor toward his private quarters. Passing the kitchens, C. caught a glimpse of the food taster's boy.

III: The Food Taster's Boy

Later, he couldn't say for certain what he saw in the child. Some fleeting spark of defiance around the eyes, like a single wicked star glimmering in a black-hole night. Some sign of intelligence in the face, some steel in the posture, where he stood just inside the doorway of the kitchens, watching wordlessly as C. strode past.

At the sight of him, the idea sprang into C.'s head fully formed, in all of its cruelty and hopelessness.

The boy was taken first, and lashed to the floor.

His father, the food taster, was delivered up, trussed and gagged, and after him, the wife, naked and bound.

The depredations C. performed upon the food taster and the wife out-stripped any he had done before. Not in their cruelty, for he had performed many cruelties in his long vicious slog from obscurity to domination, but in their variety and sheer imaginative force.

And C. did these things himself, by hand. The guards were dismissed from the room. He himself wielded the blade and the hook, the gas and the heat, the boot heel and the prong. The food taster's boy witnessed every stroke, every lash, each twist of the knife. Saw the imaginative uses of electricity, of water, of the bladed floor, and the kitchen dog.

It lasted a very long time.

He was no hero, the food taster's boy. He was a child. He wept and he moaned, he begged as children beg, stomping his little bare feet and slapping his hands on the horrible floor, stickied with the blood of those he most loved.

Surely, if there had been a spark of defiance, it had been brutally dimmed, if not snuffed. Not for the last time, C. (bent with the exertion of many hours) wondered if he had made a mistake, if all of this was for nothing. But he continued, and never said a word; he offered no explanations, never called this a punishment for any crime. A display, that is, of pure, arbitrary, and personal horror.

A display for the benefit of the food taster's boy.

IV: Waiting

In the decade that followed, C. continued as he was, carrying the memory of the food taster's boy with him always, like a secret jewel clasped in a closed fist. At night, he dreamed rich dreams of the food taster's boy, of his ragged baby's face, tear-clouded and wild with grief, his tiny mouth a distorted wail. He dreamt of that face growing older, filling out, the boy becoming stronger—hardened by time, by rage . . .

By day, he lingered on the gravel roof of Glory One, staring into distances, sweeping his spyglass. Waiting.

Waiting for the food taster's boy to return.

This waiting, he knew, was a form of faith, and almost certainly in vain. C. had issued no orders concerning the food taster's boy; no squadron to track his movements, to watch him from a distance, to send back reports, to ensure that he lived. No—for in that version of events, the child would be but another acrobat, a dancing girl, another play ghostwritten by C. for his own enjoyment.

What he needed from the food taster's boy, he could only get by performing the act of creation, and then standing back, an uncaring God. The boy had been reduced to rubble and then let go, a ragged and horrified orphan, hurled by his scruff from the gates of Glory One to stumble to whatever mercy he could find in the parched world. With nothing. Only a memory—of what had happened, and how. Nothing in his pockets, and nothing in his breast but hatred.

It was hatred, C. whispered to himself, hatred and vengeance that would keep the food taster's boy alive, and bring him home.

• • • •

The scenarios he imagined ran the gamut of plausibility: some utterly preposterous, some carrying the faint silvery gleam of the possible.

The food taster's boy would return at the head of a great army, on horseback or in the cockpit of a hijacked viperclaw. Or perhaps at the controls of some flying death-dealing supermachine of his own invention, shooting barrel-rounds from the sky, raining barrier breakers on Glory One. This would require a scramble to action for the often-drilled but never-employed higher-level guards. It would require C. himself to take to the skies, to slip into the cockpit and feel the swoosh and roar of air beneath the wing . . . eyes closed, mouth open, he tasted the smoke and blast powder of aerial combat.

Or the food taster's boy would return alone, under cloak of night. He would short-circuit the alarms and dispatch each guard with a hushed and brutal neck-breaking blow, creep into C.'s chamber and hover above him until he woke. And then combat, hand to hand, the choking grasps and pummeling kicks, the wizened old soldier facing off in the darkness with the vengeance-mad young man, his body honed to an iron edge by years of bitterness.

The thought of it sent C. yearning to the window, leaning against the glass. The thought of it sent him to the rattle-box, carried him again and again up to the gravel roof of Glory One. He stood at the northern lip with his spyglass and told himself the food taster's boy was out there, hidden in some garret, encamped in a dank fen, preparing to make his move.

Late at night, C. knew with bitter certitude that all this was a joke, a taunting cruelty he had played upon himself. The food taster's boy was a rotting pile of bones, dead in a ditch years ago, starved or murdered. Or mad, raving through the dirt street of one of these broken villages, poorer and more pathetic than any of the rest of them.

. . . .

Brutal black winters changing to chemical summers changing to dead gray autumns, years passing in the burnt-out world. And in those years, a certain efficiency returned to C.'s movements: a swiftness and decision in his step, a sharpness in his gaze—all attributable, he knew, to the subtle thrill, known to himself alone, of what he had loosed upon the world.

Sometimes, at night, C. sang to the food taster's boy: low, rasping melodies, unheard.

V: The Return

And when he came, in a shatter of glass and a bloody howl, it took seconds—less than seconds—it took *instants* for C. to know that all was wasted. The years and the hope, all wasted.

The food taster's boy was an animal, a horrid slavering creature, sloping and grunting, moving on all fours through the room, saliva and mucous dripping in thick tendrils from the corners of his mouth, a crooked mess of mandible and fang. His hair was long and knotted and filthy and he stank of rot and shit. When he kicked into the room, he had blood on his lips; he had not dispatched the guards with cunning martial blows, but devoured them, as a dog or hyena falls with violence on its prey. His thick fingertips scuttled across the floorboards as he moved like some landbound cephalopod through the room, baring his teeth, moaning gutturally, moving crab-ways at C.

"Ahh," C. moaned, holding up his hands, his chin trembling.

The food taster's boy flexed his upper body like a gorilla. He growled and spat. C. had a sudden vision of years in the woods, a demented, friendless child; an outcast from Glory, untouchable; exiled from human contact, foraging and rooting. A beast's existence. And now he had returned, not as a monomaniacal mastermind returning to take his vengeance, but like a bear that wends its way atavistically home.

"Ahh," C. said again, stepping backward. He had within arm's reach a small army's worth of weaponry: optically guided knives and three gauges of hand-cannon and a close-range incendiary device of terrible power. But he did not reach for a trigger, did not move. He stared at the food taster's boy and cried.

"My child," he said. "My child."

The food taster's boy advanced, closed the last feet between them, pushed his malformed body up against C.'s. One of his eyes bulged queerly from his head, like a tumor, grayish and watery. His nostrils flared. His forehead pulsed. Behind him, through the south-facing window, C. saw the lights of fast-approaching viperclaws, a squadron, charging through the sky, to his rescue. The food taster's boy had short-circuited no alarms.

"Oh my child," C. repeated. "My boy."

In a moment, the window would be kicked in, strikers would flow into the room and the food taster's boy destroyed.

And then . . .

What then?

C. moved forward instead of away, got to his knees and sprawled his body into the foul embrace of the food taster's boy. He might have whispered "I'm sorry," or only known it. He saw the lights of the viperclaws hovering now outside the windows, heard the urgent hollering of soldiers.

He leaned back, opening up his neck to the sharpened teeth of the boy.

The food taster's boy whispered a word, his hot foul breath fogging onto C.'s cheek, droplets of rank saliva in his ear. One clear and human word: "No."

Ben H. Winters is the bestselling author of two posthumous "mash-up" collaborations: Sense and Sensibility and Sea Monsters *(with Jane Austen) and* Android Karenina *(with Leo Tolstoy). He is also the author of the pre-apocalyptic murder mystery* The Lost Policeman, *the supernatural thriller* Bedbugs, *and two middle-grade novels:* The Secret Life of Ms. Finkleman *and* The Mystery of the Missing Everything. *To learn more, visit benhwinters.com.*

ACKNOWLEDGMENTS

Many thanks to the following:

Jim Frenkel at Tor Books for publishing this anthology, and for shepherding the book through the publication process. Helen Chin for her copyediting prowess, production editor Kevin Sweeney, Heather Saunders for designing the book, and Nathan Weaver for guiding the book through production.

My former agent, Jenny Rappaport, who sold this book and otherwise helped me launch my anthology career, and my current agent, Joe Monti, for keeping it going. Thanks, too, to Joe for the incredible amount of support he's provided since taking me on as a client—he's gone above and beyond the call of duty. To any writers reading this: you'd be lucky to have Joe in your corner.

Ben Templesmith, for the megalomaniacal cover art.

Wendy N. Wagner for her assistance wrangling the header notes.

Gordon Van Gelder, the Dr. Frankenstein to my Igor. I never would be where I am today without his tutelage. Gordon, you created a monster!

My amazing wife, Christie, and my mom, Marianne, for all their love and support, and their endless enthusiasm for all my new projects.

My dear friends Robert Bland, Desirina Boskovich, Christopher M. Cevasco, Douglas E. Cohen, Jordan Hamessley, Andrea Kail, David Barr Kirtley, and Matt London.

The readers and reviewers who loved my other anthologies, making it possible for me to do more.

And last, but certainly not least: a big thanks to all of the authors whose stories appear in this anthology.

ABOUT THE EDITOR

John Joseph Adams (www.johnjosephadams.com) is the bestselling editor of many anthologies, such as *Epic, Other Worlds Than These, Armored, Under the Moons of Mars: New Adventures on Barsoom, Lightspeed: Year One, Brave New Worlds, Wastelands, The Living Dead, The Living Dead 2, The Way of the Wizard, By Blood We Live, Federations,* and *The Improbable Adventures of Sherlock Holmes.* He is a four-time finalist for the Hugo Award and a three-time finalist for the World Fantasy Award. In addition to his anthology work, John is also the publisher and editor of the magazines *Lightspeed* and *Nightmare,* and is the cohost of Wired.com's *The Geek's Guide to the Galaxy* podcast.

For more information about John and *The Mad Scientist's Guide to World Domination,* go to www.johnjosephadams/mad-scientists-guide.